MIKE MAIHACK

CLEOPATRA IN SPACE

BOOK ONE
TARGET PRACTICE

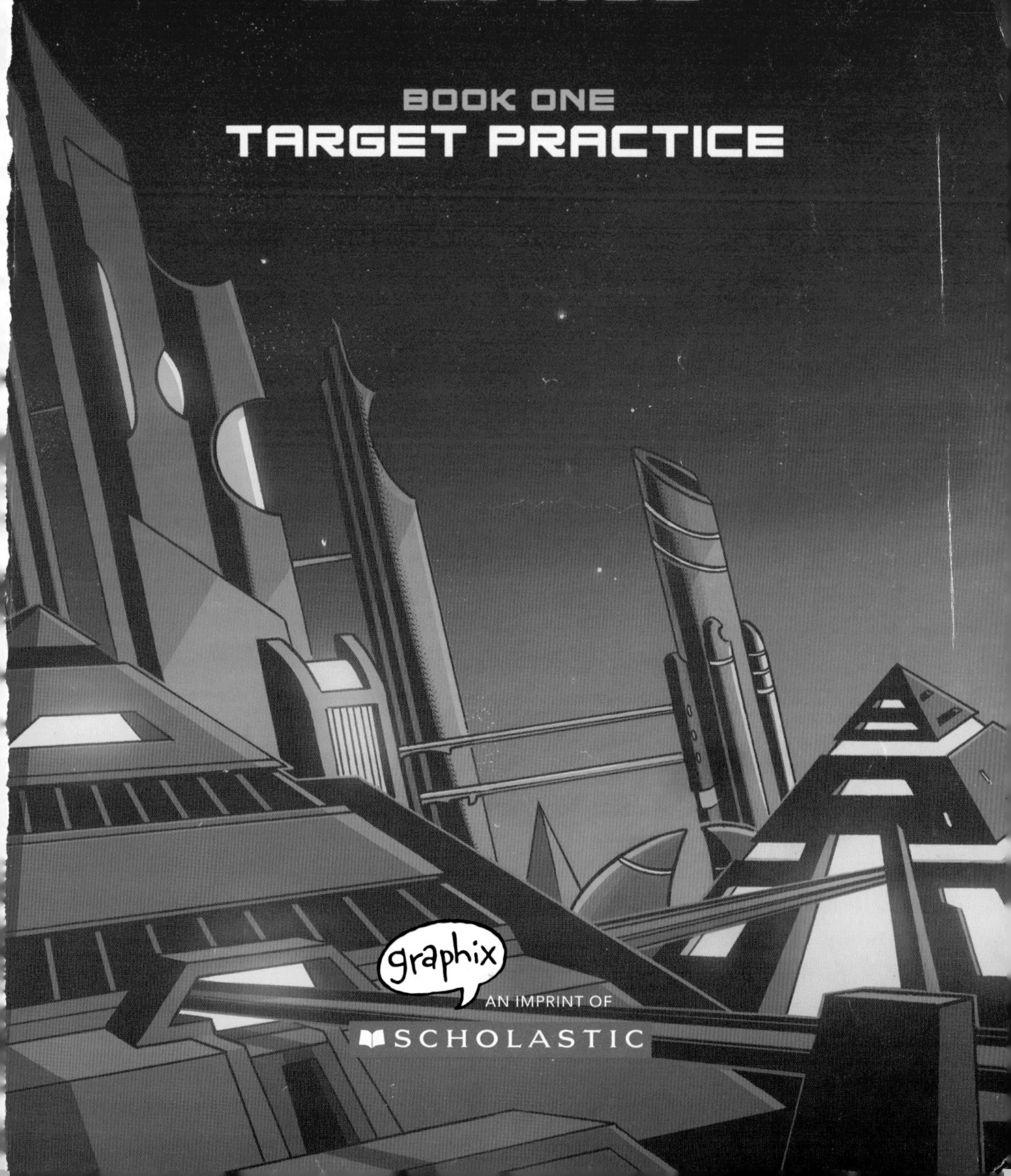

graphix
AN IMPRINT OF
SCHOLASTIC

Library of Congress Control Number: 2013934374

ISBN 978-0-545-52842-9 (hardcover)
ISBN 978-0-545-52843-6 (paperback)

10 9 8 7 6 5 4   16 17 18
First edition, May 2014
Edited by Cassandra Pelham
Book design by Phil Falco
Creative Director: David Saylor
Printed in Malaysia   108

For Oliver Prime

CHAPTER ONE

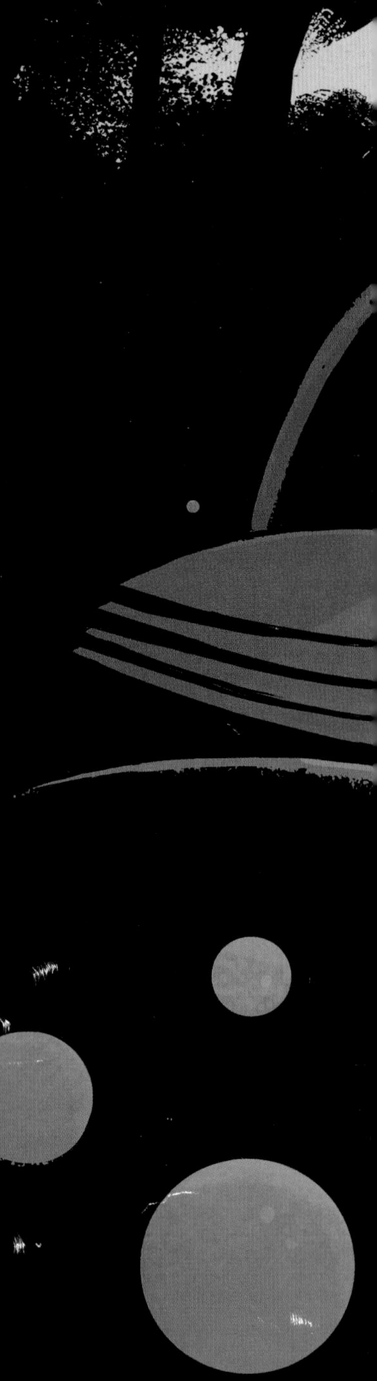

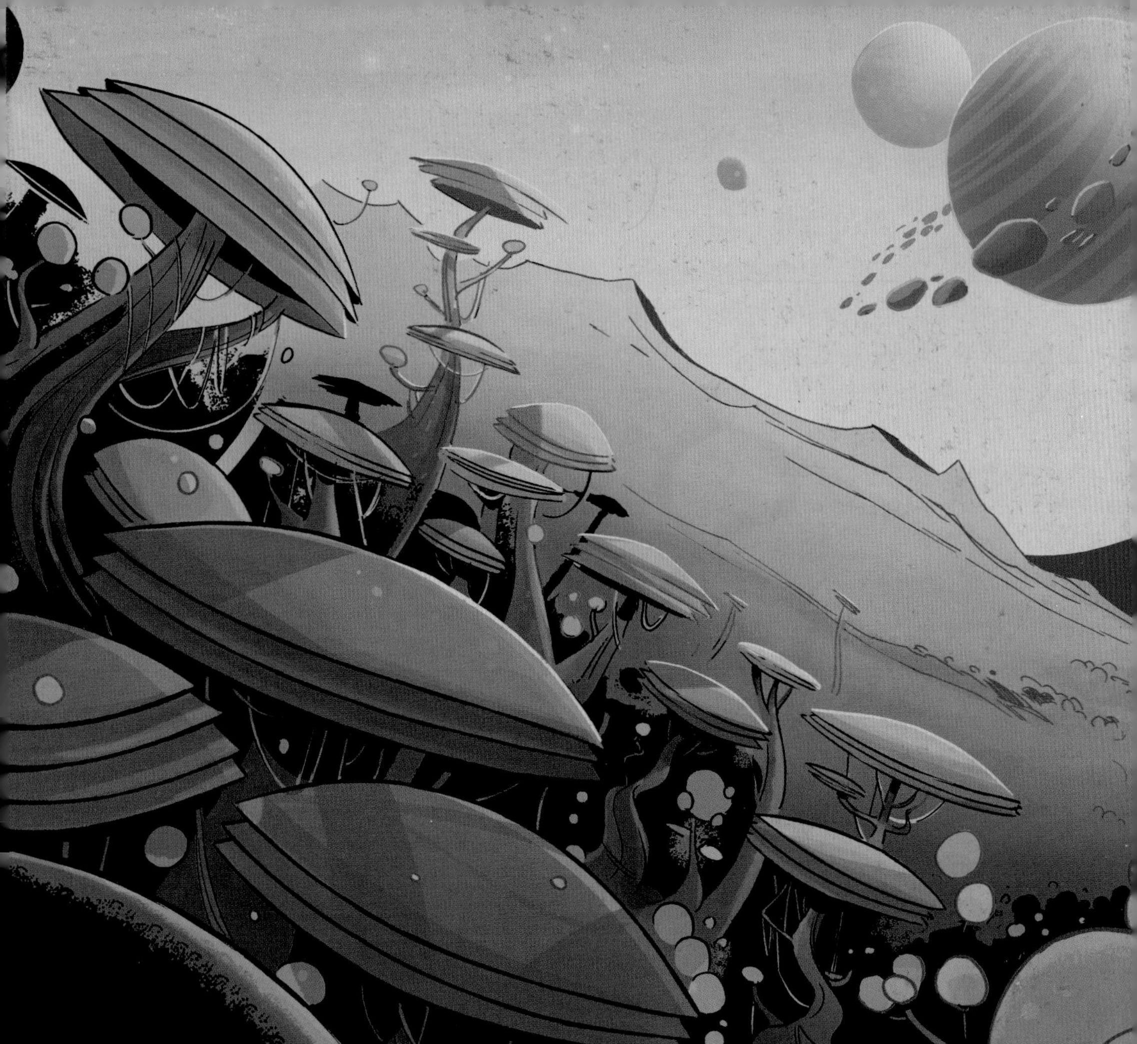

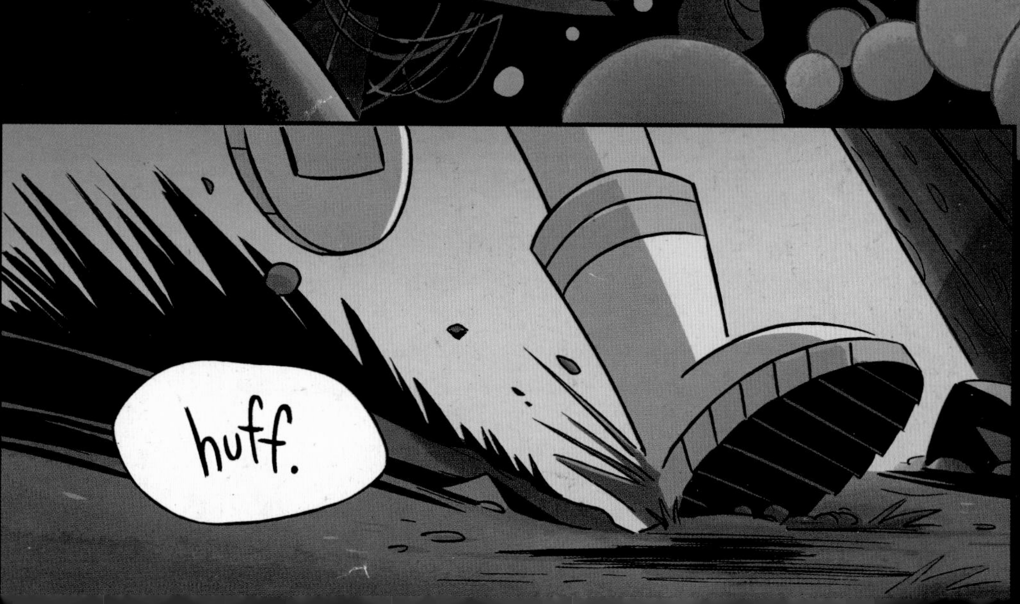
huff.

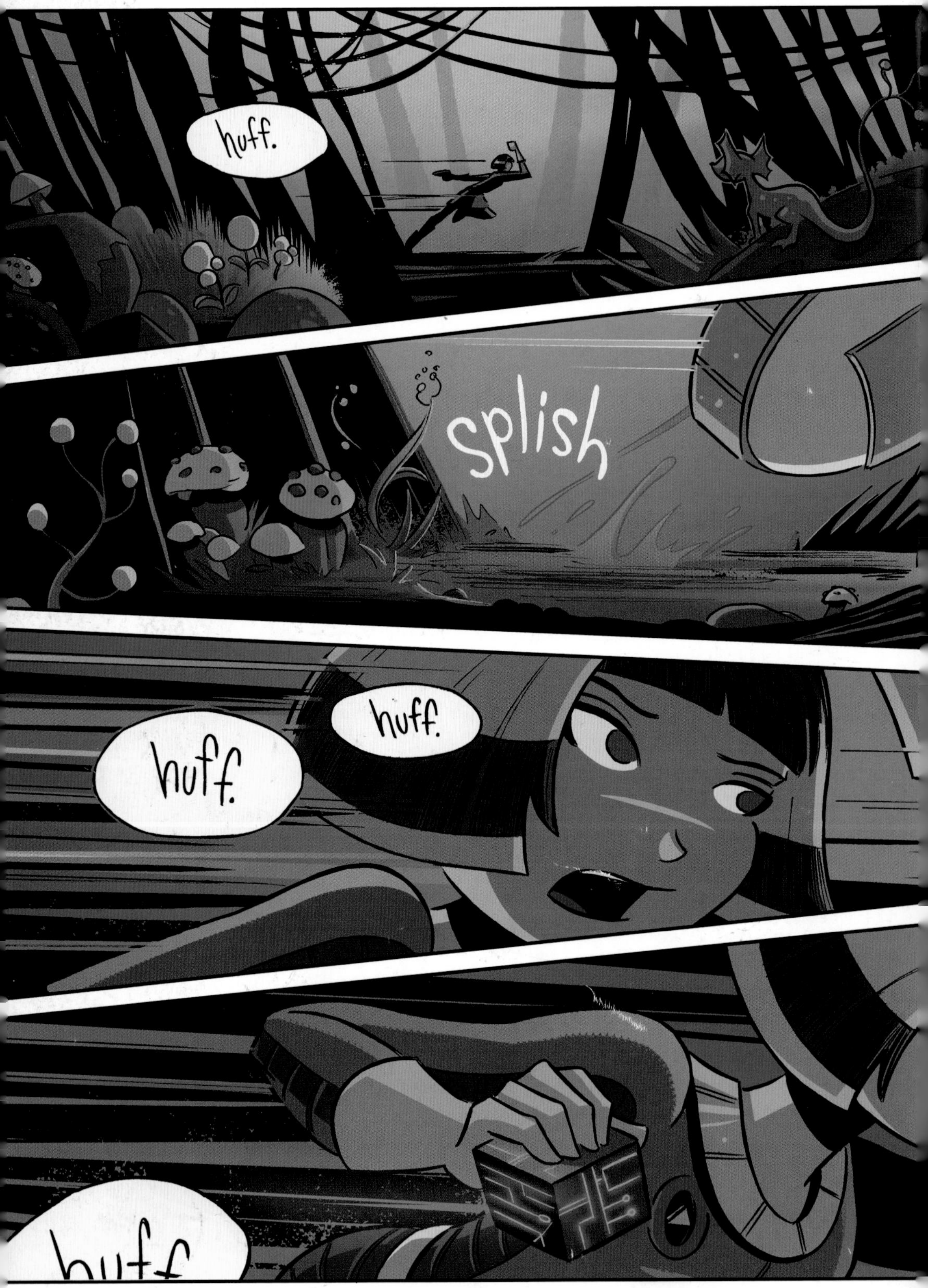
huff.
splish
huff.
huff.
huff

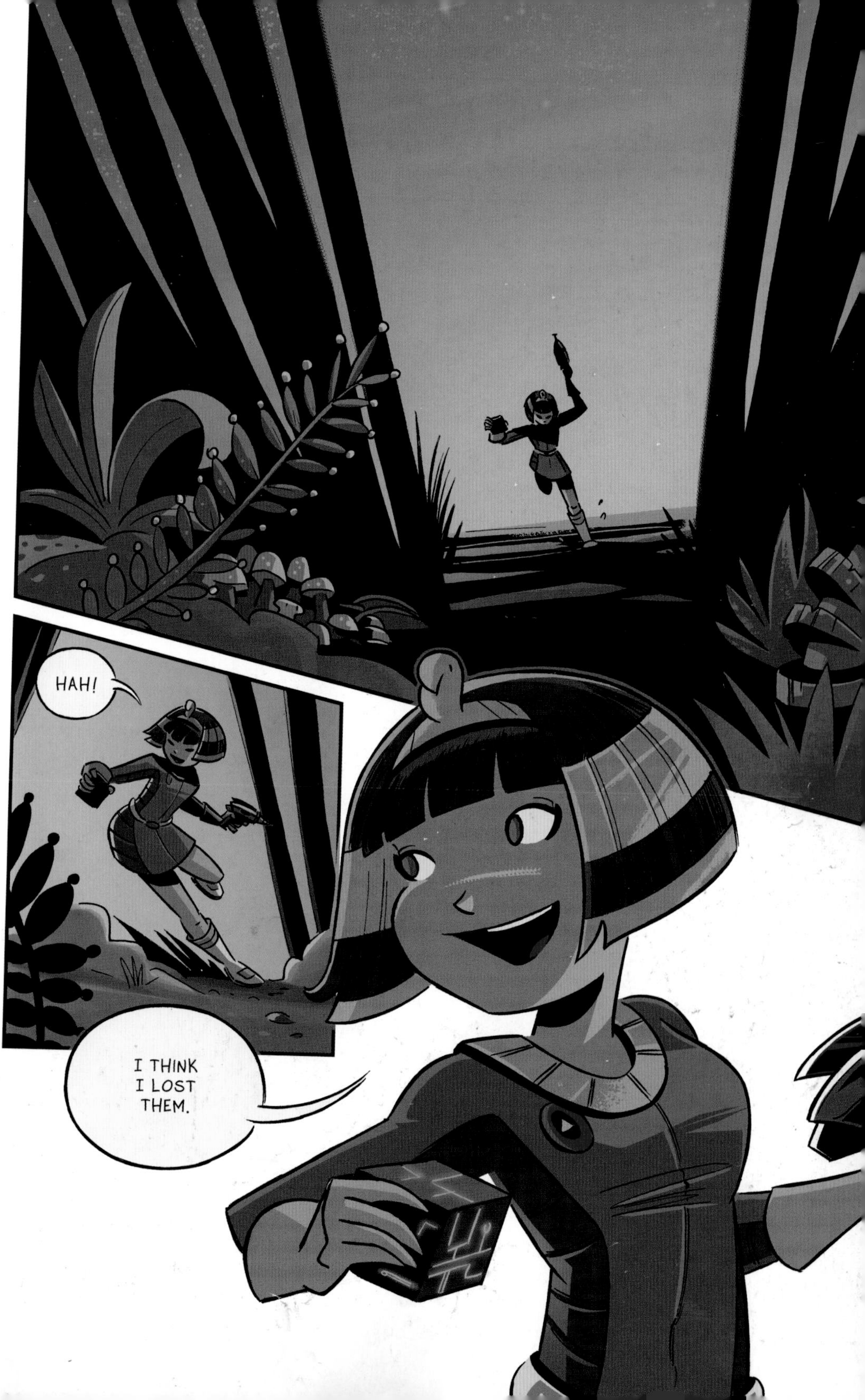
HAH!
I THINK I LOST THEM.

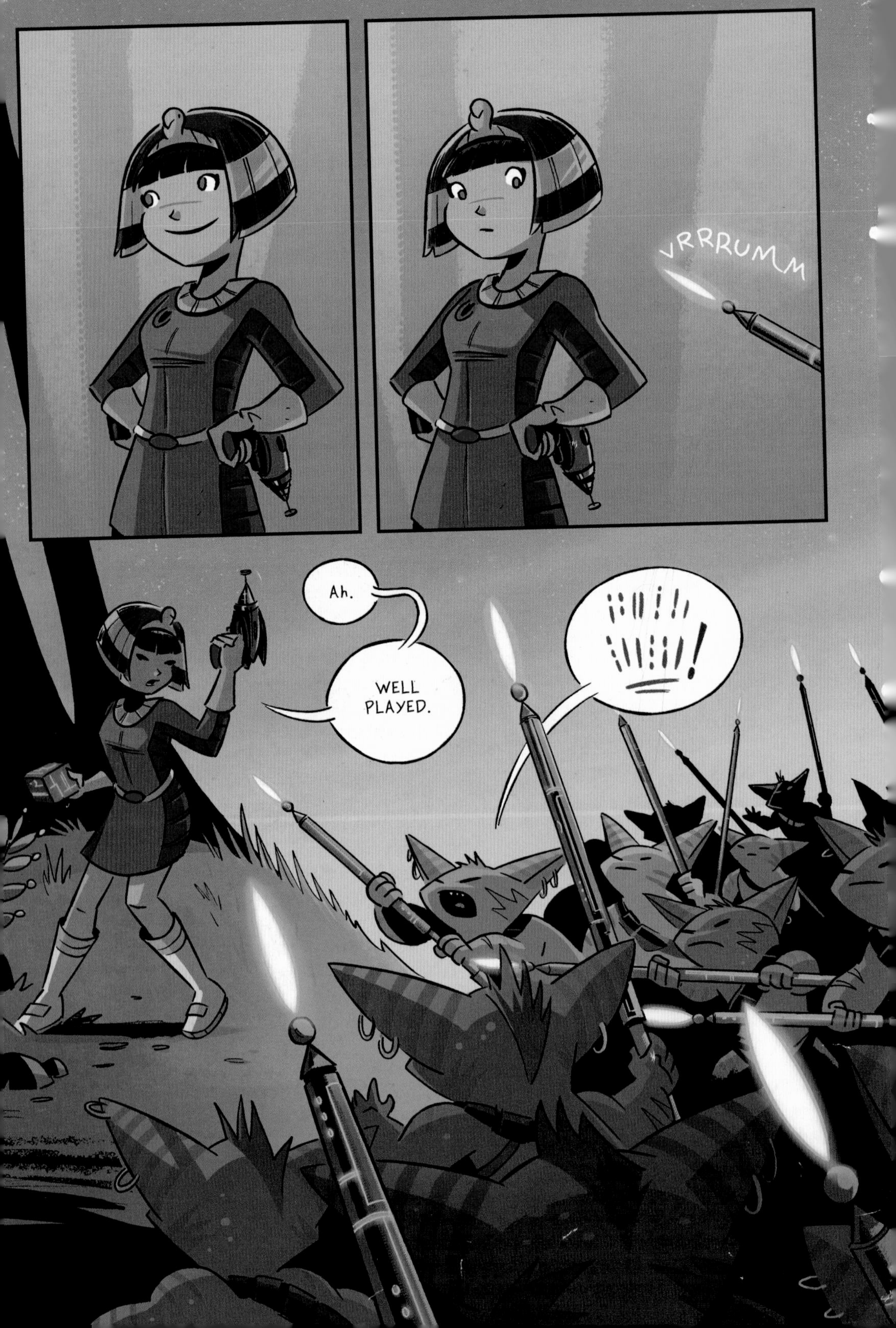
VRRRUMM
Ah.
WELL PLAYED.

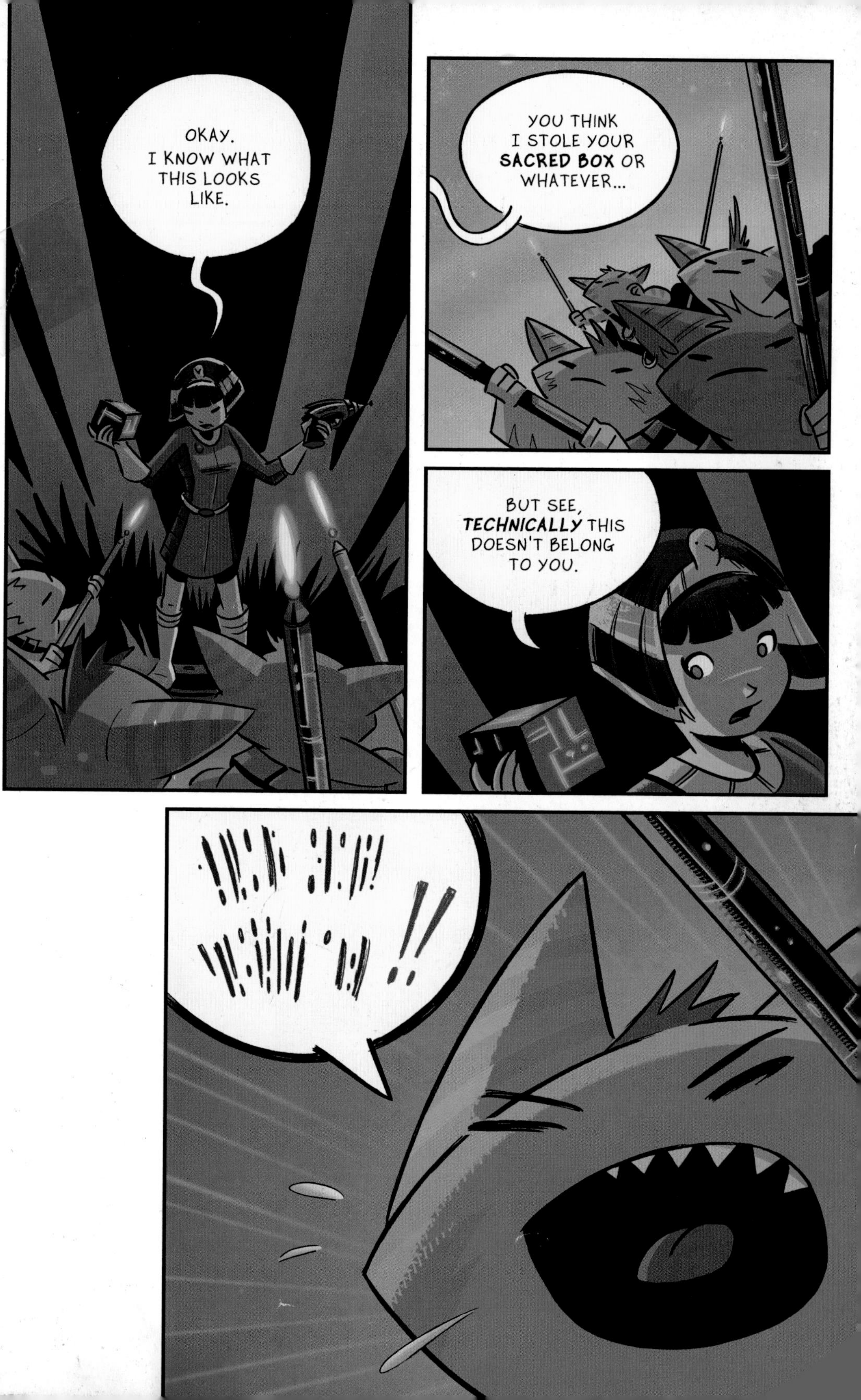
OKAY.
I KNOW WHAT THIS LOOKS LIKE.
YOU THINK I STOLE YOUR **SACRED BOX** OR WHATEVER...
BUT SEE, ***TECHNICALLY*** THIS DOESN'T BELONG TO YOU.

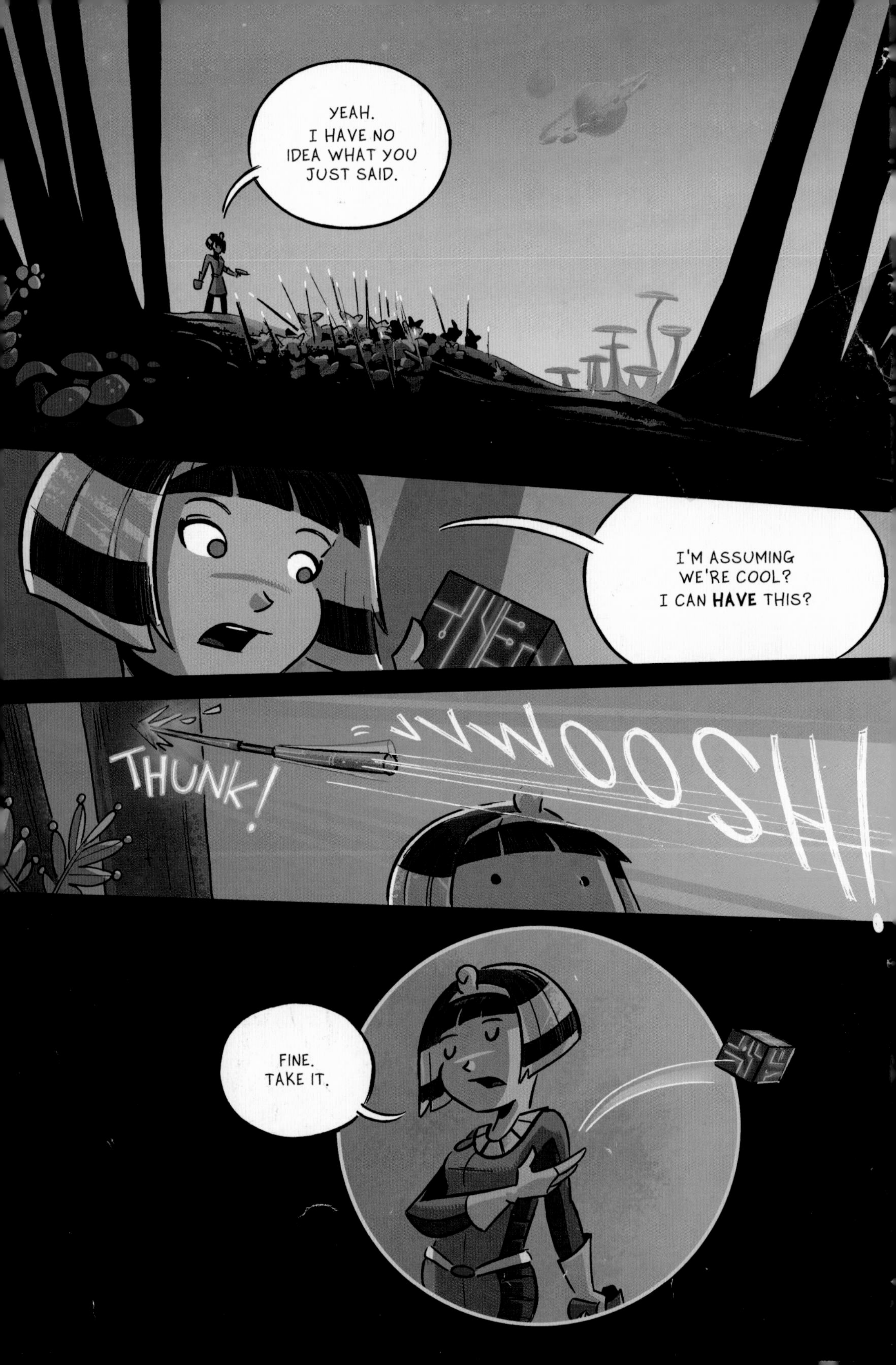
YEAH. I HAVE NO IDEA WHAT YOU JUST SAID.
I'M ASSUMING WE'RE COOL? I CAN **HAVE** THIS?
VVWOOOSH!
THUNK!
FINE. TAKE IT.

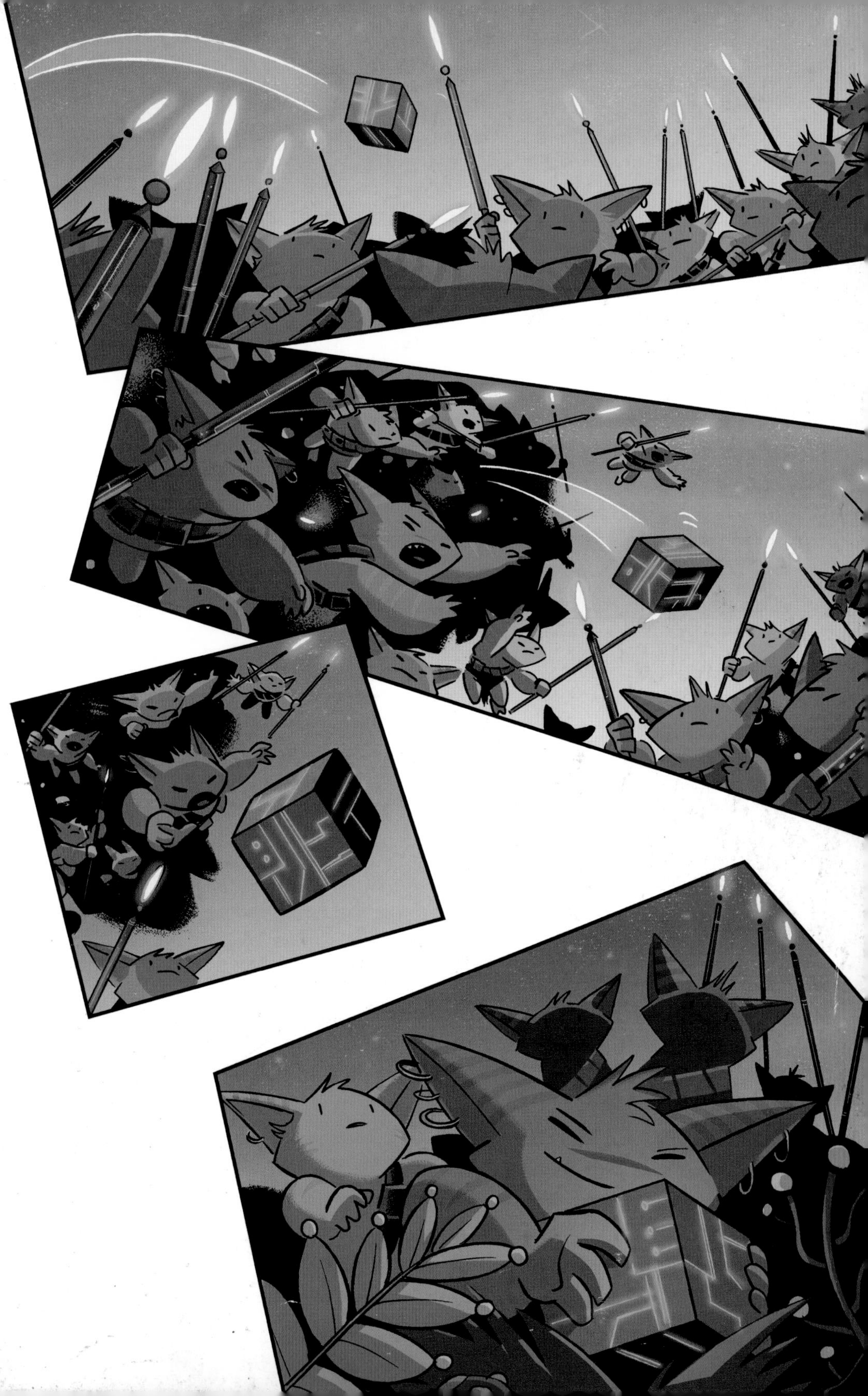

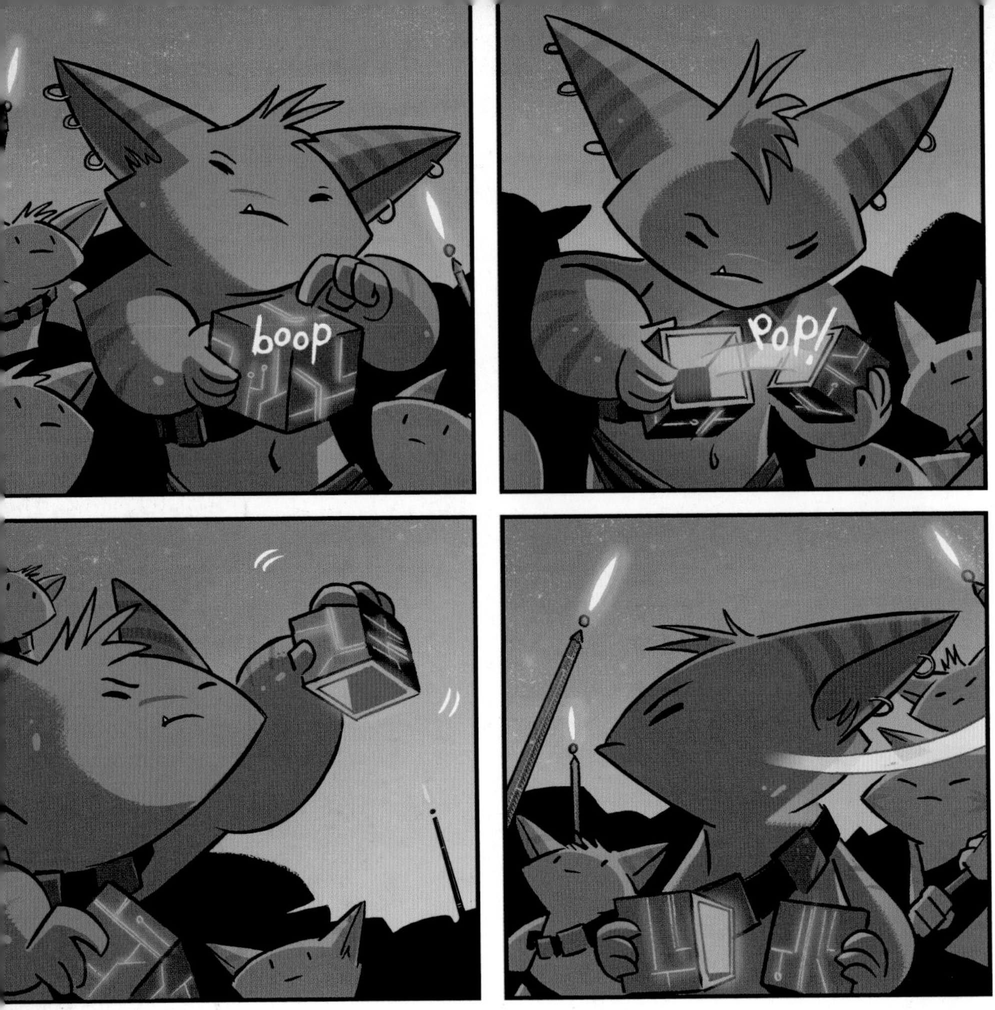
boop
pop!

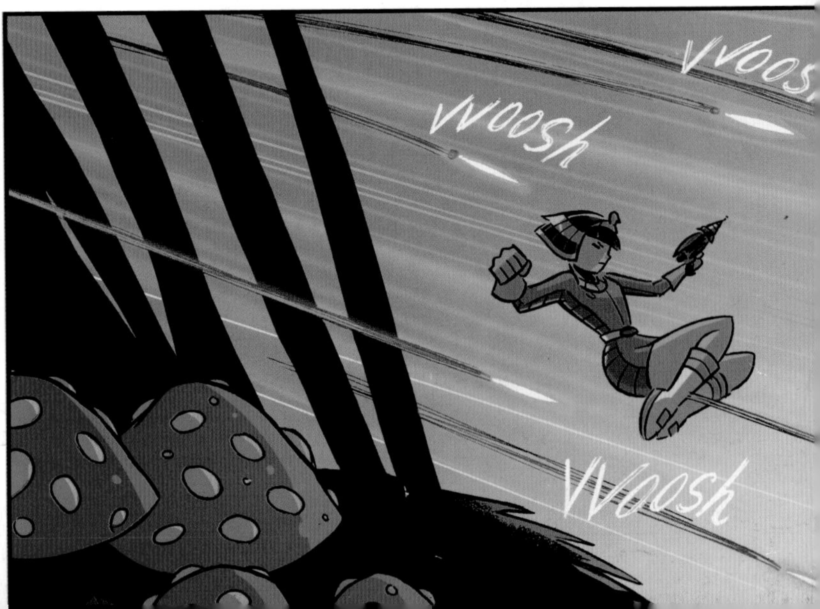
VVOOSH
VVOOSH
VVOOSH

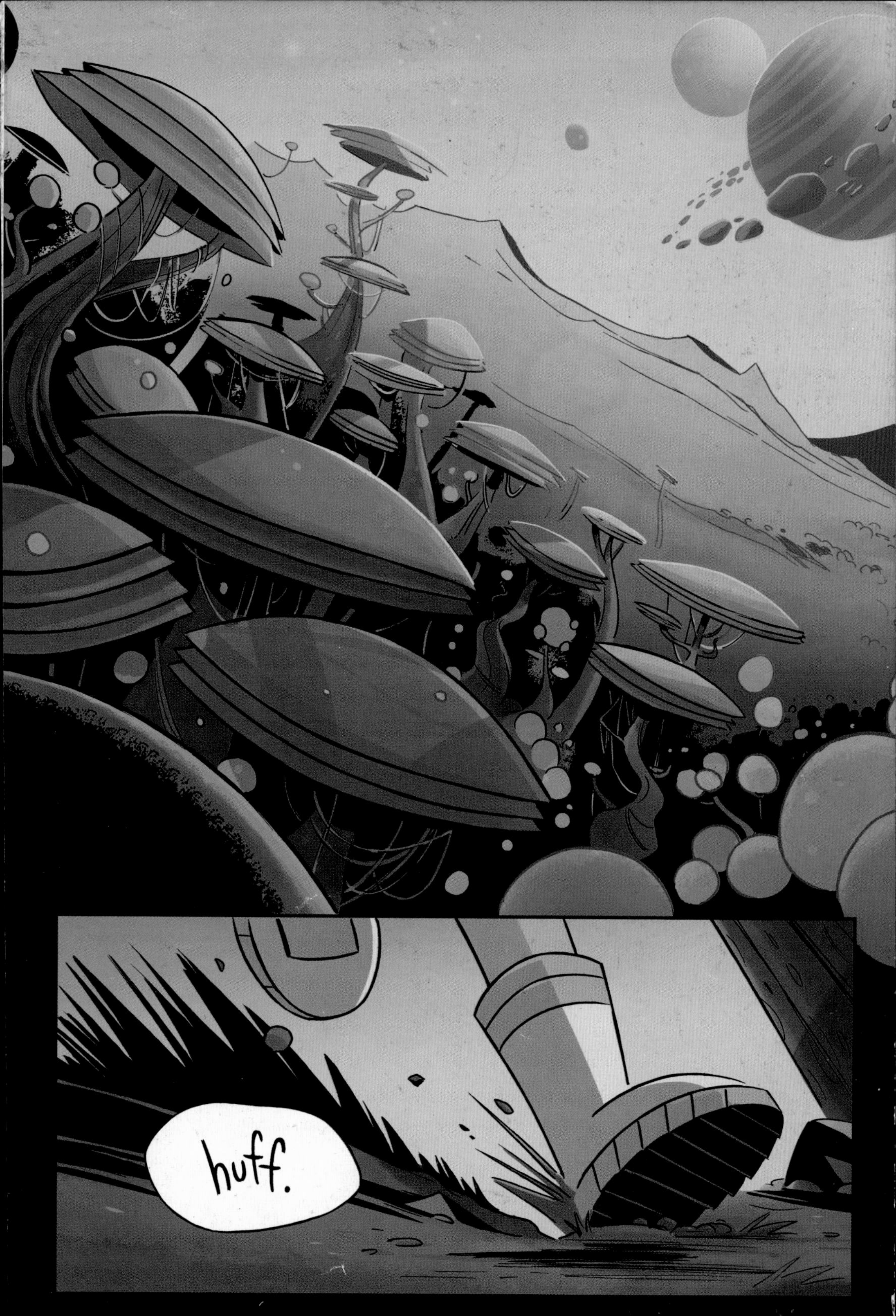
huff.

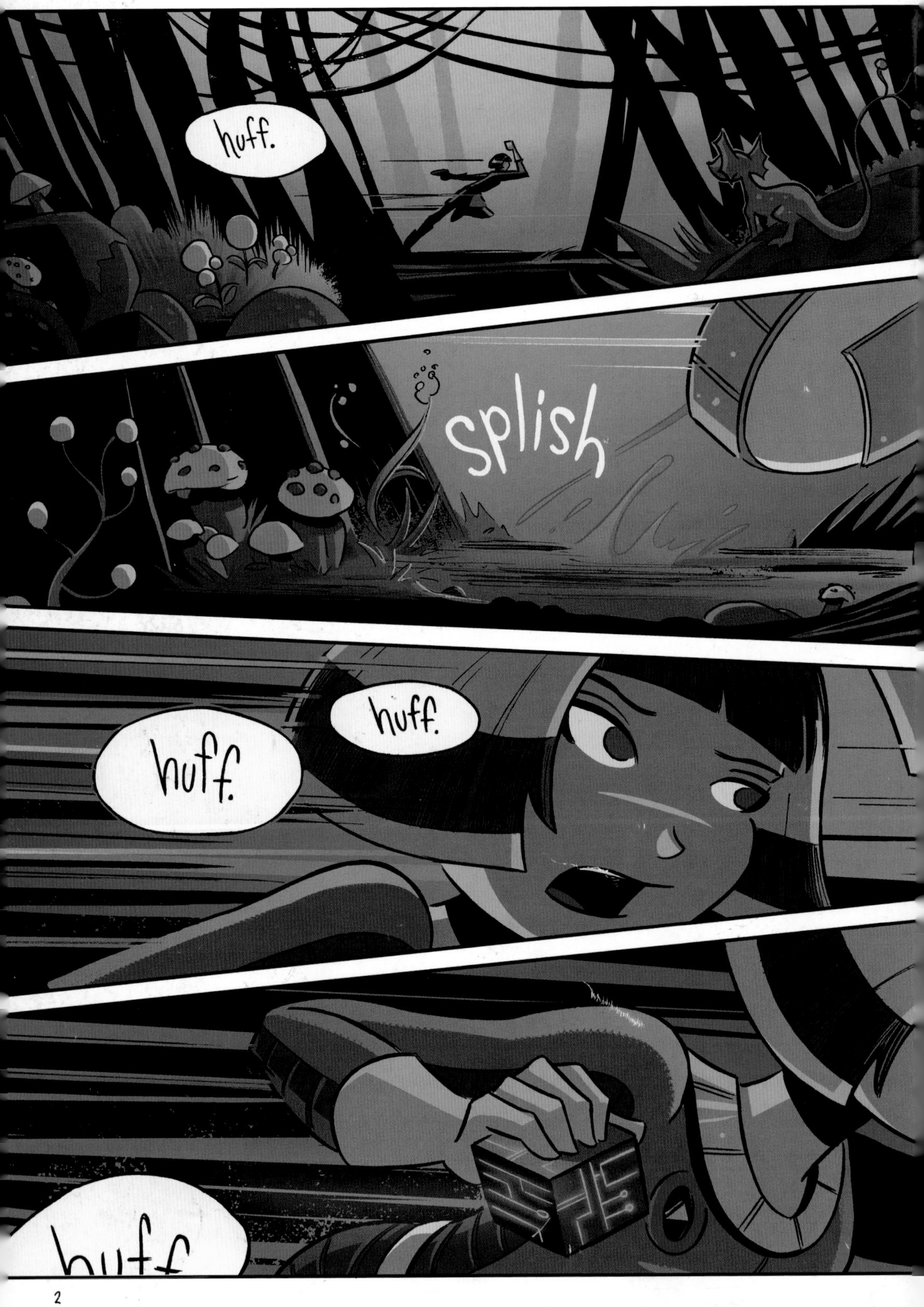
huff.
splish
huff.
huff.
huff

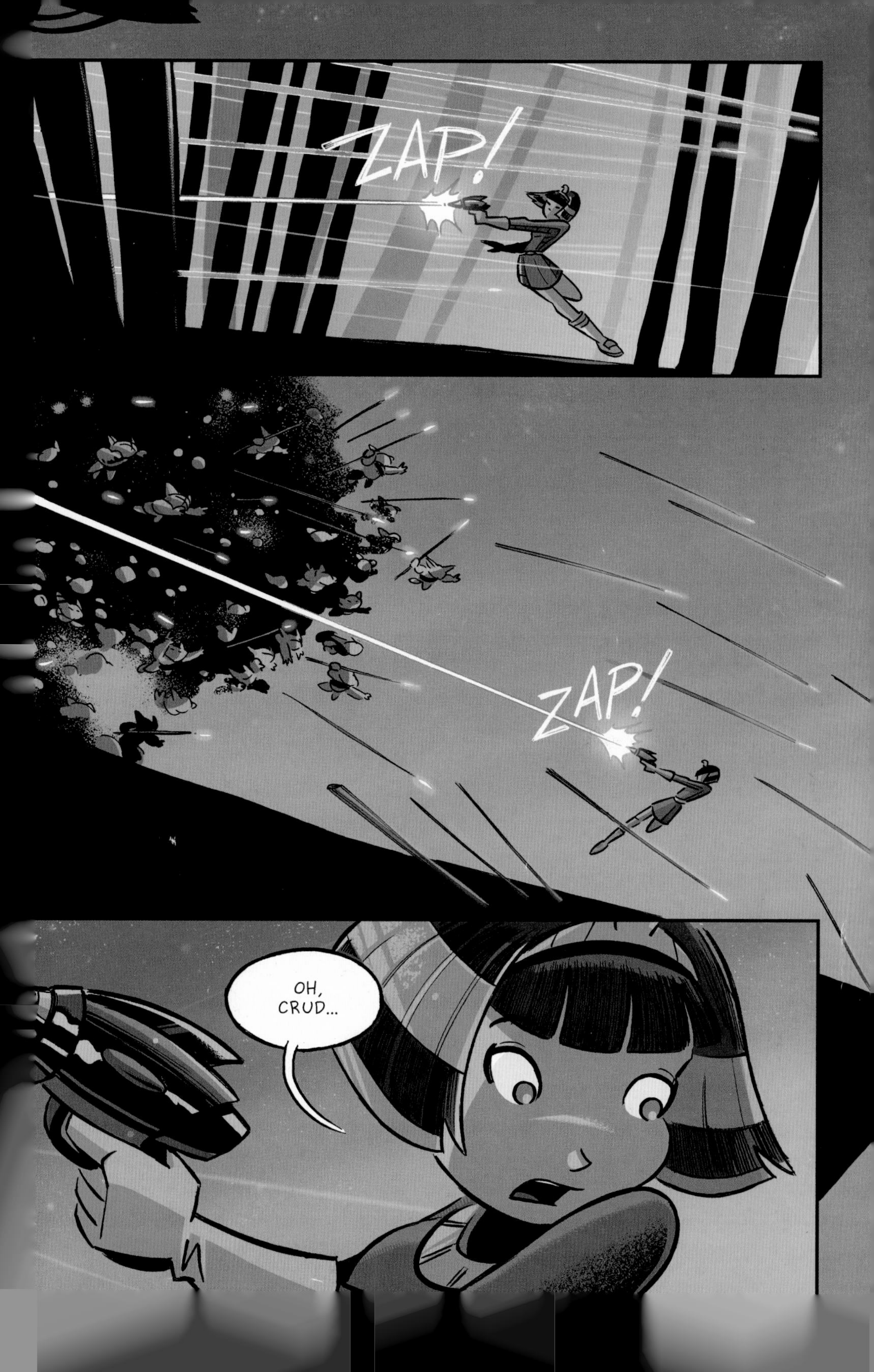
ZAP!
ZAP!
OH, CRUD...

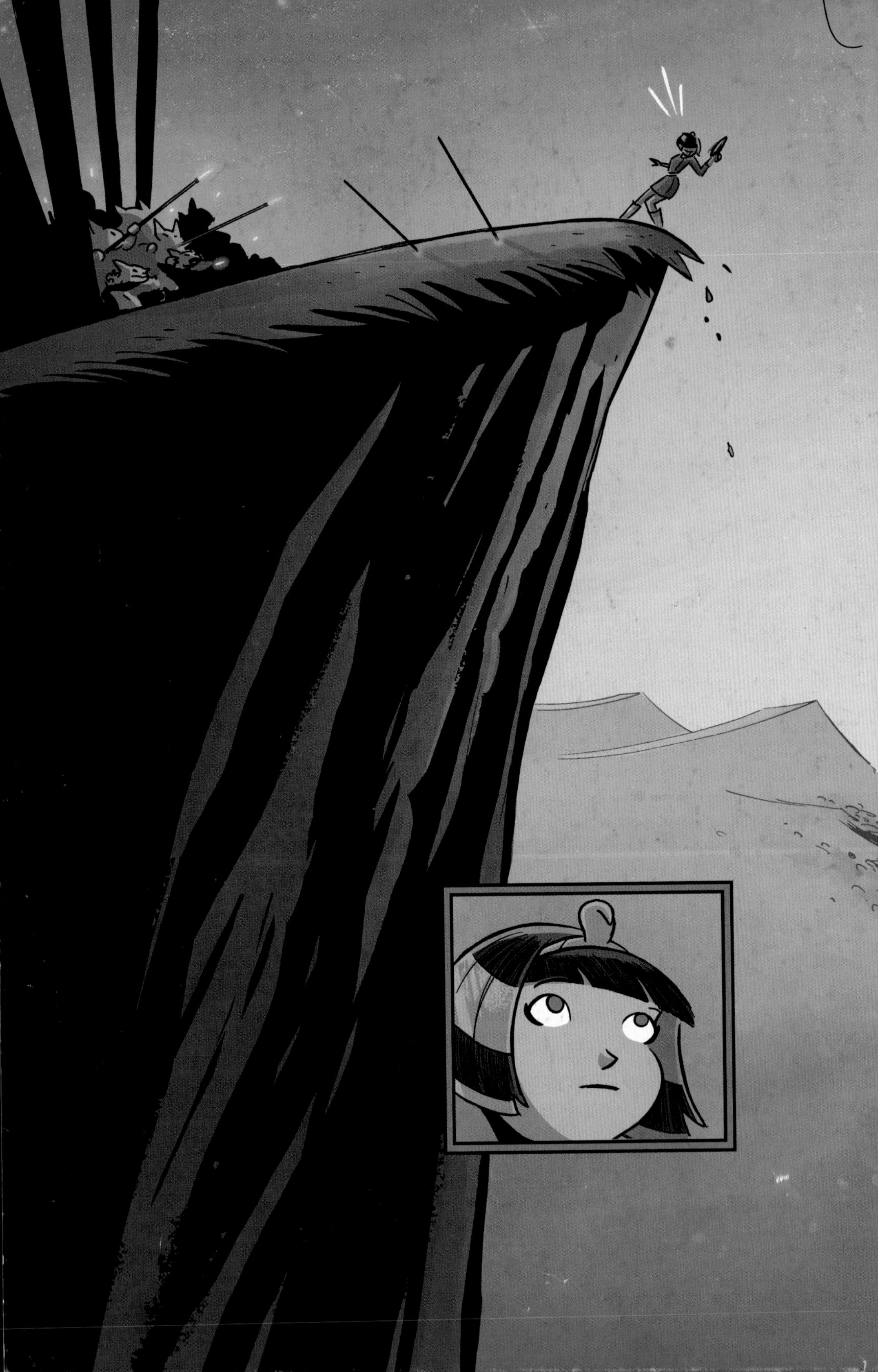

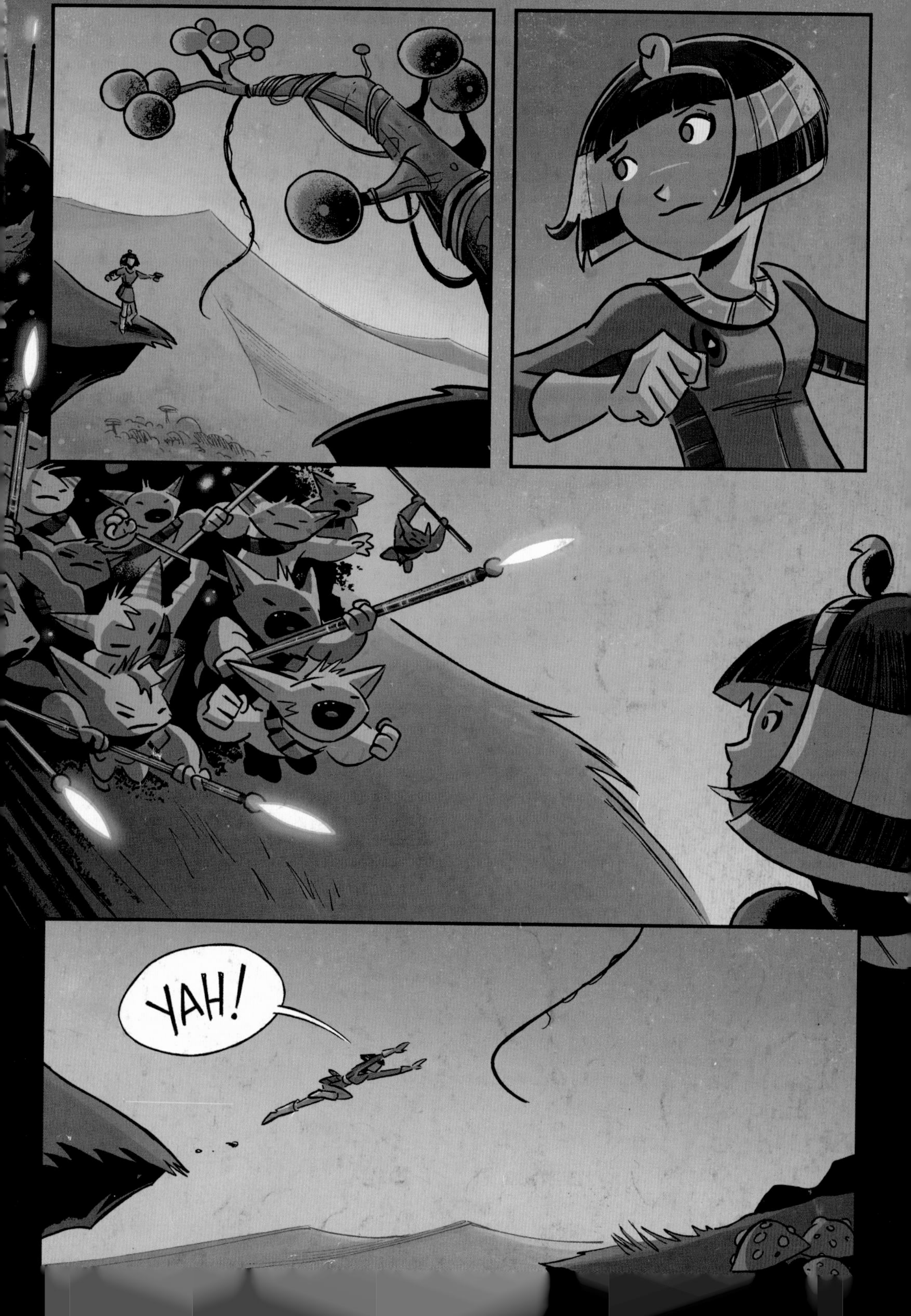
YAH!

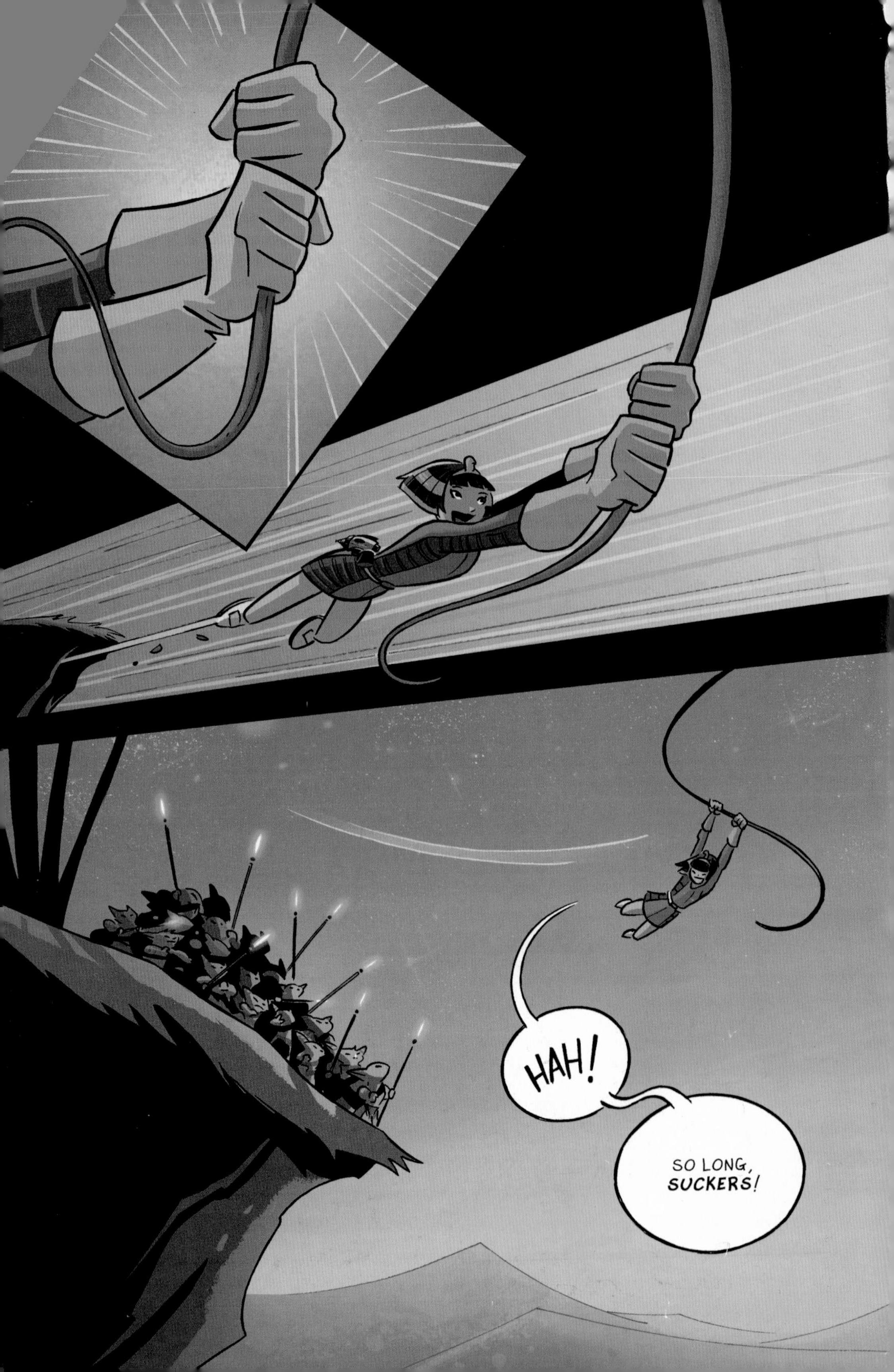
HAH!
SO LONG, SUCKERS!

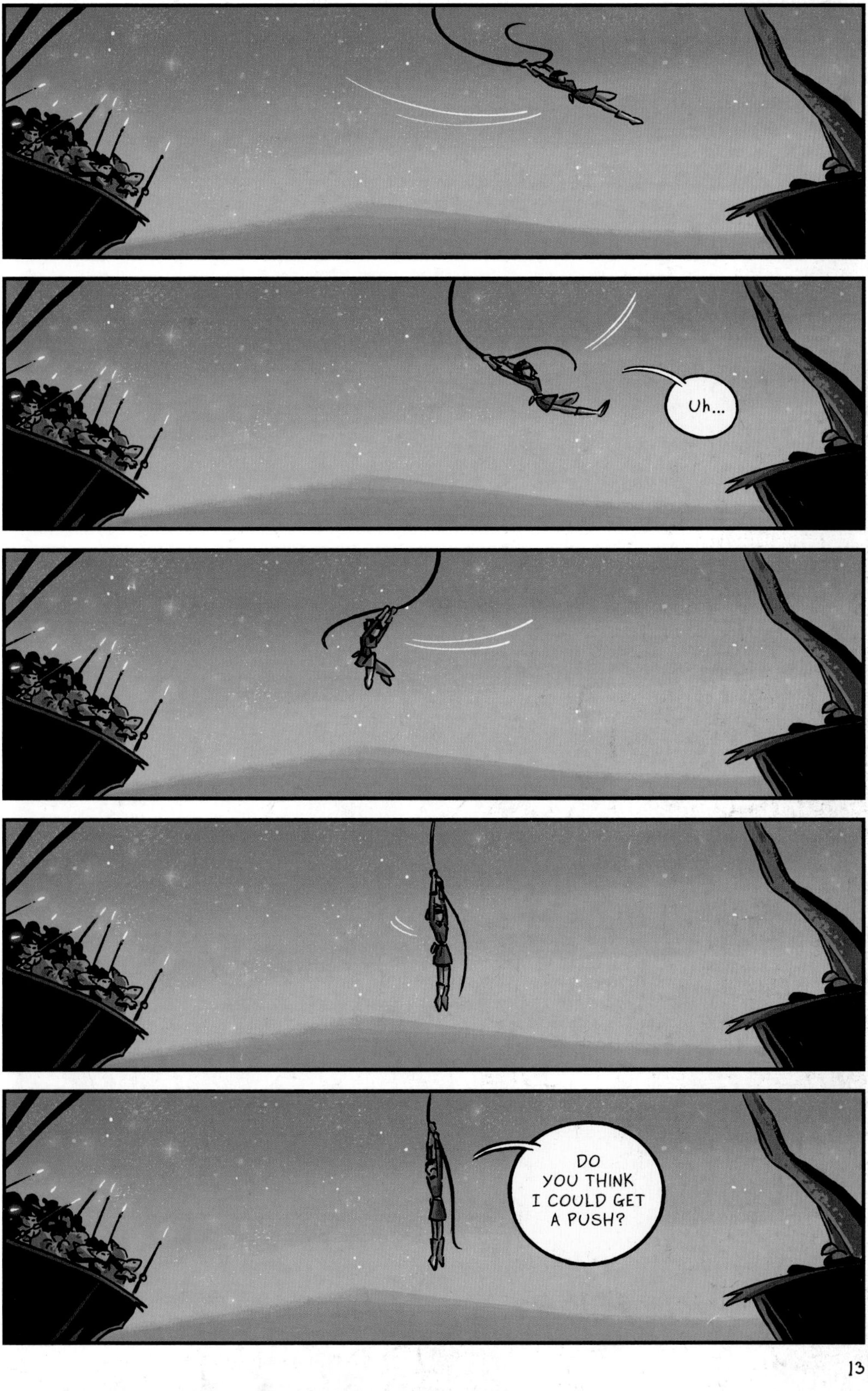
Uh...
DO YOU THINK I COULD GET A PUSH?

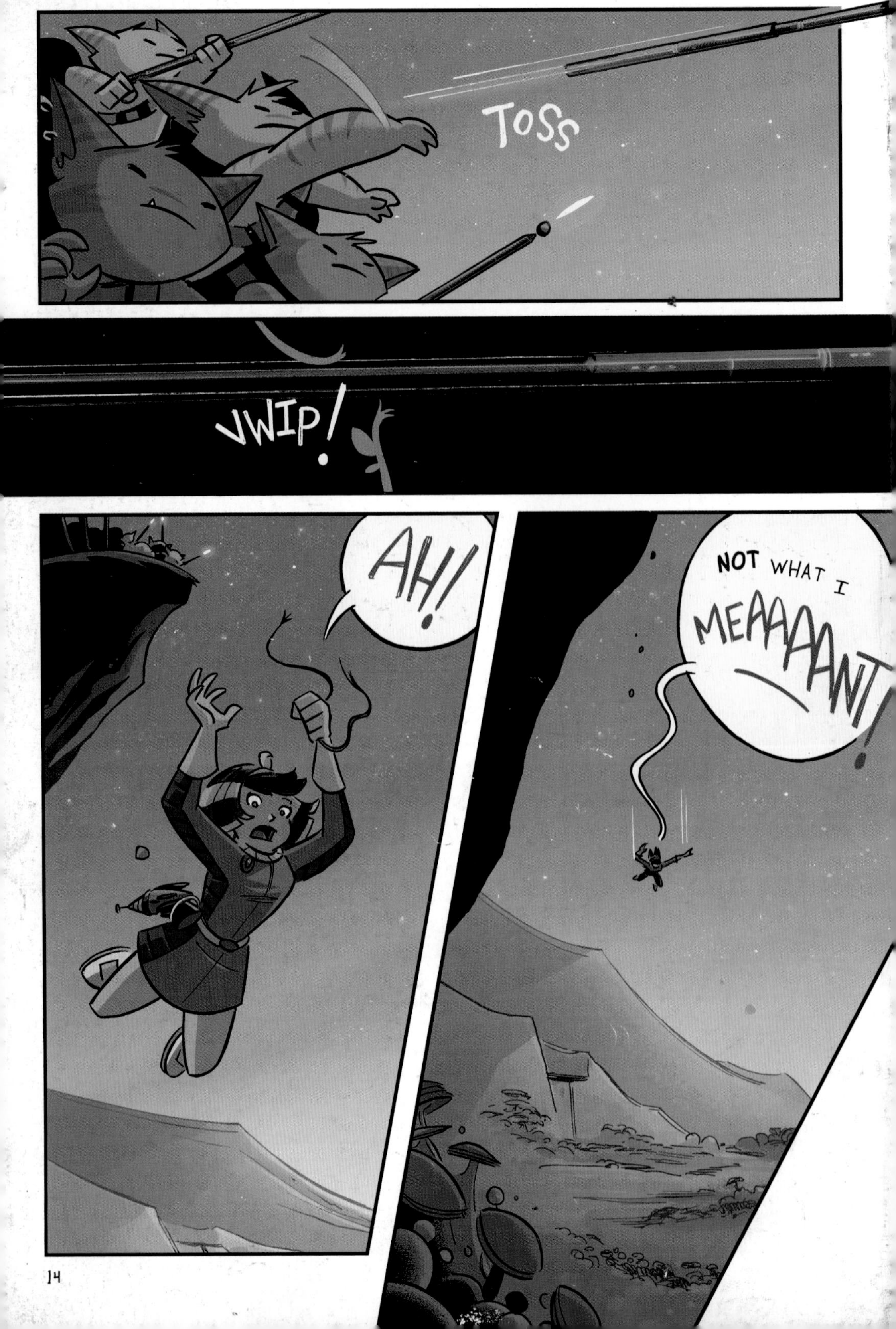
TOSS
VWIP!
AH!
NOT WHAT I MEAAAAANT!

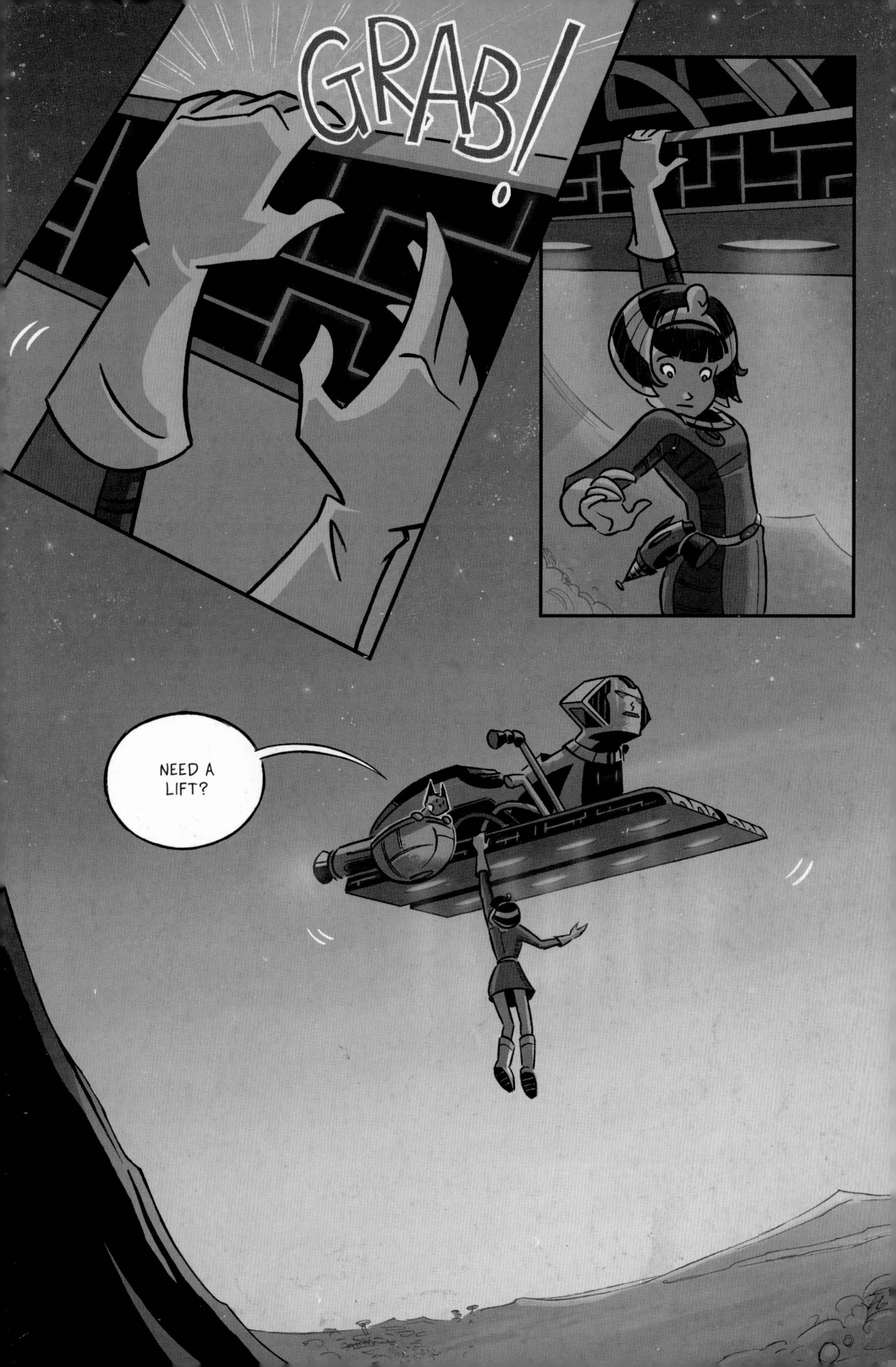
GRAB!
NEED A LIFT?

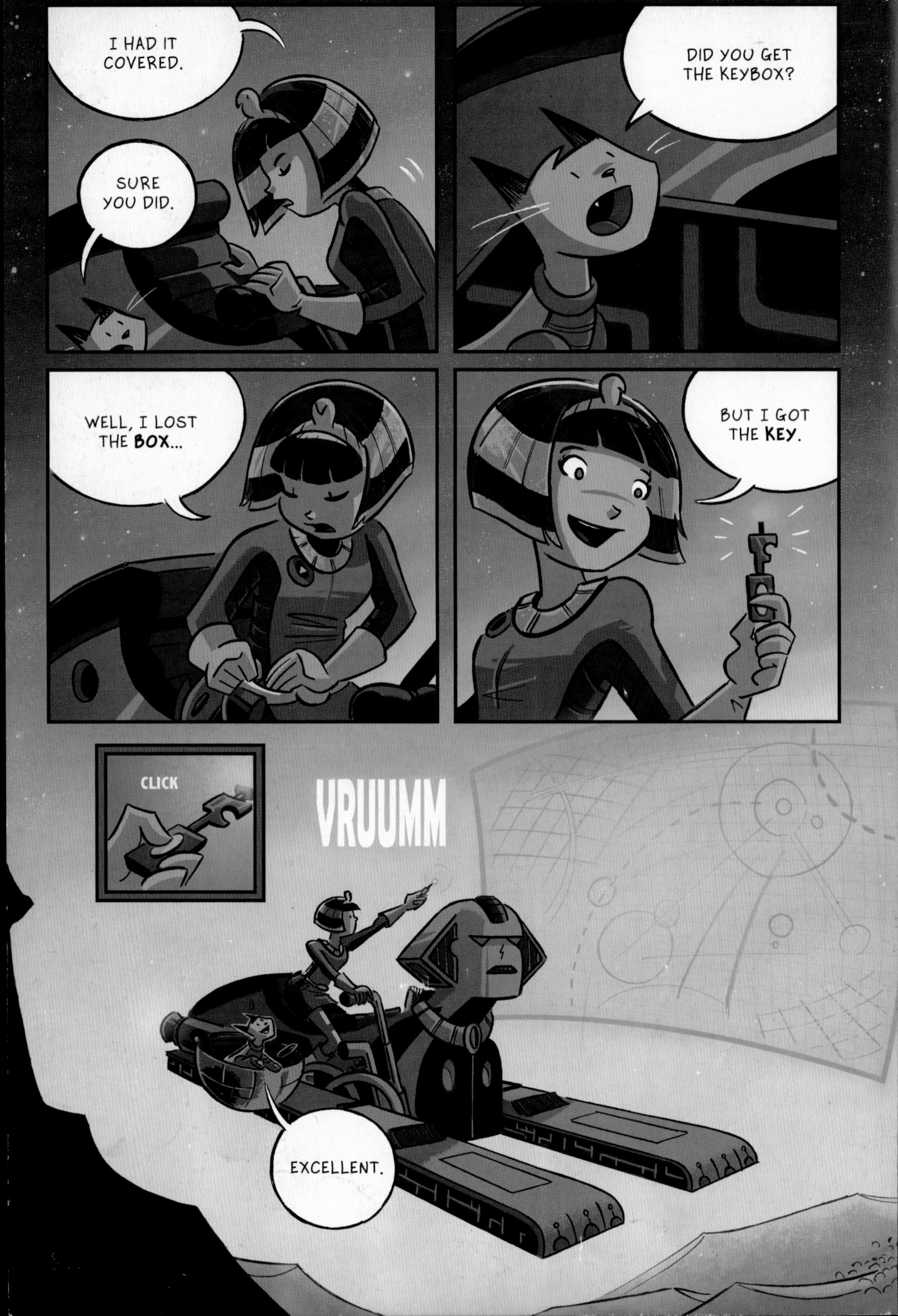
I HAD IT COVERED.
SURE YOU DID.
DID YOU GET THE KEYBOX?
WELL, I LOST THE **BOX**...
BUT I GOT THE **KEY**.
CLICK
VRUUMM
EXCELLENT.

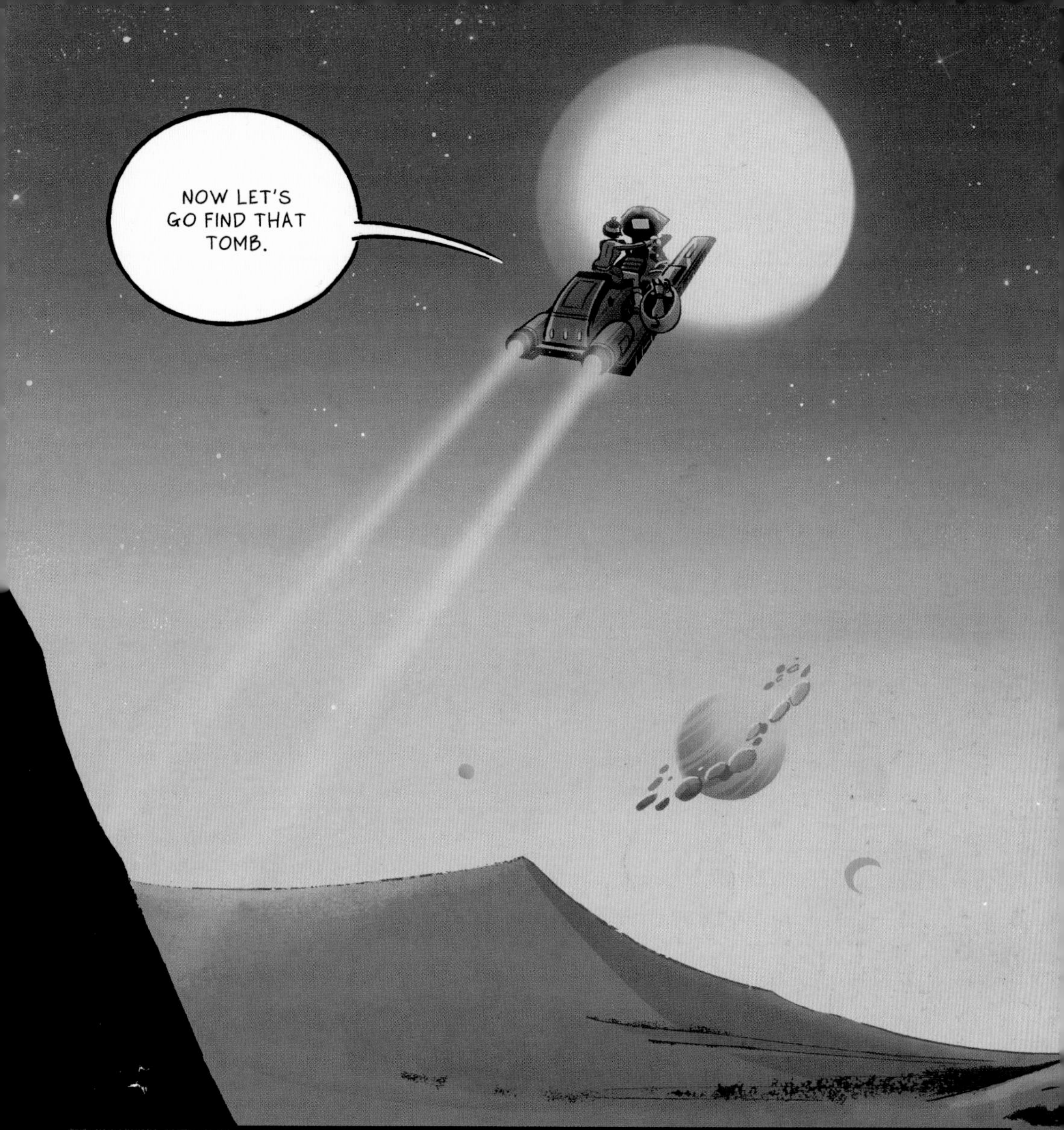
NOW LET'S GO FIND THAT TOMB.

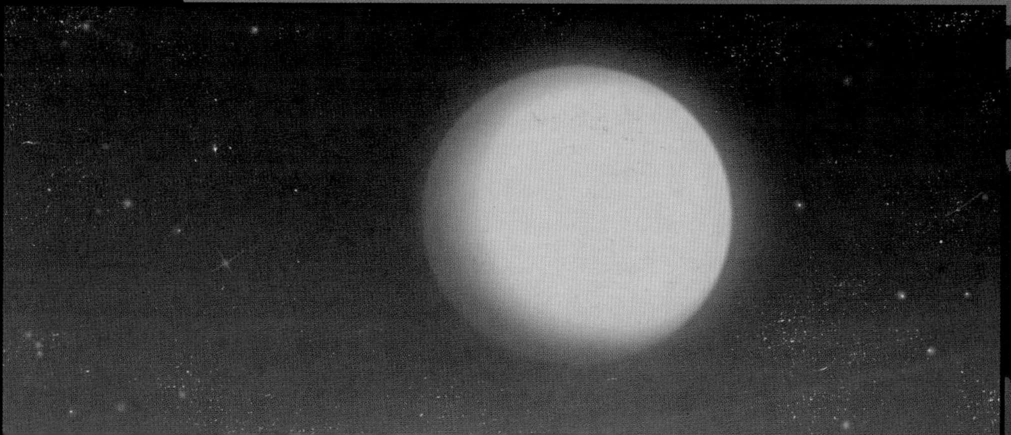

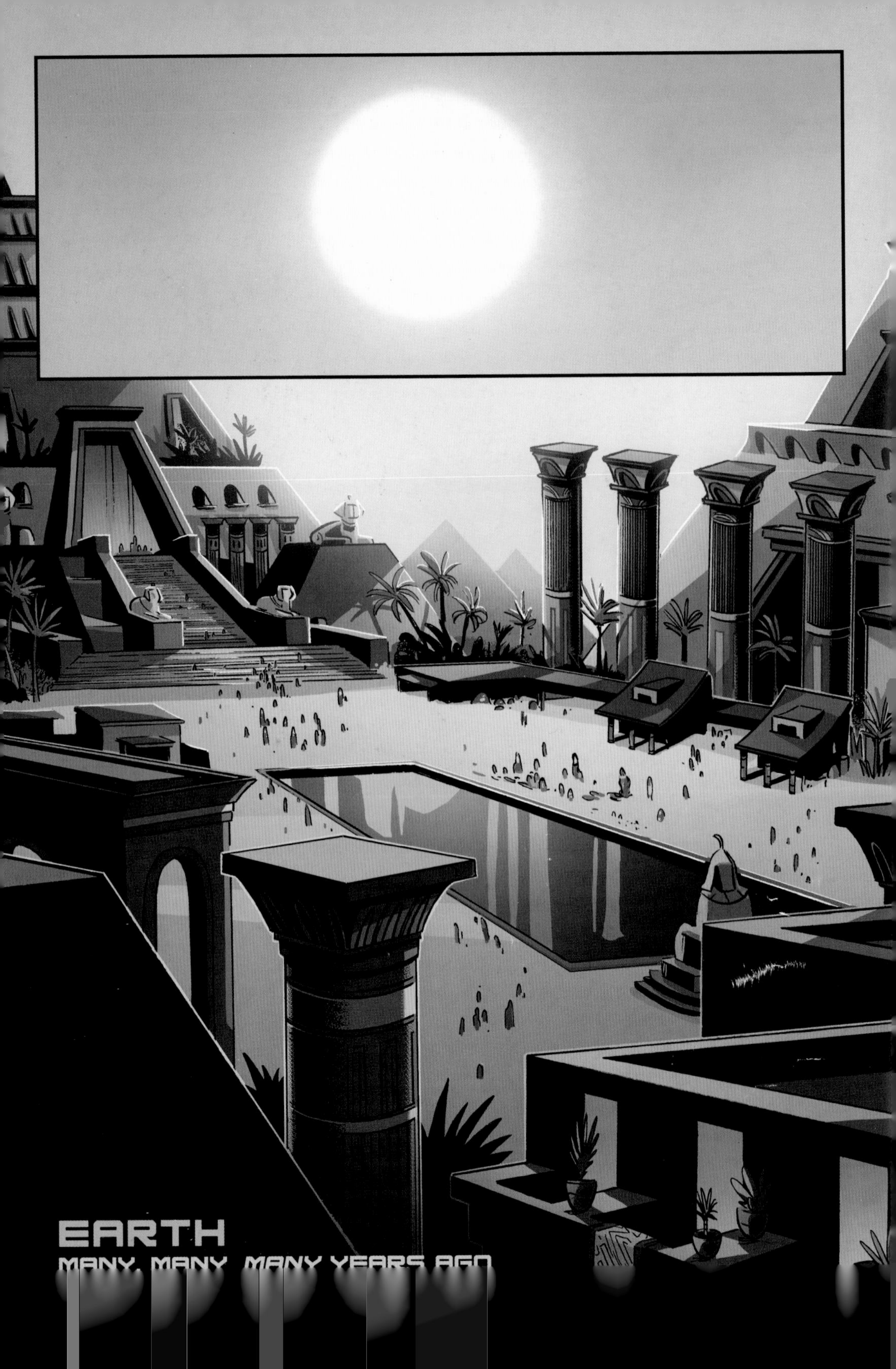
EARTH
MANY, MANY, MANY YEARS AGO

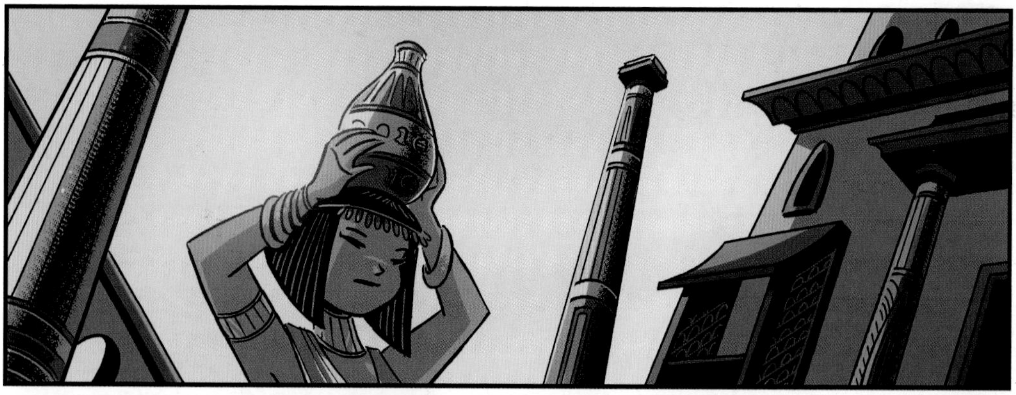
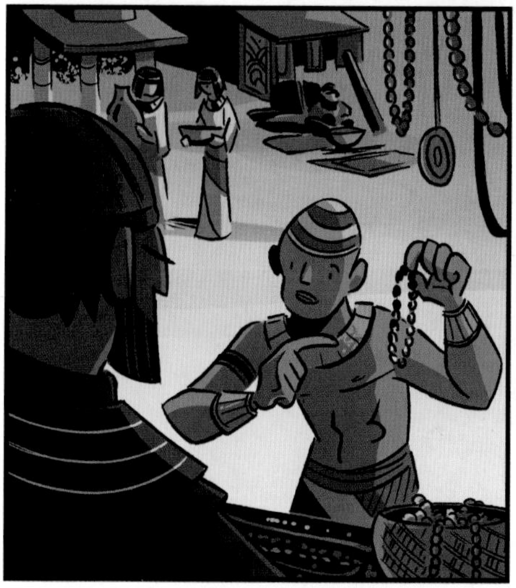
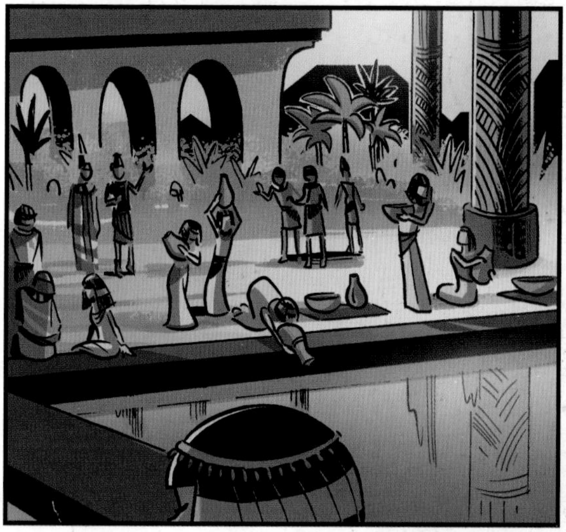
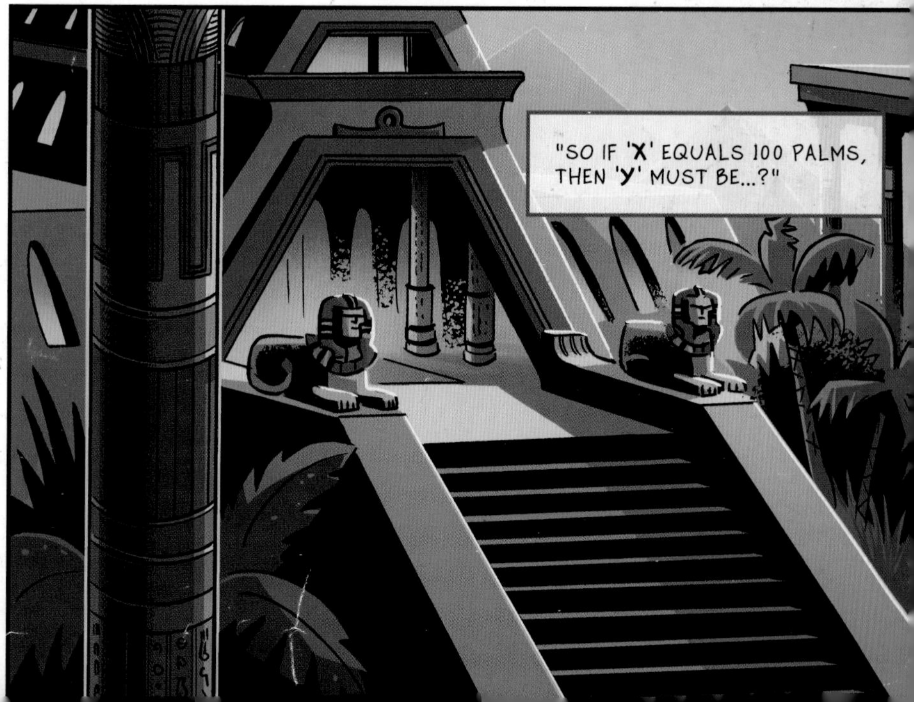
"SO IF 'X' EQUALS 100 PALMS, THEN 'Y' MUST BE...?"

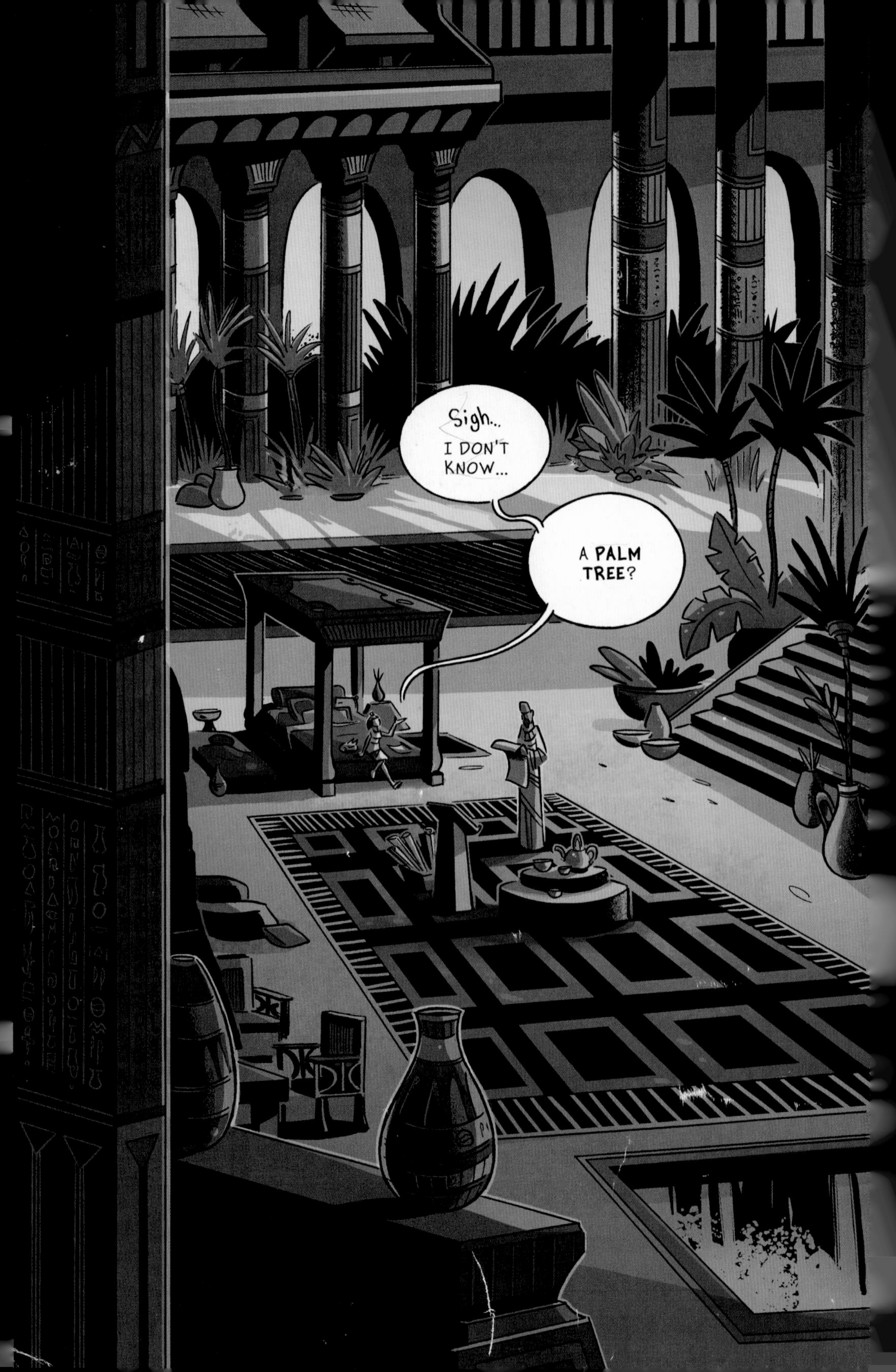
Sigh... I DON'T KNOW...
A PALM TREE?

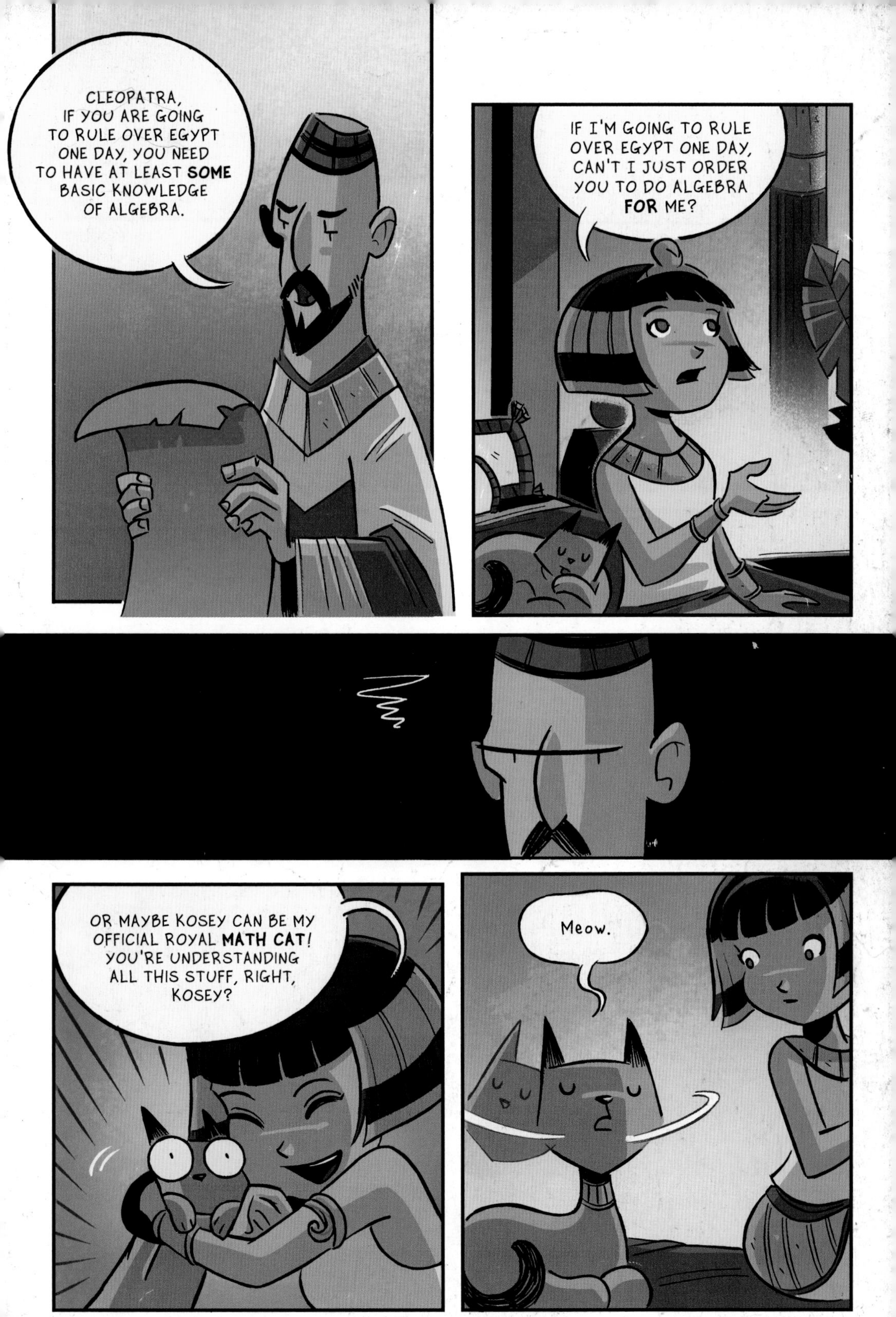
CLEOPATRA, IF YOU ARE GOING TO RULE OVER EGYPT ONE DAY, YOU NEED TO HAVE AT LEAST **SOME** BASIC KNOWLEDGE OF ALGEBRA.
IF I'M GOING TO RULE OVER EGYPT ONE DAY, CAN'T I JUST ORDER YOU TO DO ALGEBRA **FOR** ME?
OR MAYBE KOSEY CAN BE MY OFFICIAL ROYAL **MATH CAT**! YOU'RE UNDERSTANDING ALL THIS STUFF, RIGHT, KOSEY?
Meow.

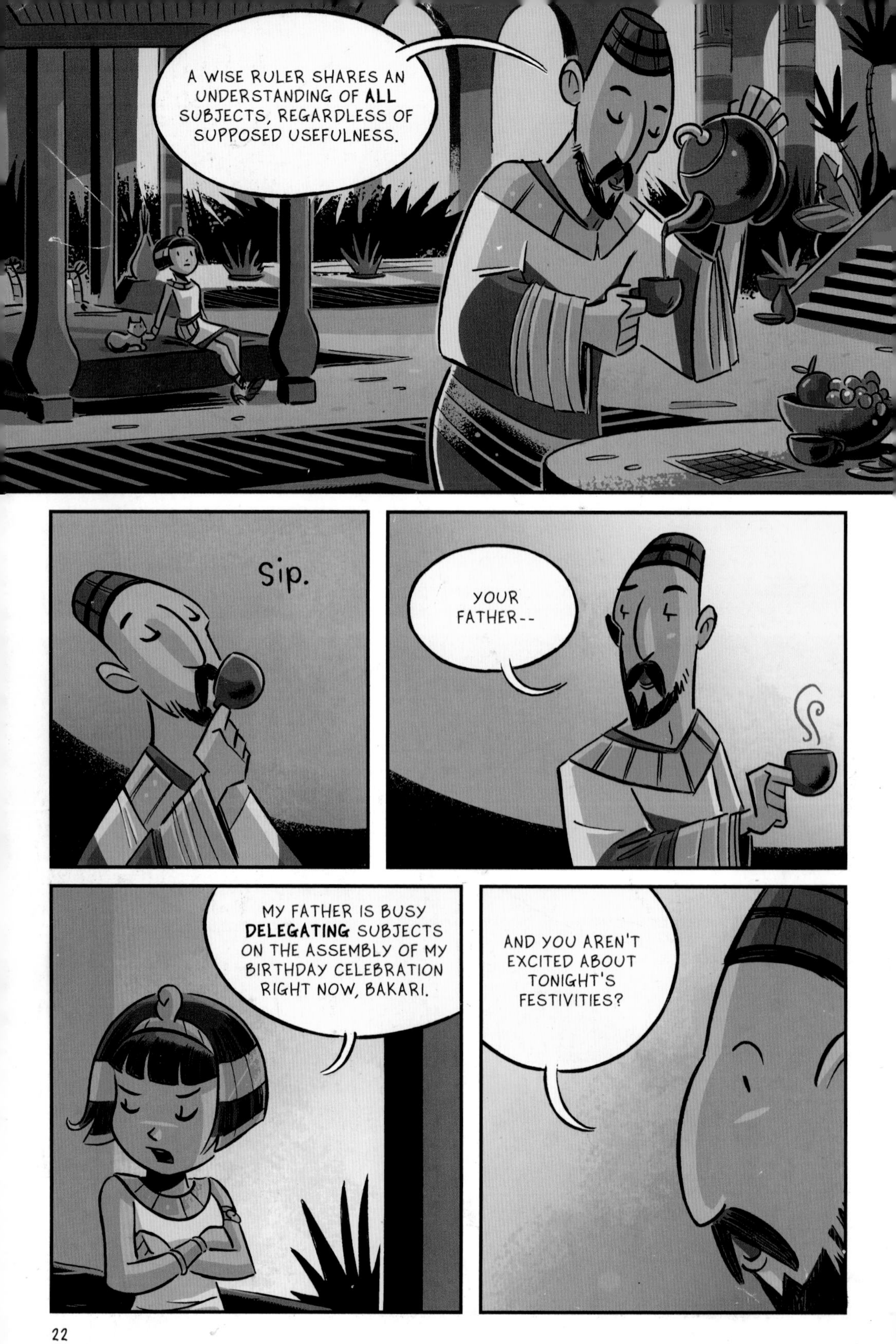
A WISE RULER SHARES AN UNDERSTANDING OF **ALL** SUBJECTS, REGARDLESS OF SUPPOSED USEFULNESS.
Sip.
YOUR FATHER--
MY FATHER IS BUSY **DELEGATING** SUBJECTS ON THE ASSEMBLY OF MY BIRTHDAY CELEBRATION RIGHT NOW, BAKARI.
AND YOU AREN'T EXCITED ABOUT TONIGHT'S FESTIVITIES?

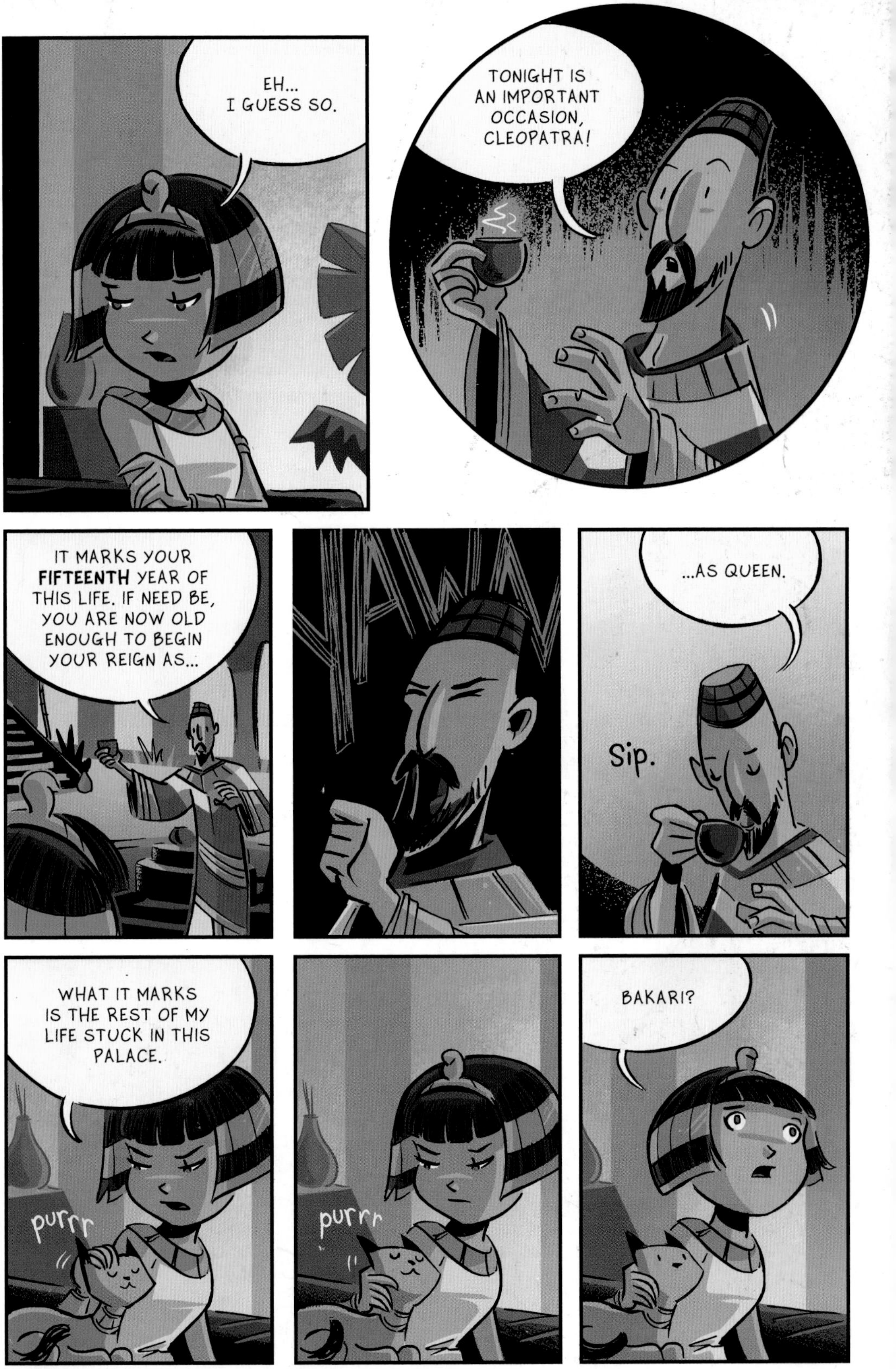
EH...
I GUESS SO.
TONIGHT IS AN IMPORTANT OCCASION, CLEOPATRA!
IT MARKS YOUR **FIFTEENTH** YEAR OF THIS LIFE. IF NEED BE, YOU ARE NOW OLD ENOUGH TO BEGIN YOUR REIGN AS...
...AS QUEEN.
Sip.
WHAT IT MARKS IS THE REST OF MY LIFE STUCK IN THIS PALACE.
purrr
purrr
BAKARI?

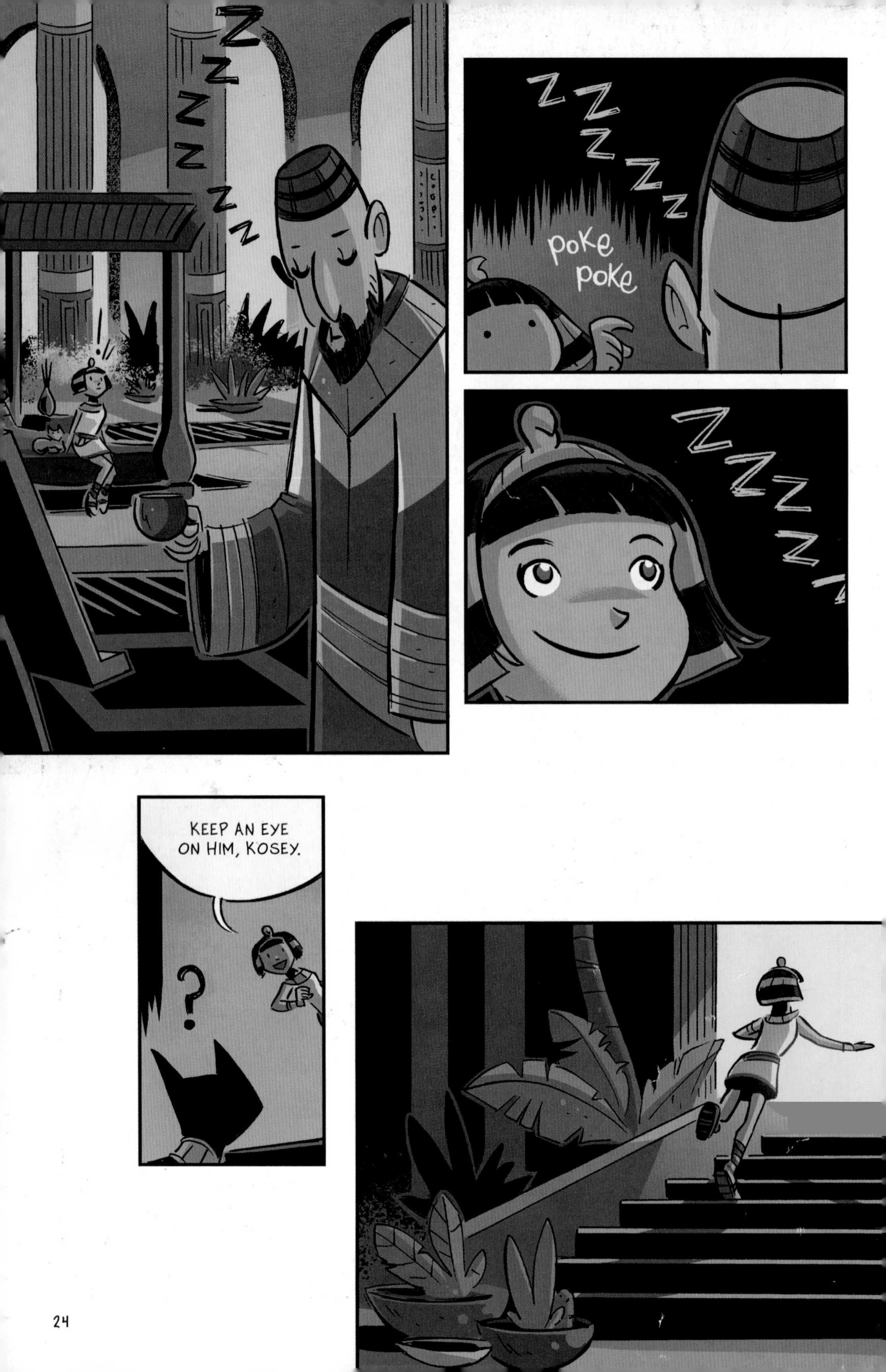
ZZZZZZ
ZZZZZZ
POKE POKE
ZZZZZ
KEEP AN EYE ON HIM, KOSEY.
?

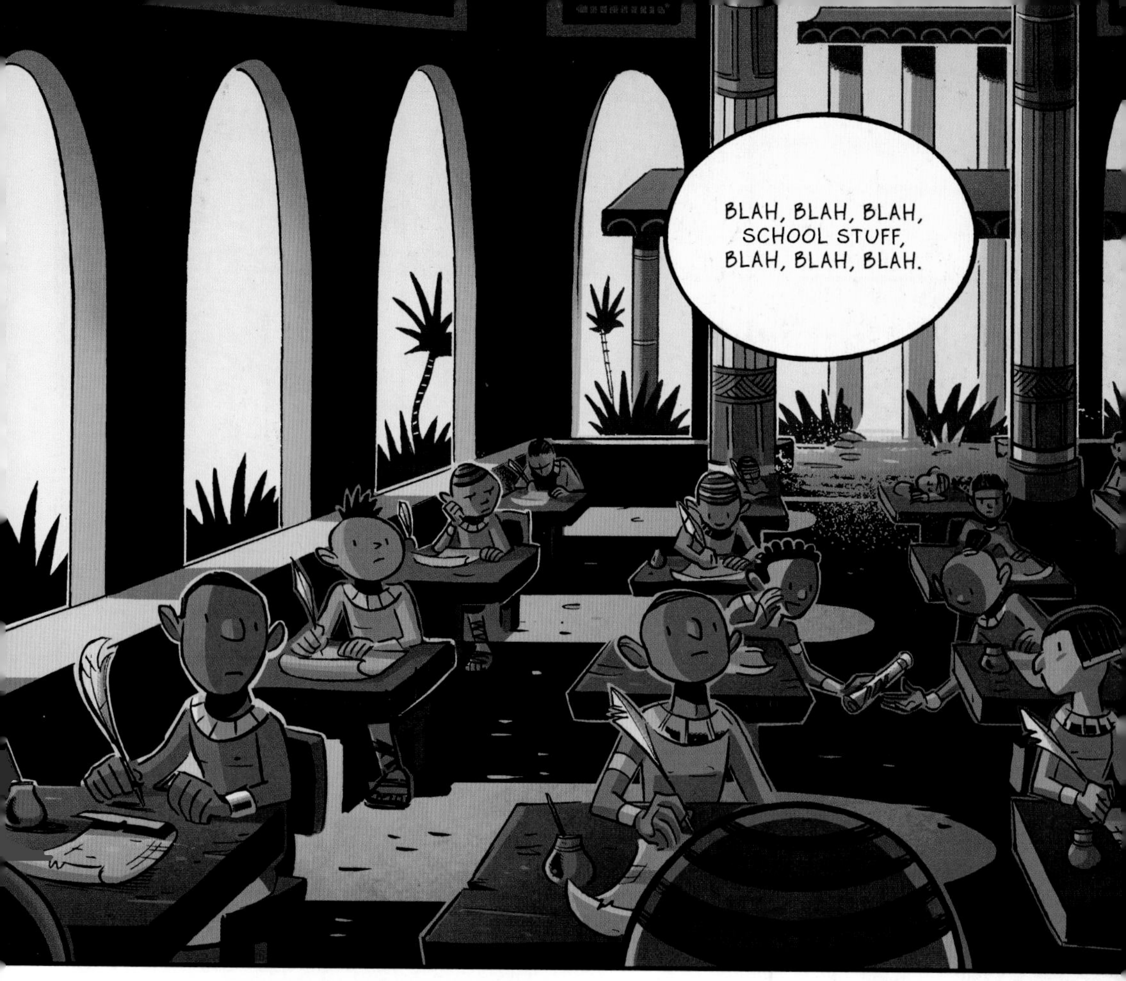
BLAH, BLAH, BLAH,
SCHOOL STUFF,
BLAH, BLAH, BLAH.

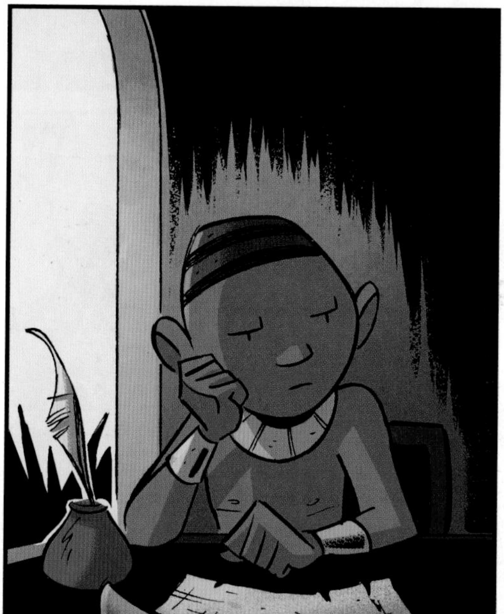

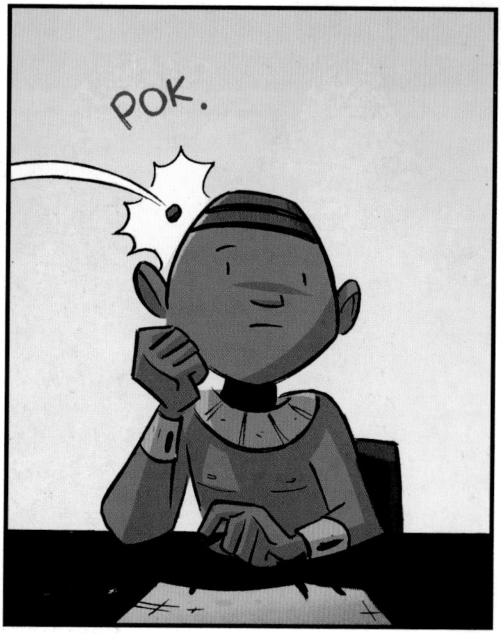
POK.

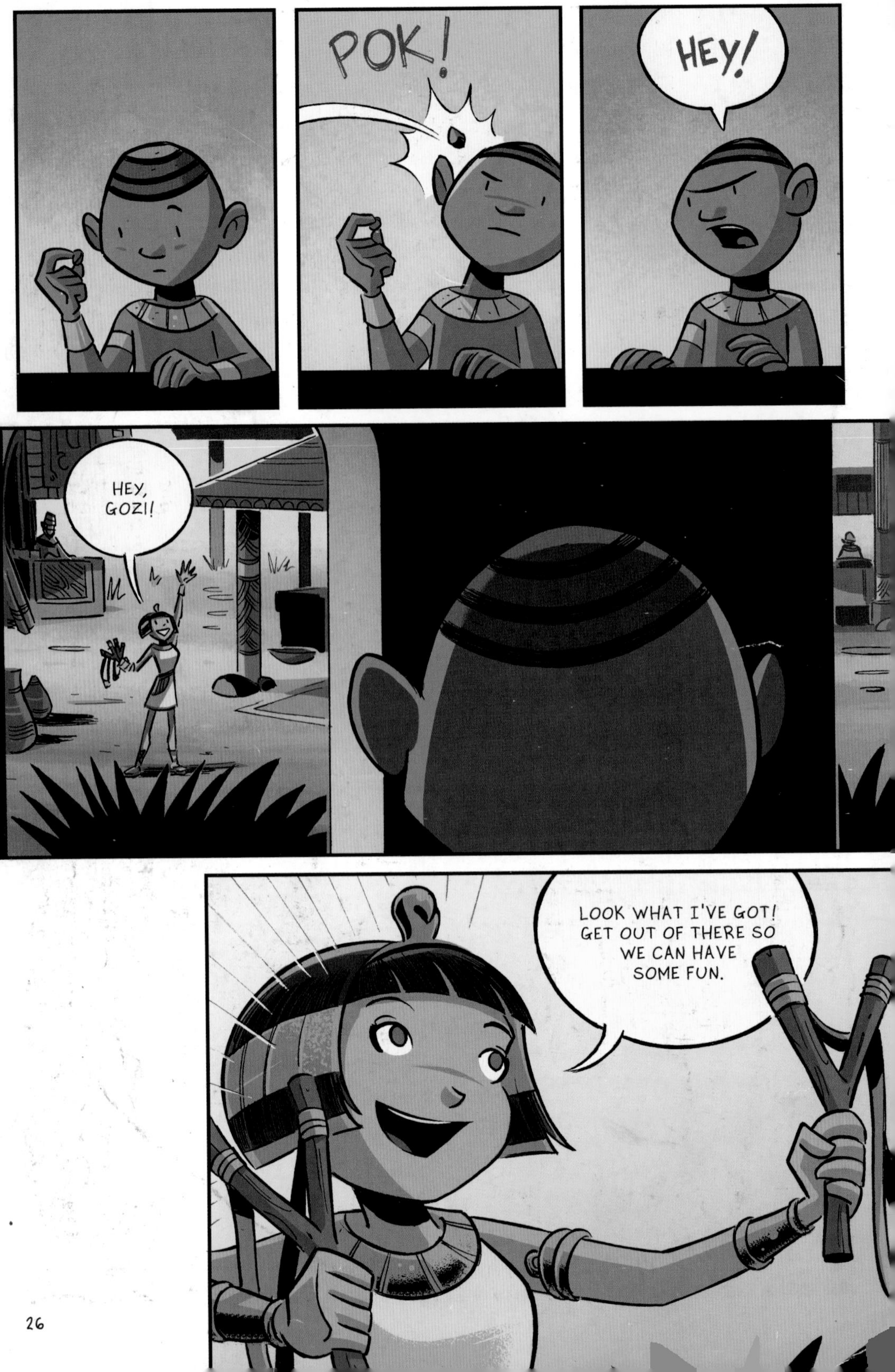
POK!
HEY!
HEY, GOZI!
LOOK WHAT I'VE GOT! GET OUT OF THERE SO WE CAN HAVE SOME FUN.

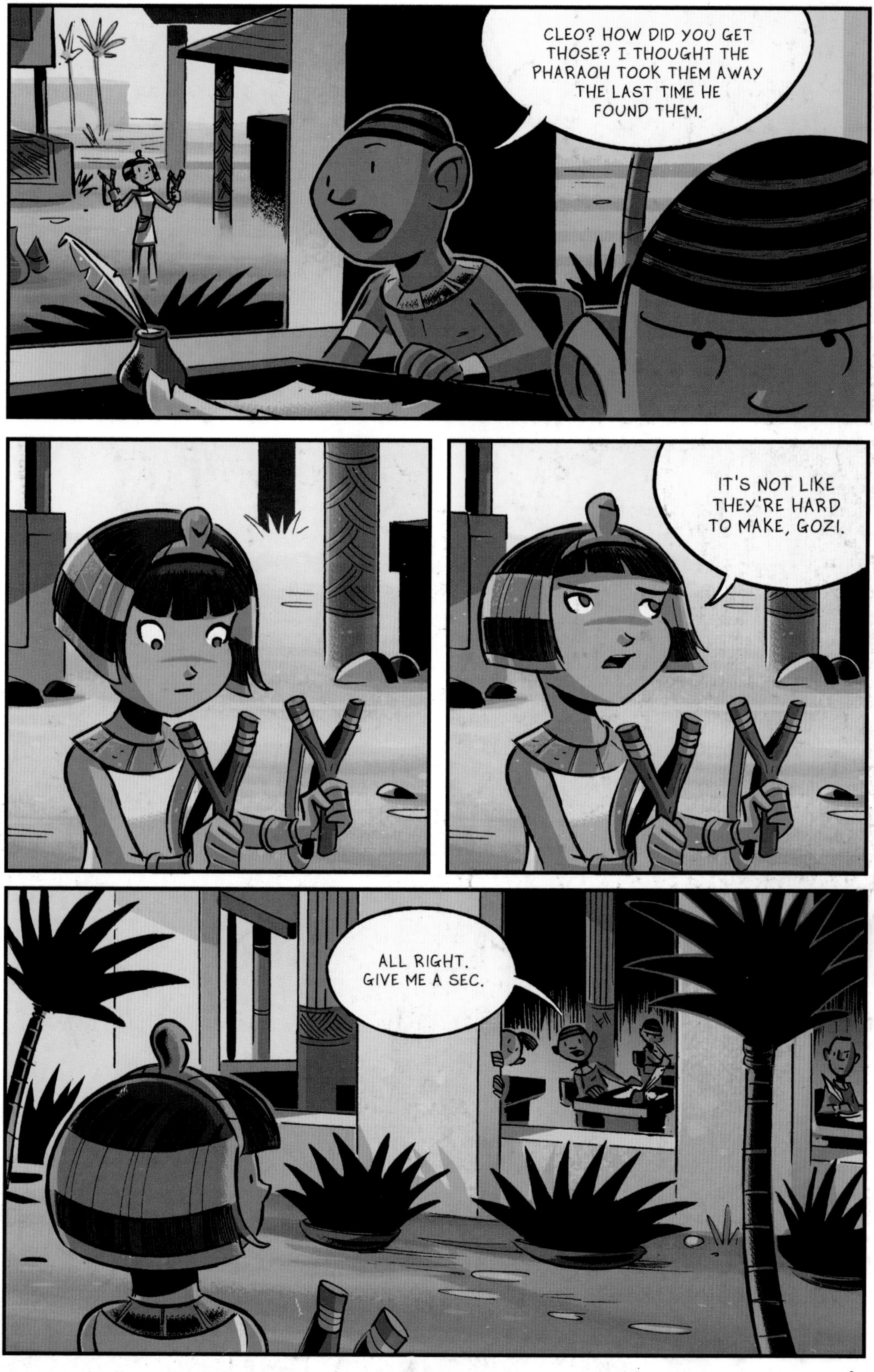
CLEO? HOW DID YOU GET THOSE? I THOUGHT THE PHARAOH TOOK THEM AWAY THE LAST TIME HE FOUND THEM.
IT'S NOT LIKE THEY'RE HARD TO MAKE, GOZI.
ALL RIGHT. GIVE ME A SEC.

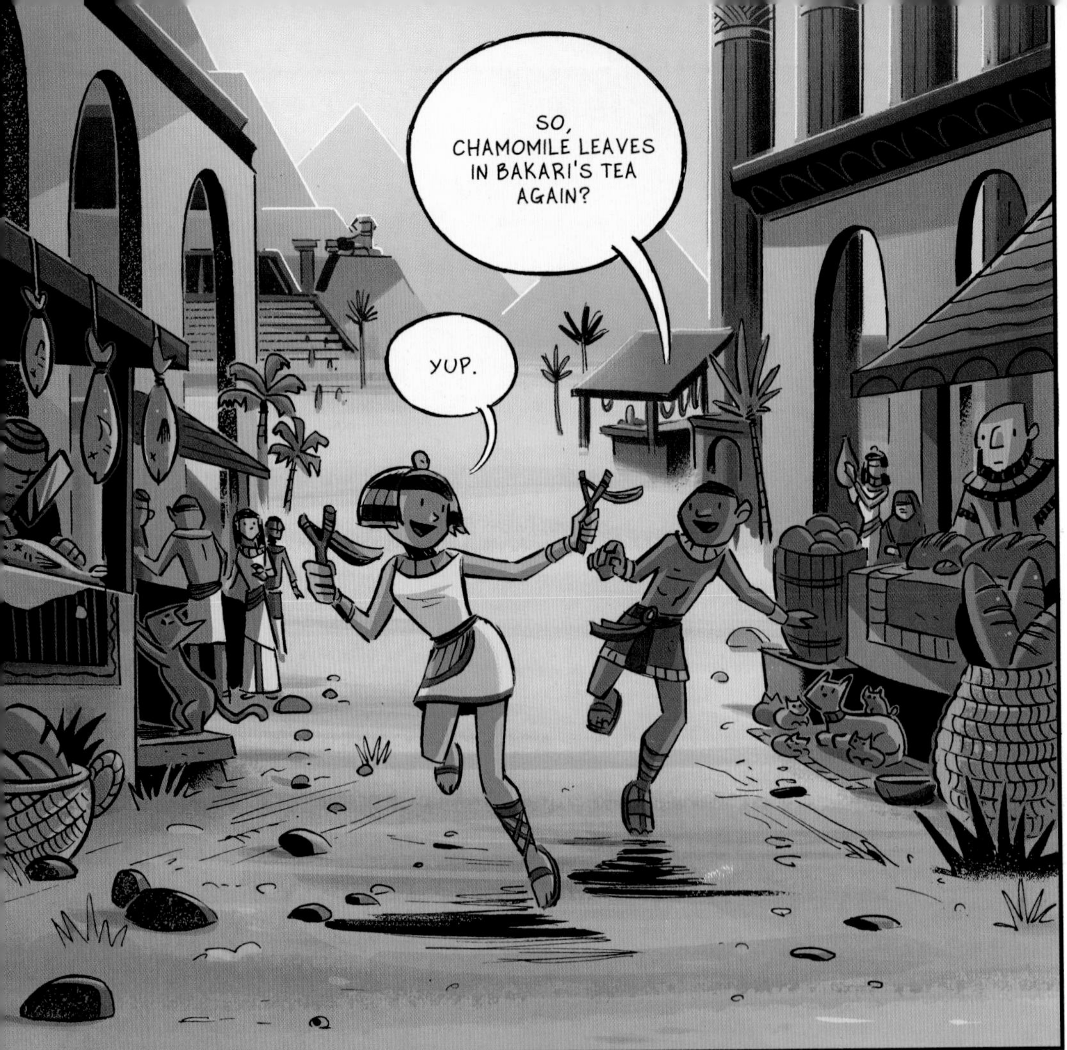
SO, CHAMOMILE LEAVES IN BAKARI'S TEA AGAIN?
YUP.

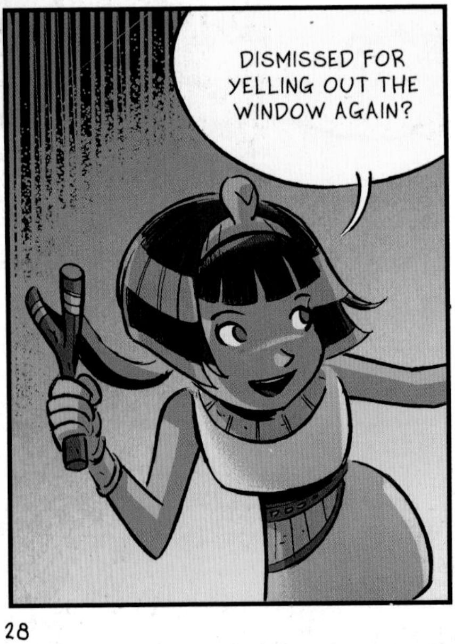
DISMISSED FOR YELLING OUT THE WINDOW AGAIN?

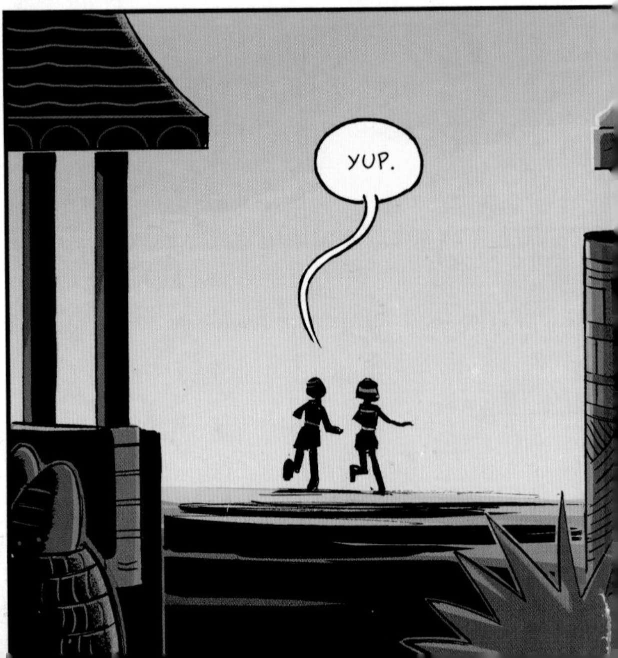
YUP.

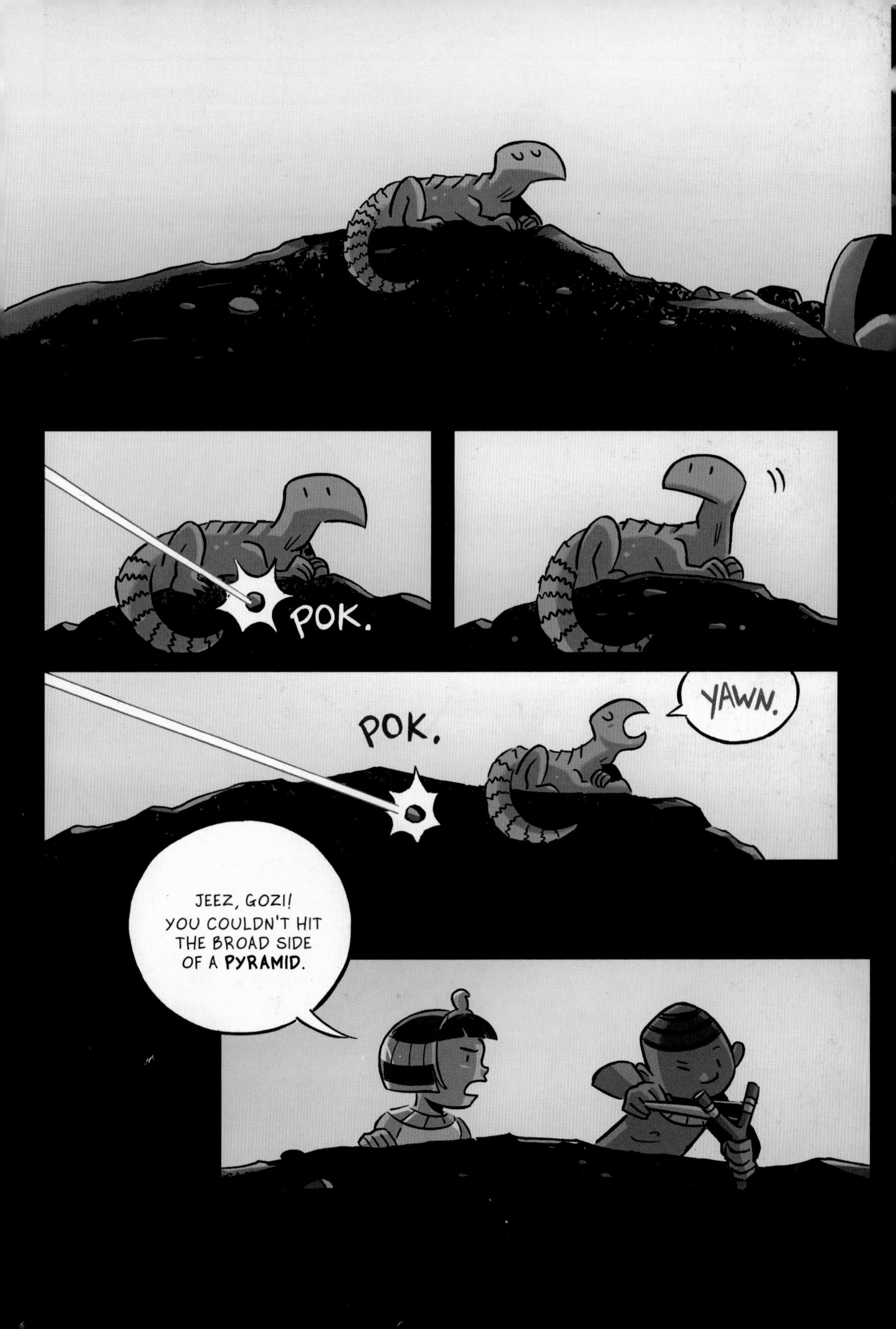
POK.
POK.
YAWN.
JEEZ, GOZI! YOU COULDN'T HIT THE BROAD SIDE OF A **PYRAMID**.

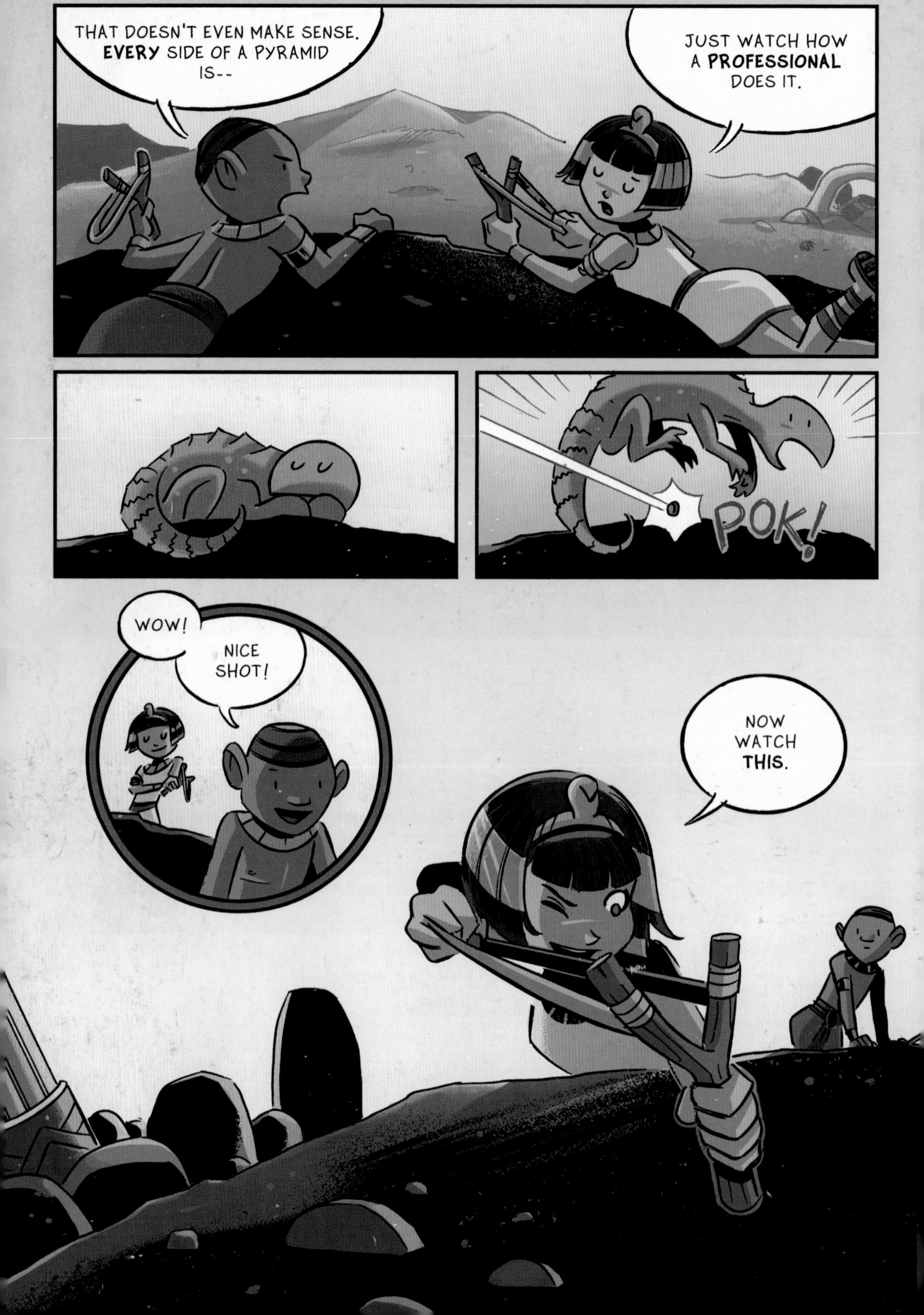
THAT DOESN'T EVEN MAKE SENSE. EVERY SIDE OF A PYRAMID IS--
JUST WATCH HOW A PROFESSIONAL DOES IT.
POK!
WOW!
NICE SHOT!
NOW WATCH THIS.

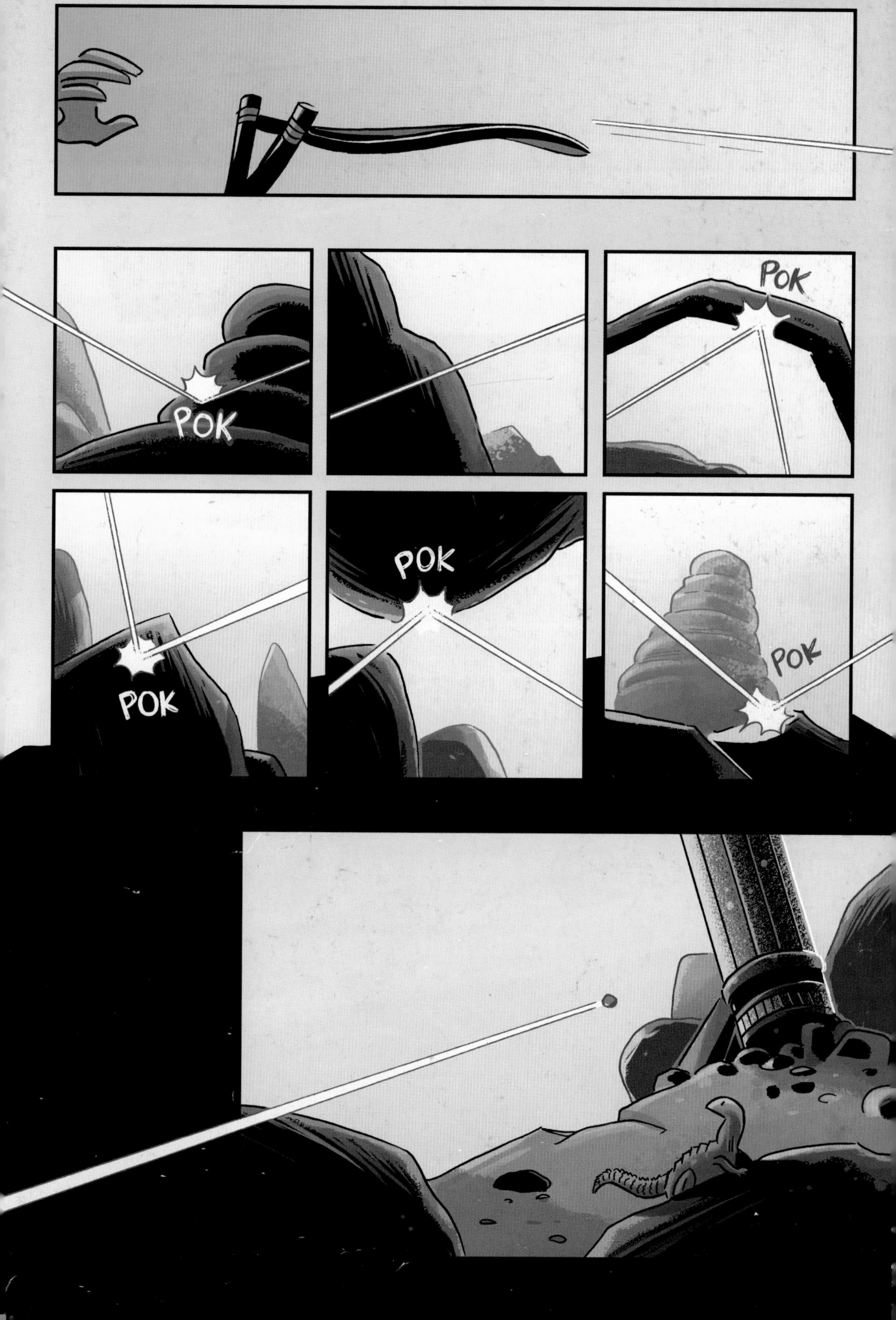
POK
POK
POK
POK
POK

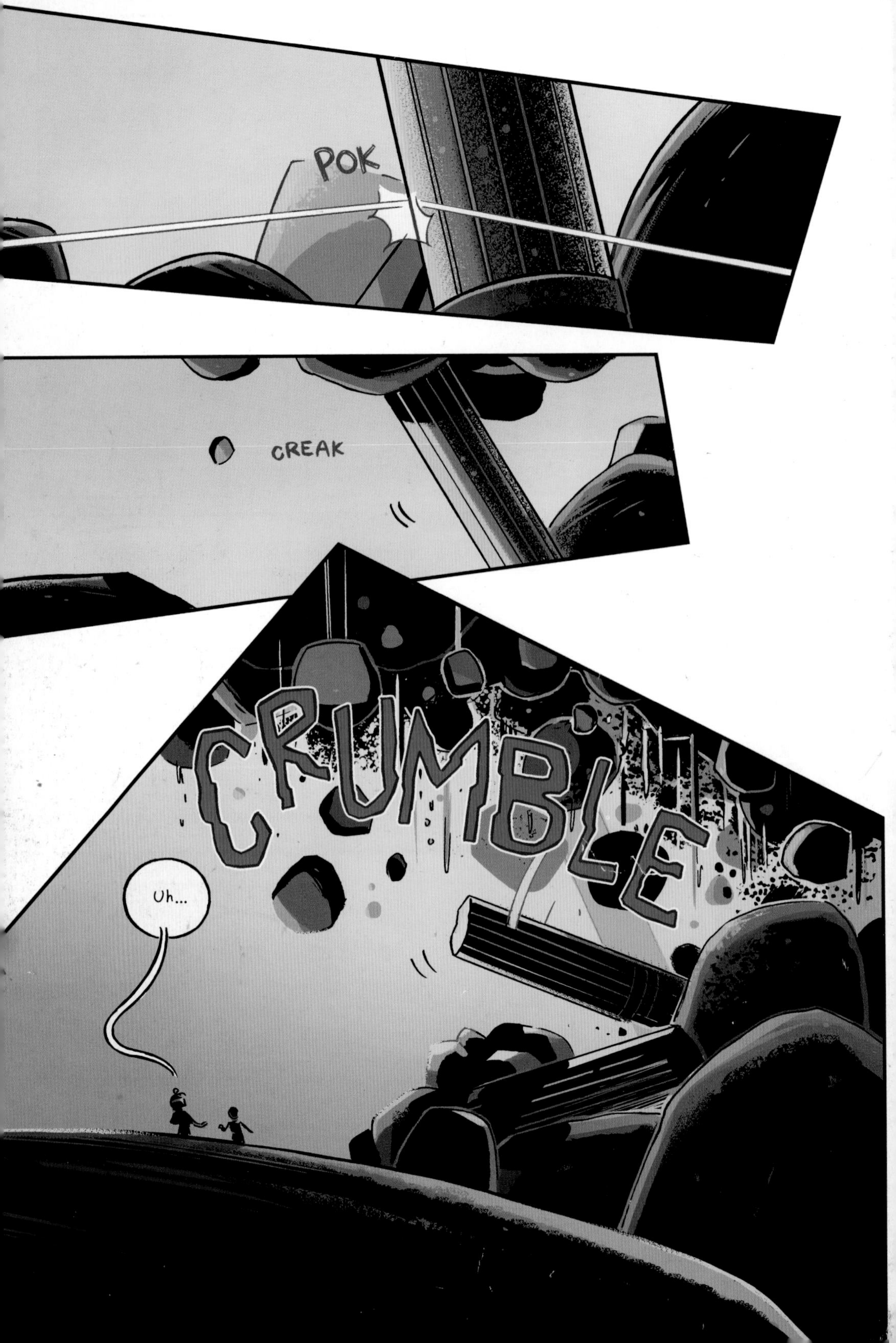
POK
CREAK
CRUMBLE
Uh...

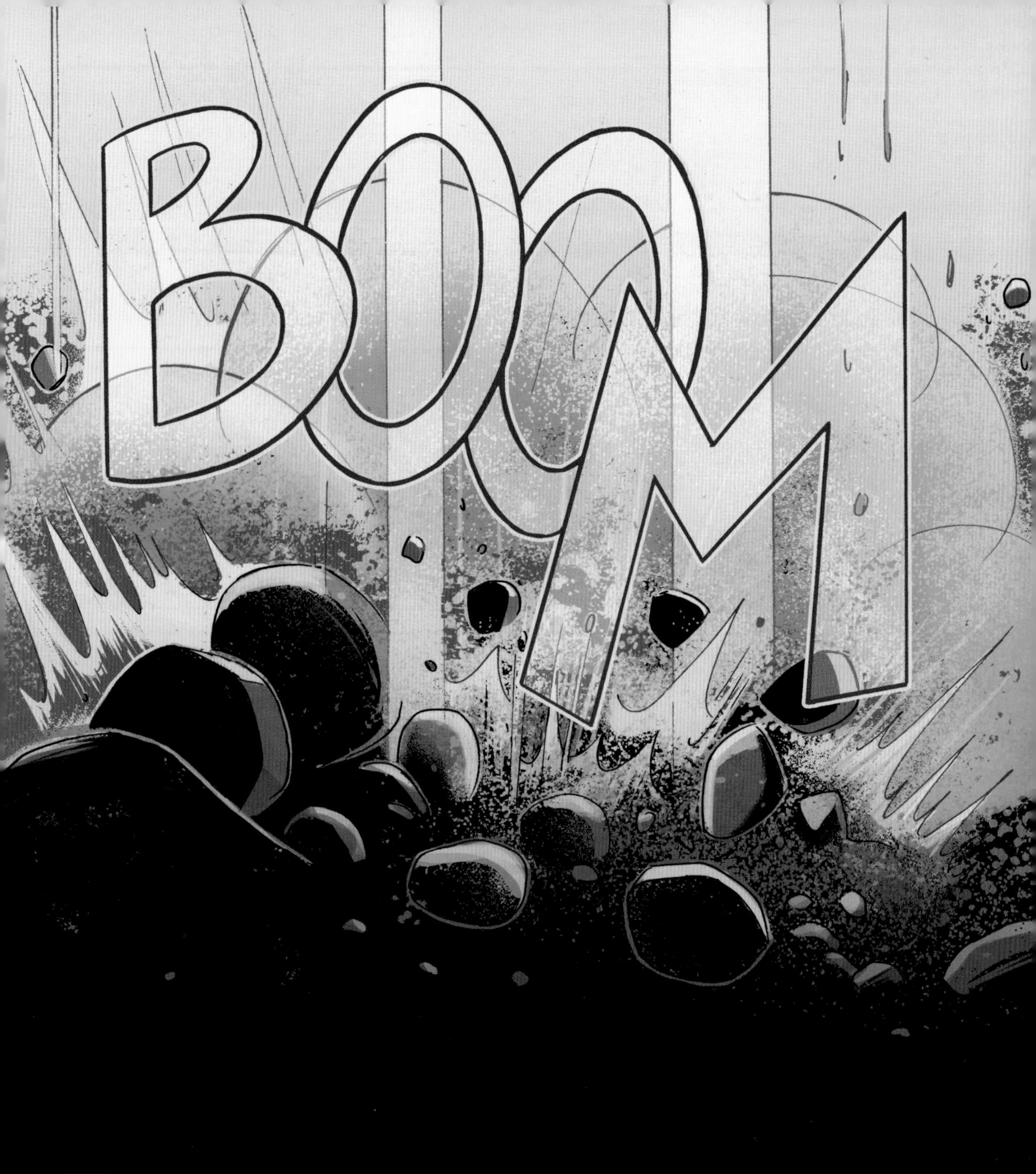
BOOM

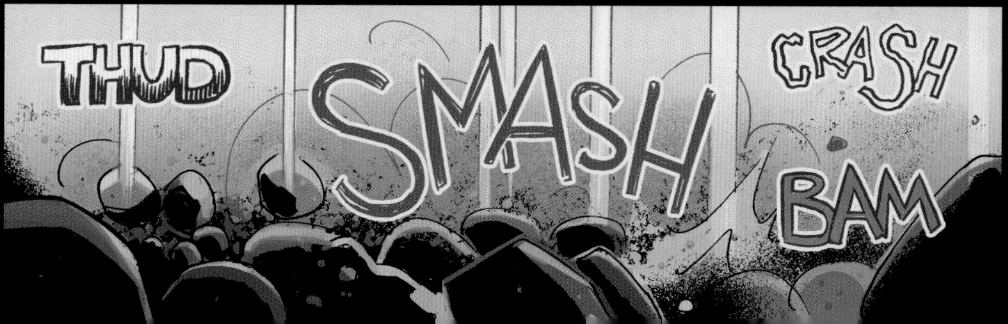
THUD
SMASH
CRASH
BAM

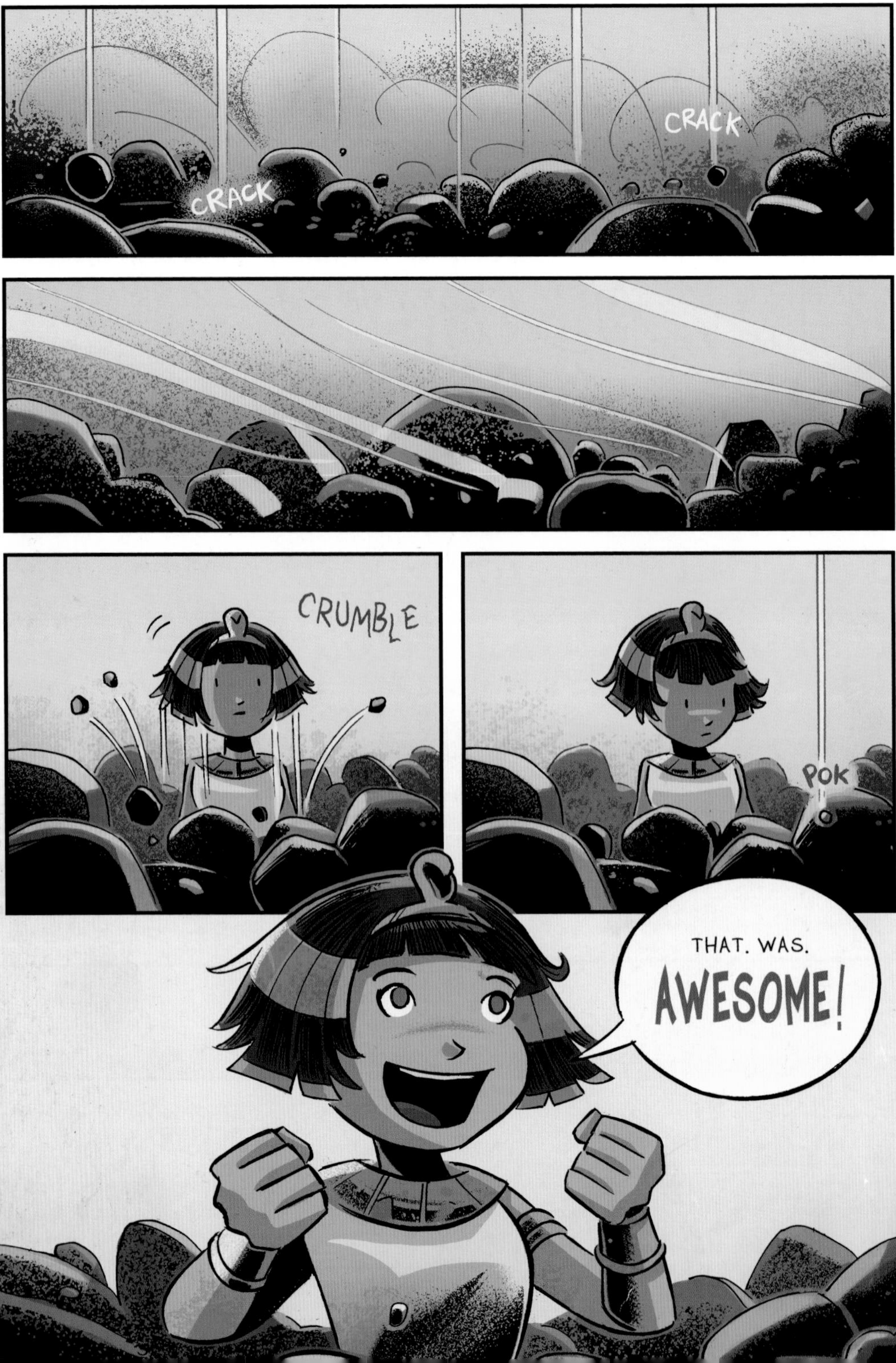
CRACK
CRACK
CRUMBLE
POK
THAT. WAS.
AWESOME!

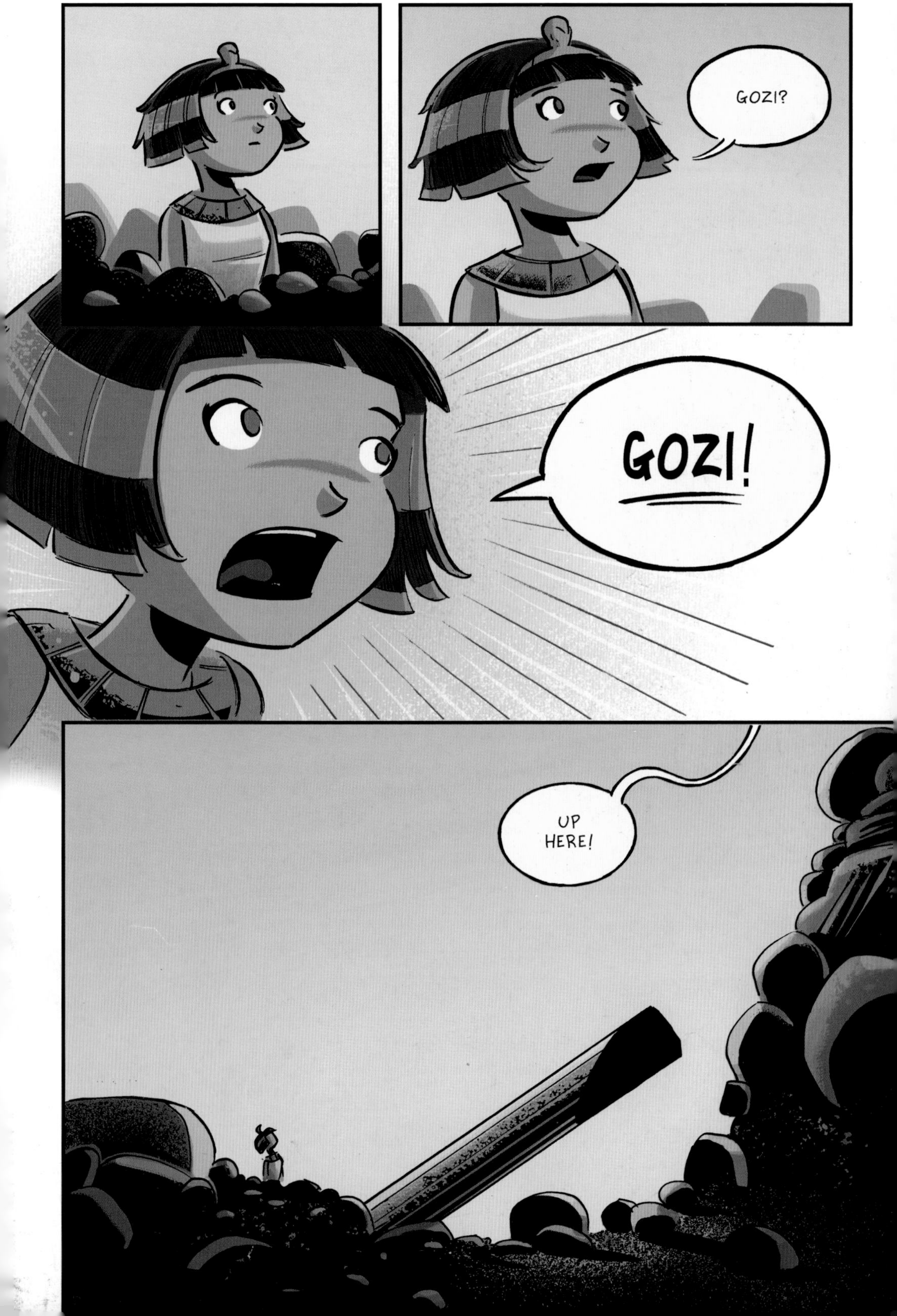
GOZI?
GOZI!
UP HERE!

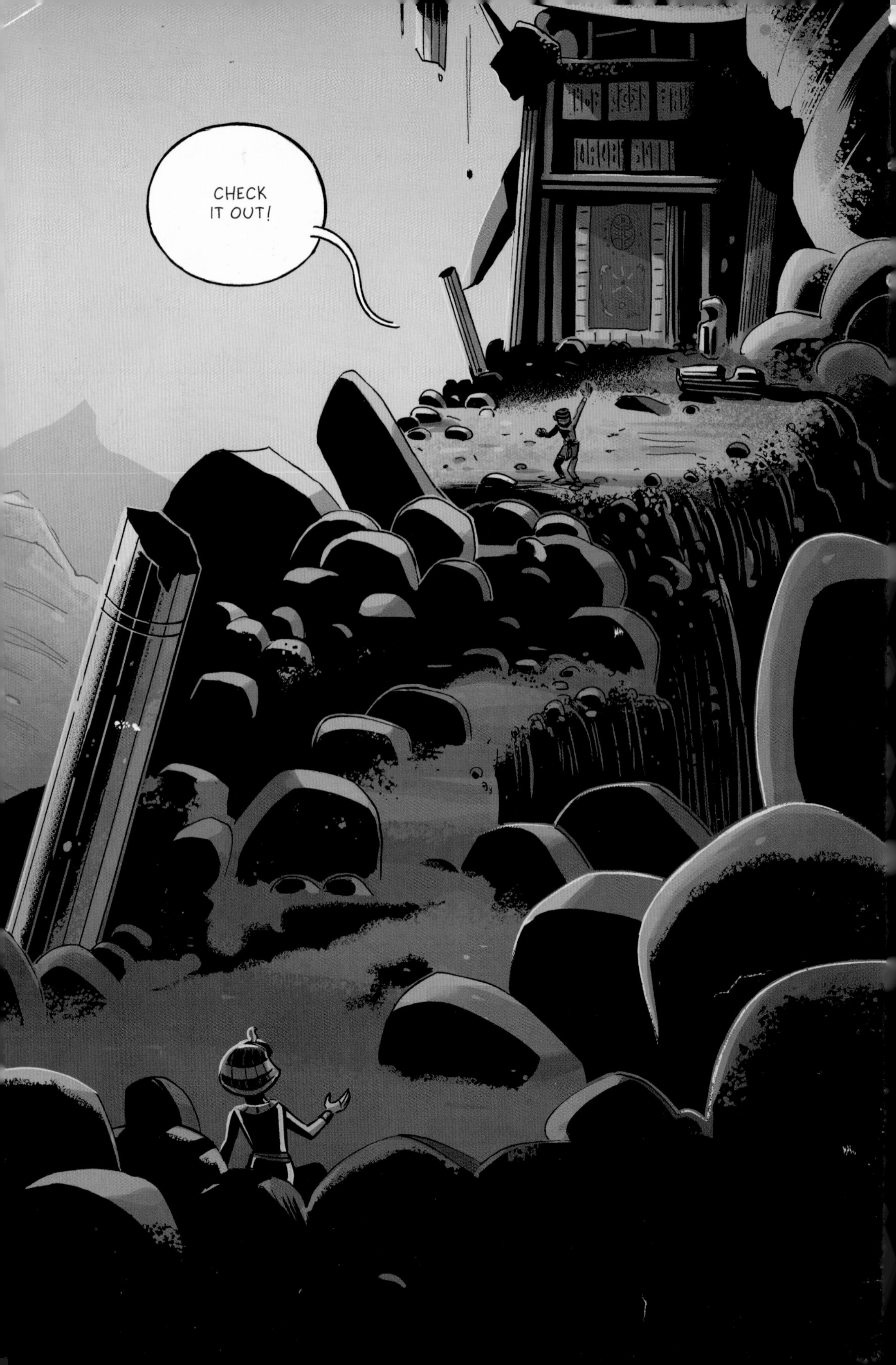
CHECK IT OUT!

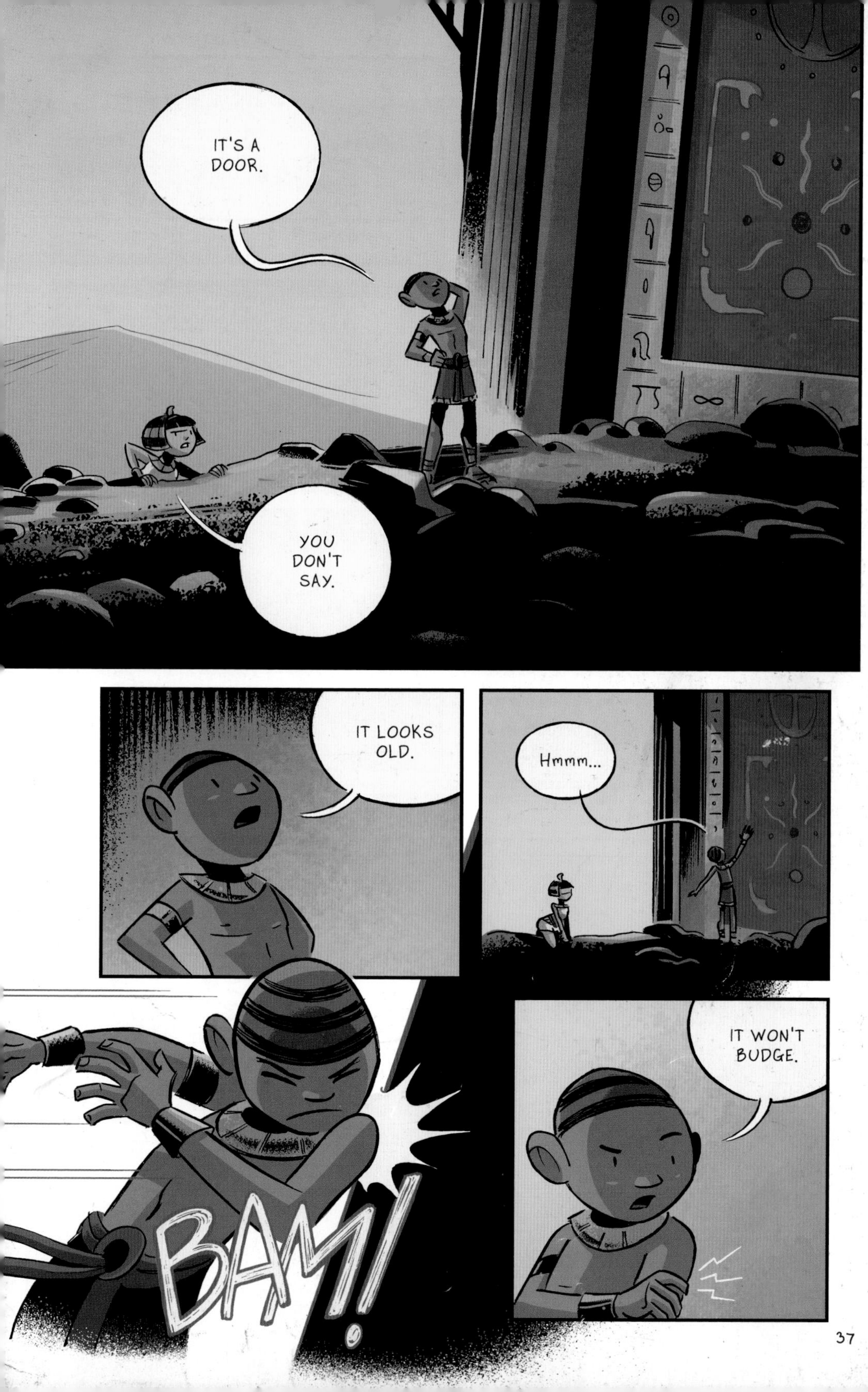
IT'S A DOOR.
YOU DON'T SAY.
IT LOOKS OLD.
Hmmm...
BAM!
IT WON'T BUDGE.

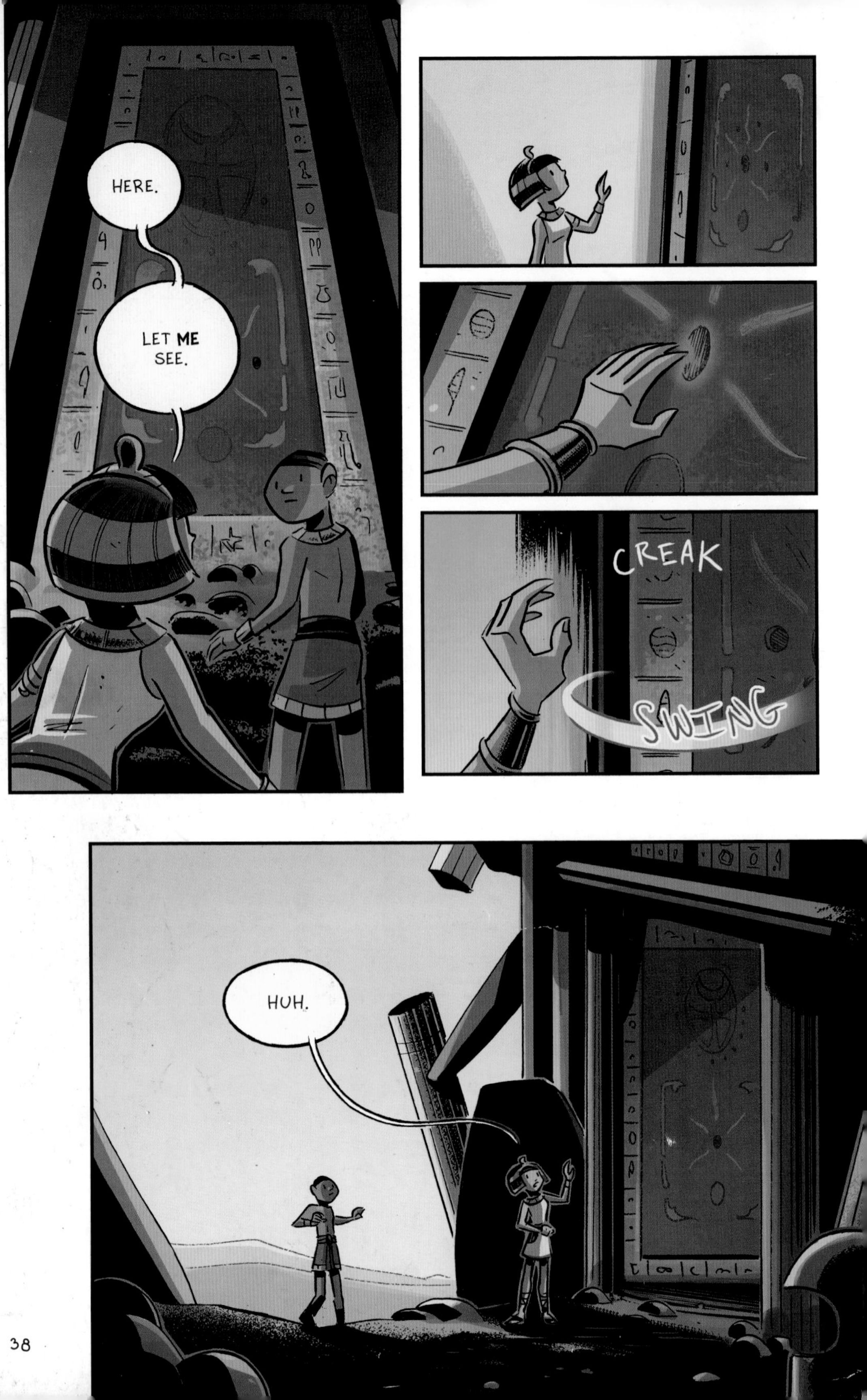
HERE.
LET **ME** SEE.
CREAK
SWING
HUH.

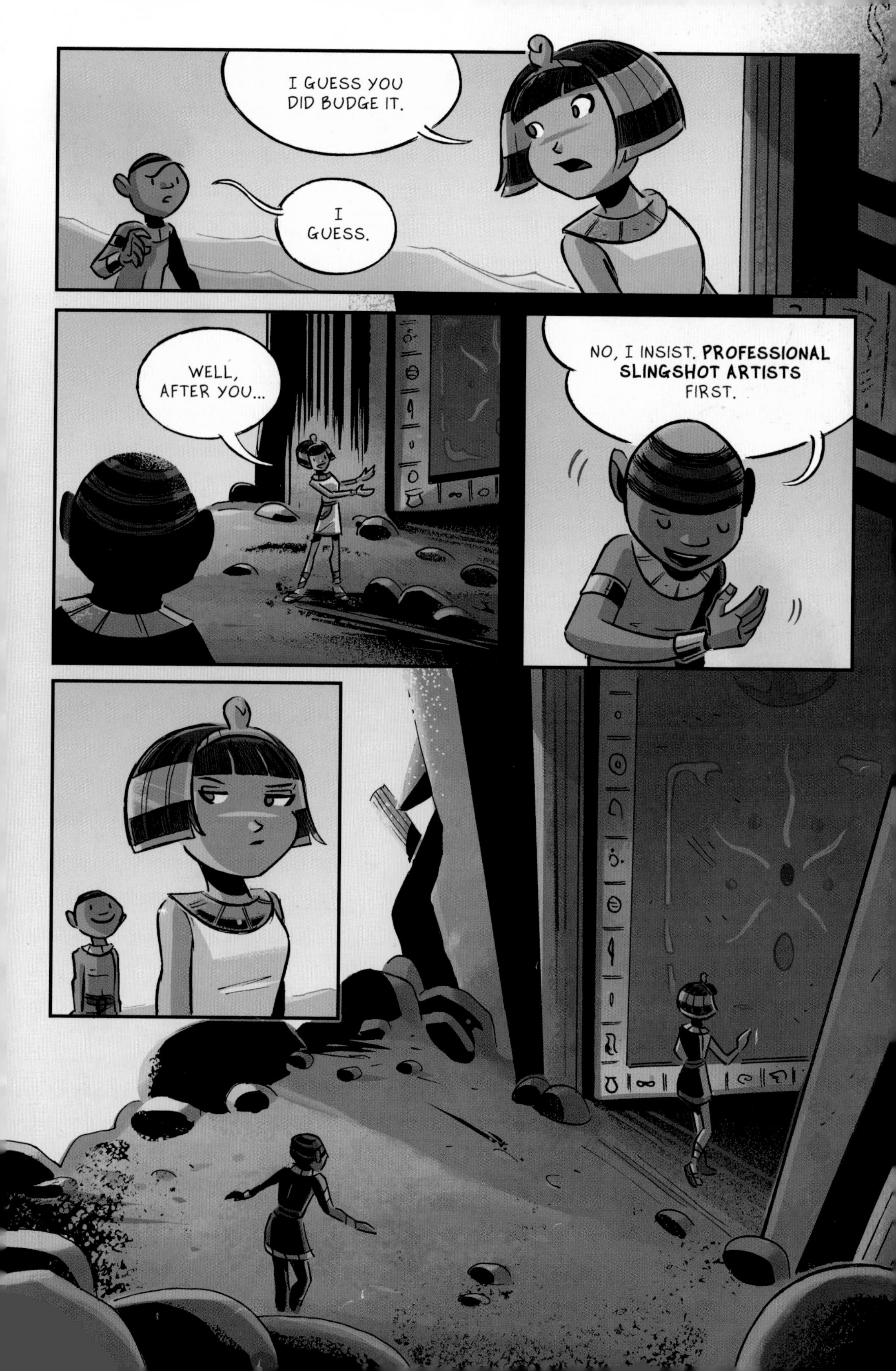
I GUESS YOU DID BUDGE IT.
I GUESS.
WELL, AFTER YOU...
NO, I INSIST. PROFESSIONAL SLINGSHOT ARTISTS FIRST.

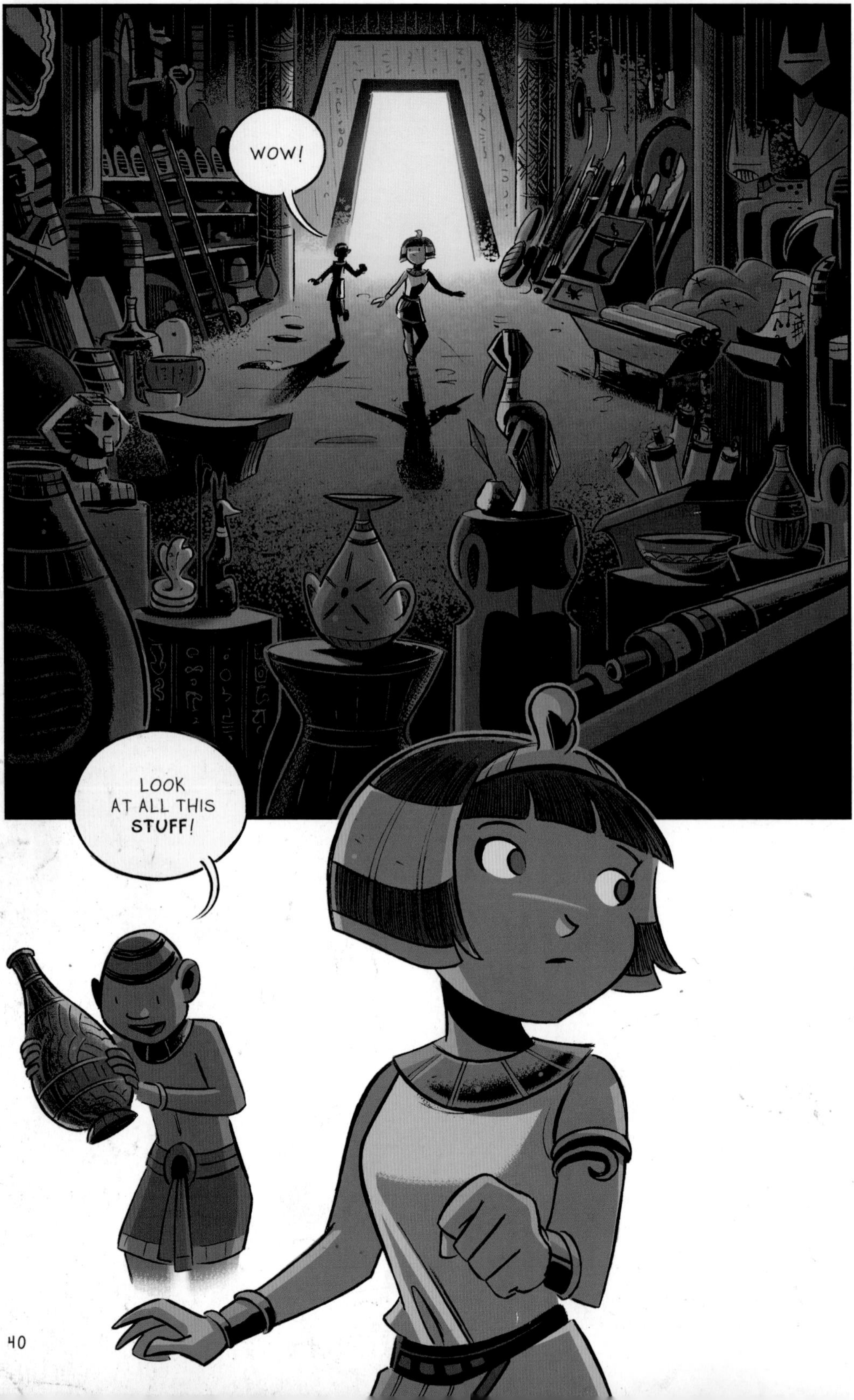
WOW!
LOOK AT ALL THIS **STUFF**!

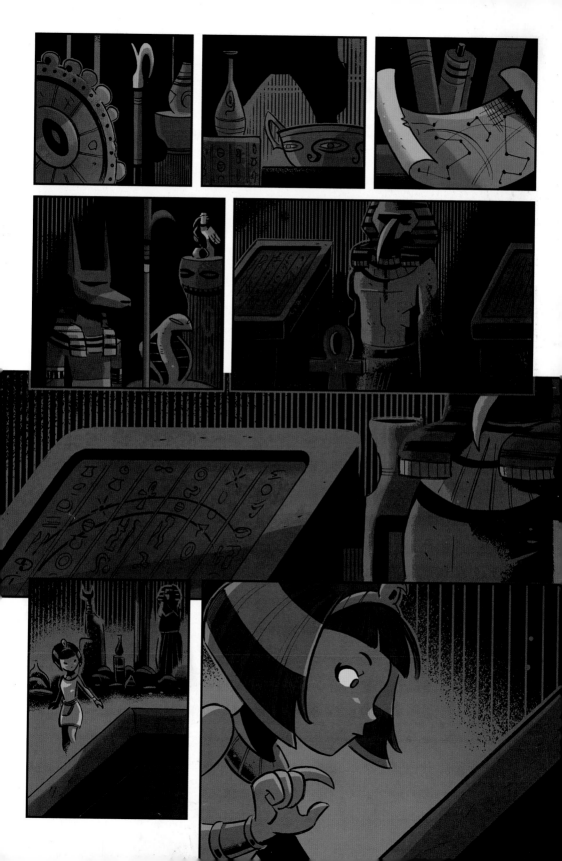

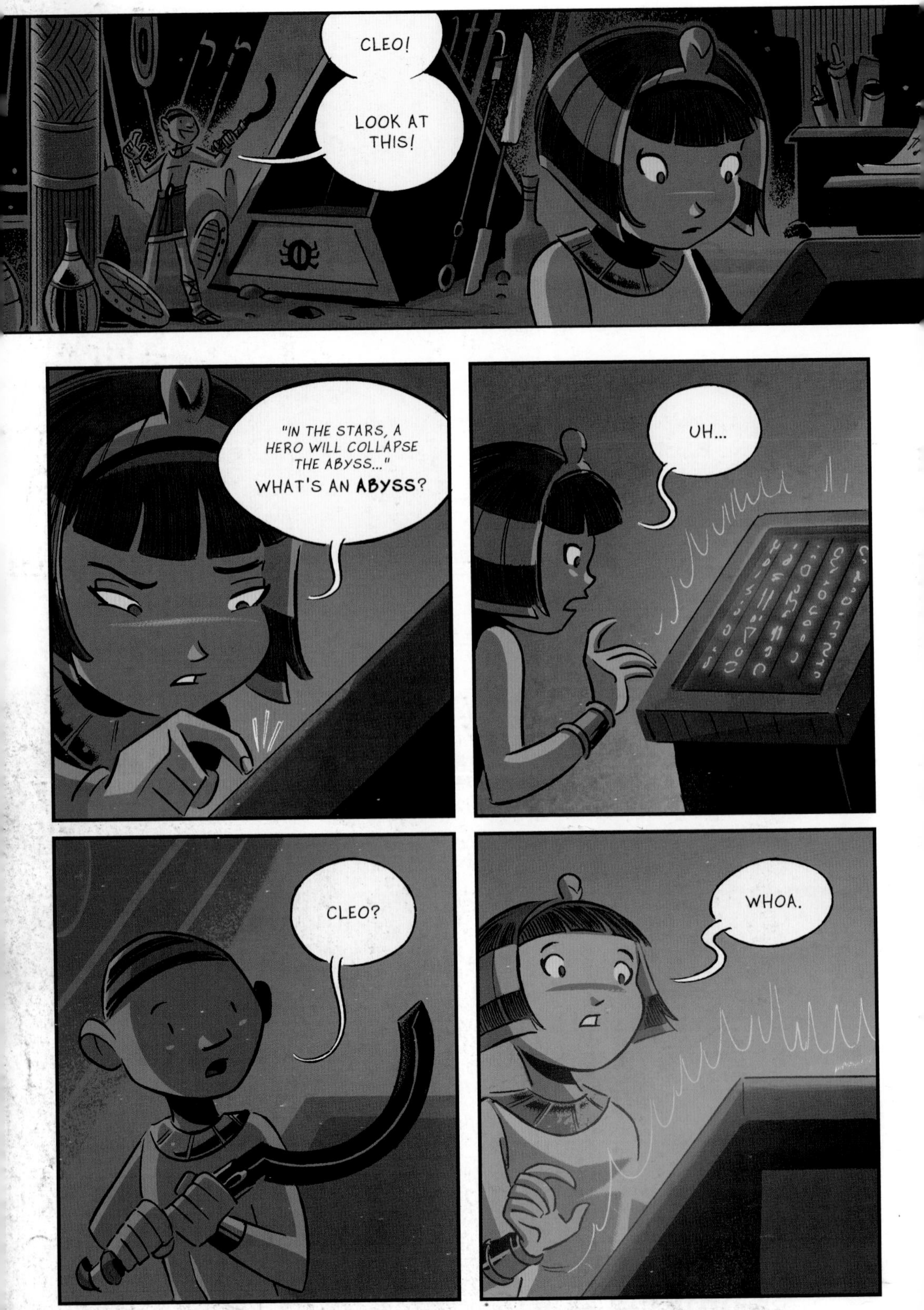
CLEO!
LOOK AT THIS!
"IN THE STARS, A HERO WILL COLLAPSE THE ABYSS..." WHAT'S AN ABYSS?
UH...
CLEO?
WHOA.

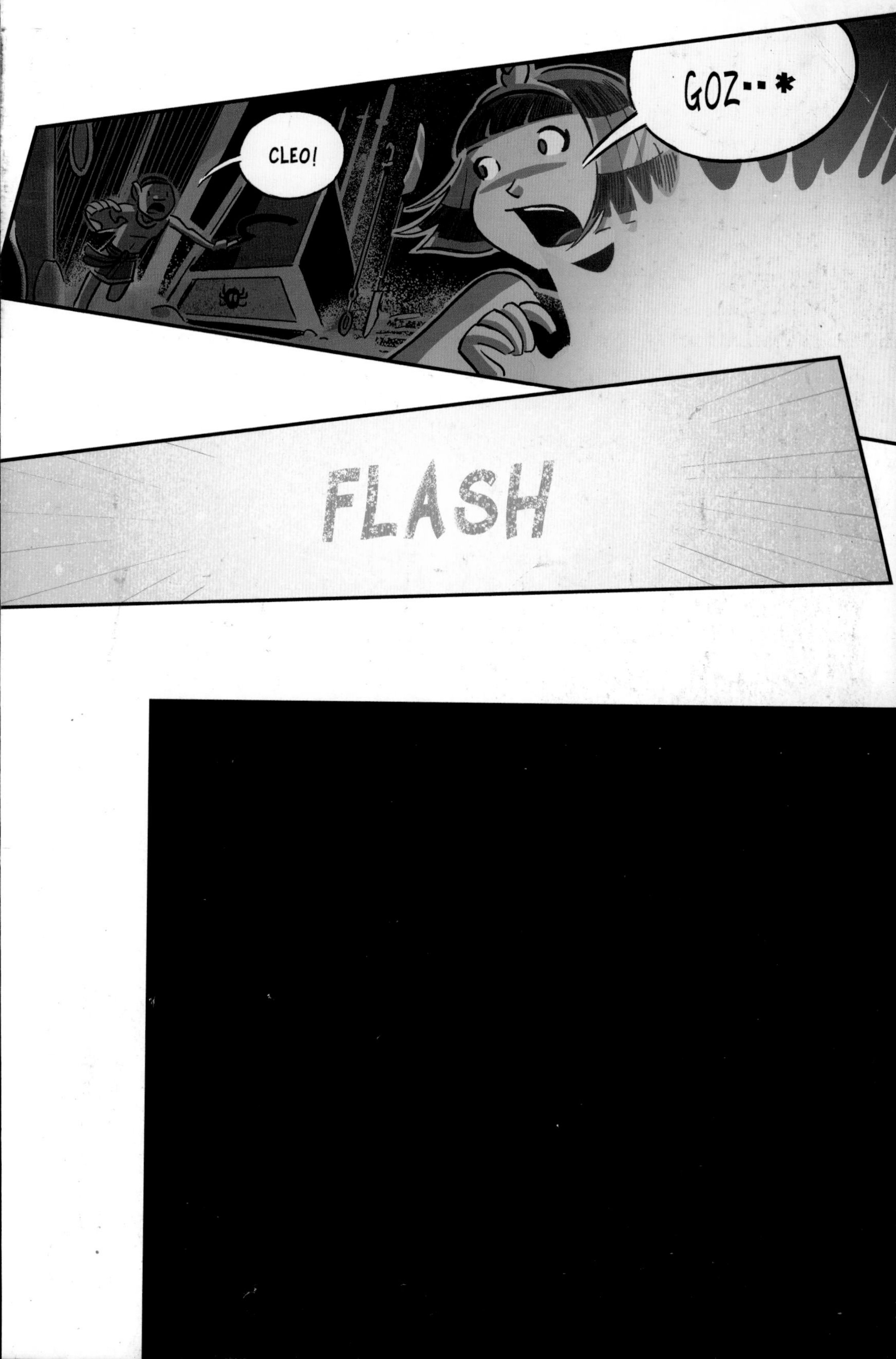
CLEO!
GOZ..*
FLASH

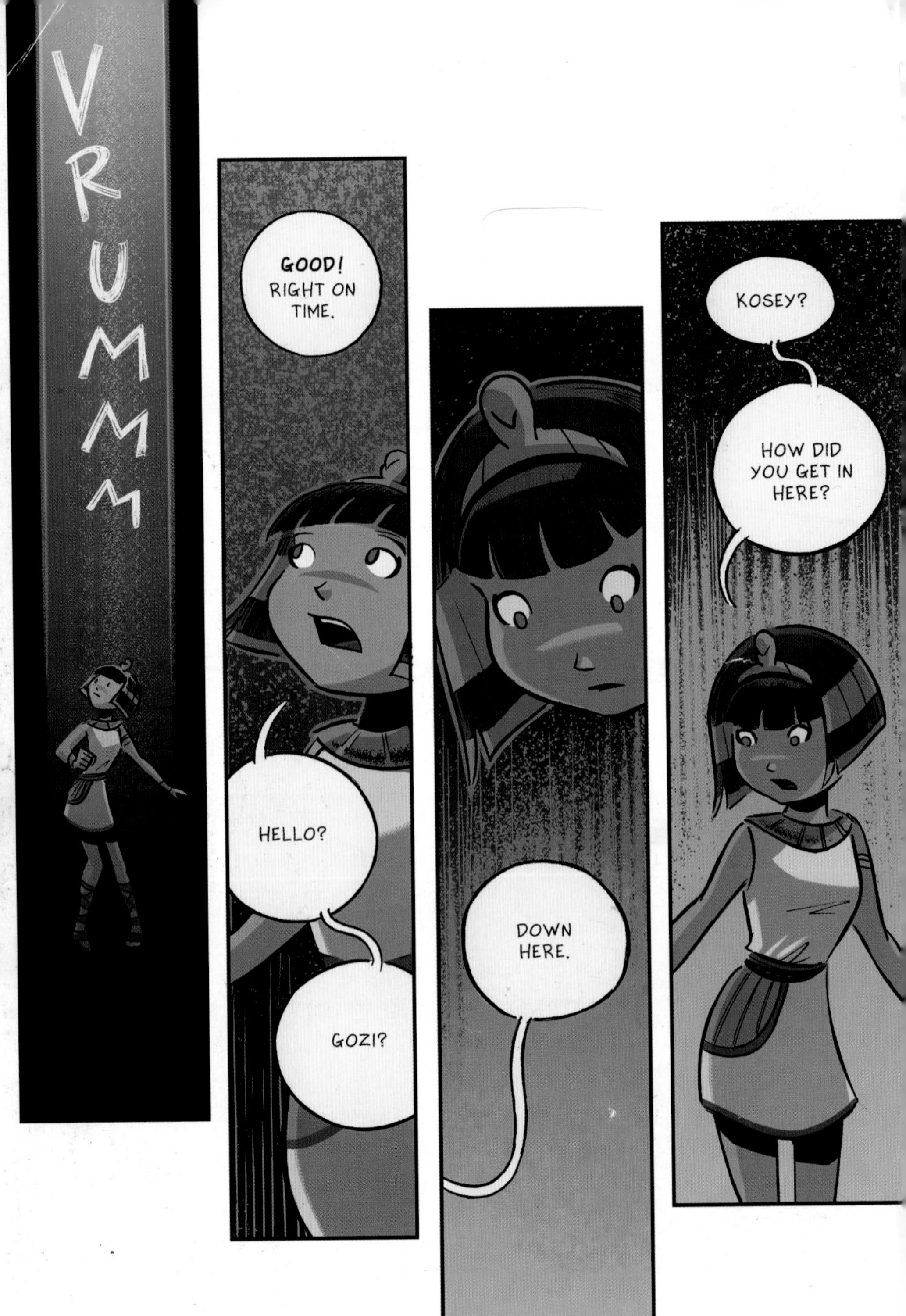
VRUMMM
GOOD! RIGHT ON TIME.
HELLO?
GOZI?
DOWN HERE.
KOSEY?
HOW DID YOU GET IN HERE?

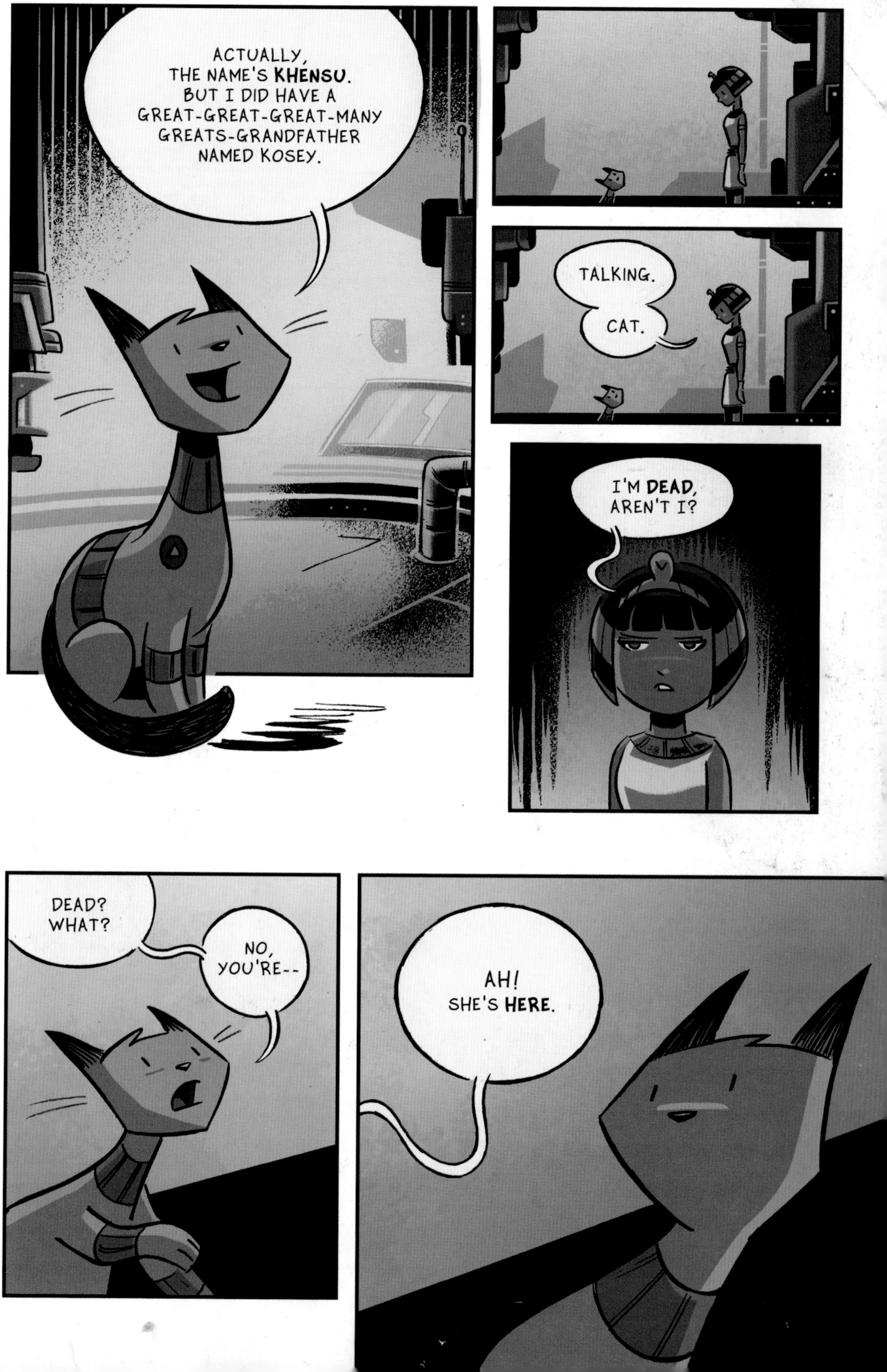
ACTUALLY, THE NAME'S **KHENSU**. BUT I DID HAVE A GREAT-GREAT-GREAT-MANY GREATS-GRANDFATHER NAMED KOSEY.
TALKING.
CAT.
I'M **DEAD**, AREN'T I?
DEAD? WHAT?
NO, YOU'RE--
AH! SHE'S **HERE**.

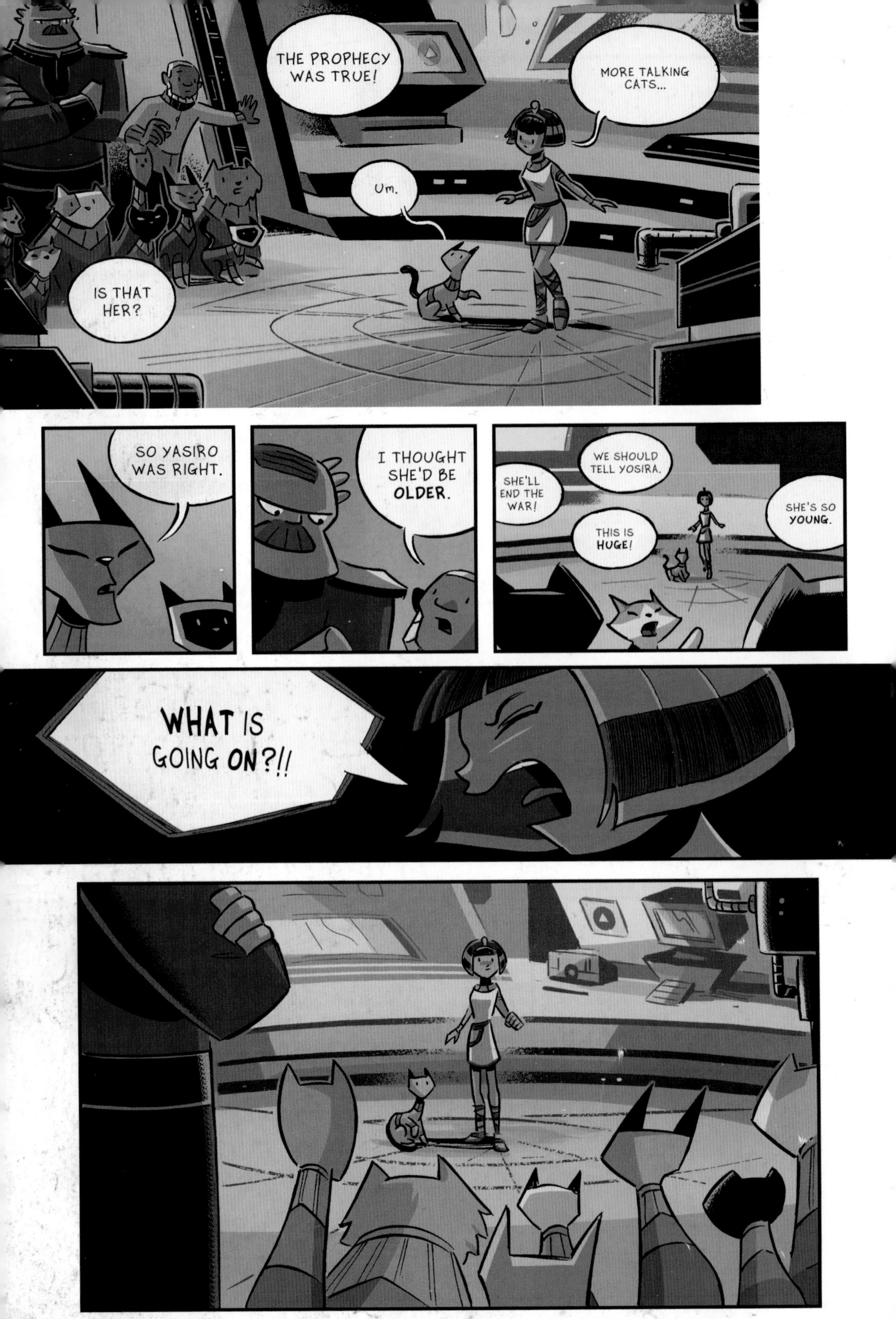
THE PROPHECY WAS TRUE!
MORE TALKING CATS...
Um.
IS THAT HER?
SO YASIRO WAS RIGHT.
I THOUGHT SHE'D BE **OLDER**.
SHE'LL END THE WAR!
WE SHOULD TELL YOSIRA.
THIS IS **HUGE**!
SHE'S SO **YOUNG**.
WHAT IS GOING **ON**?!!

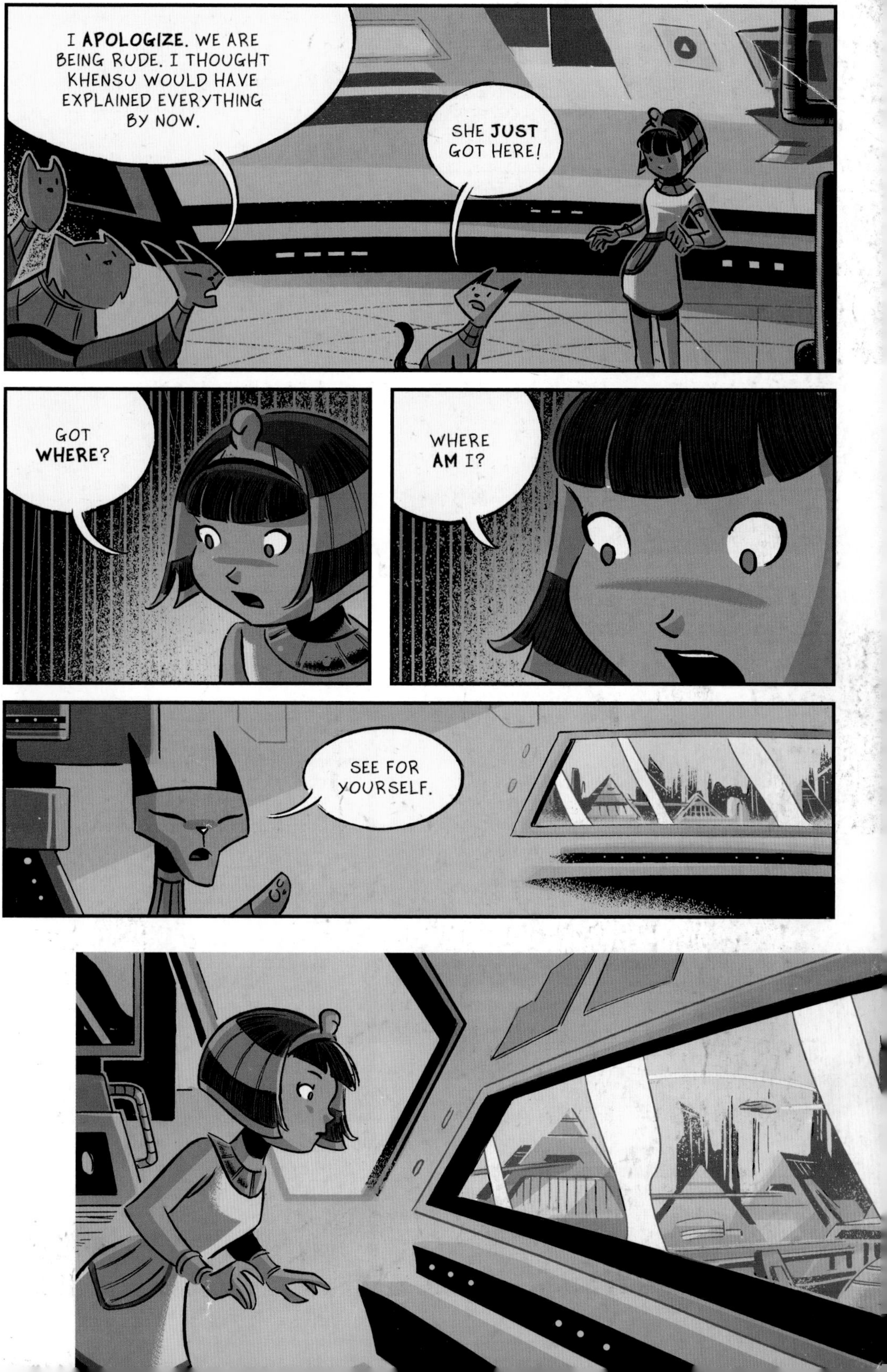

I **APOLOGIZE**. WE ARE BEING RUDE. I THOUGHT KHENSU WOULD HAVE EXPLAINED EVERYTHING BY NOW.
SHE **JUST** GOT HERE!
GOT **WHERE**?
WHERE **AM** I?
SEE FOR YOURSELF.

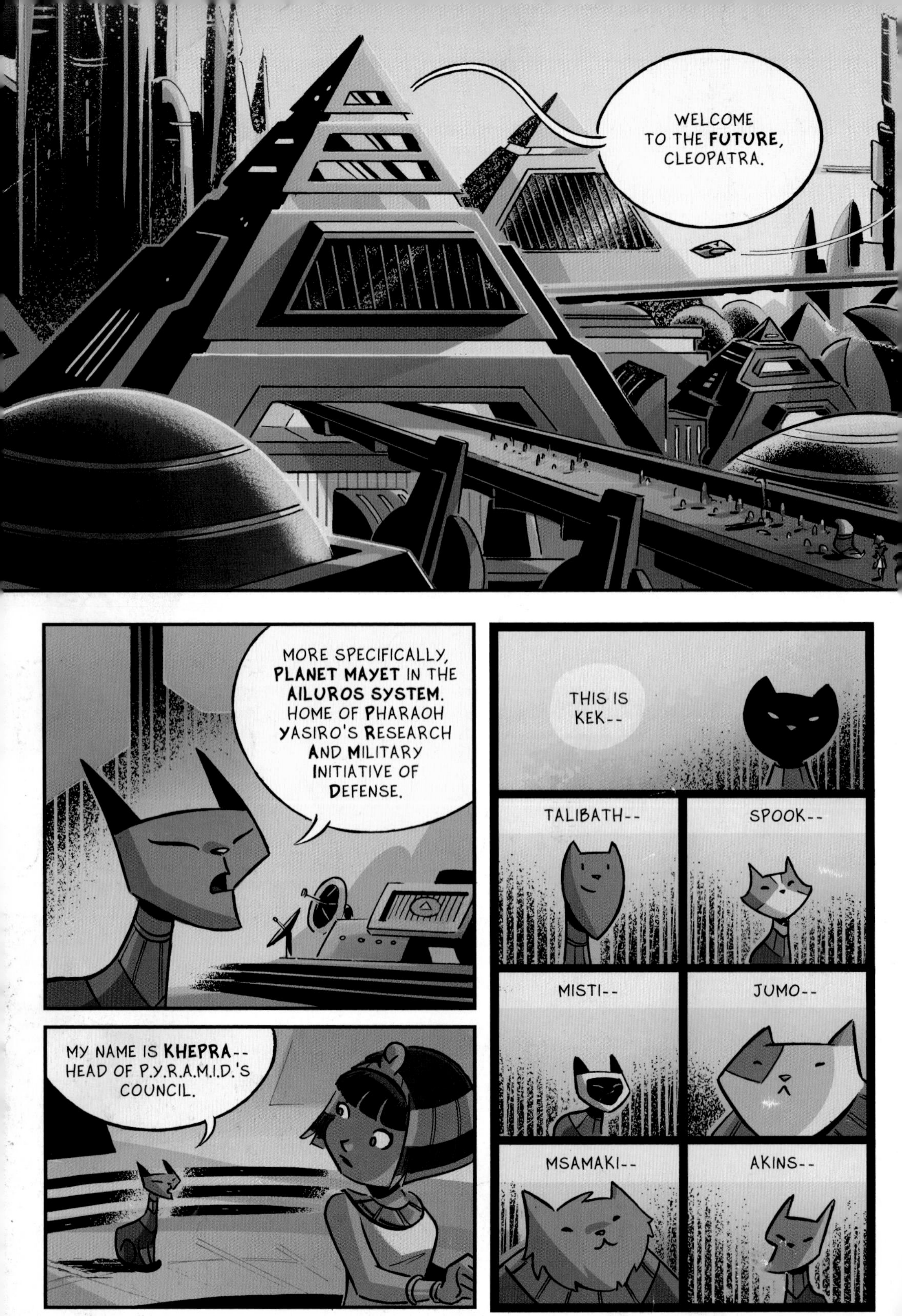
WELCOME TO THE FUTURE, CLEOPATRA.
MORE SPECIFICALLY, PLANET MAYET IN THE AILUROS SYSTEM. HOME OF PHARAOH YASIRO'S RESEARCH AND MILITARY INITIATIVE OF DEFENSE.
MY NAME IS KHEPRA-- HEAD OF P.Y.R.A.M.I.D.'S COUNCIL.
THIS IS KEK--
TALIBATH--
SPOOK--
MISTI--
JUMO--
MSAMAKI--
AKINS--

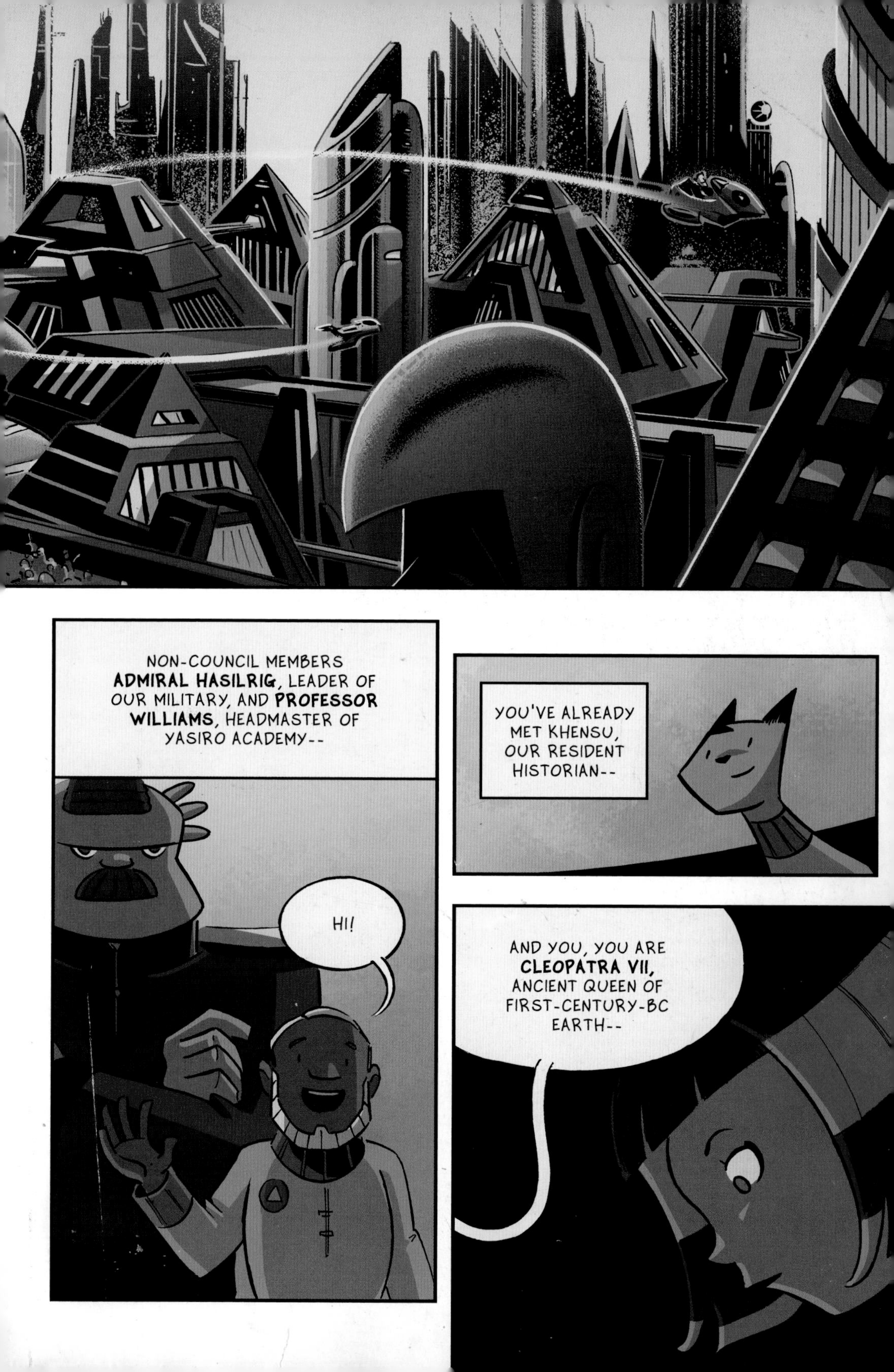
NON-COUNCIL MEMBERS **ADMIRAL HASILRIG**, LEADER OF OUR MILITARY, AND **PROFESSOR WILLIAMS**, HEADMASTER OF YASIRO ACADEMY--
HI!
YOU'VE ALREADY MET KHENSU, OUR RESIDENT HISTORIAN--
AND YOU, YOU ARE **CLEOPATRA VII,** ANCIENT QUEEN OF FIRST-CENTURY-BC EARTH--

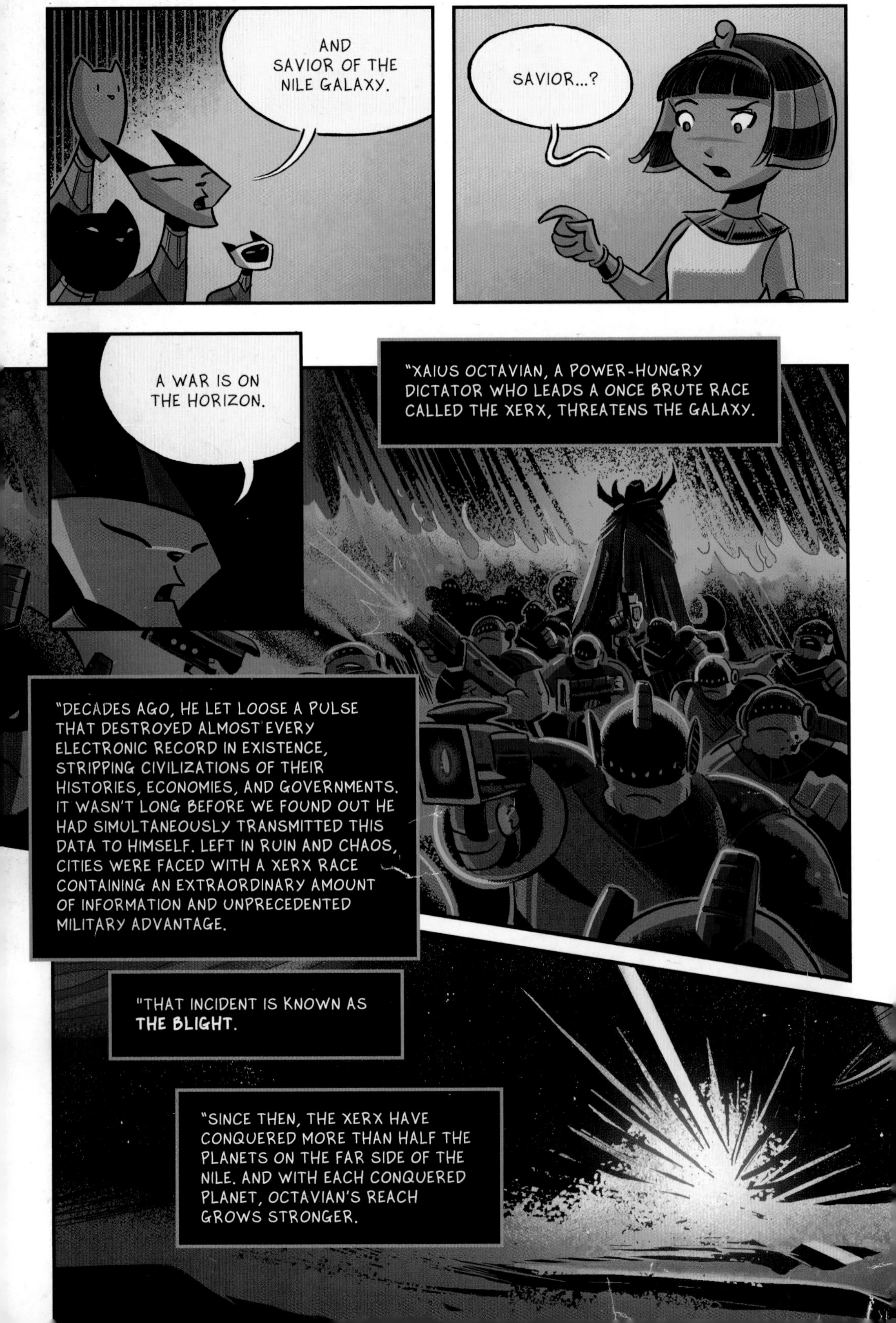
AND SAVIOR OF THE NILE GALAXY.
SAVIOR...?
A WAR IS ON THE HORIZON.
"XAIUS OCTAVIAN, A POWER-HUNGRY DICTATOR WHO LEADS A ONCE BRUTE RACE CALLED THE XERX, THREATENS THE GALAXY.
"DECADES AGO, HE LET LOOSE A PULSE THAT DESTROYED ALMOST EVERY ELECTRONIC RECORD IN EXISTENCE, STRIPPING CIVILIZATIONS OF THEIR HISTORIES, ECONOMIES, AND GOVERNMENTS. IT WASN'T LONG BEFORE WE FOUND OUT HE HAD SIMULTANEOUSLY TRANSMITTED THIS DATA TO HIMSELF. LEFT IN RUIN AND CHAOS, CITIES WERE FACED WITH A XERX RACE CONTAINING AN EXTRAORDINARY AMOUNT OF INFORMATION AND UNPRECEDENTED MILITARY ADVANTAGE.
"THAT INCIDENT IS KNOWN AS **THE BLIGHT**.
"SINCE THEN, THE XERX HAVE CONQUERED MORE THAN HALF THE PLANETS ON THE FAR SIDE OF THE NILE. AND WITH EACH CONQUERED PLANET, OCTAVIAN'S REACH GROWS STRONGER.

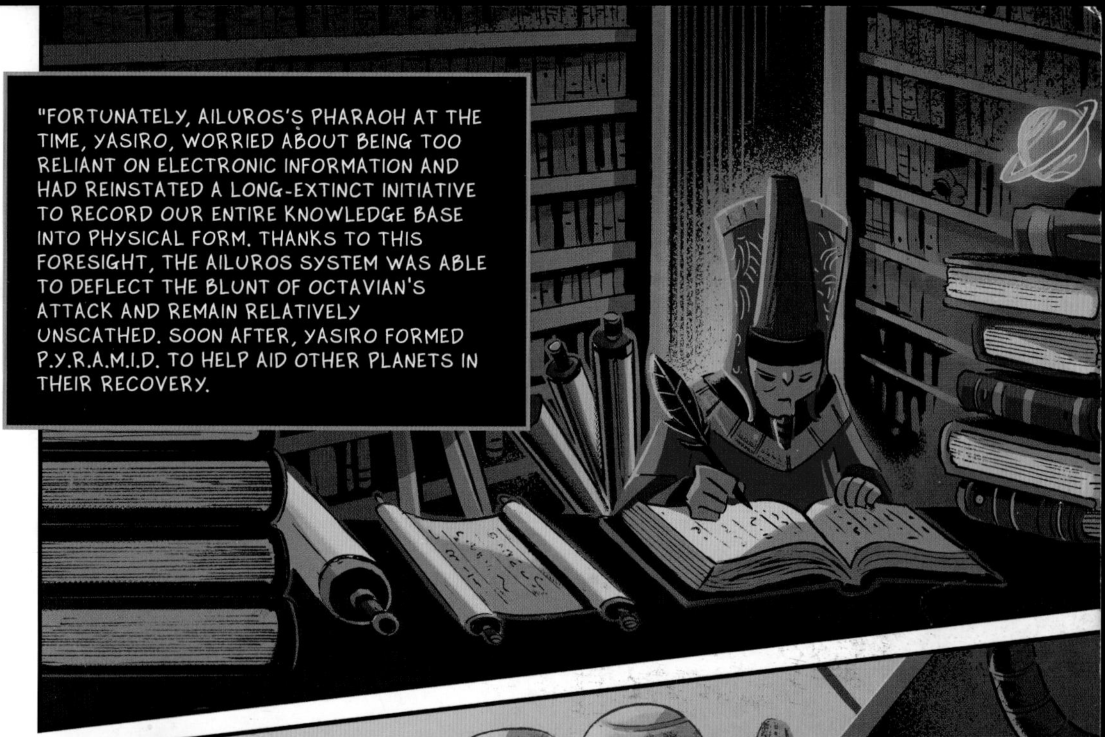
"FORTUNATELY, AILUROS'S PHARAOH AT THE TIME, YASIRO, WORRIED ABOUT BEING TOO RELIANT ON ELECTRONIC INFORMATION AND HAD REINSTATED A LONG-EXTINCT INITIATIVE TO RECORD OUR ENTIRE KNOWLEDGE BASE INTO PHYSICAL FORM. THANKS TO THIS FORESIGHT, THE AILUROS SYSTEM WAS ABLE TO DEFLECT THE BLUNT OF OCTAVIAN'S ATTACK AND REMAIN RELATIVELY UNSCATHED. SOON AFTER, YASIRO FORMED P.Y.R.A.M.I.D. TO HELP AID OTHER PLANETS IN THEIR RECOVERY.

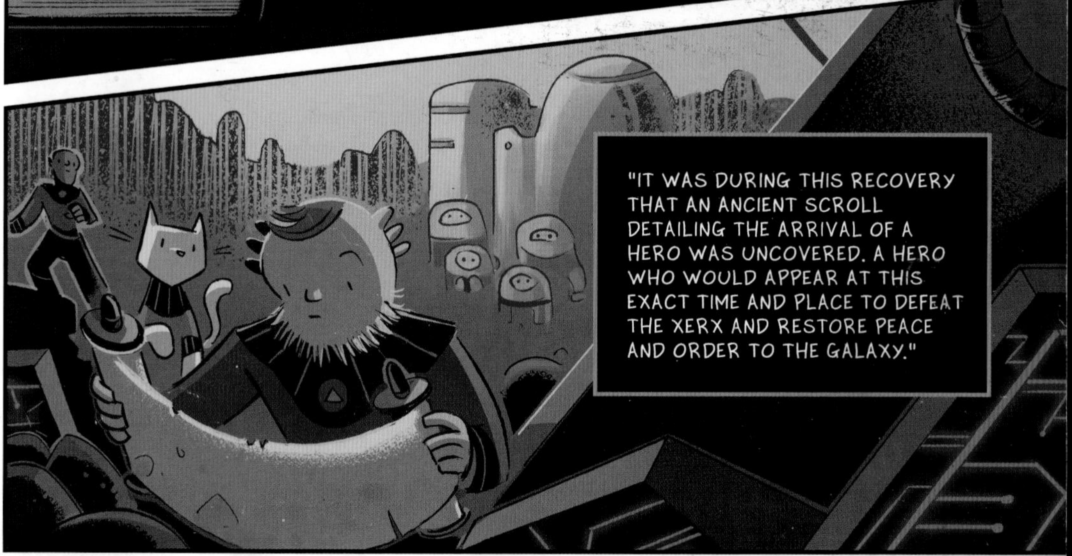
"IT WAS DURING THIS RECOVERY THAT AN ANCIENT SCROLL DETAILING THE ARRIVAL OF A HERO WAS UNCOVERED. A HERO WHO WOULD APPEAR AT THIS EXACT TIME AND PLACE TO DEFEAT THE XERX AND RESTORE PEACE AND ORDER TO THE GALAXY."

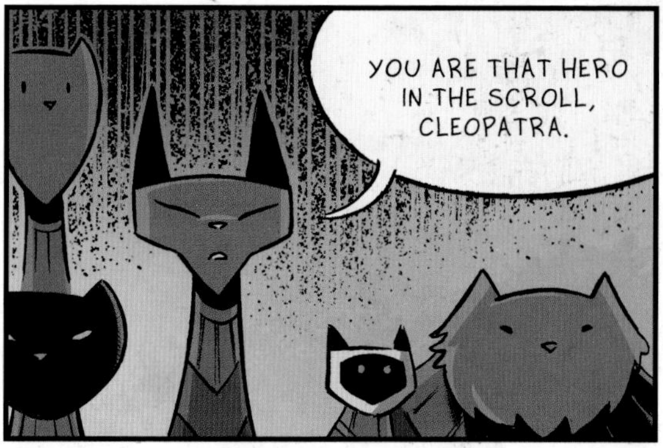
YOU ARE THAT HERO IN THE SCROLL, CLEOPATRA.

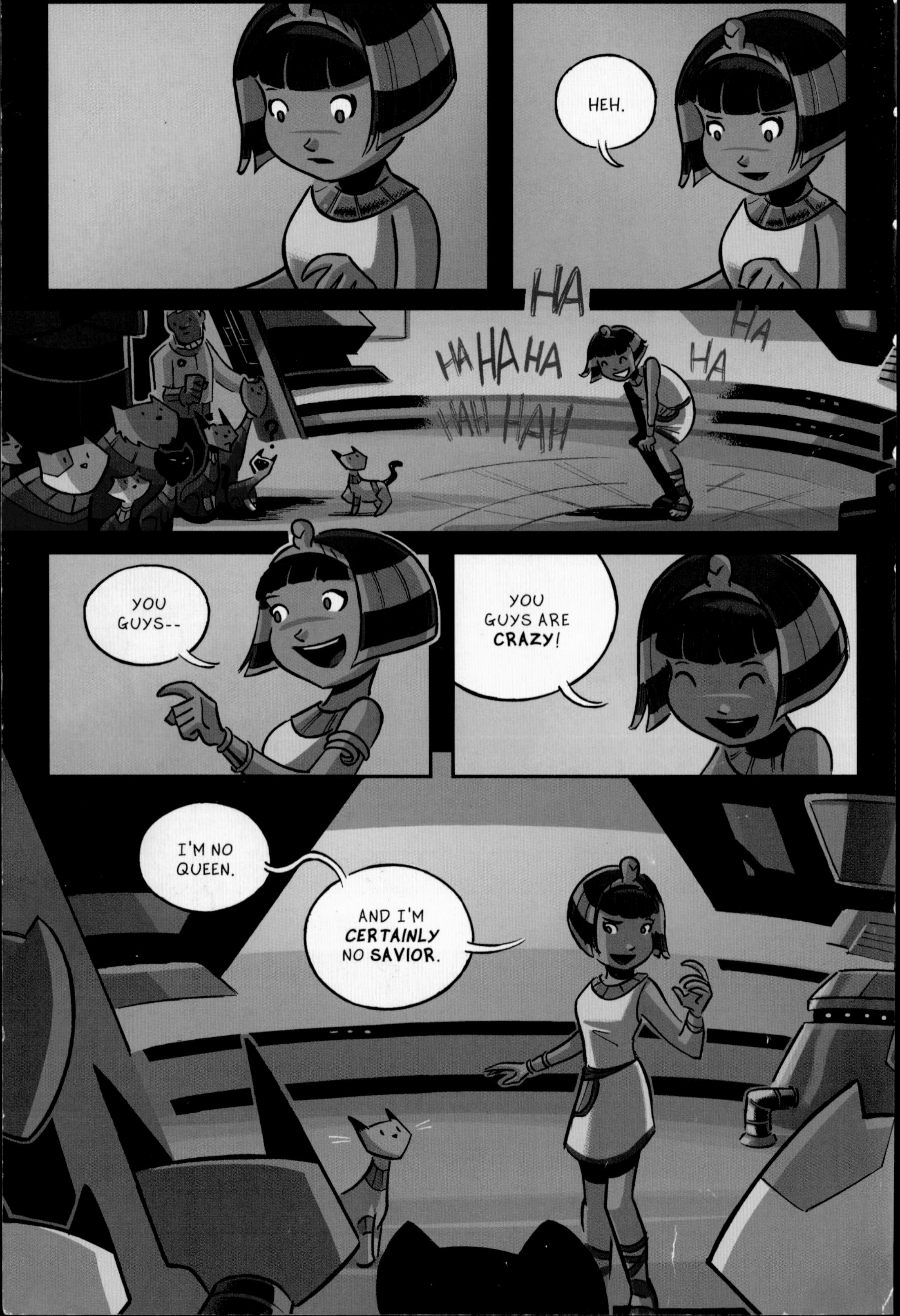

HEH.
HA
HA HA HA
HAH HAH
HA
HA
YOU GUYS--
YOU GUYS ARE **CRAZY**!
I'M NO QUEEN.
AND I'M **CERTAINLY** NO **SAVIOR**.

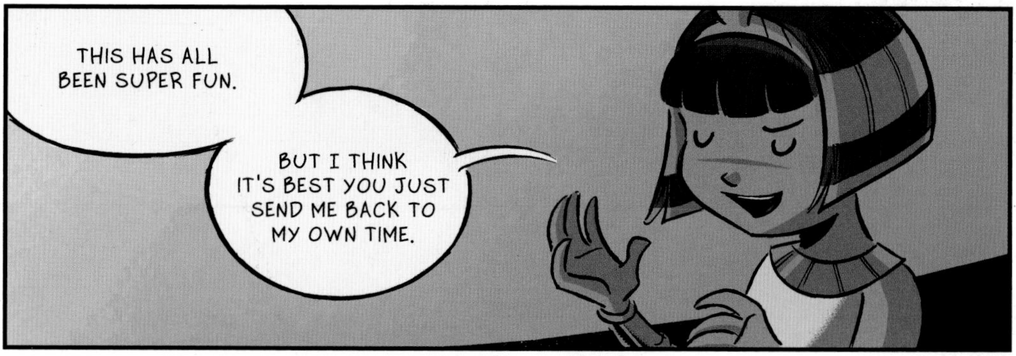
THIS HAS ALL BEEN SUPER FUN.
BUT I THINK IT'S BEST YOU JUST SEND ME BACK TO MY OWN TIME.

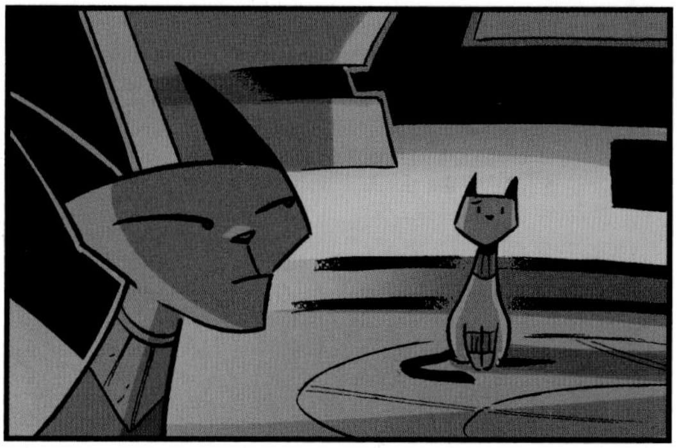

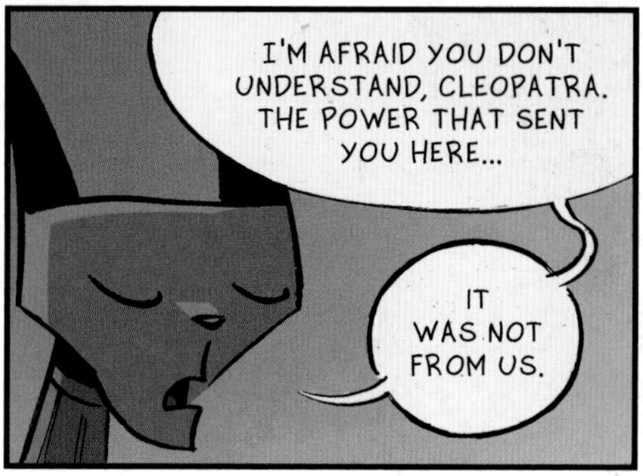
I'M AFRAID YOU DON'T UNDERSTAND, CLEOPATRA. THE POWER THAT SENT YOU HERE...
IT WAS NOT FROM US.

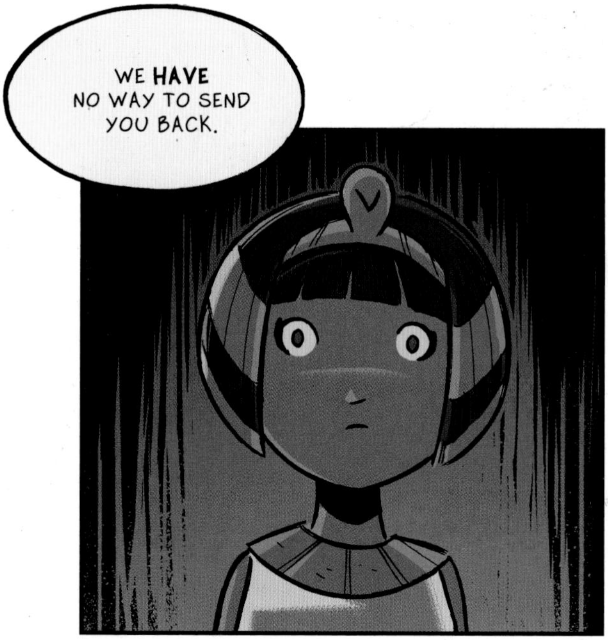
WE **HAVE** NO WAY TO SEND YOU BACK.

CHAPTER TWO

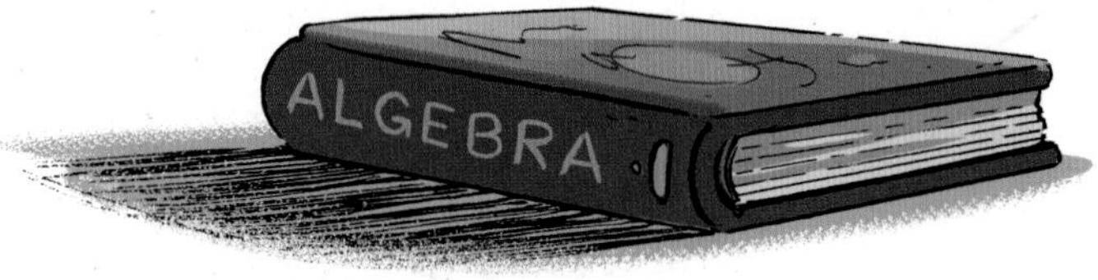
ALGEBRA

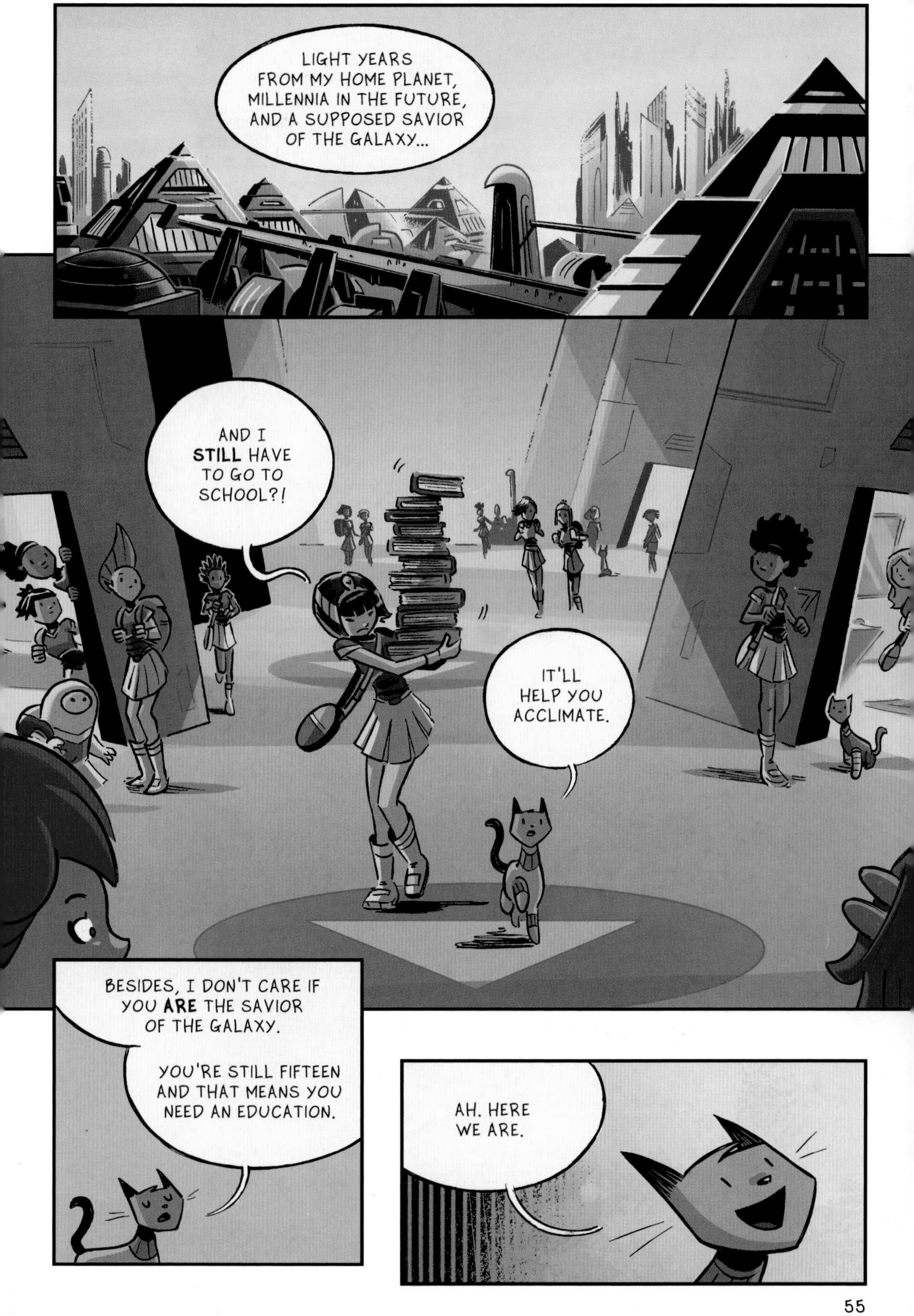
LIGHT YEARS FROM MY HOME PLANET, MILLENNIA IN THE FUTURE, AND A SUPPOSED SAVIOR OF THE GALAXY...
AND I **STILL** HAVE TO GO TO SCHOOL?!
IT'LL HELP YOU ACCLIMATE.
BESIDES, I DON'T CARE IF YOU **ARE** THE SAVIOR OF THE GALAXY.
YOU'RE STILL FIFTEEN AND THAT MEANS YOU NEED AN EDUCATION.
AH. HERE WE ARE.

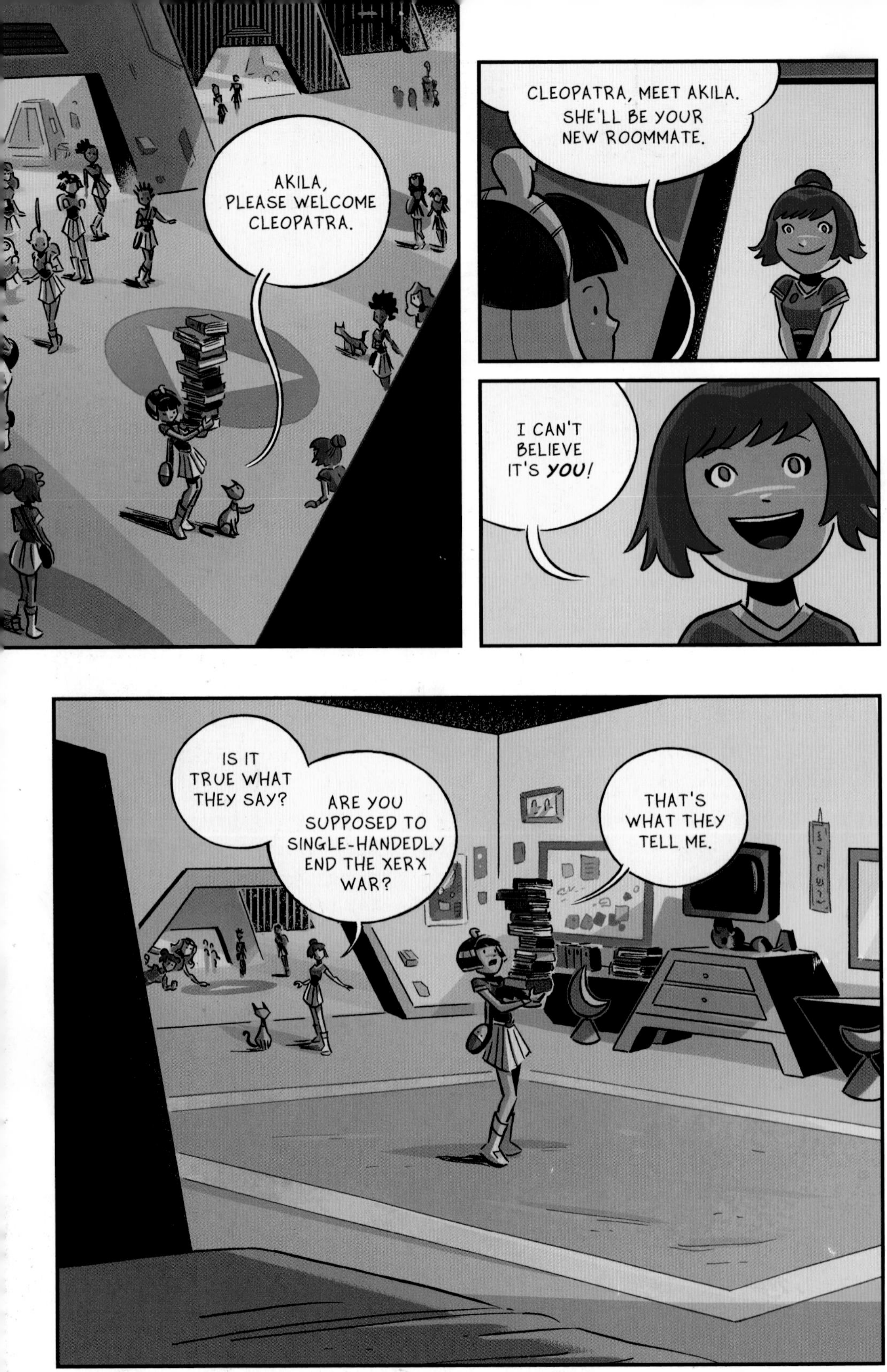
AKILA, PLEASE WELCOME CLEOPATRA.
CLEOPATRA, MEET AKILA. SHE'LL BE YOUR NEW ROOMMATE.
I CAN'T BELIEVE IT'S *YOU*!
IS IT TRUE WHAT THEY SAY?
ARE YOU SUPPOSED TO SINGLE-HANDEDLY END THE XERX WAR?
THAT'S WHAT THEY TELL ME.

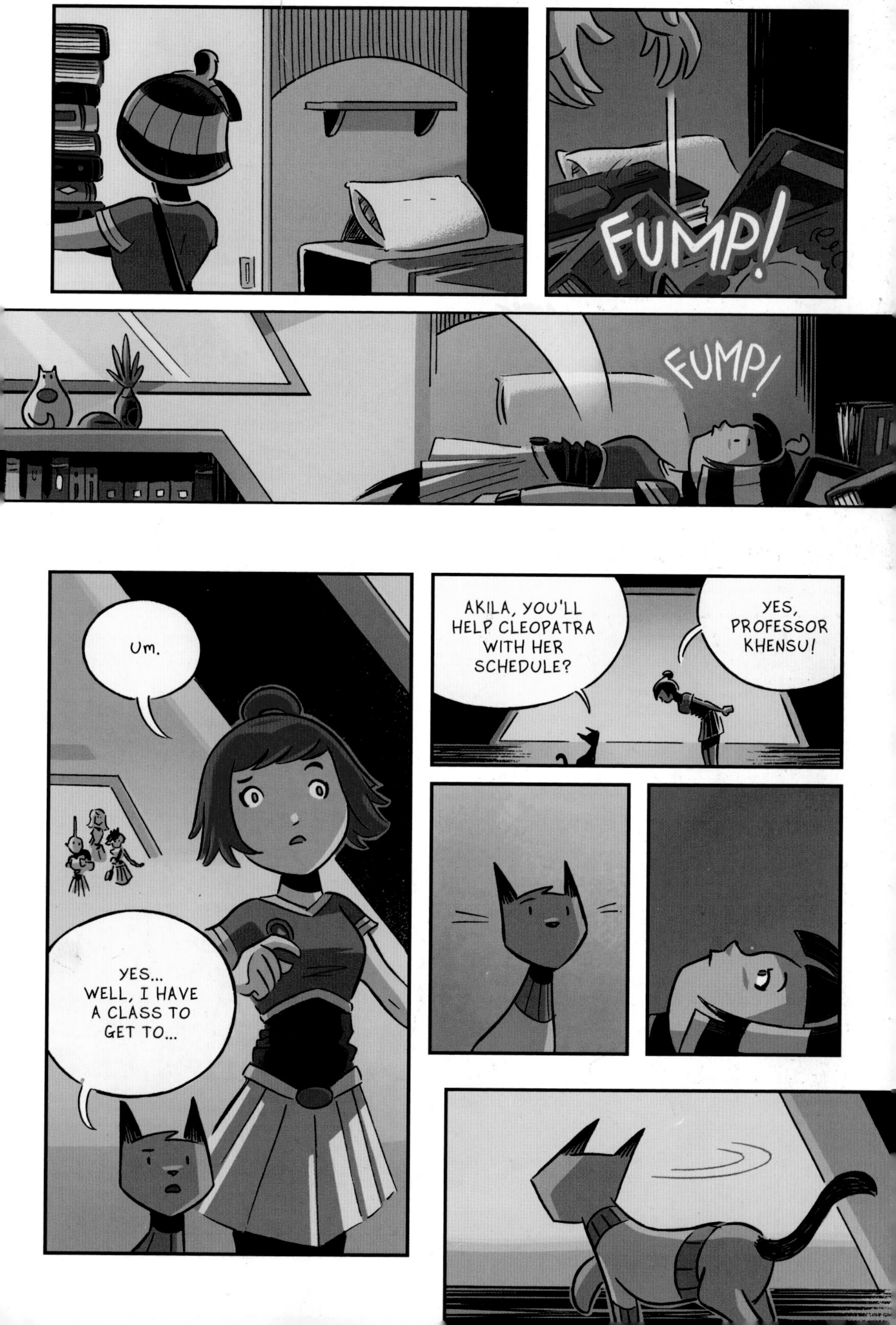
FUMP!
FUMP!
Um.
YES... WELL, I HAVE A CLASS TO GET TO...
AKILA, YOU'LL HELP CLEOPATRA WITH HER SCHEDULE?
YES, PROFESSOR KHENSU!

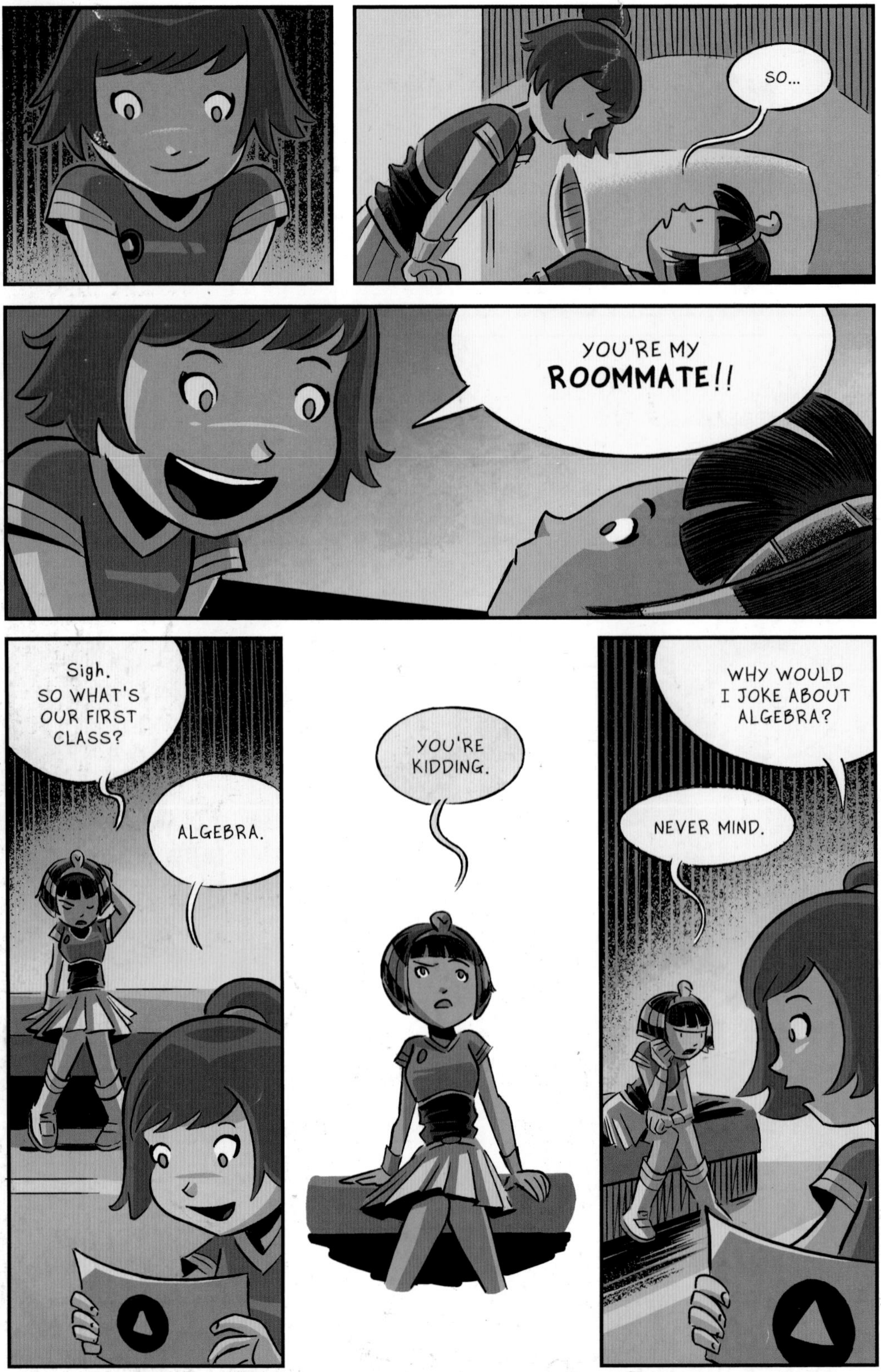
SO...
YOU'RE MY ROOMMATE!!
Sigh. SO WHAT'S OUR FIRST CLASS?
ALGEBRA.
YOU'RE KIDDING.
WHY WOULD I JOKE ABOUT ALGEBRA?
NEVER MIND.

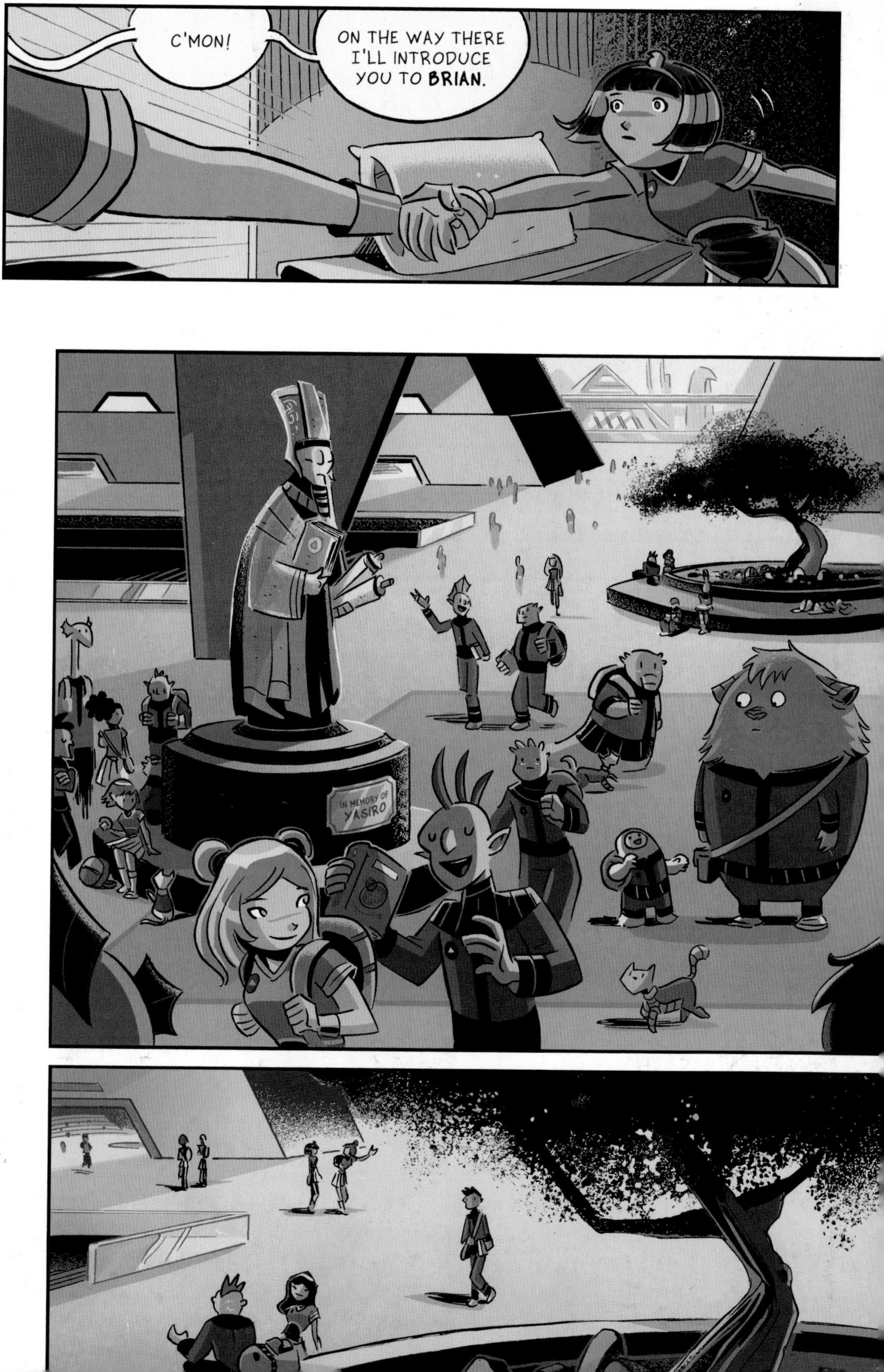
C'MON!
ON THE WAY THERE I'LL INTRODUCE YOU TO **BRIAN**.
IN MEMORY OF YASIRO

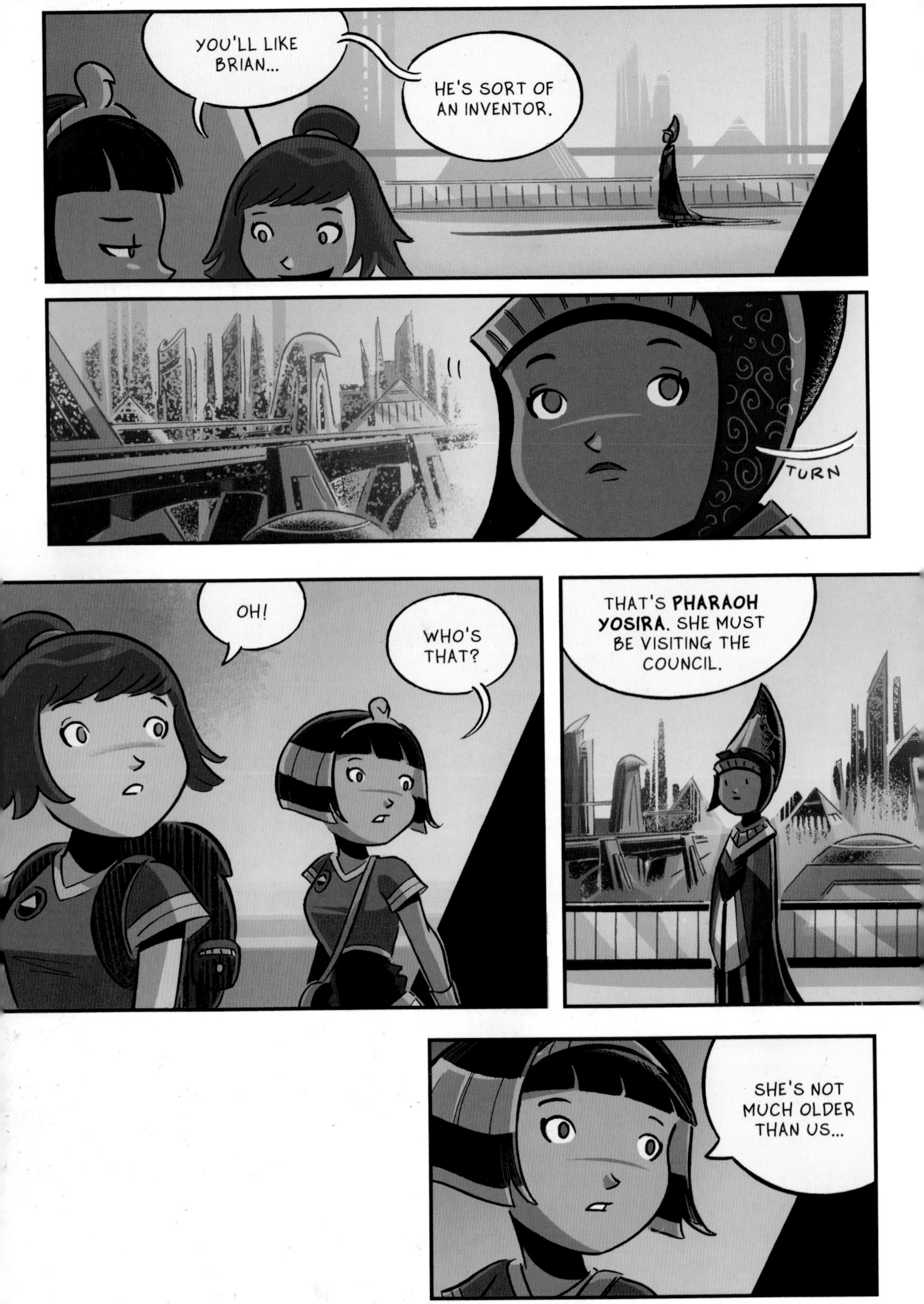

YOU'LL LIKE BRIAN...
HE'S SORT OF AN INVENTOR.
TURN
OH!
WHO'S THAT?
THAT'S **PHARAOH YOSIRA**. SHE MUST BE VISITING THE COUNCIL.
SHE'S NOT MUCH OLDER THAN US...

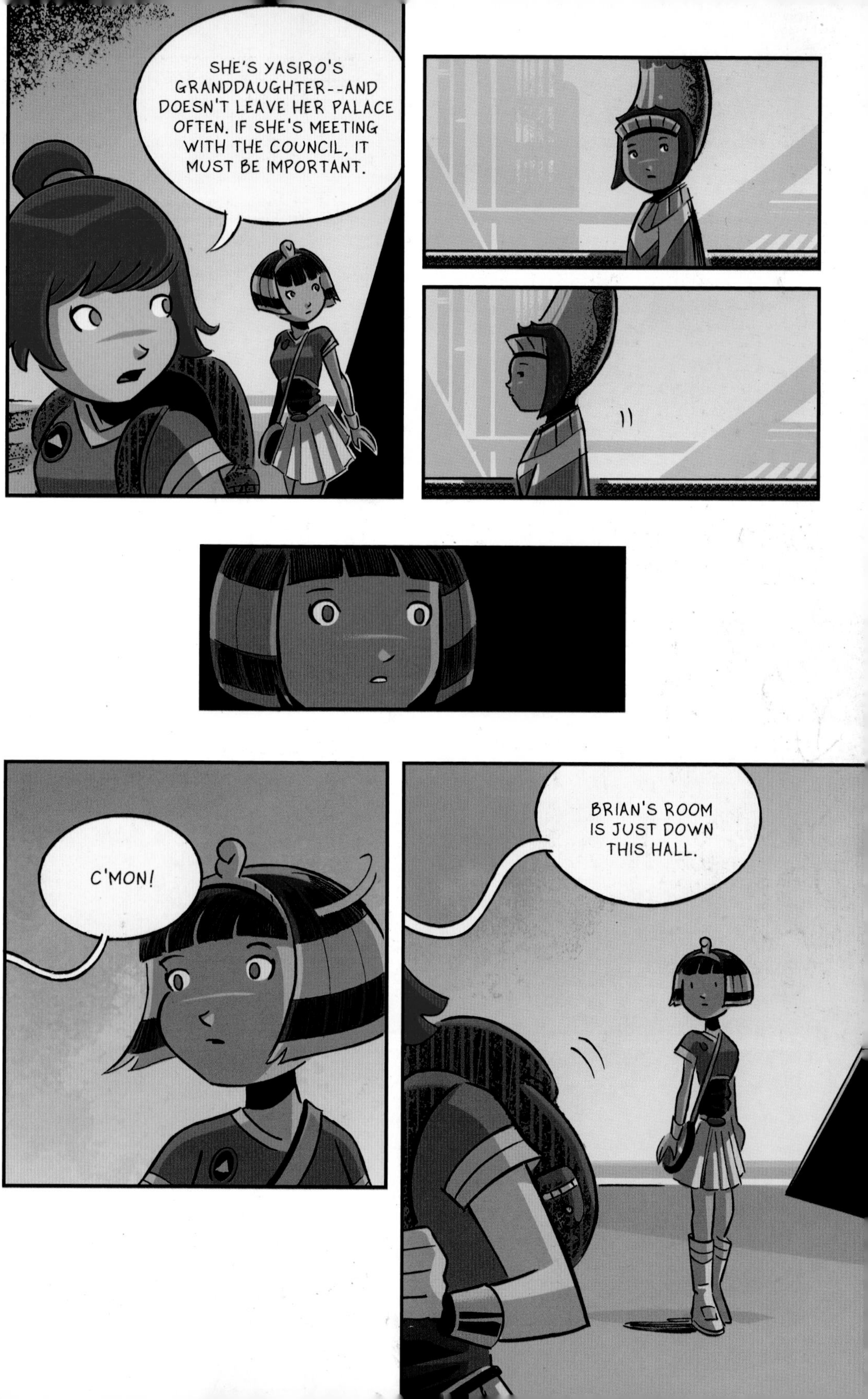
SHE'S YASIRO'S GRANDDAUGHTER--AND DOESN'T LEAVE HER PALACE OFTEN. IF SHE'S MEETING WITH THE COUNCIL, IT MUST BE IMPORTANT.
C'MON!
BRIAN'S ROOM IS JUST DOWN THIS HALL.

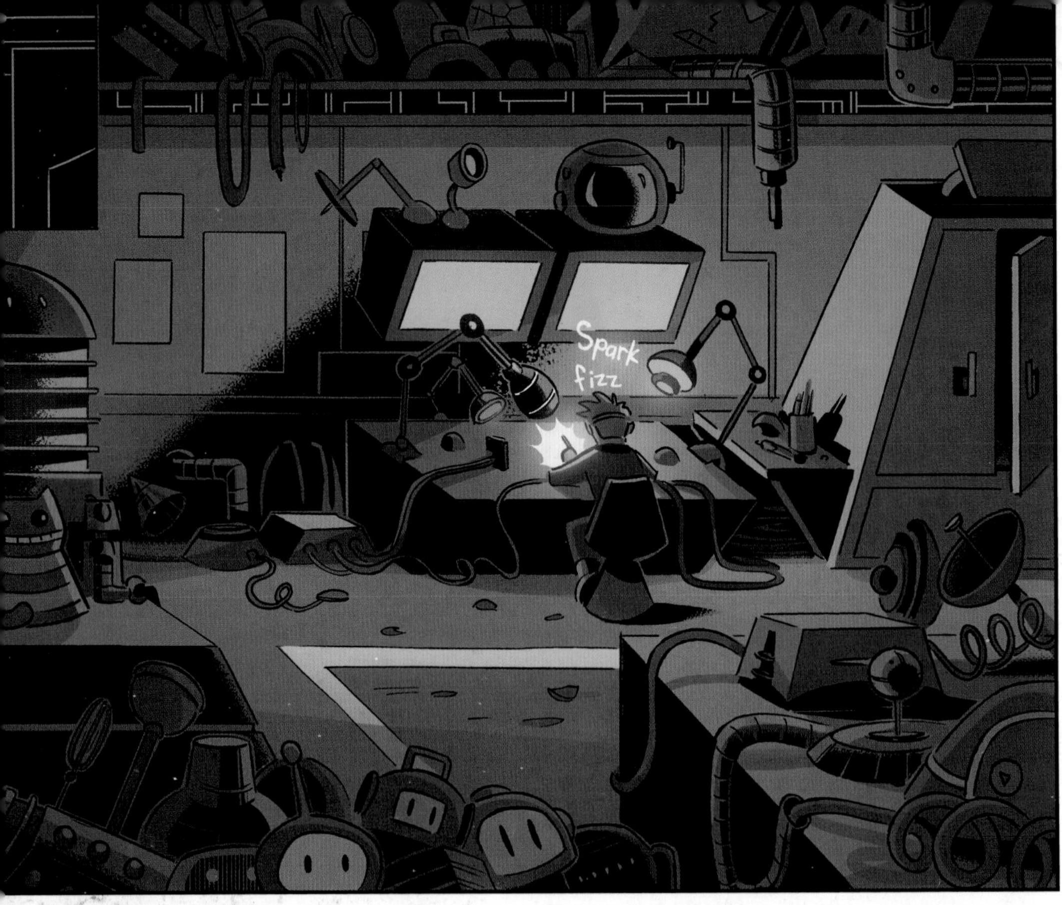
Spark
fizz

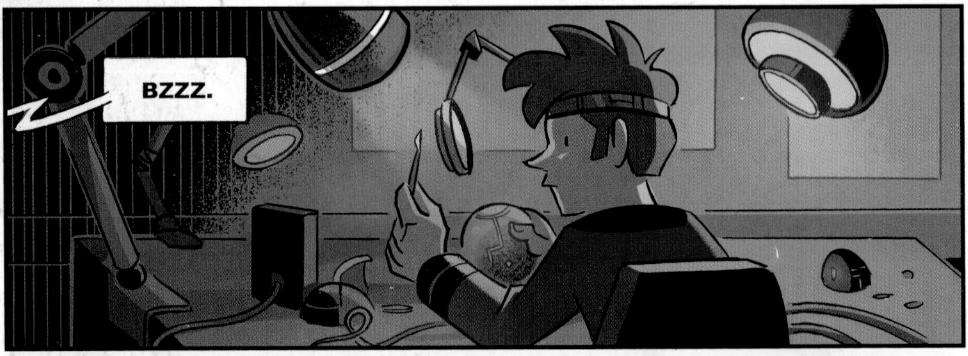
BZZZ.

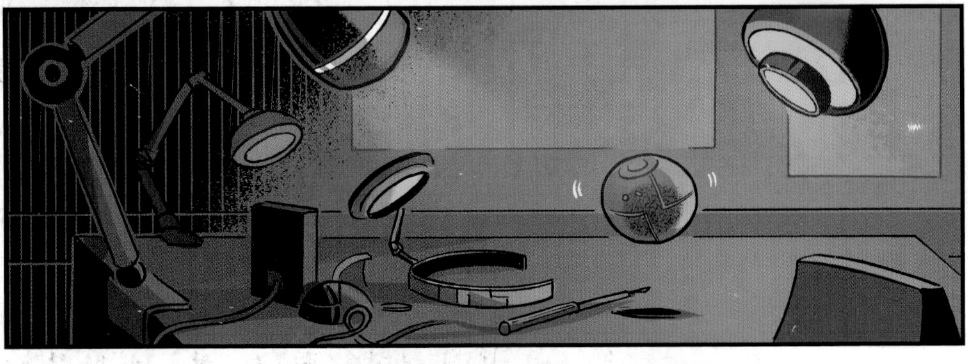

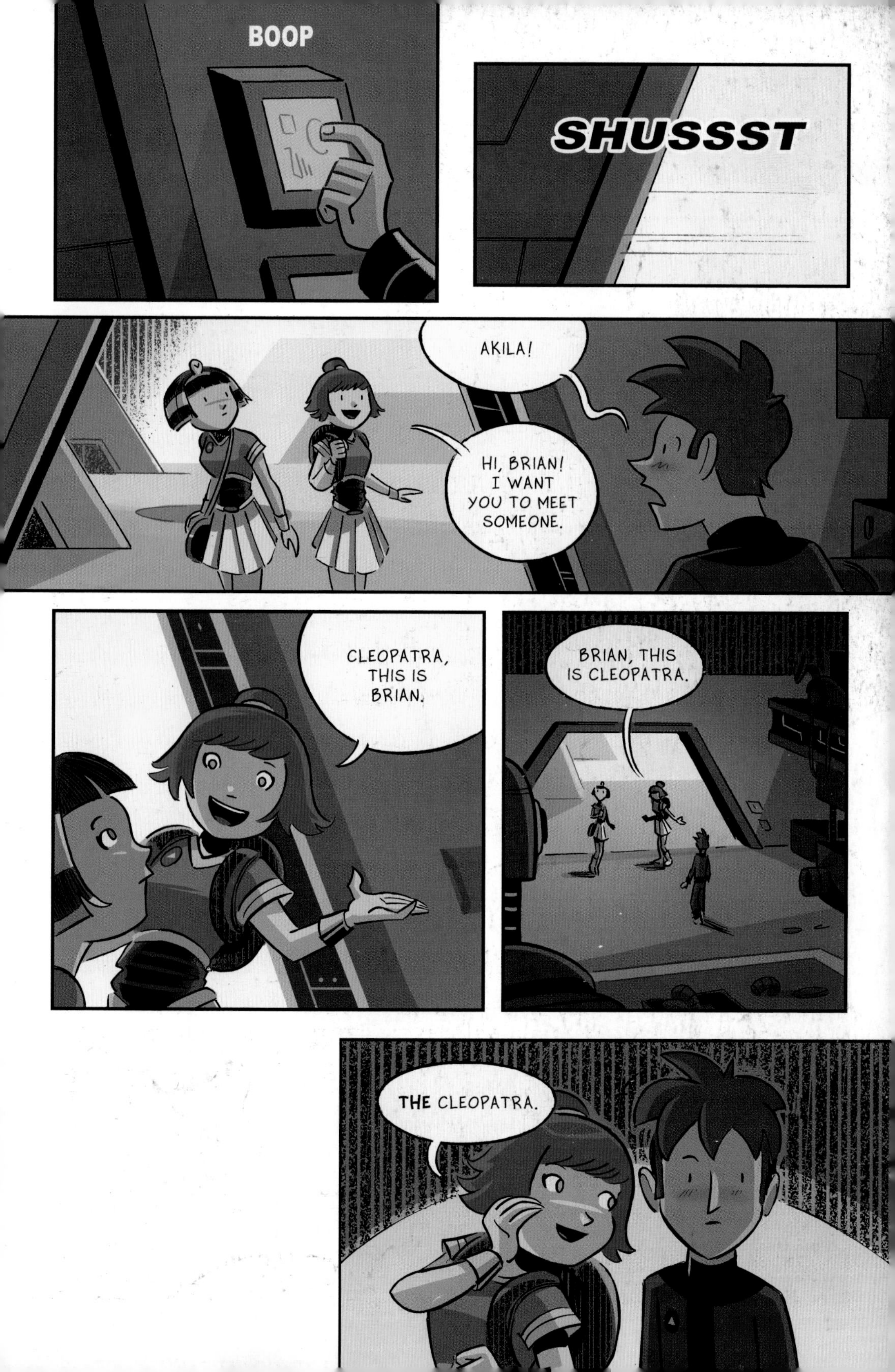
BOOP
SHUSSST
AKILA!
HI, BRIAN! I WANT YOU TO MEET SOMEONE.
CLEOPATRA, THIS IS BRIAN.
BRIAN, THIS IS CLEOPATRA.
THE CLEOPATRA.

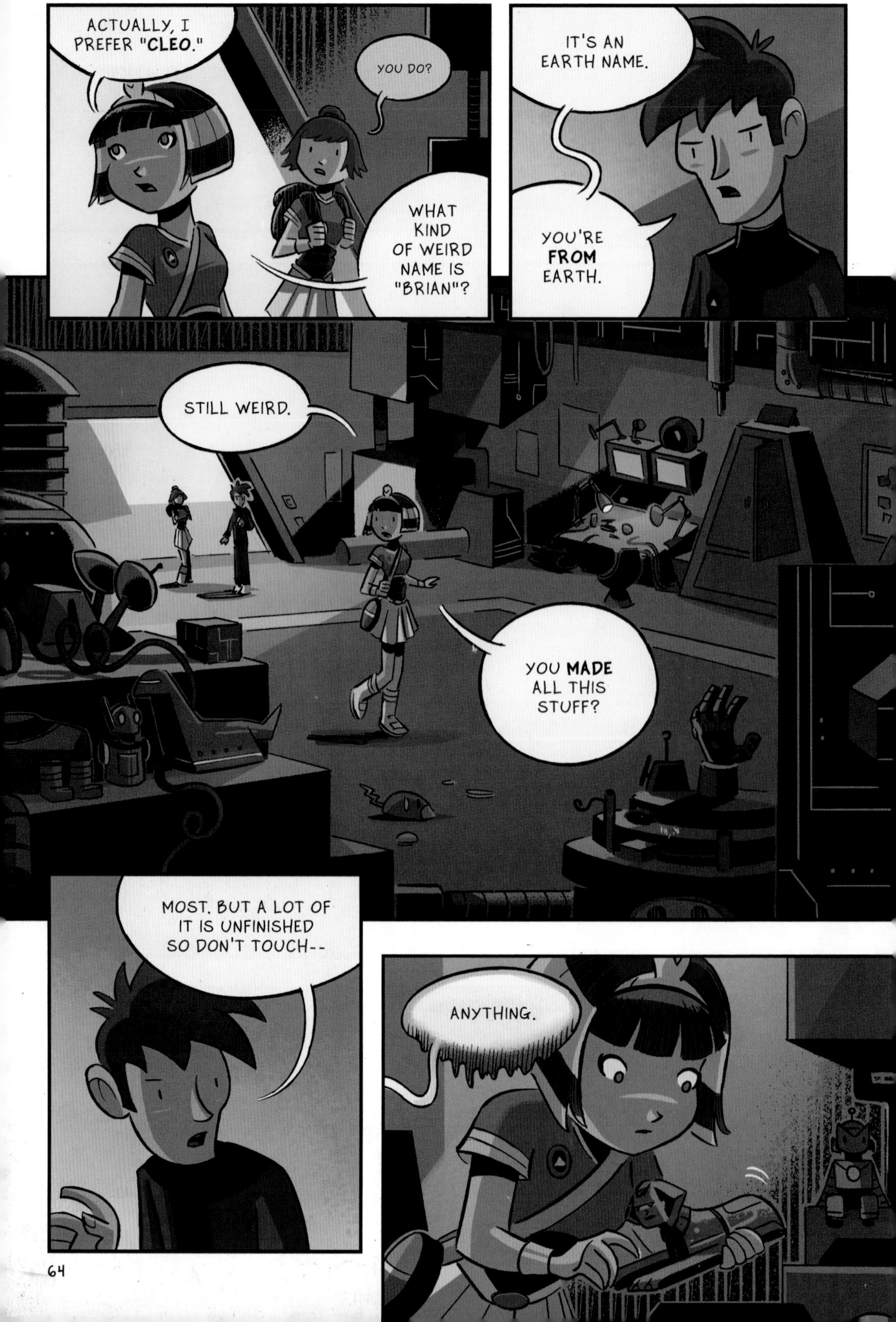
ACTUALLY, I PREFER "CLEO."
YOU DO?
WHAT KIND OF WEIRD NAME IS "BRIAN"?
IT'S AN EARTH NAME.
YOU'RE FROM EARTH.
STILL WEIRD.
YOU MADE ALL THIS STUFF?
MOST. BUT A LOT OF IT IS UNFINISHED SO DON'T TOUCH--
ANYTHING.

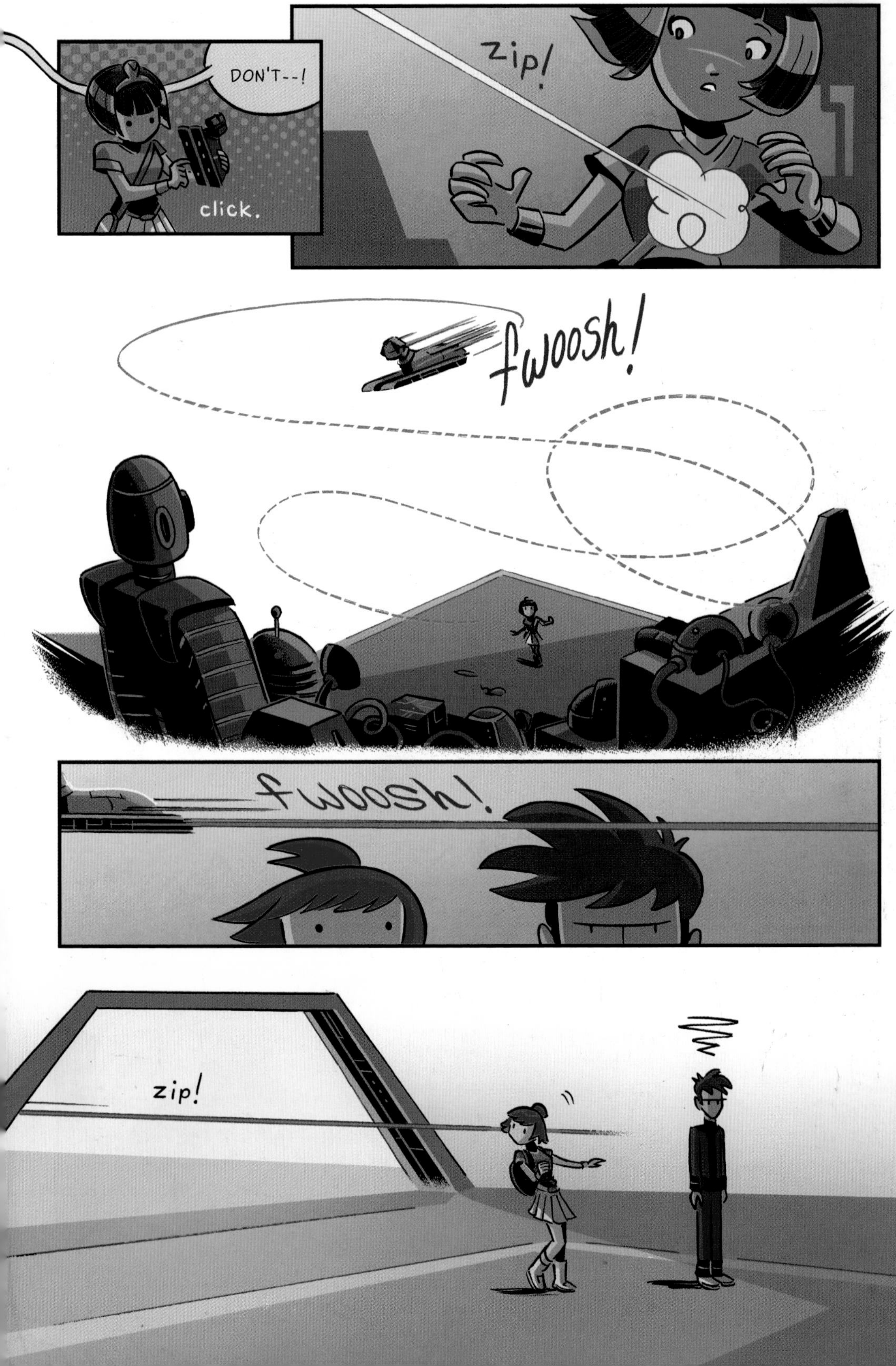
DON'T--!
click.
zip!
fwoosh!
fwoosh!
zip!

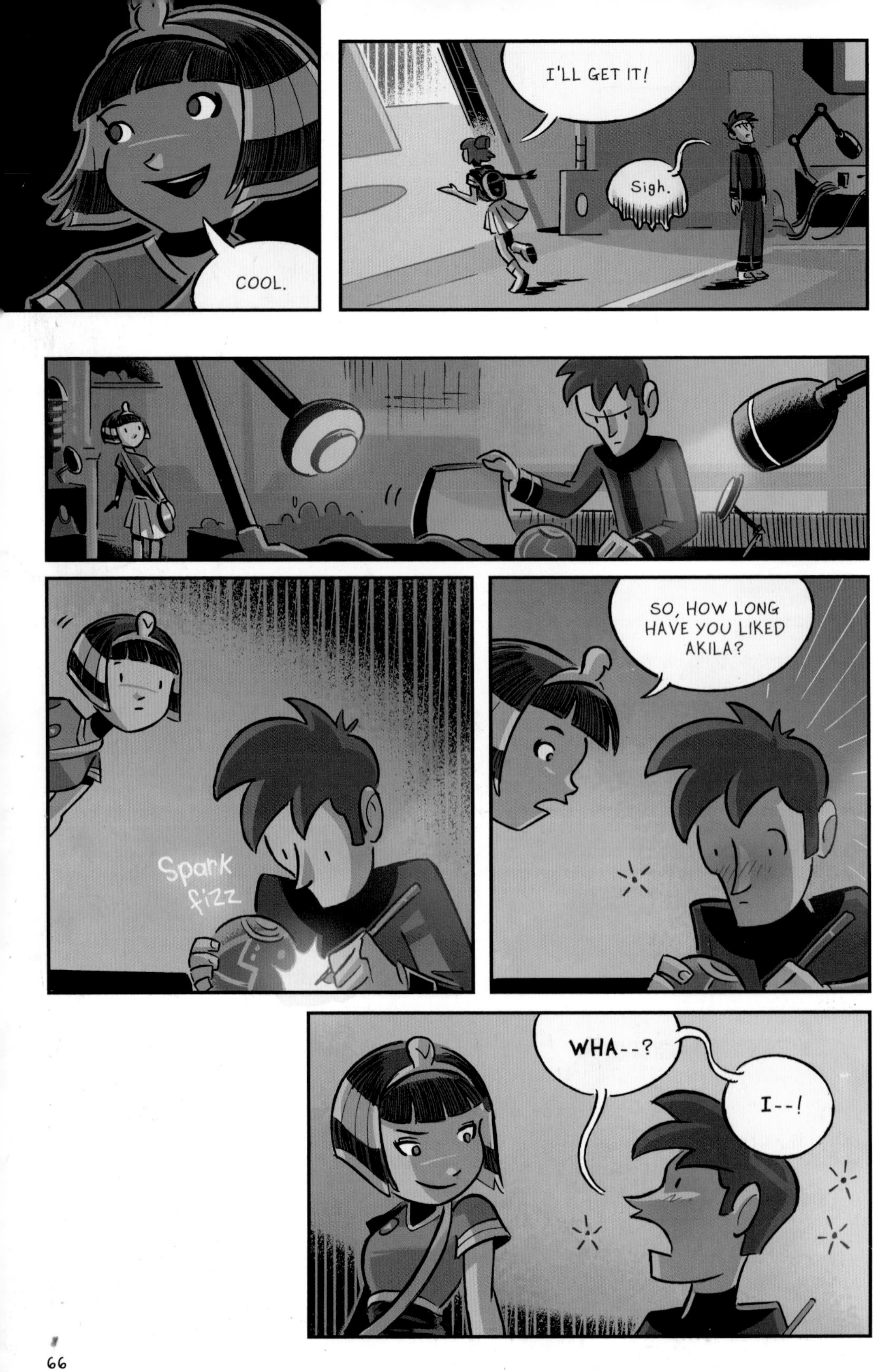
COOL.
I'LL GET IT!
Sigh.
Spark
fizz
SO, HOW LONG HAVE YOU LIKED AKILA?
WHA--?
I--!

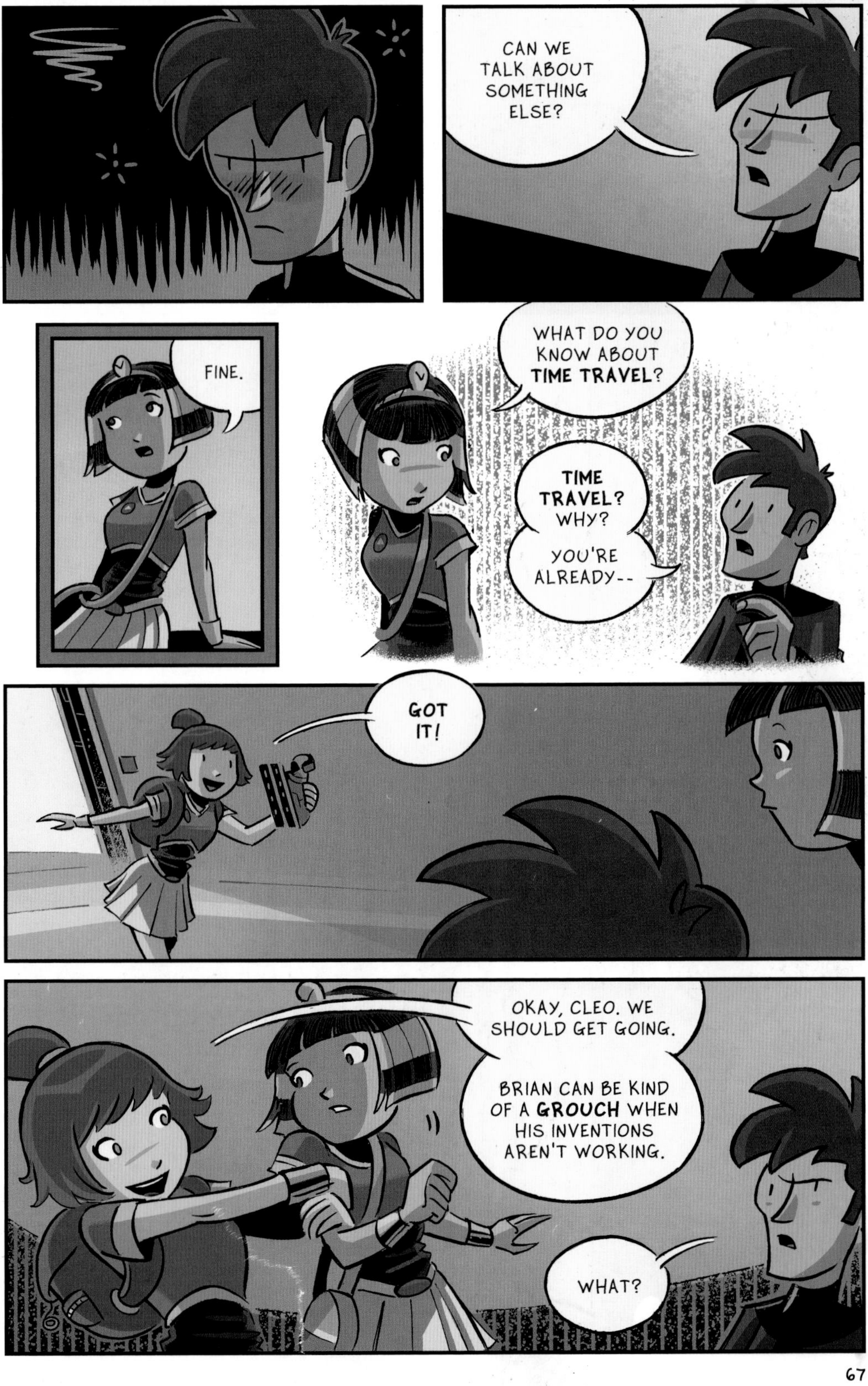
CAN WE TALK ABOUT SOMETHING ELSE?
FINE.
WHAT DO YOU KNOW ABOUT **TIME TRAVEL**?
TIME TRAVEL? WHY?
YOU'RE ALREADY--
GOT IT!
OKAY, CLEO. WE SHOULD GET GOING.
BRIAN CAN BE KIND OF A **GROUCH** WHEN HIS INVENTIONS AREN'T WORKING.
WHAT?

MY INVENTIONS ARE WORKING.
BLEEP
VZZZZSH
Sputter
FIZZ
THUD

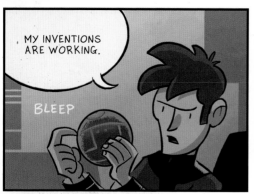

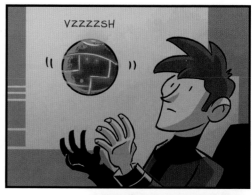

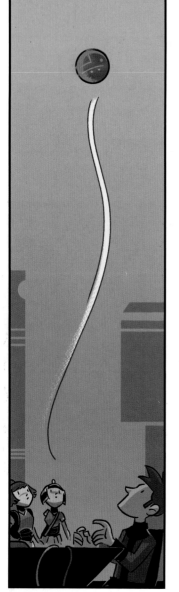

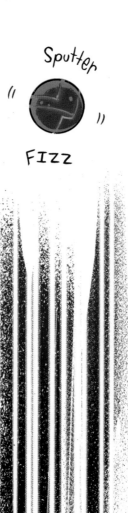

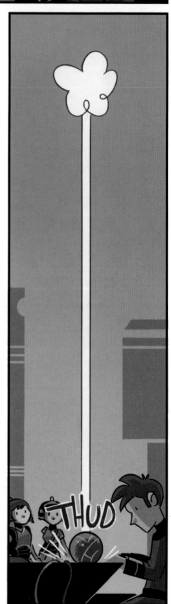

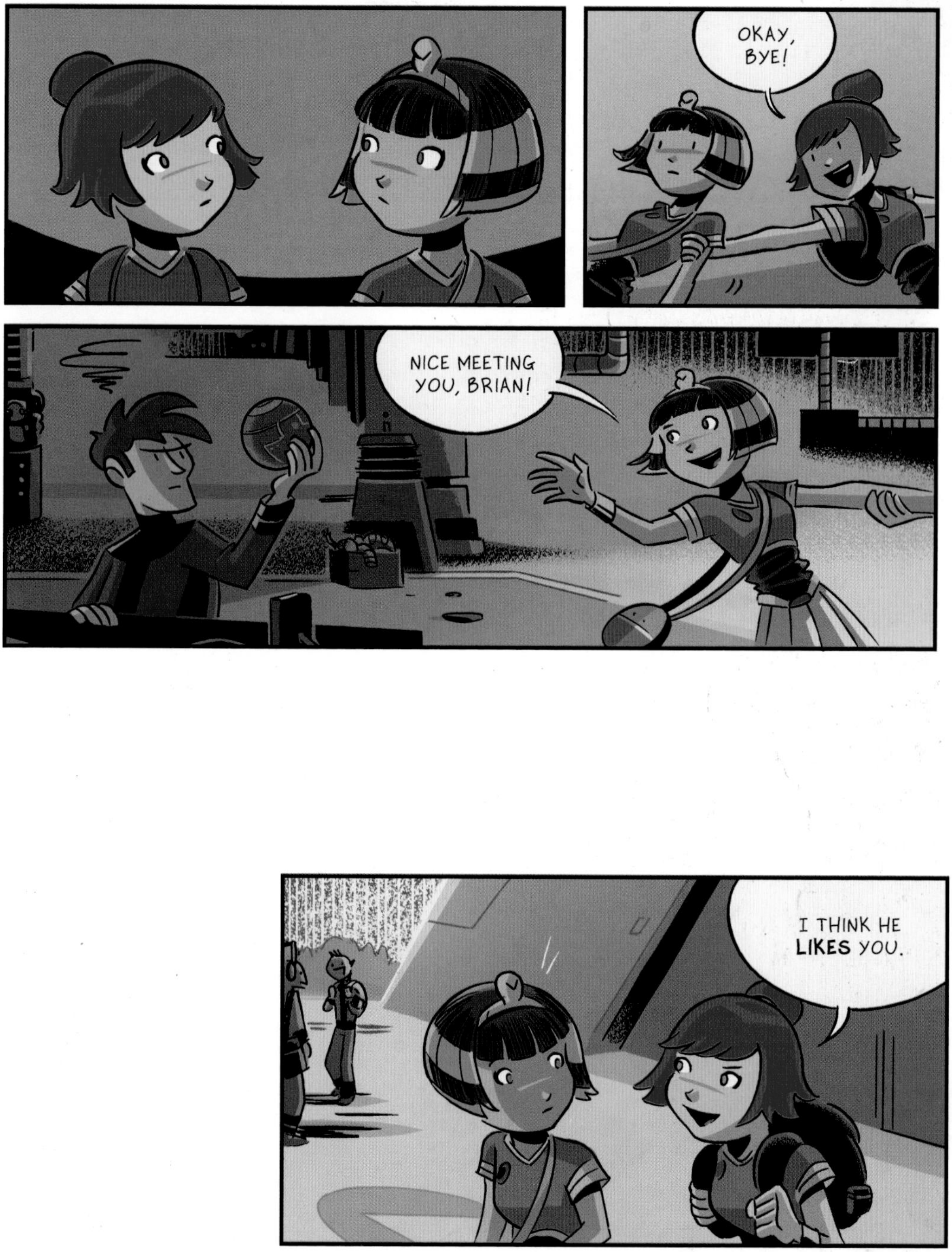
OKAY, BYE!
NICE MEETING YOU, BRIAN!
I THINK HE LIKES YOU.

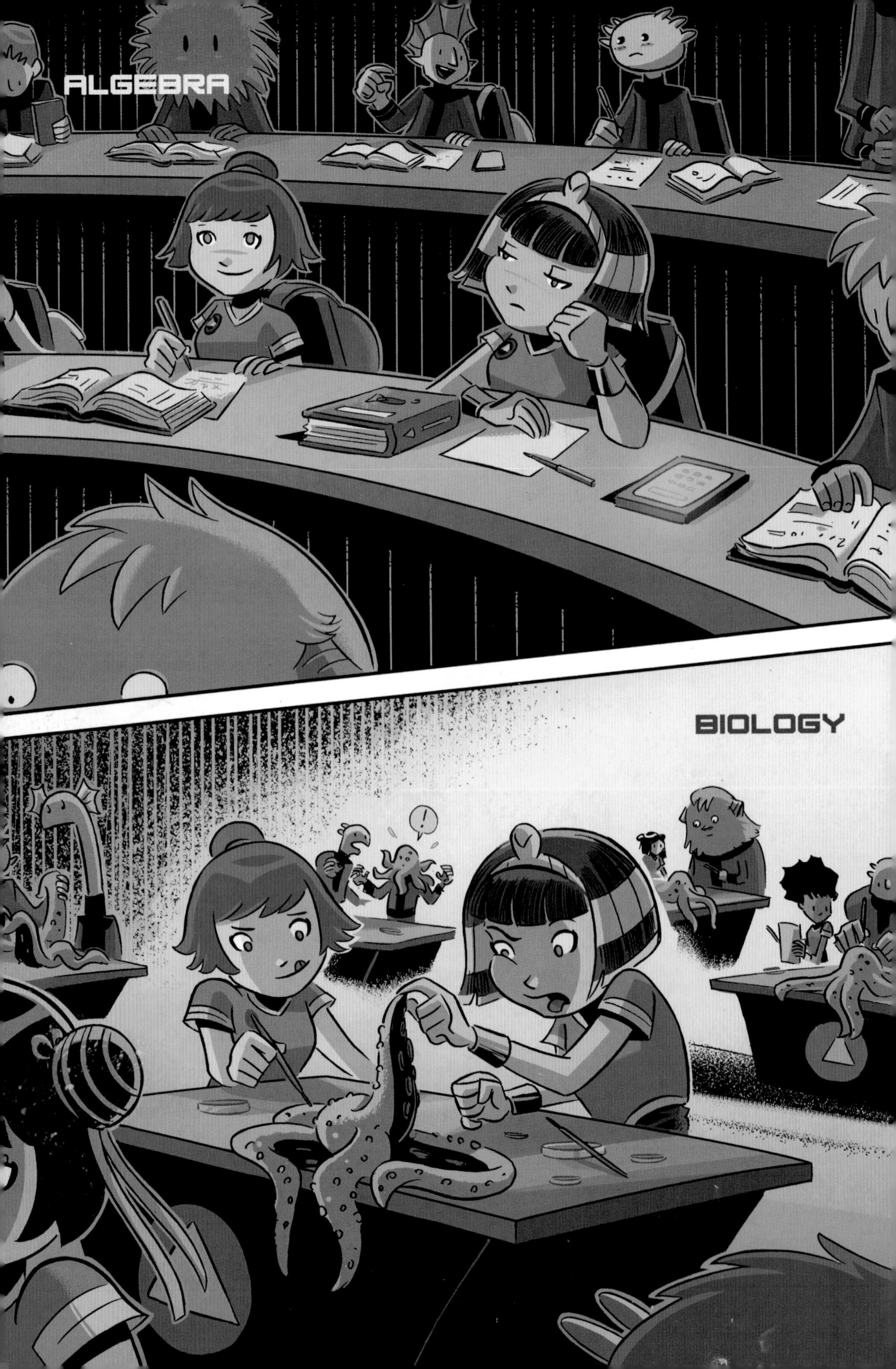
ALGEBRA
BIOLOGY
!

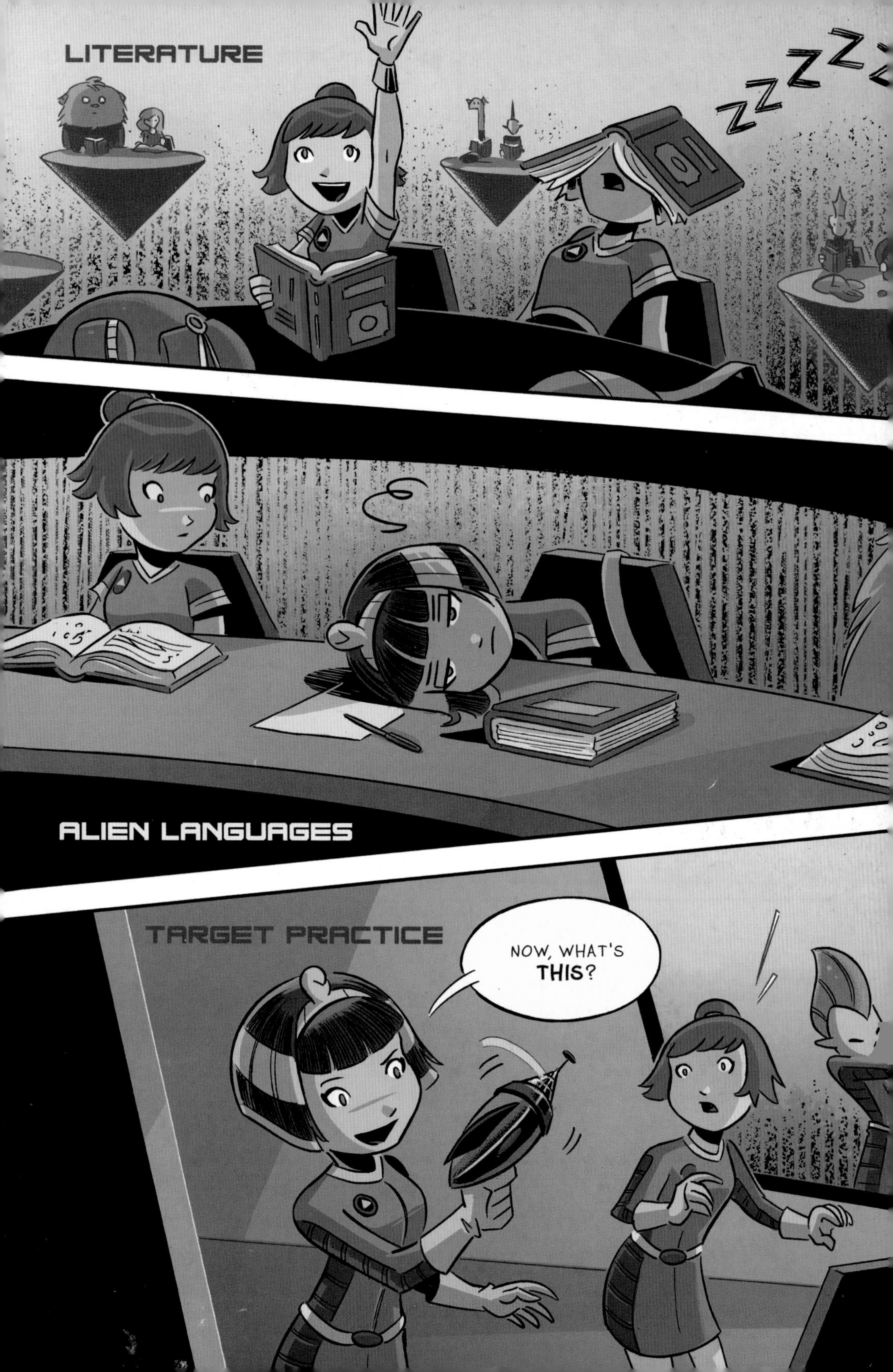
LITERATURE
ZZZZZ
ALIEN LANGUAGES
TARGET PRACTICE
NOW, WHAT'S **THIS**?

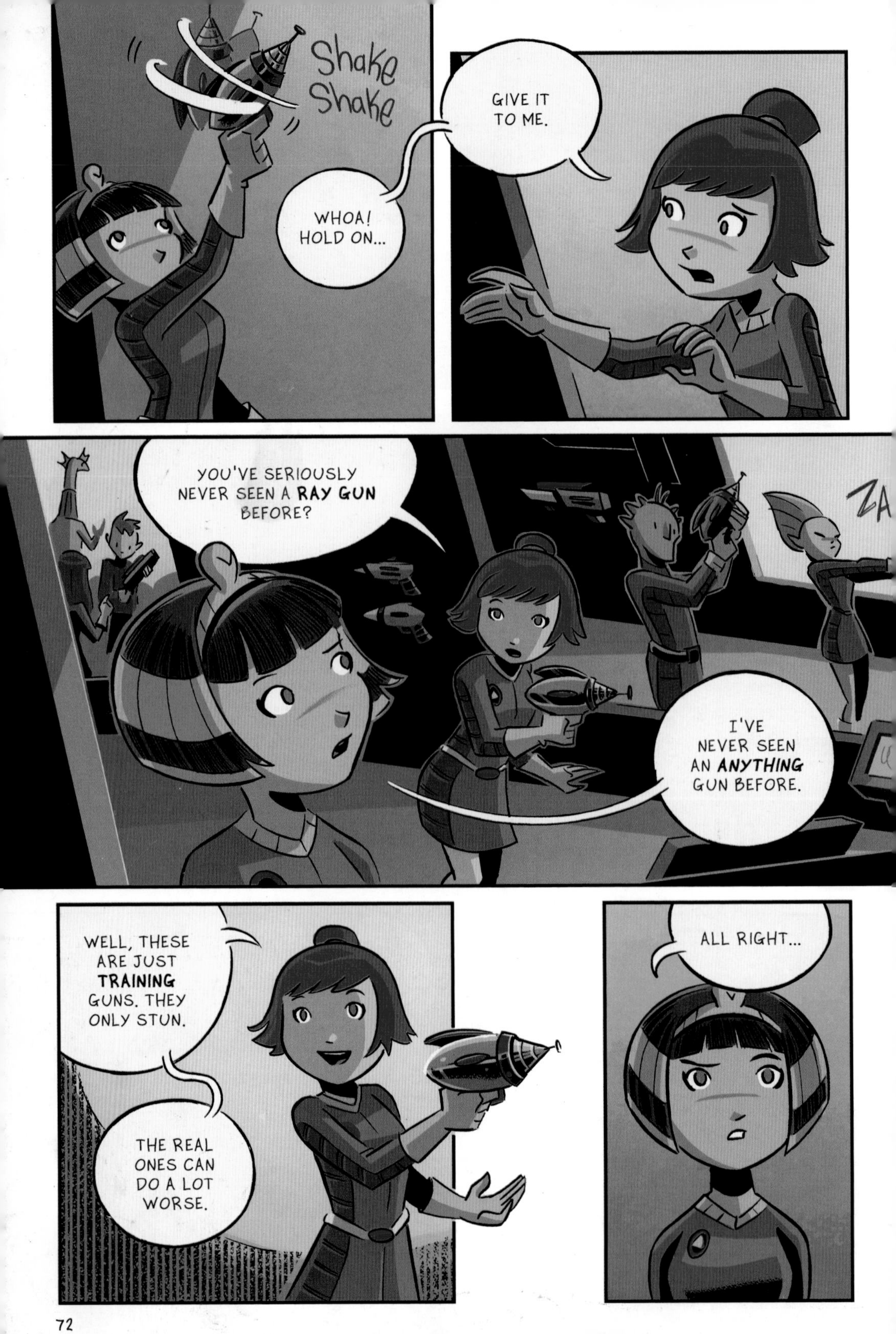
Shake
Shake
GIVE IT TO ME.
WHOA! HOLD ON...
YOU'VE SERIOUSLY NEVER SEEN A RAY GUN BEFORE?
I'VE NEVER SEEN AN ANYTHING GUN BEFORE.
WELL, THESE ARE JUST TRAINING GUNS. THEY ONLY STUN.
THE REAL ONES CAN DO A LOT WORSE.
ALL RIGHT...

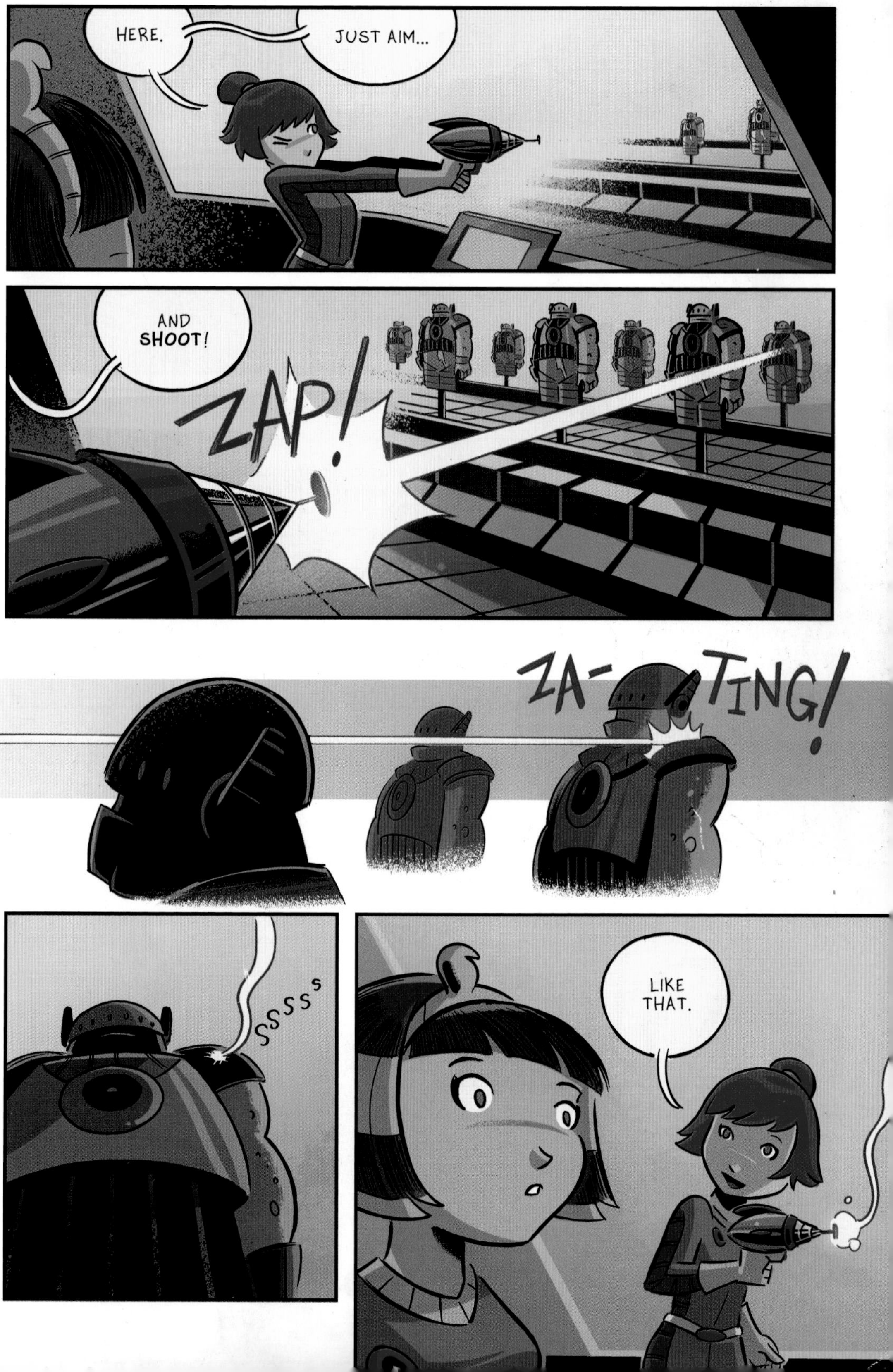

HERE.
JUST AIM...
AND SHOOT!
ZAP!
ZA-TING!
SSSSS
LIKE THAT.

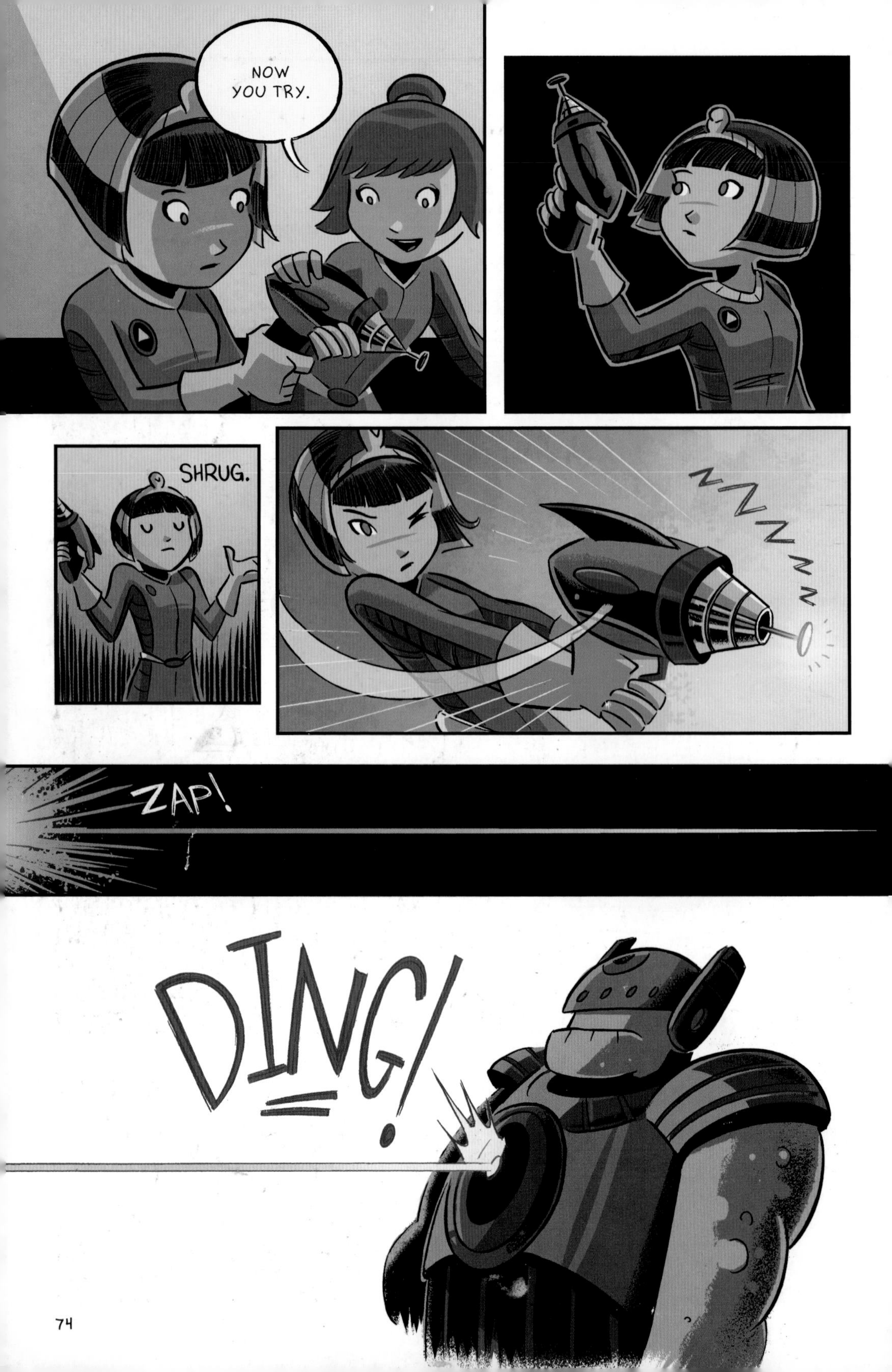
NOW YOU TRY.
SHRUG.
ZNNNNNN
ZAP!
DING!

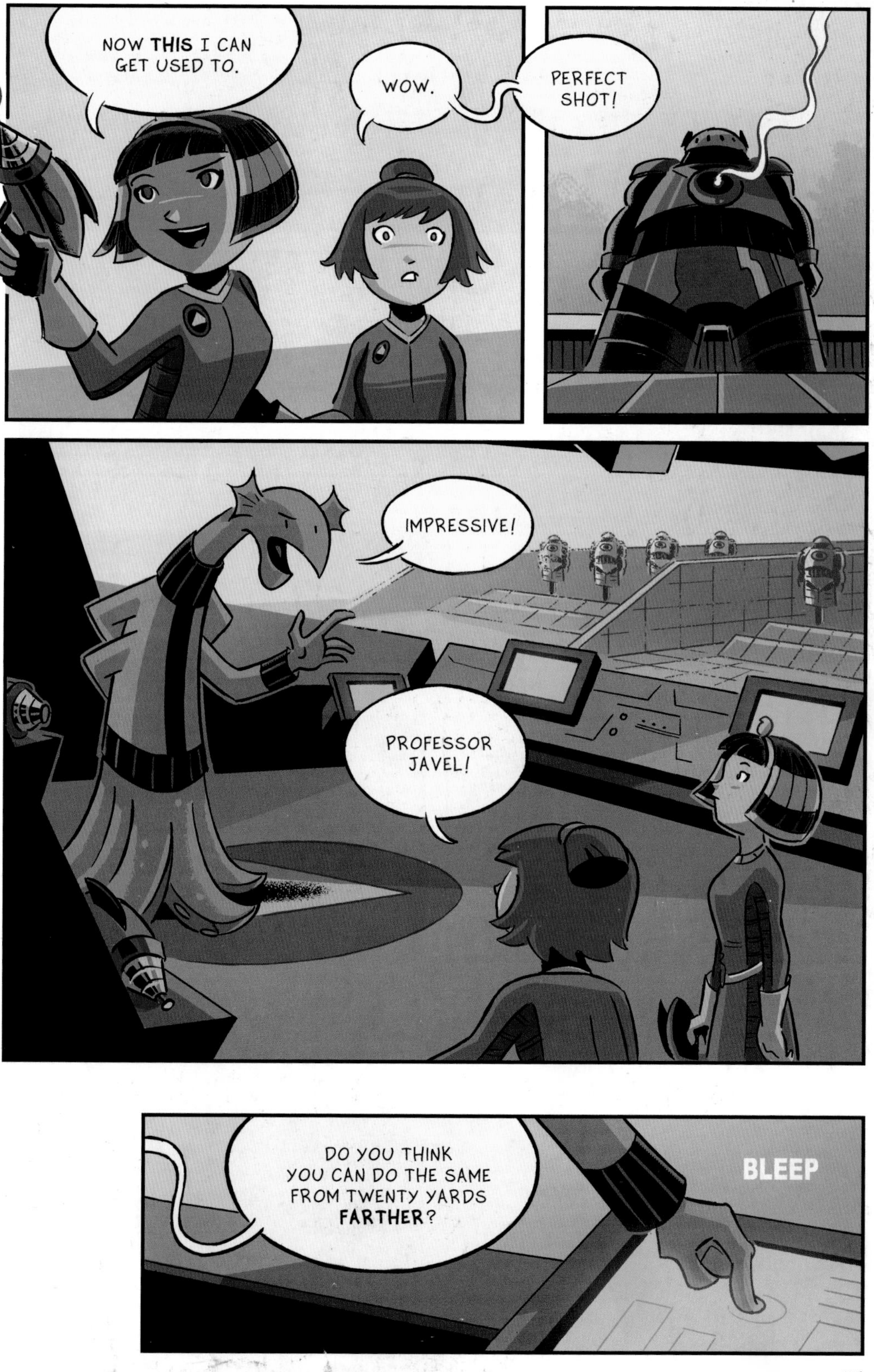
NOW **THIS** I CAN GET USED TO.
WOW.
PERFECT SHOT!
IMPRESSIVE!
PROFESSOR JAVEL!
DO YOU THINK YOU CAN DO THE SAME FROM TWENTY YARDS **FARTHER**?
BLEEP

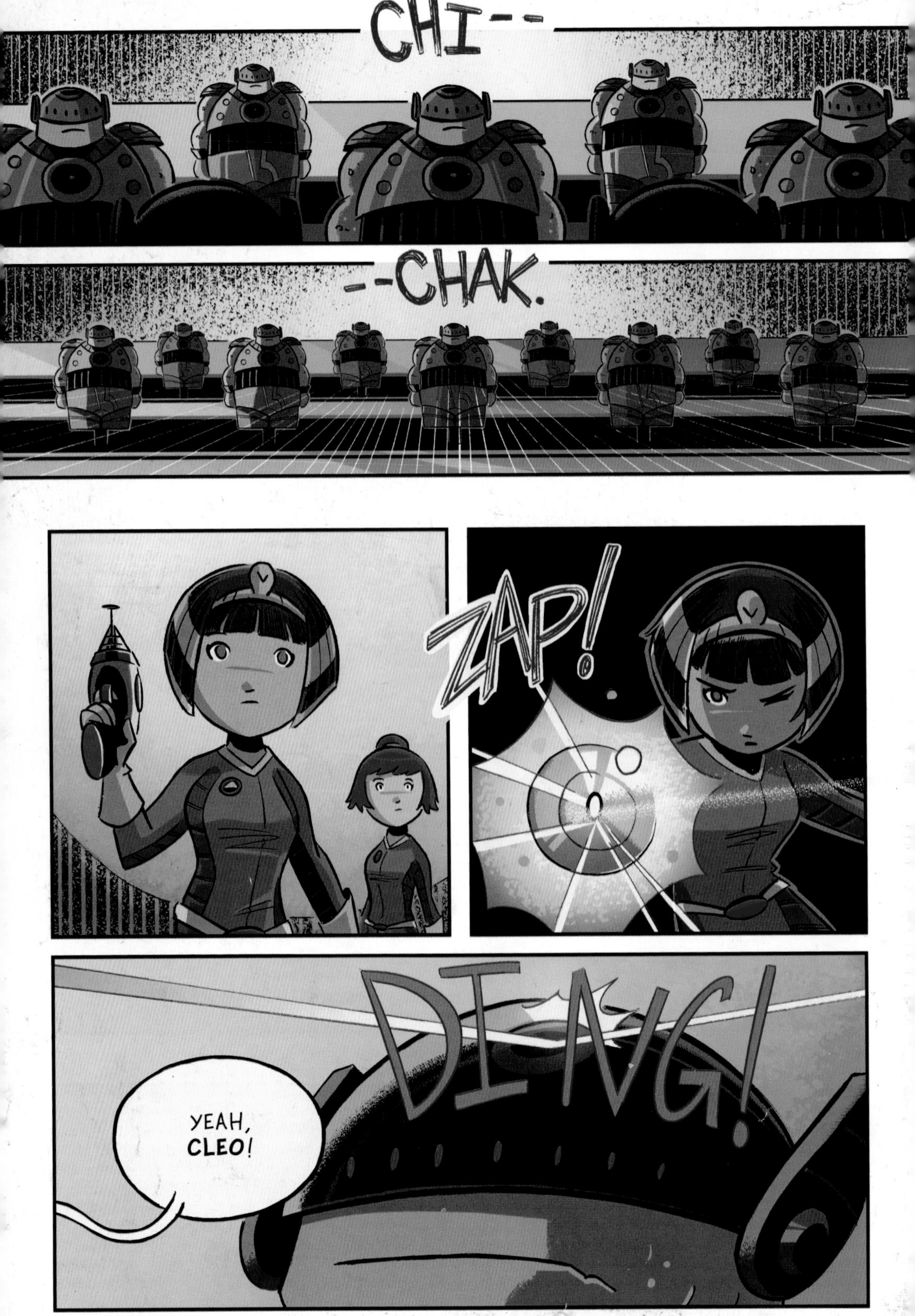
CHI--
--CHAK.
ZAP!
DING!
YEAH, CLEO!

Hrmph.

HOW WOULD THE CLASS LIKE TO SEE A LITTLE **COMPETITION**?

YOUR INSTRUCTOR VERSUS THE NEW CADET?

YEAH! WOO! YEAH!

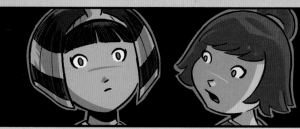

DON'T WORRY. HE DID THIS LAST SEMESTER, TOO. IT'S JUST HIS WAY OF KEEPING THE CLASS IN LINE.

FACING ONE XERX SOLDIER SHOULD BE CHALLENGING ENOUGH, BUT IF YOU EVER ENCOUNTER A WHOLE **BATTALION** OF XERX, IT'S IMPORTANT NOT TO WASTE YOUR SHOTS. OTHERWISE YOUR RAY GUN MAY RUN OUT OF CHARGE BEFORE YOU'VE DEFEATED YOUR ENEMY.

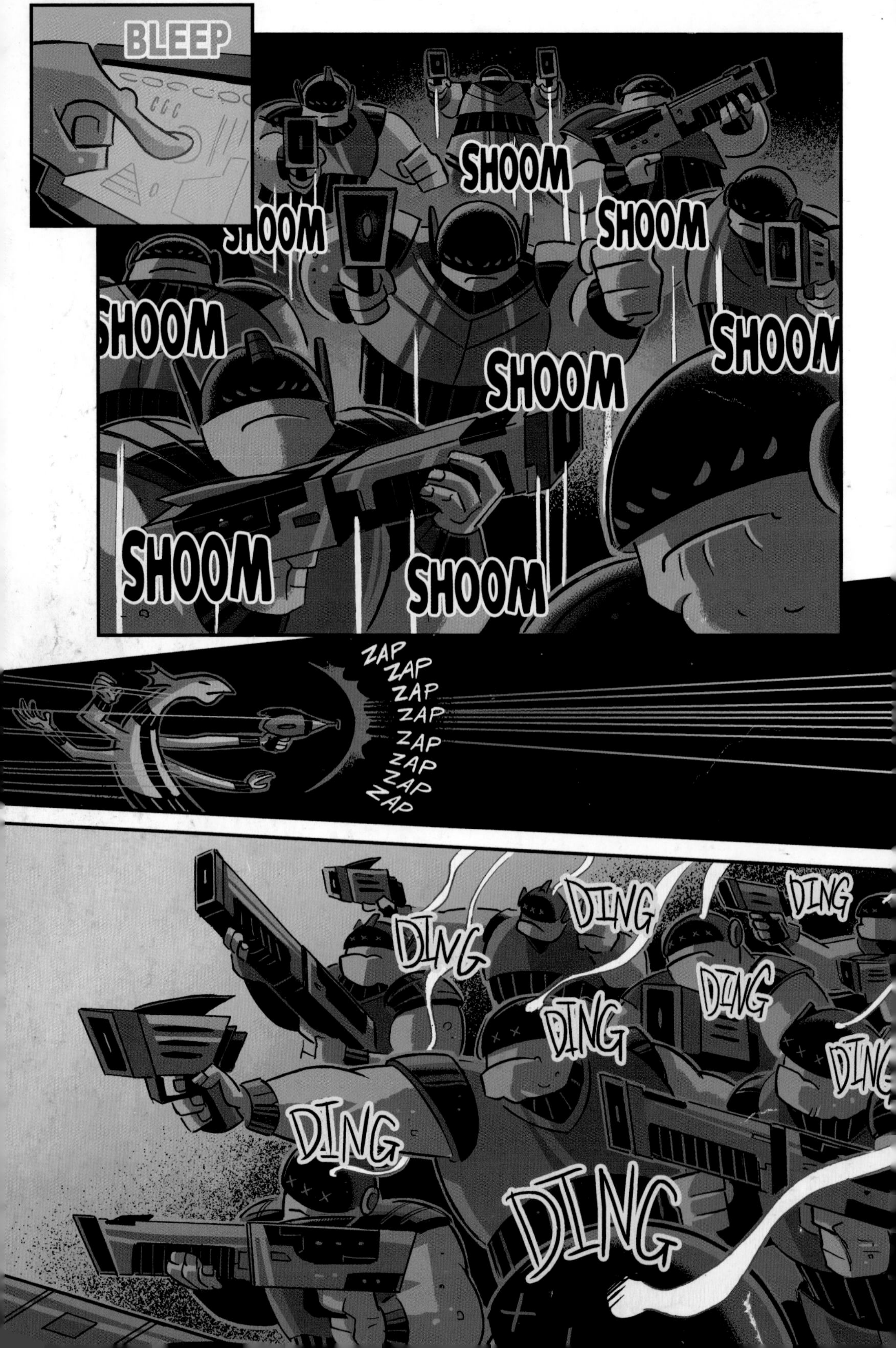
BLEEP
SHOOM
SHOOM
SHOOM
SHOOM
SHOOM
SHOOM
SHOOM
SHOOM
ZAP
ZAP
ZAP
ZAP
ZAP
ZAP
ZAP
ZAP
DING
DING
DING
DING
DING
DING
DING
DING

EIGHT SHOTS. EIGHT STUNNED XERX.

LET'S SEE IF YOU CAN FARE BETTER, CADET.

BLEEP

SHOOM SHOOM SHOOM SHOOM SHOOM SHOOM SHOOM SHOOM

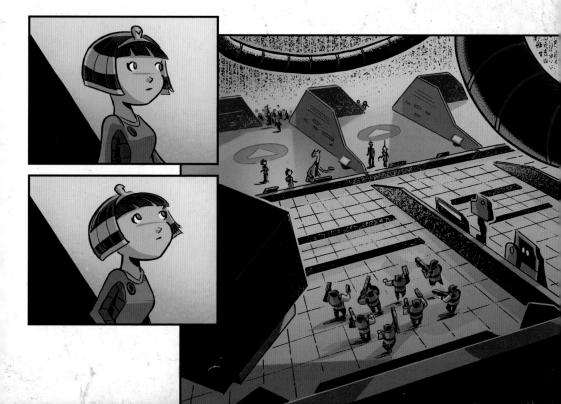

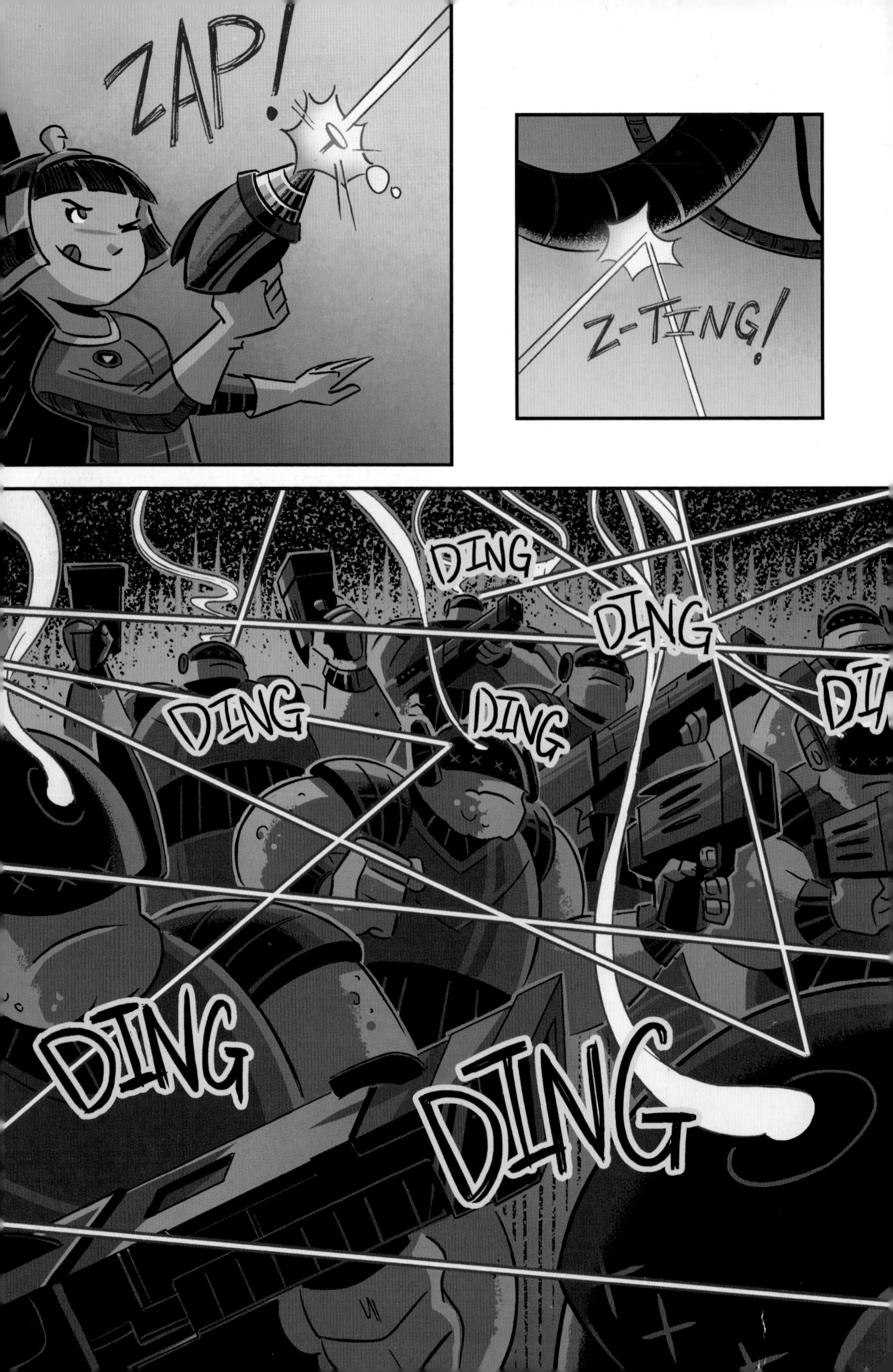
ZAP!
Z-TING!
DING
DING
DING
DING
DI
DING
DING

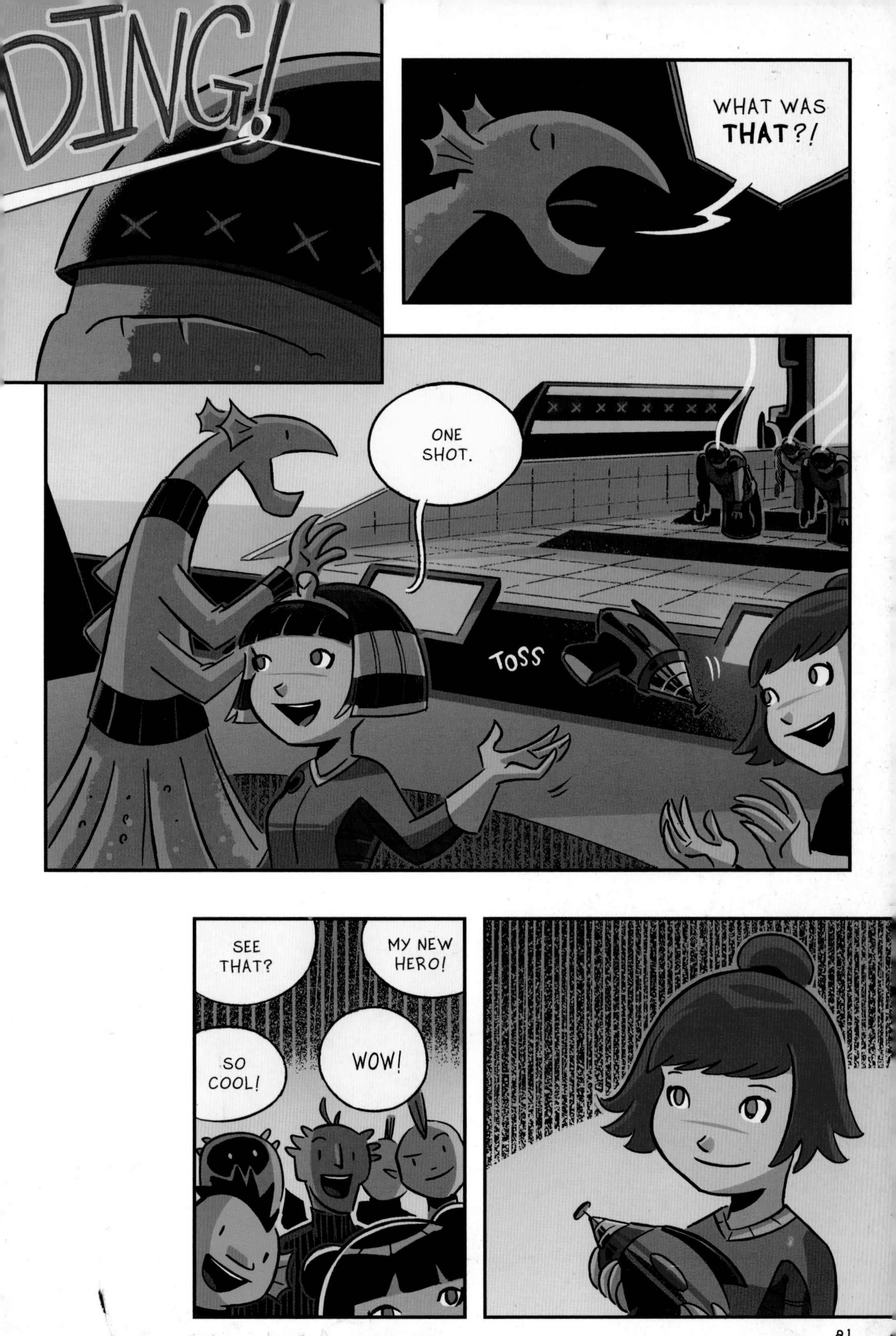
DING!
WHAT WAS THAT?!
ONE SHOT.
TOSS
SEE THAT?
MY NEW HERO!
SO COOL!
WOW!

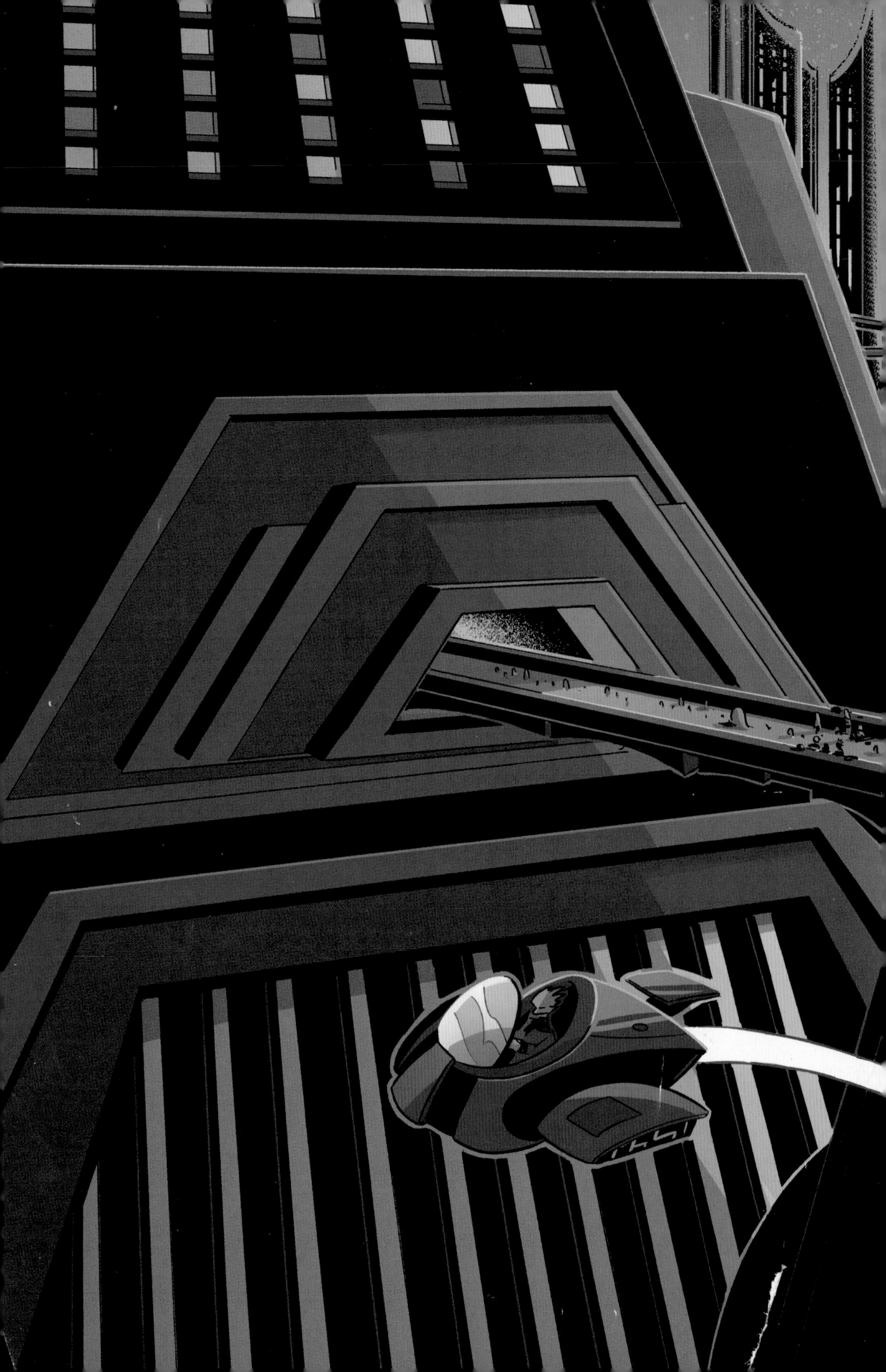

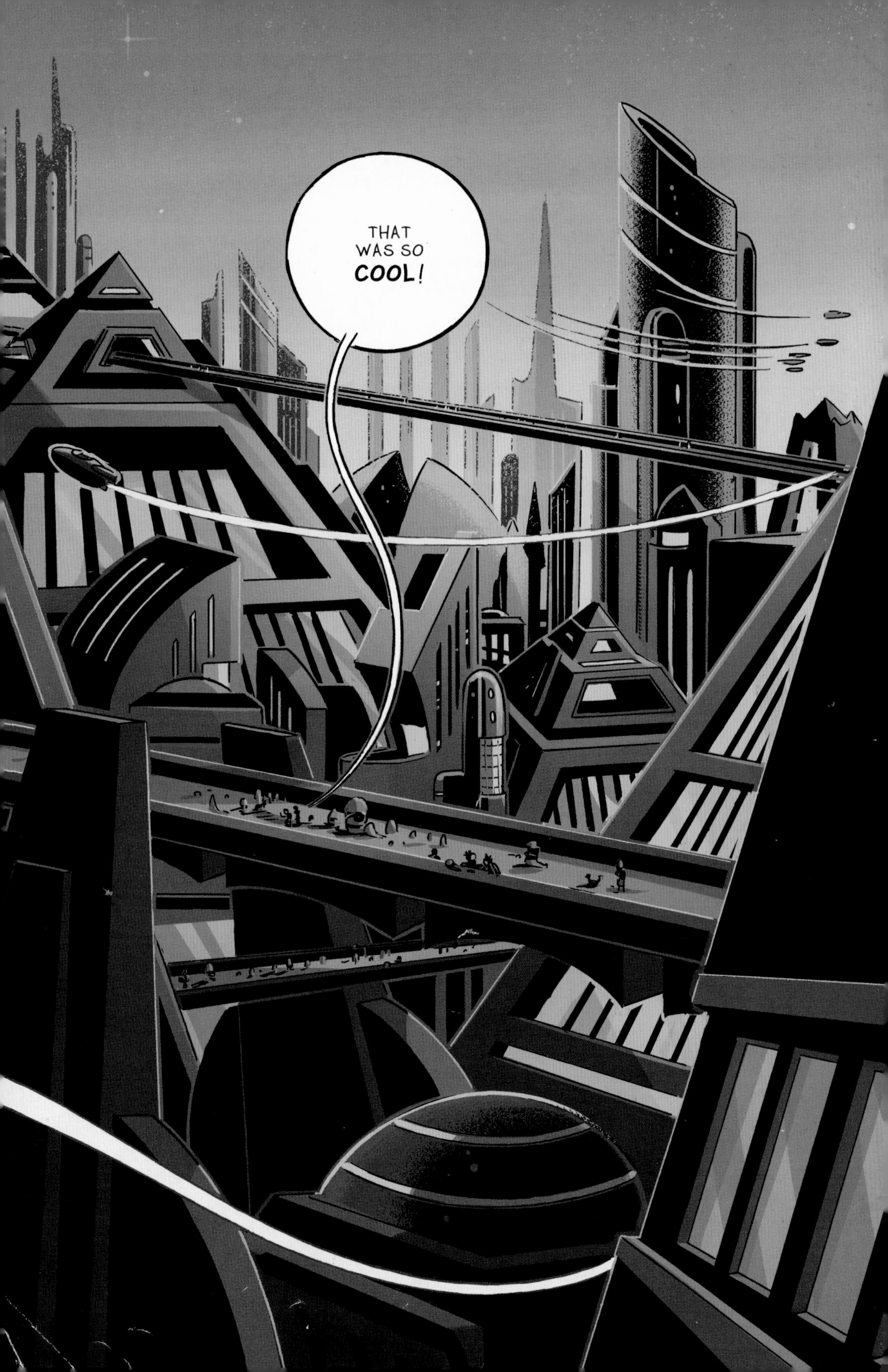
THAT WAS SO **COOL**!

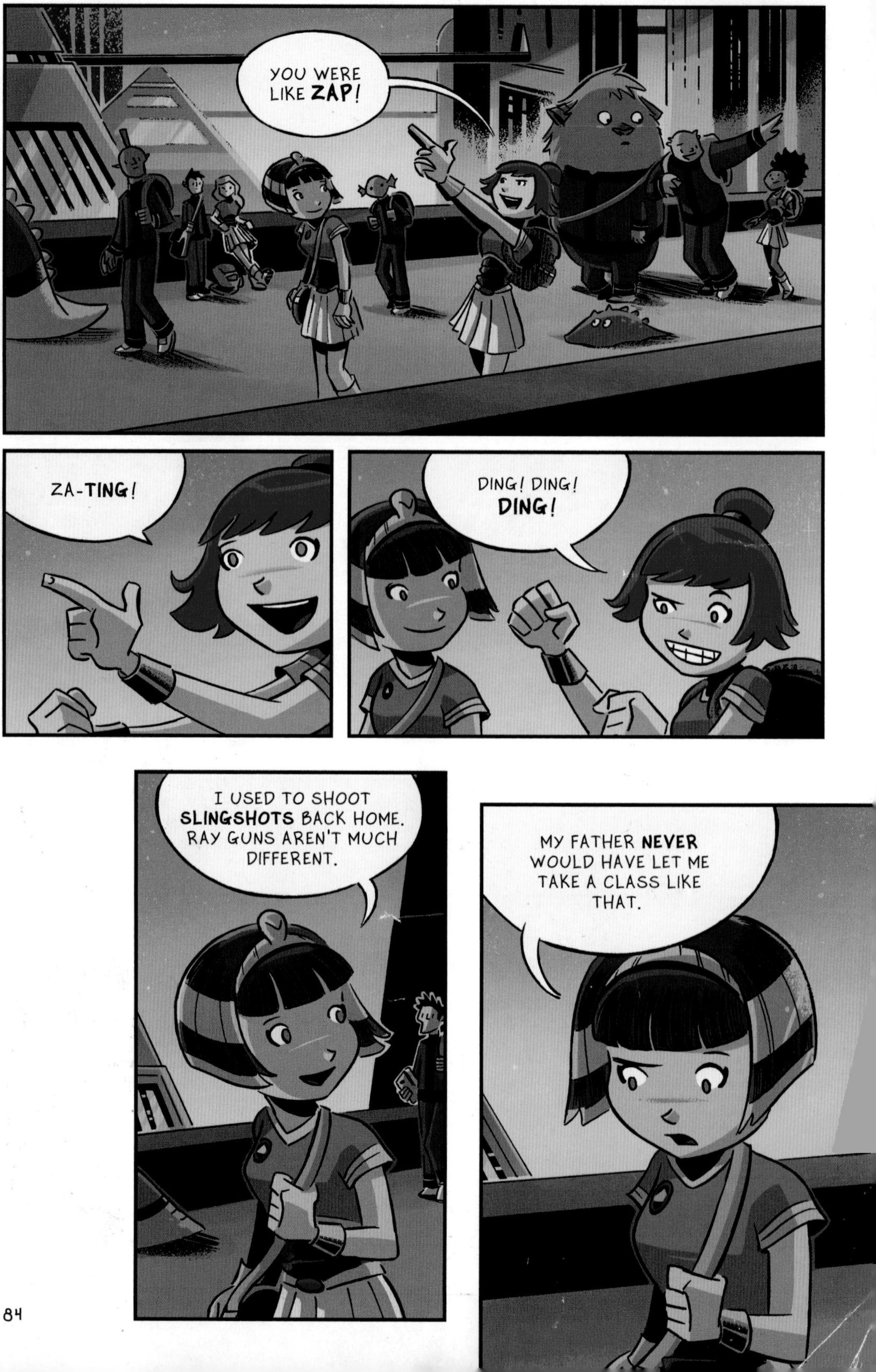
YOU WERE LIKE ZAP!
ZA-TING!
DING! DING! DING!
I USED TO SHOOT SLINGSHOTS BACK HOME. RAY GUNS AREN'T MUCH DIFFERENT.
MY FATHER NEVER WOULD HAVE LET ME TAKE A CLASS LIKE THAT.

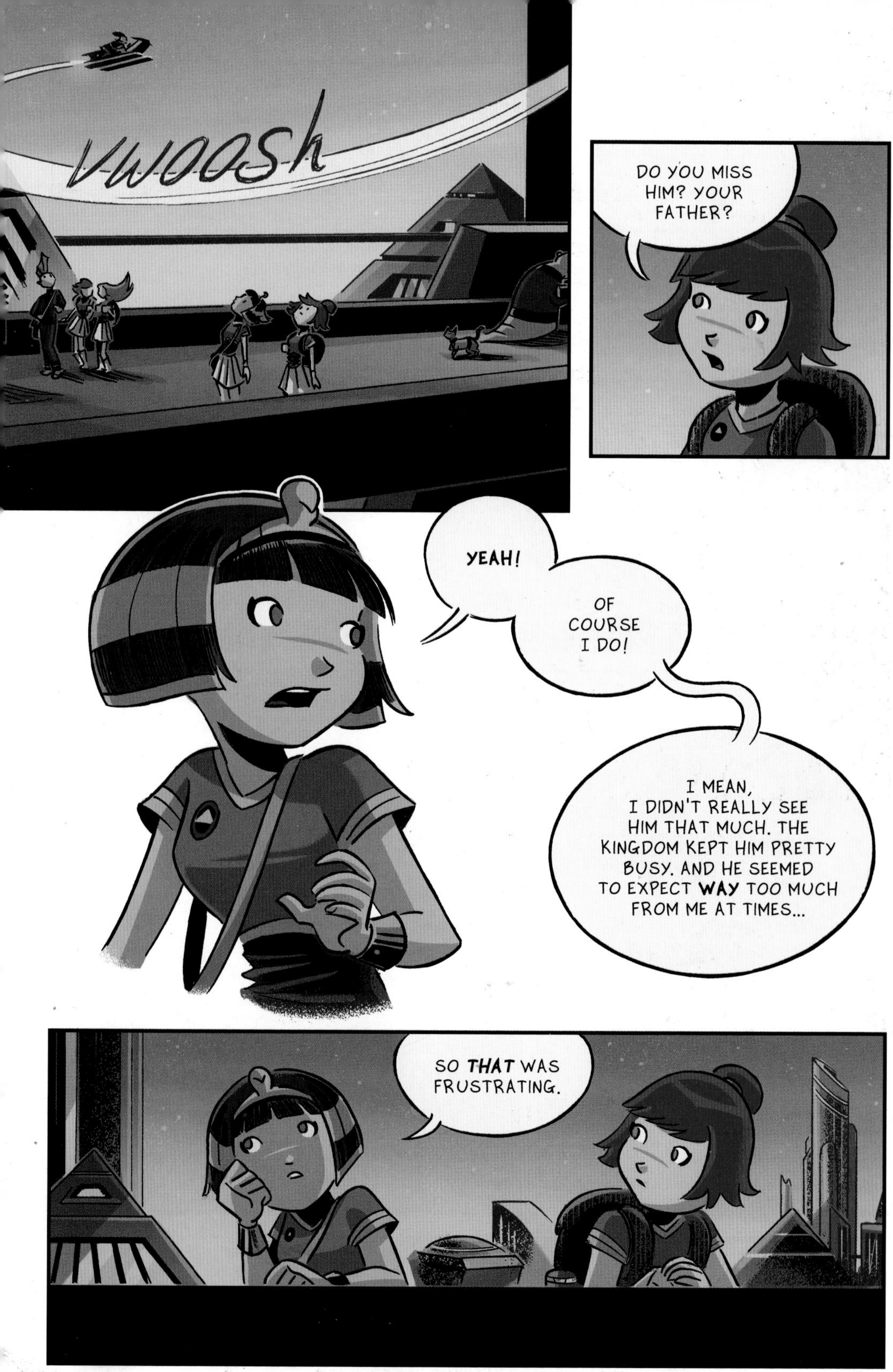
VWOOSH
DO YOU MISS HIM? YOUR FATHER?
YEAH!
OF COURSE I DO!
I MEAN, I DIDN'T REALLY SEE HIM THAT MUCH. THE KINGDOM KEPT HIM PRETTY BUSY. AND HE SEEMED TO EXPECT WAY TOO MUCH FROM ME AT TIMES...
SO THAT WAS FRUSTRATING.

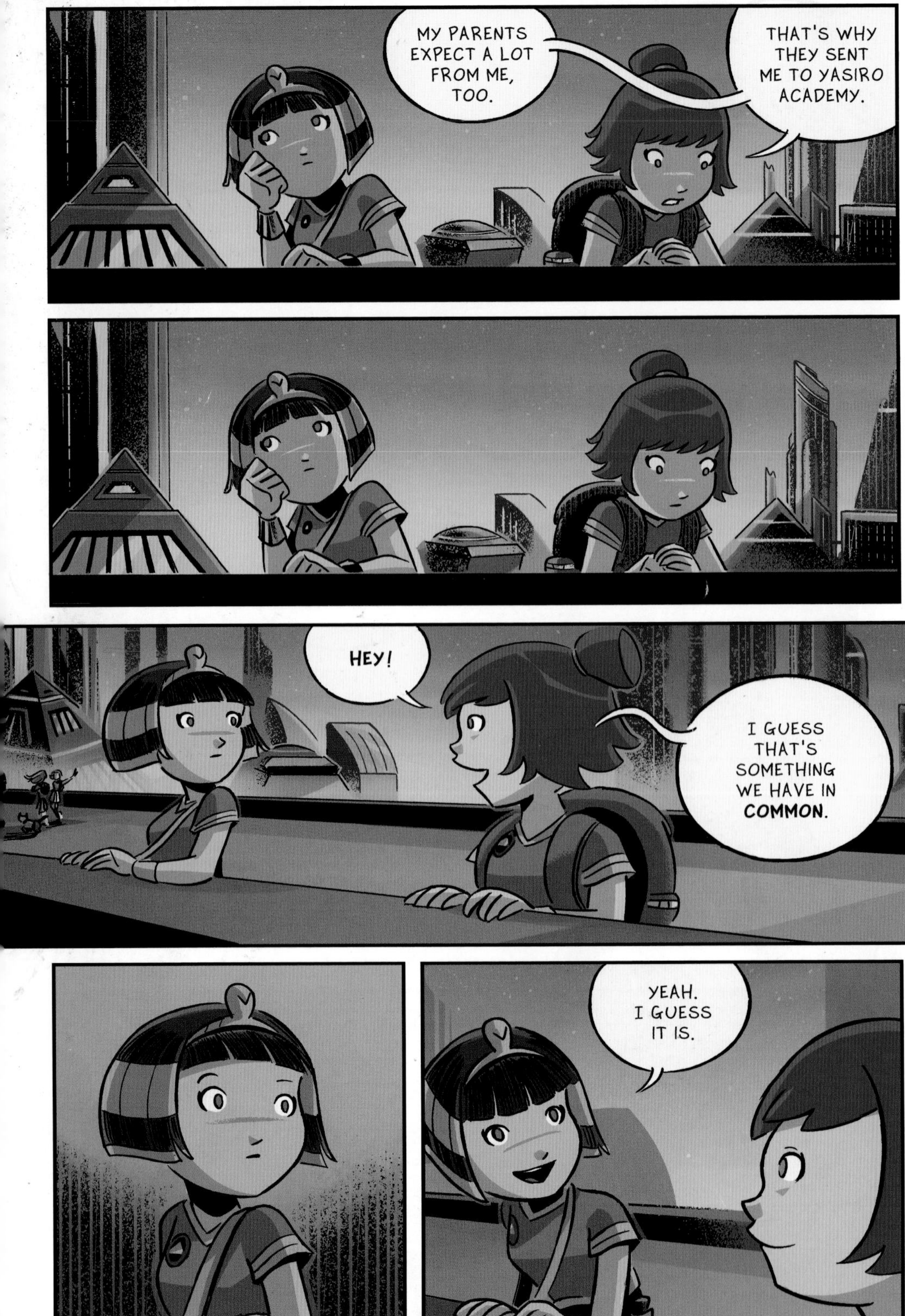
MY PARENTS EXPECT A LOT FROM ME, TOO.
THAT'S WHY THEY SENT ME TO YASIRO ACADEMY.
HEY!
I GUESS THAT'S SOMETHING WE HAVE IN **COMMON**.
YEAH. I GUESS IT IS.

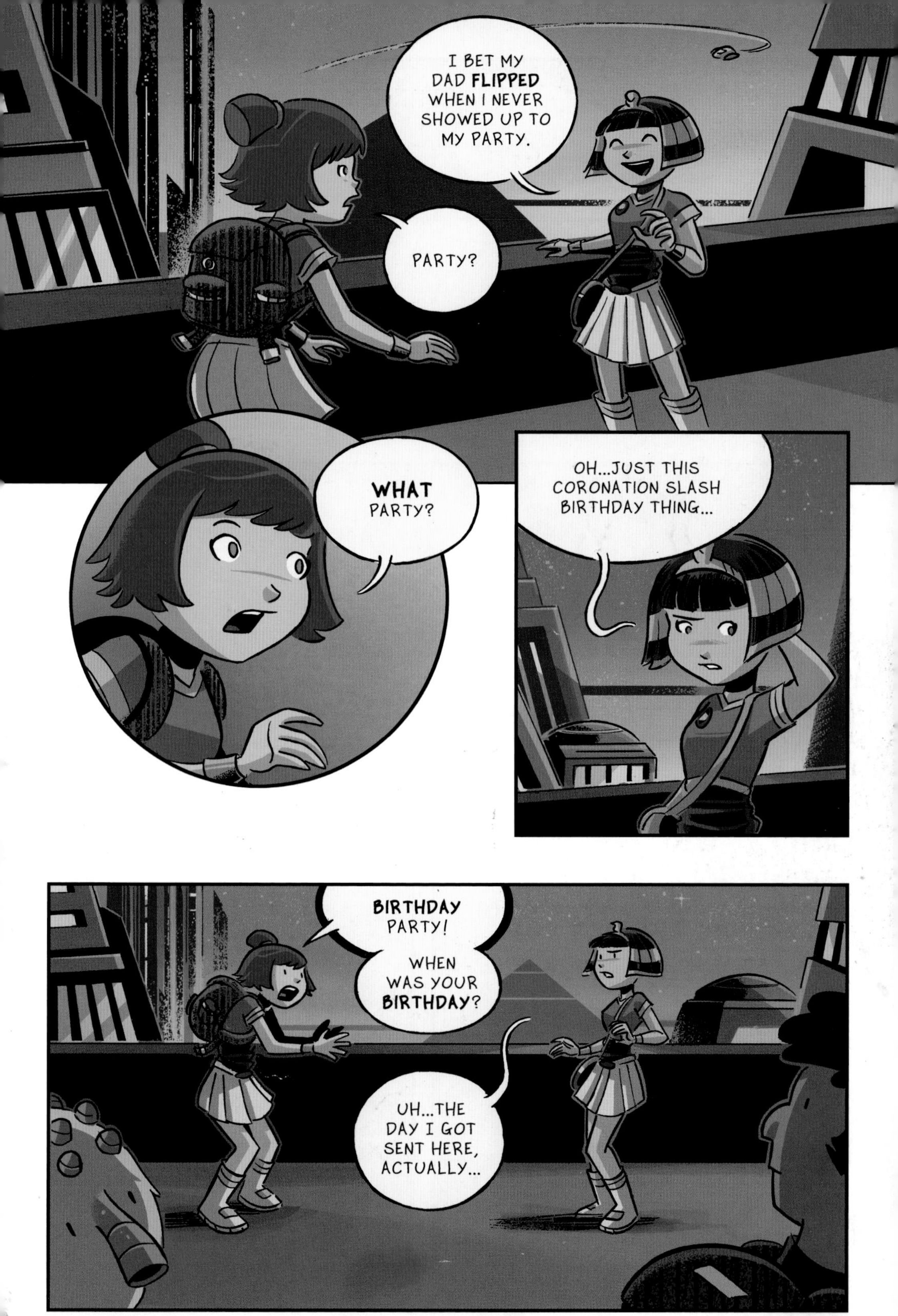
I BET MY DAD **FLIPPED** WHEN I NEVER SHOWED UP TO MY PARTY.
PARTY?
WHAT PARTY?
OH...JUST THIS CORONATION SLASH BIRTHDAY THING...
BIRTHDAY PARTY!
WHEN WAS YOUR **BIRTHDAY**?
UH...THE DAY I GOT SENT HERE, ACTUALLY...

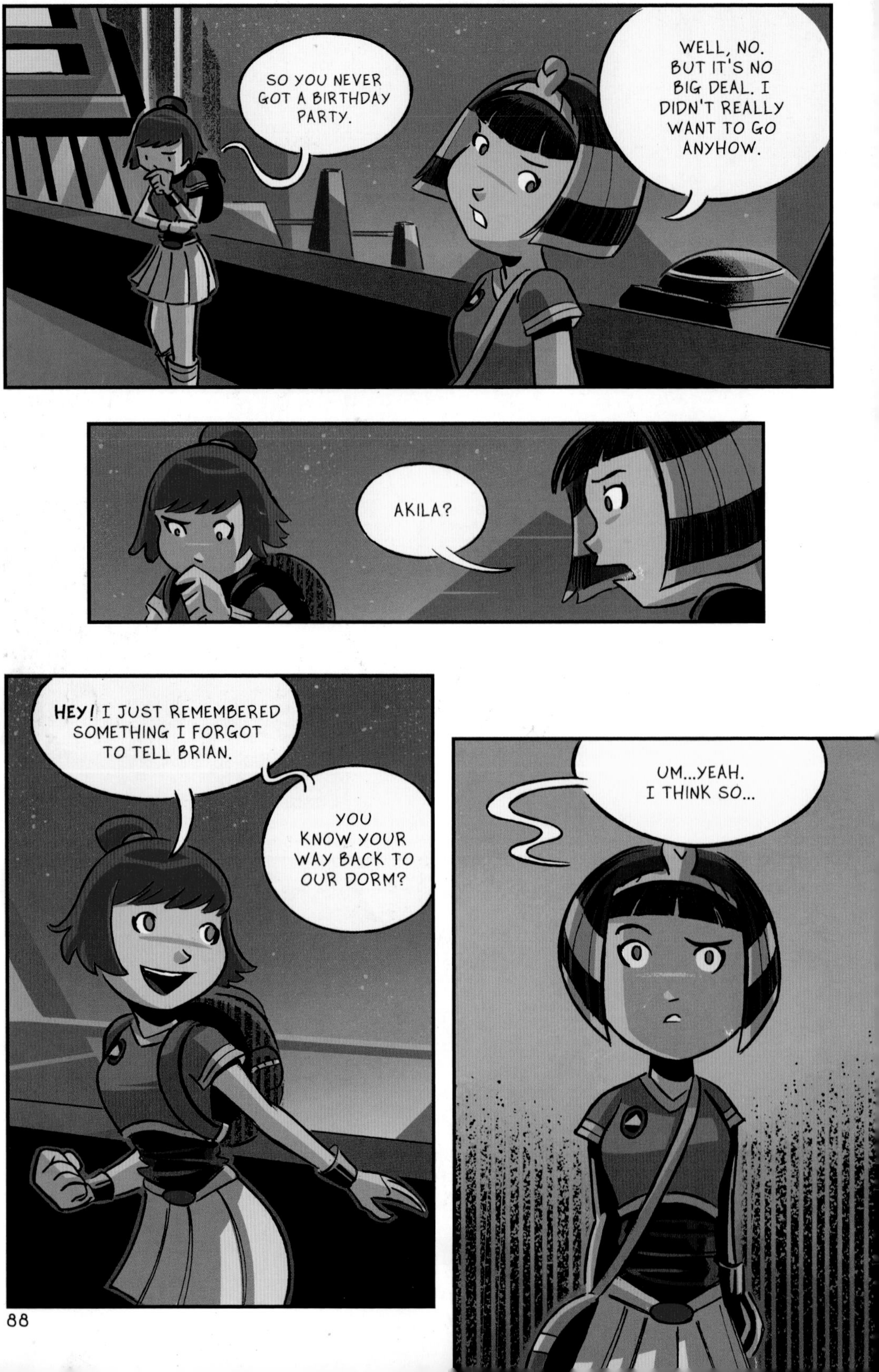
SO YOU NEVER GOT A BIRTHDAY PARTY.
WELL, NO. BUT IT'S NO BIG DEAL. I DIDN'T REALLY WANT TO GO ANYHOW.
AKILA?
HEY! I JUST REMEMBERED SOMETHING I FORGOT TO TELL BRIAN.
YOU KNOW YOUR WAY BACK TO OUR DORM?
UM...YEAH. I THINK SO...

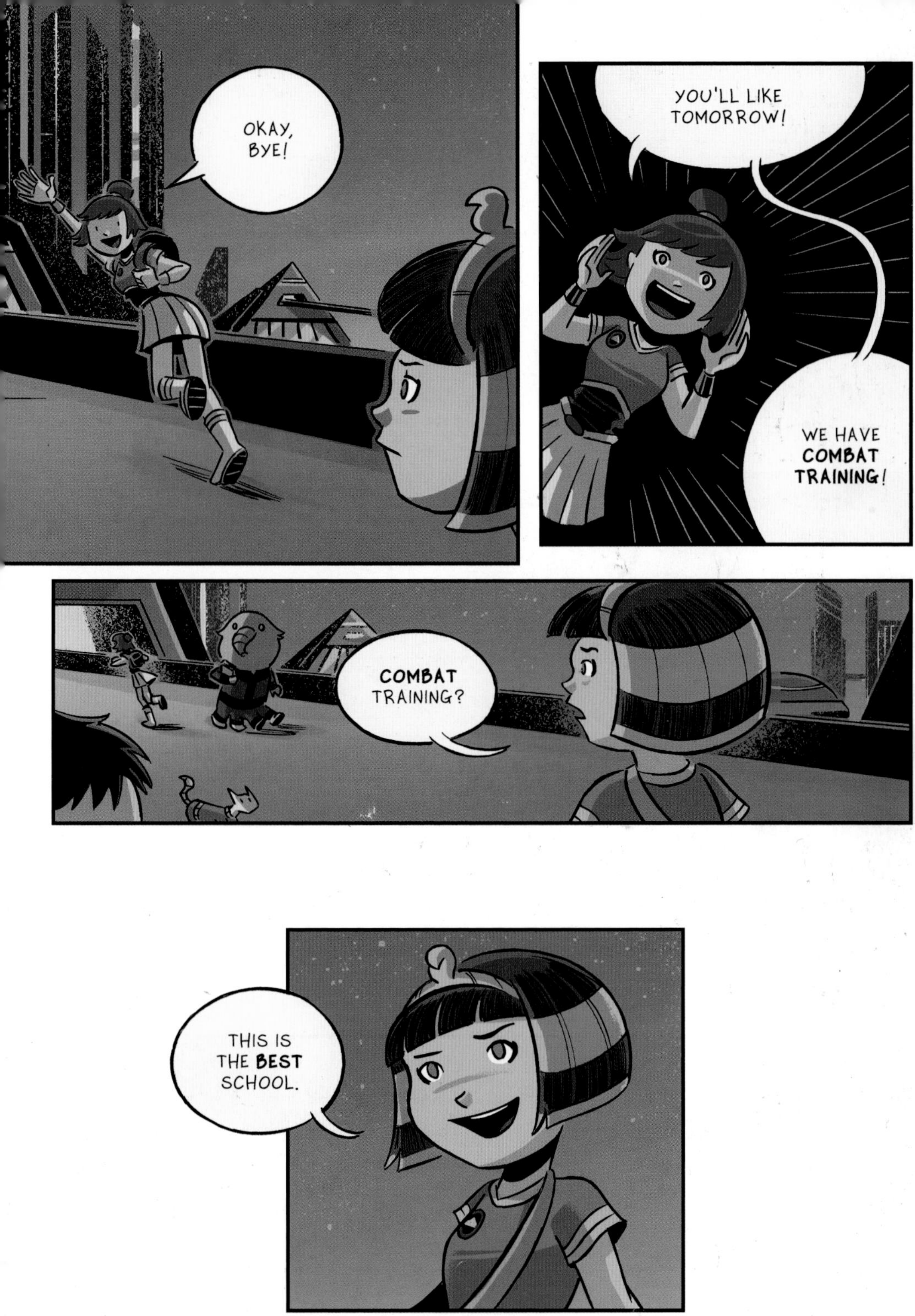
OKAY, BYE!
YOU'LL LIKE TOMORROW!
WE HAVE **COMBAT TRAINING**!
COMBAT TRAINING?
THIS IS THE **BEST** SCHOOL.

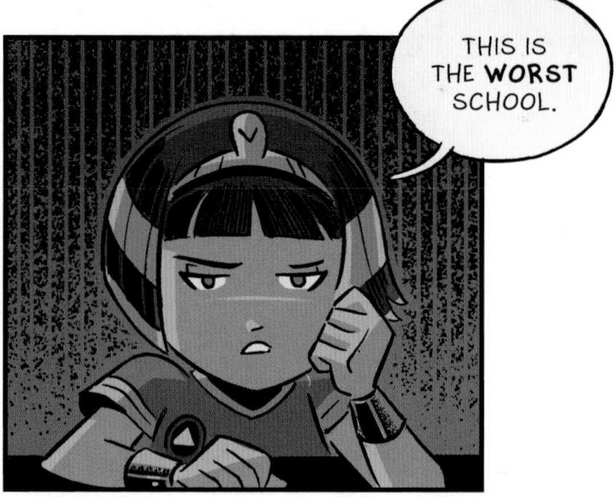
THIS IS THE **WORST** SCHOOL.

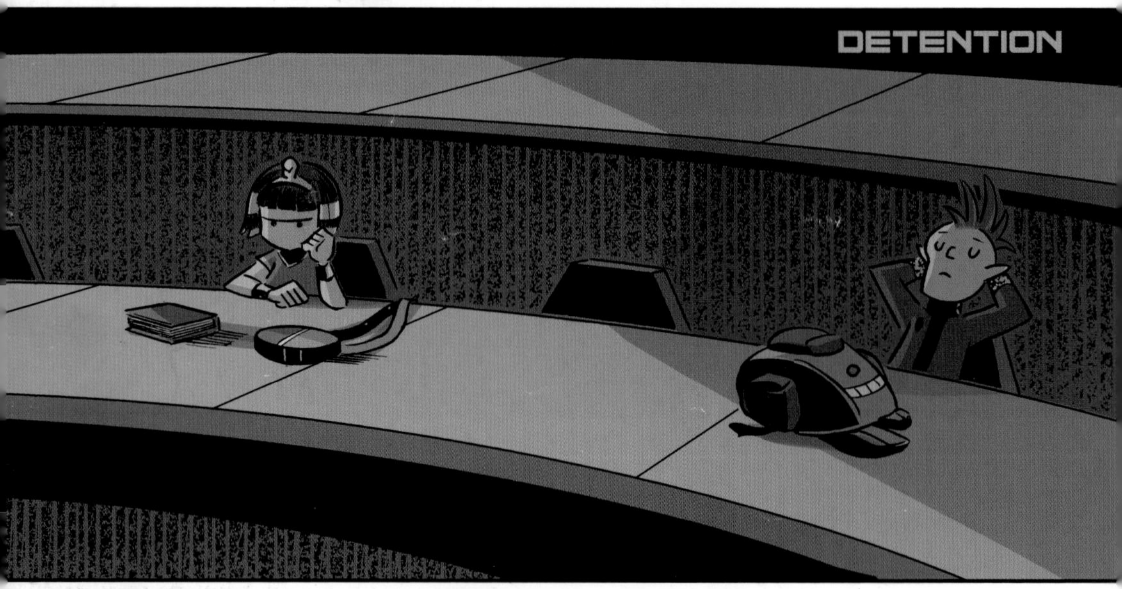
DETENTION

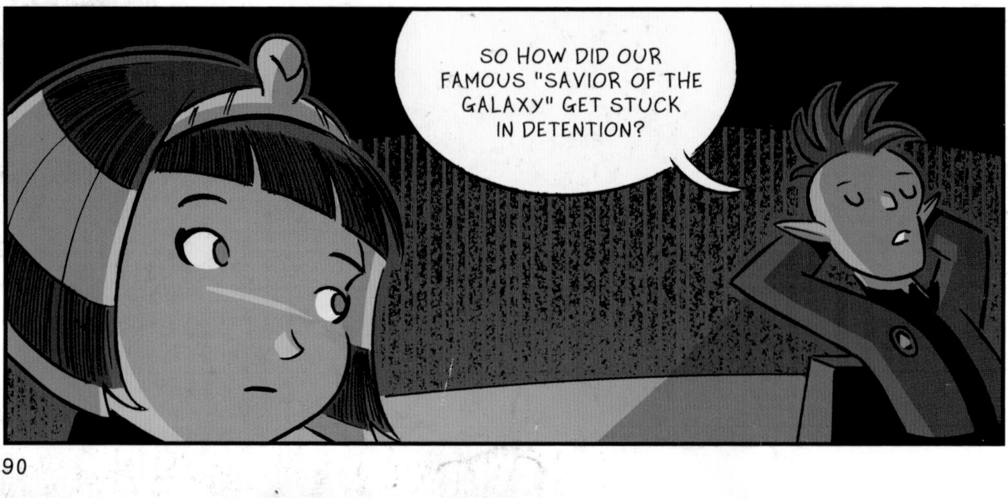
SO HOW DID OUR FAMOUS "SAVIOR OF THE GALAXY" GET STUCK IN DETENTION?

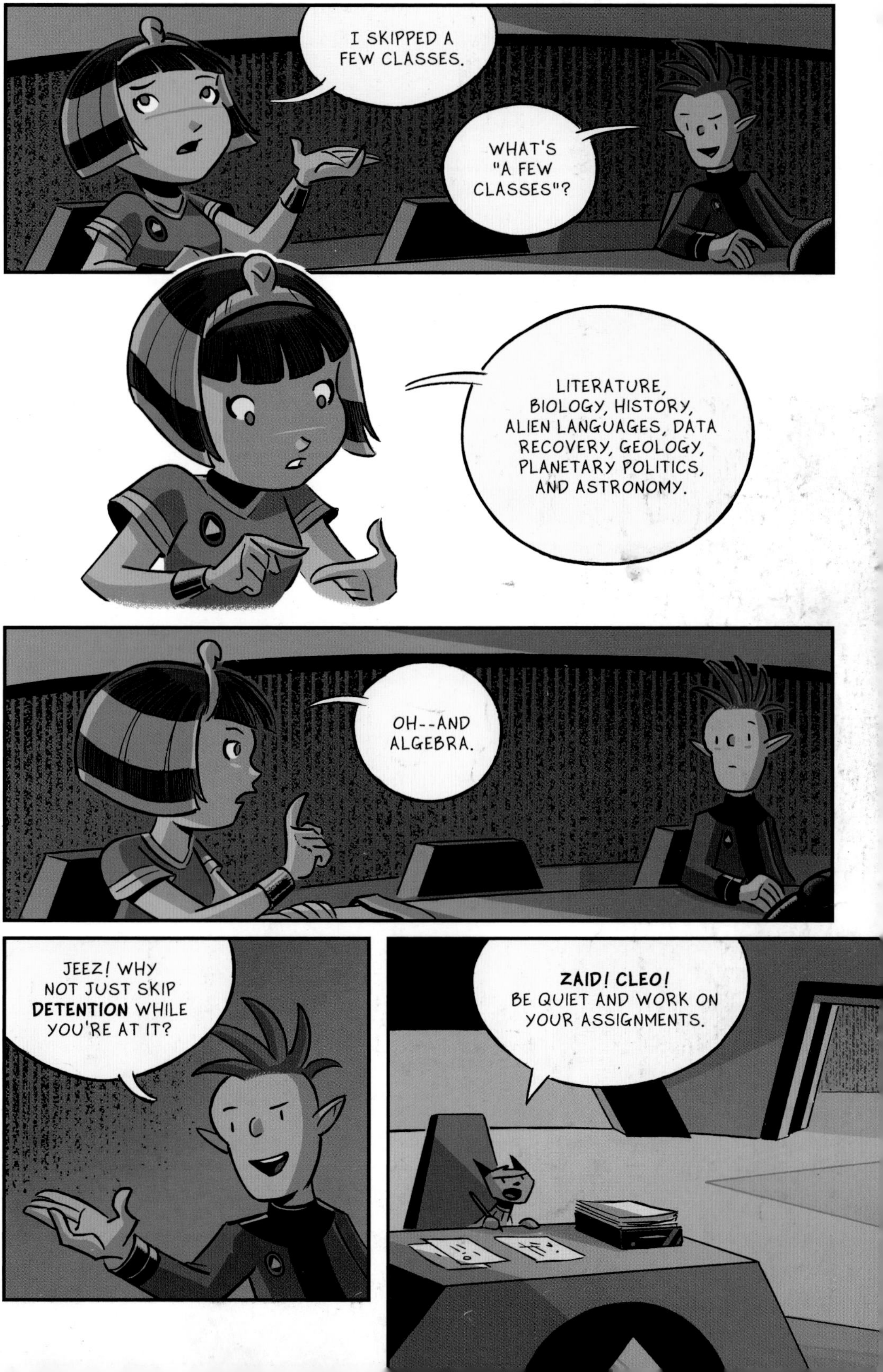
I SKIPPED A FEW CLASSES.
WHAT'S "A FEW CLASSES"?
LITERATURE, BIOLOGY, HISTORY, ALIEN LANGUAGES, DATA RECOVERY, GEOLOGY, PLANETARY POLITICS, AND ASTRONOMY.
OH--AND ALGEBRA.
JEEZ! WHY NOT JUST SKIP **DETENTION** WHILE YOU'RE AT IT?
ZAID! CLEO! BE QUIET AND WORK ON YOUR ASSIGNMENTS.

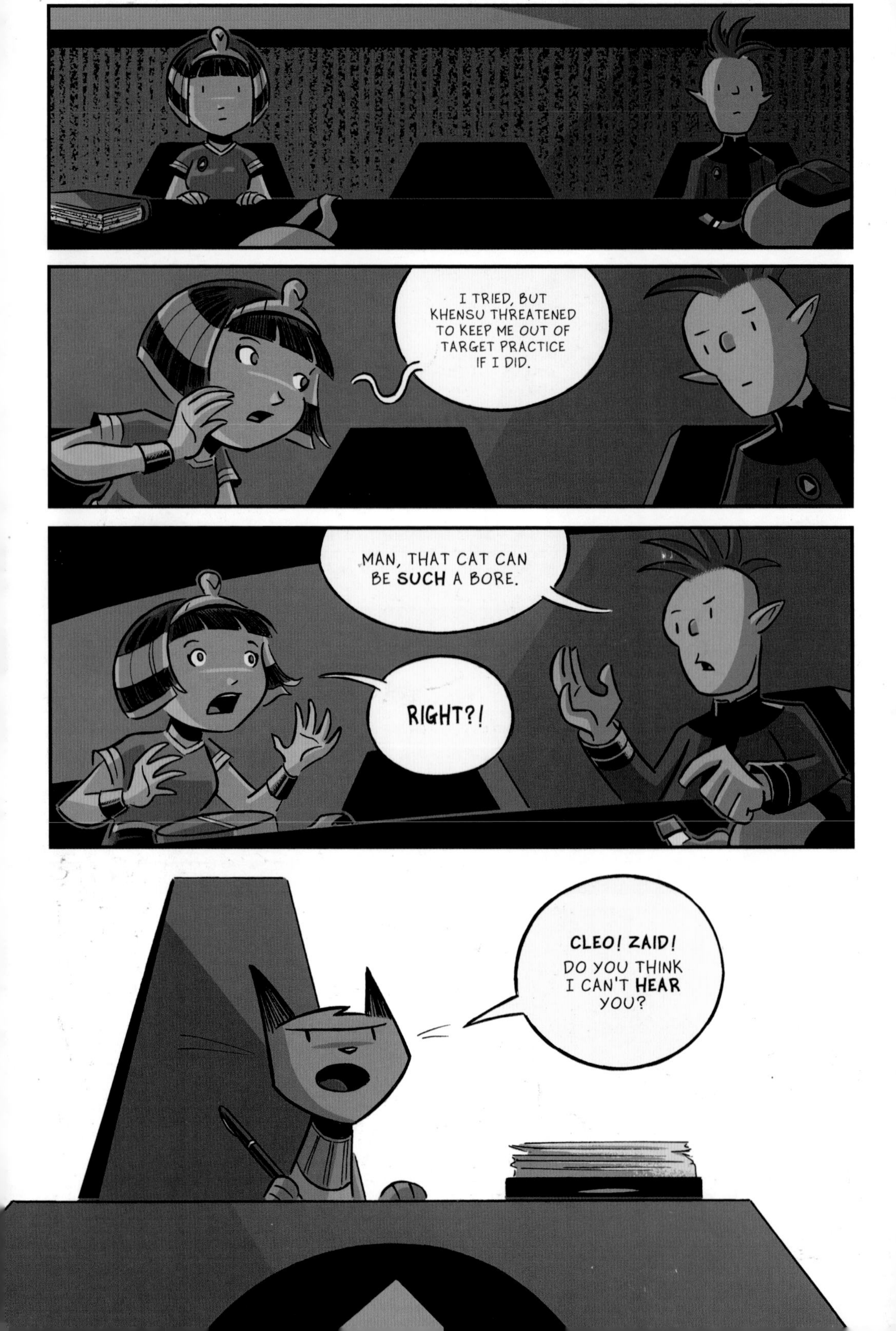

I TRIED, BUT KHENSU THREATENED TO KEEP ME OUT OF TARGET PRACTICE IF I DID.
MAN, THAT CAT CAN BE **SUCH** A BORE.
RIGHT?!
CLEO! ZAID! DO YOU THINK I CAN'T **HEAR** YOU?

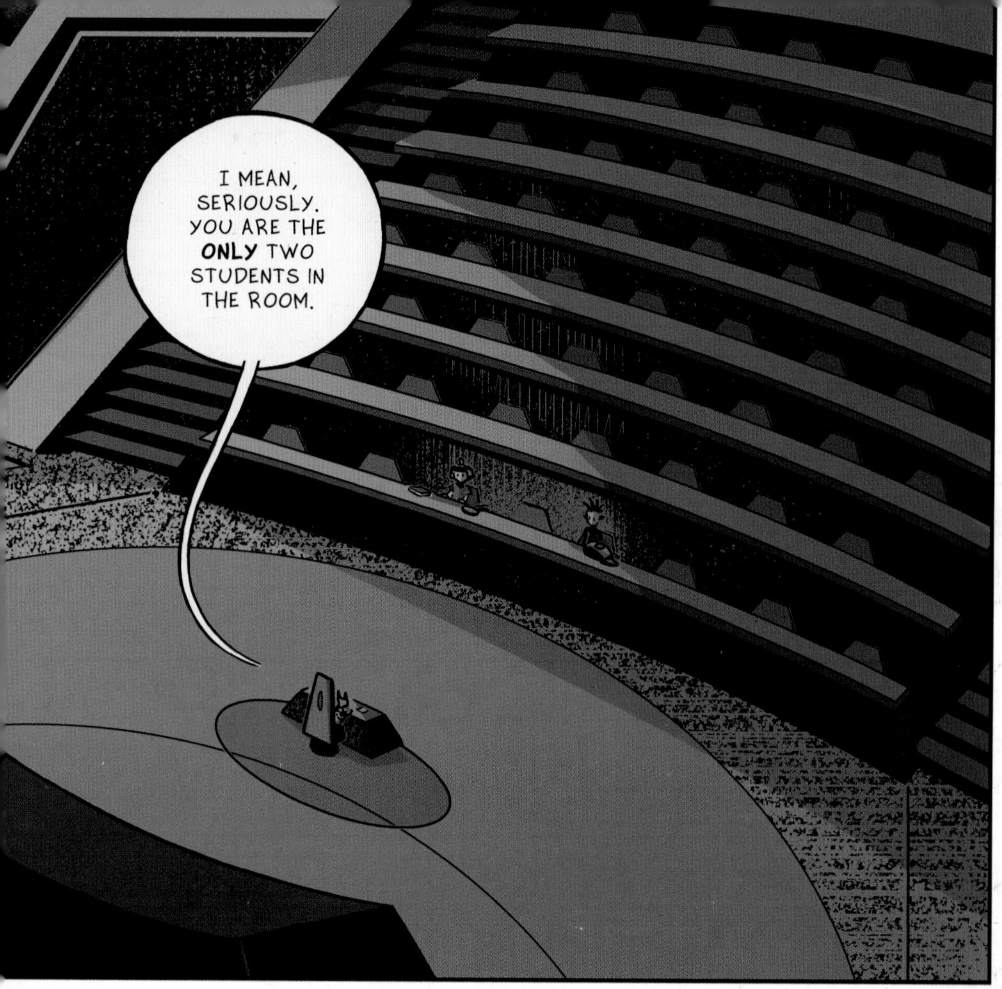
I MEAN, SERIOUSLY. YOU ARE THE **ONLY** TWO STUDENTS IN THE ROOM.

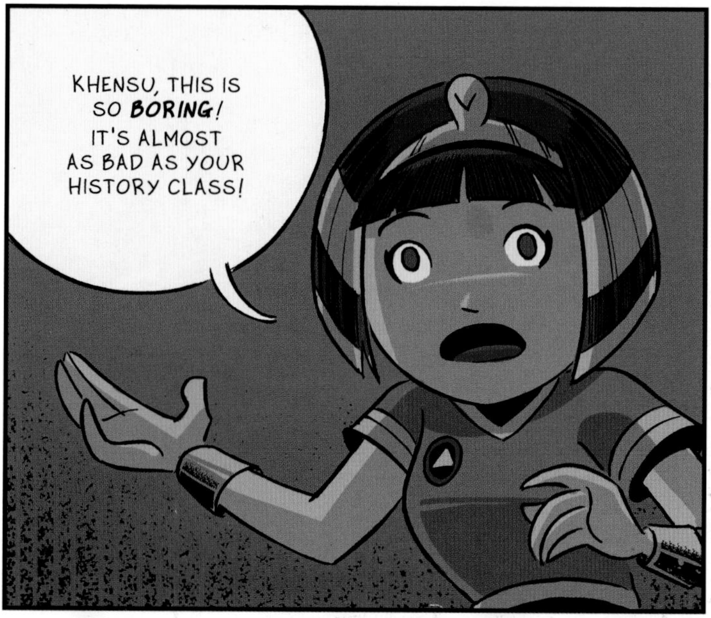
KHENSU, THIS IS SO **BORING**! IT'S ALMOST AS BAD AS YOUR HISTORY CLASS!

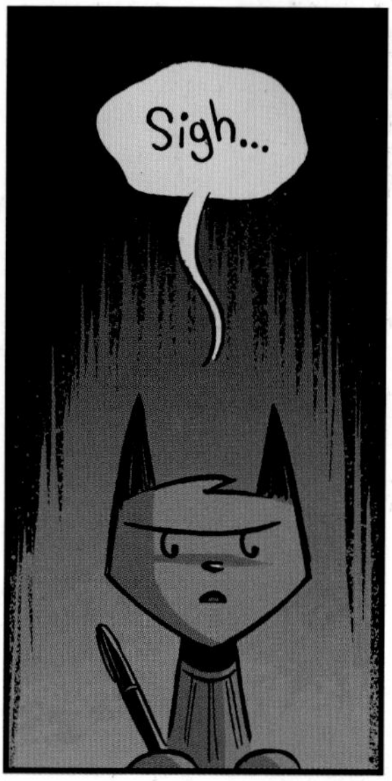
Sigh...

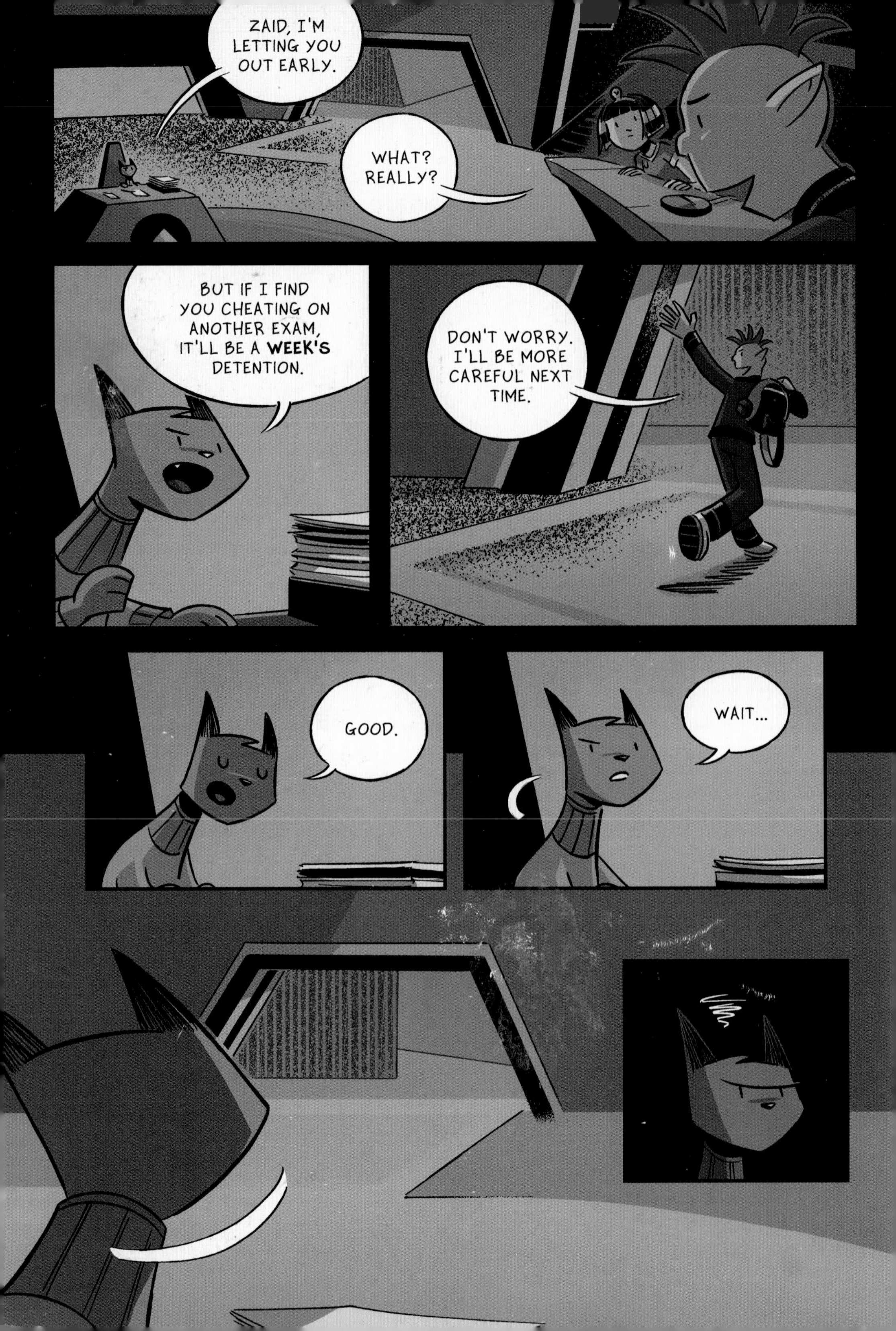
ZAID, I'M LETTING YOU OUT EARLY.
WHAT? REALLY?
BUT IF I FIND YOU CHEATING ON ANOTHER EXAM, IT'LL BE A **WEEK'S** DETENTION.
DON'T WORRY. I'LL BE MORE CAREFUL NEXT TIME.
GOOD.
WAIT...

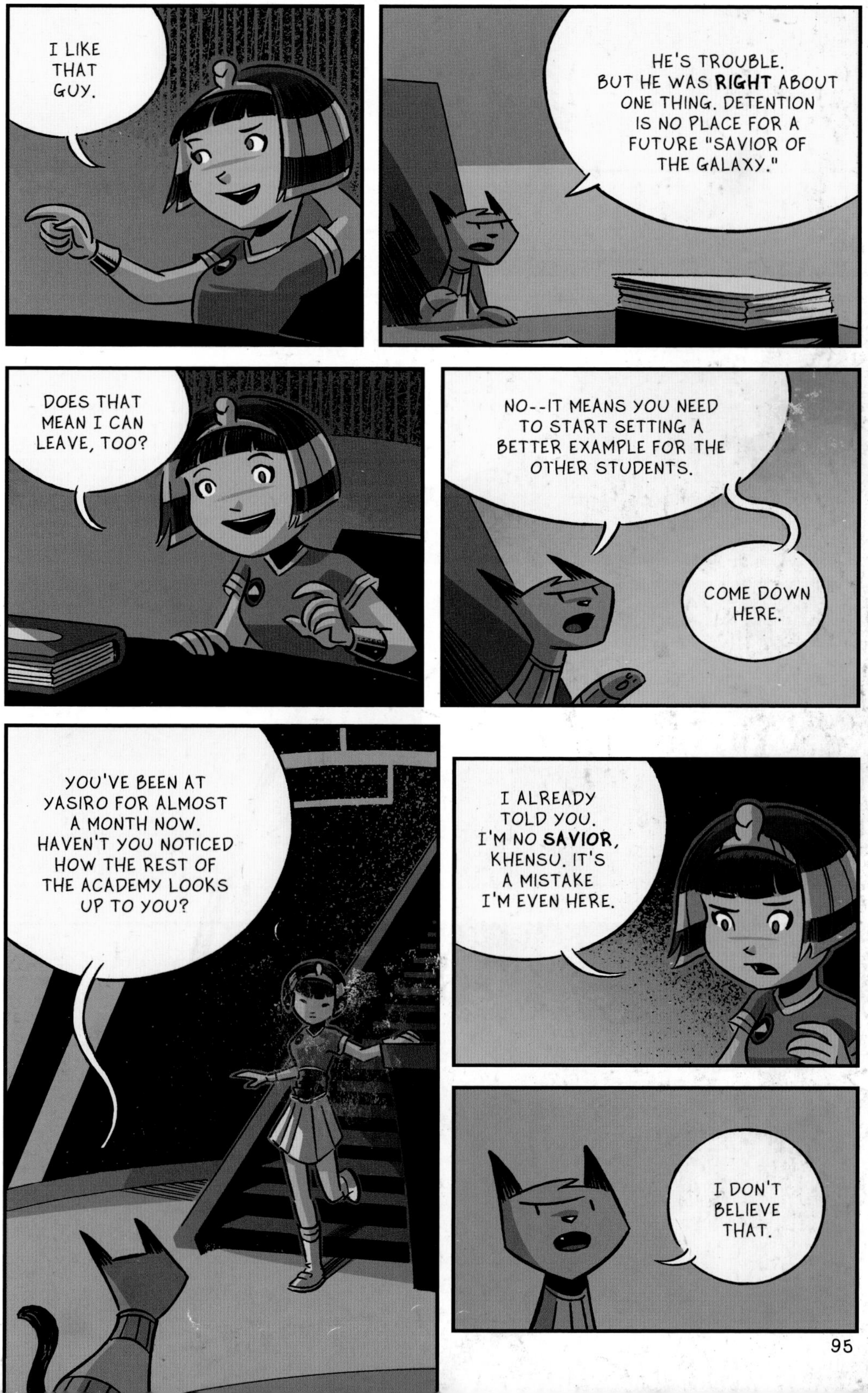
I LIKE THAT GUY.
HE'S TROUBLE. BUT HE WAS **RIGHT** ABOUT ONE THING. DETENTION IS NO PLACE FOR A FUTURE "SAVIOR OF THE GALAXY."
DOES THAT MEAN I CAN LEAVE, TOO?
NO--IT MEANS YOU NEED TO START SETTING A BETTER EXAMPLE FOR THE OTHER STUDENTS.
COME DOWN HERE.
YOU'VE BEEN AT YASIRO FOR ALMOST A MONTH NOW. HAVEN'T YOU NOTICED HOW THE REST OF THE ACADEMY LOOKS UP TO YOU?
I ALREADY TOLD YOU. I'M NO **SAVIOR**, KHENSU. IT'S A MISTAKE I'M EVEN HERE.
I DON'T BELIEVE THAT.

WHY?

BECAUSE OF THAT STUPID SCROLL?

NOT JUST THAT.

IT'S...HARD TO EXPLAIN.

LOOK--THE COUNCIL PUT ME IN CHARGE OF YOU BECAUSE THEY THOUGHT MY HISTORICAL KNOWLEDGE WAS BEST SUITED TO HELPING YOU ADAPT TO THIS NEW WORLD.

CAN YOU JUST **TRY** TO MAKE AN EFFORT? YOU MIGHT NOT FEEL WHAT WE ARE TEACHING YOU IS IMPORTANT NOW, BUT TRUST ME. SOME OF IT MIGHT SAVE YOUR LIFE ONE DAY.

MATH MIGHT SAVE MY LIFE ONE DAY?

IT'S POSSIBLE!

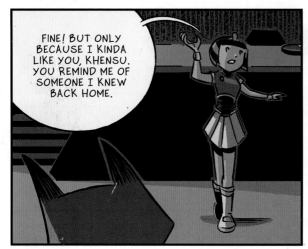

FINE! BUT ONLY BECAUSE I KINDA LIKE YOU, KHENSU. YOU REMIND ME OF SOMEONE I KNEW BACK HOME.

MY VERY-GREAT-GRANDFATHER, KOSEY?

NAH--MY TEACHER **BAKARI**. HE WAS KIND OF A BORE, TOO.

BUT HE MEANT WELL!

SEE YOU IN HISTORY TOMORROW!

WAIT!

I DIDN'T SAY YOU COULD--!

Sigh...

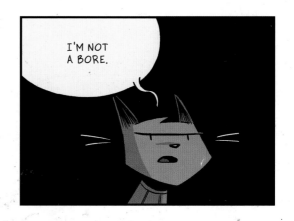

I'M NOT A BORE.

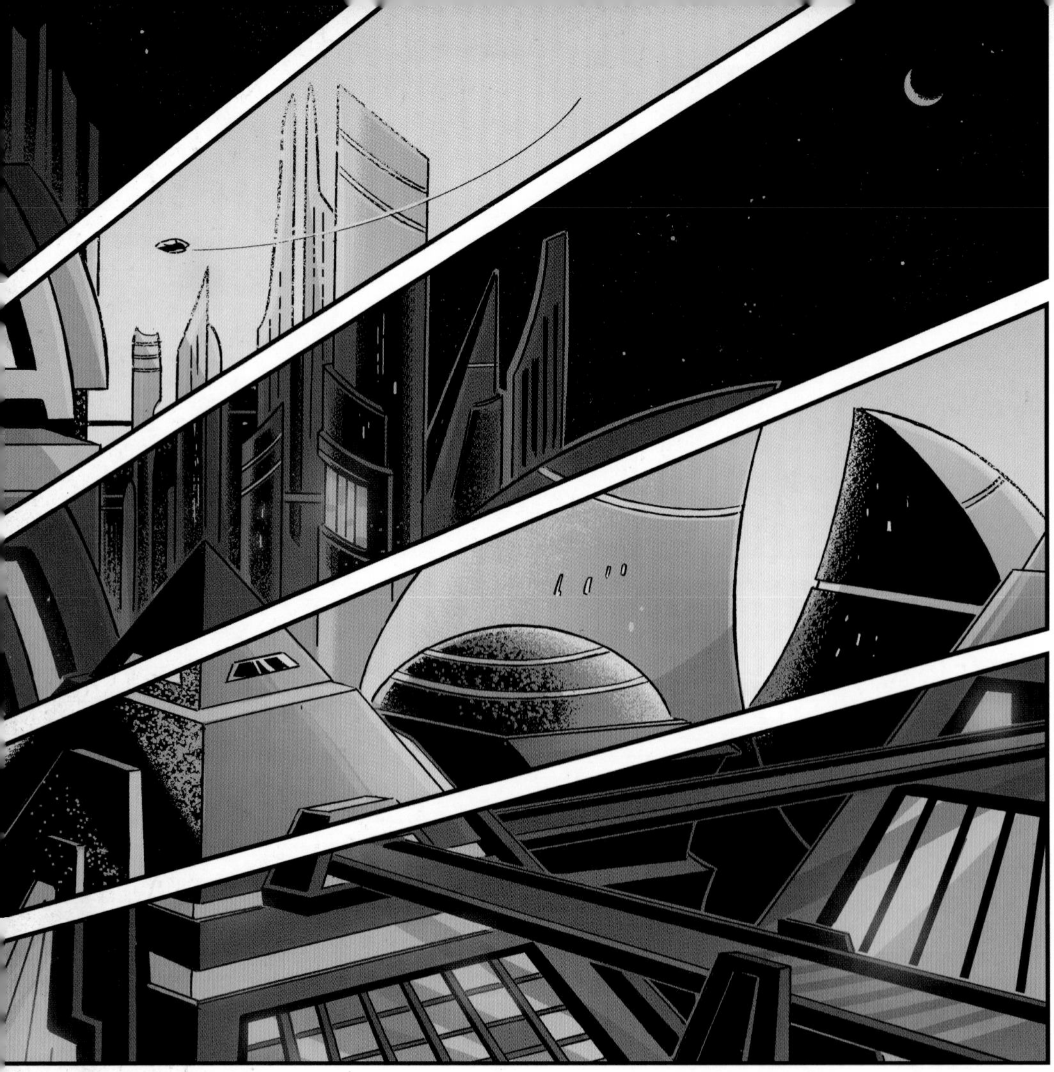

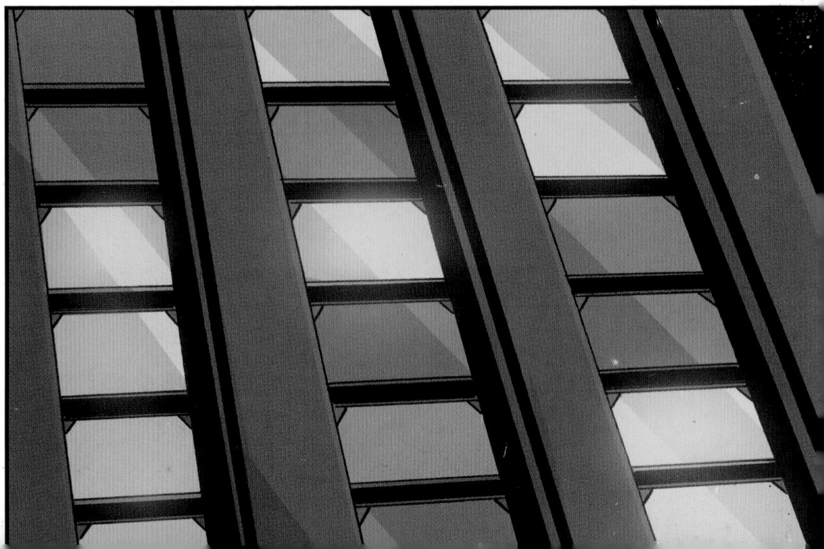

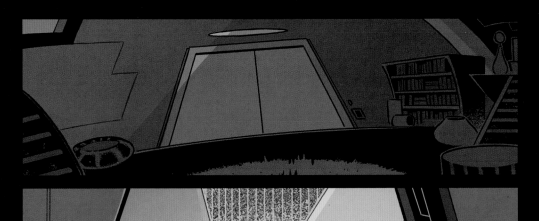

SHUFFF

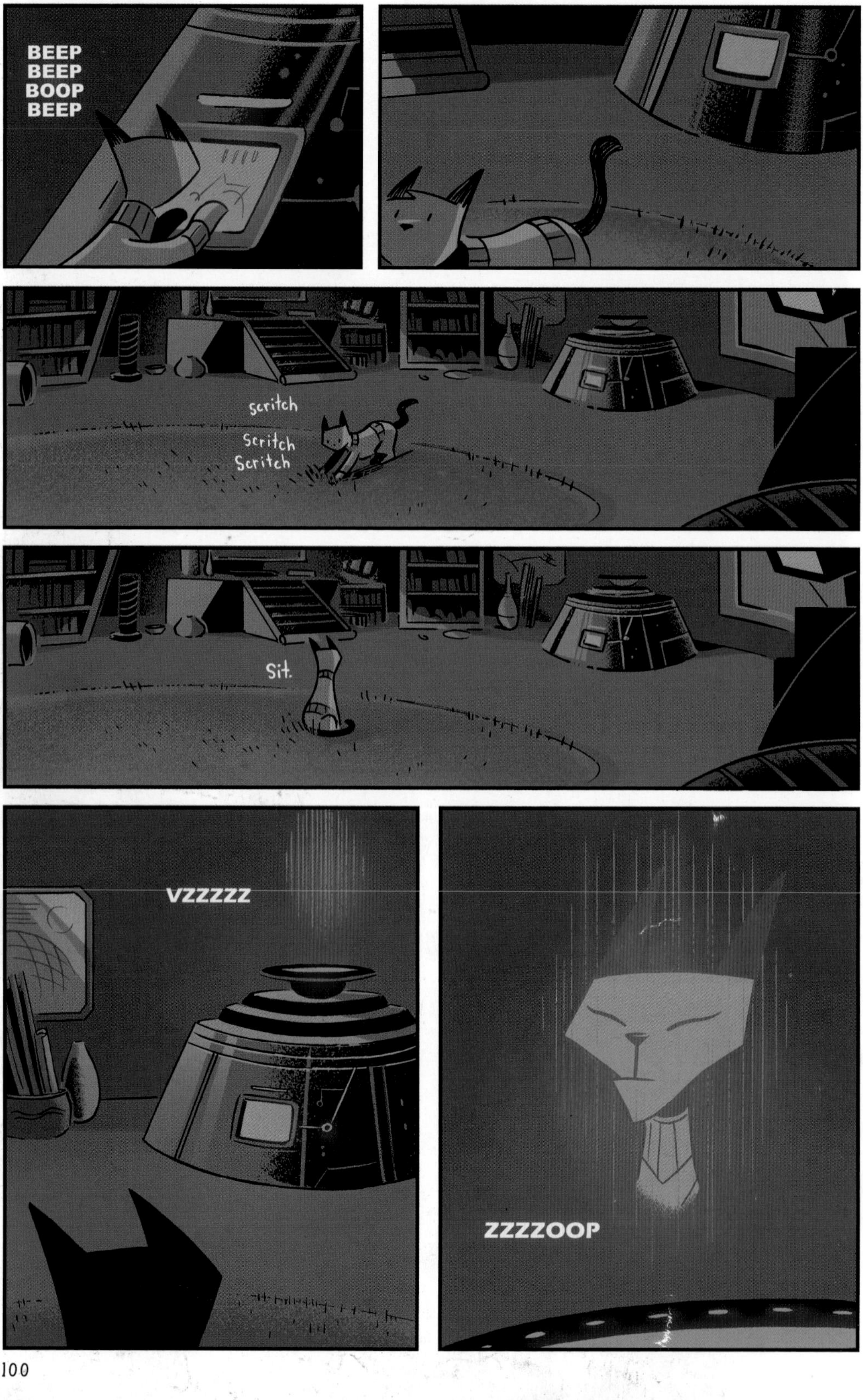
BEEP
BEEP
BOOP
BEEP
scritch
Scritch
Scritch
Sit.
VZZZZZ
ZZZZOOP

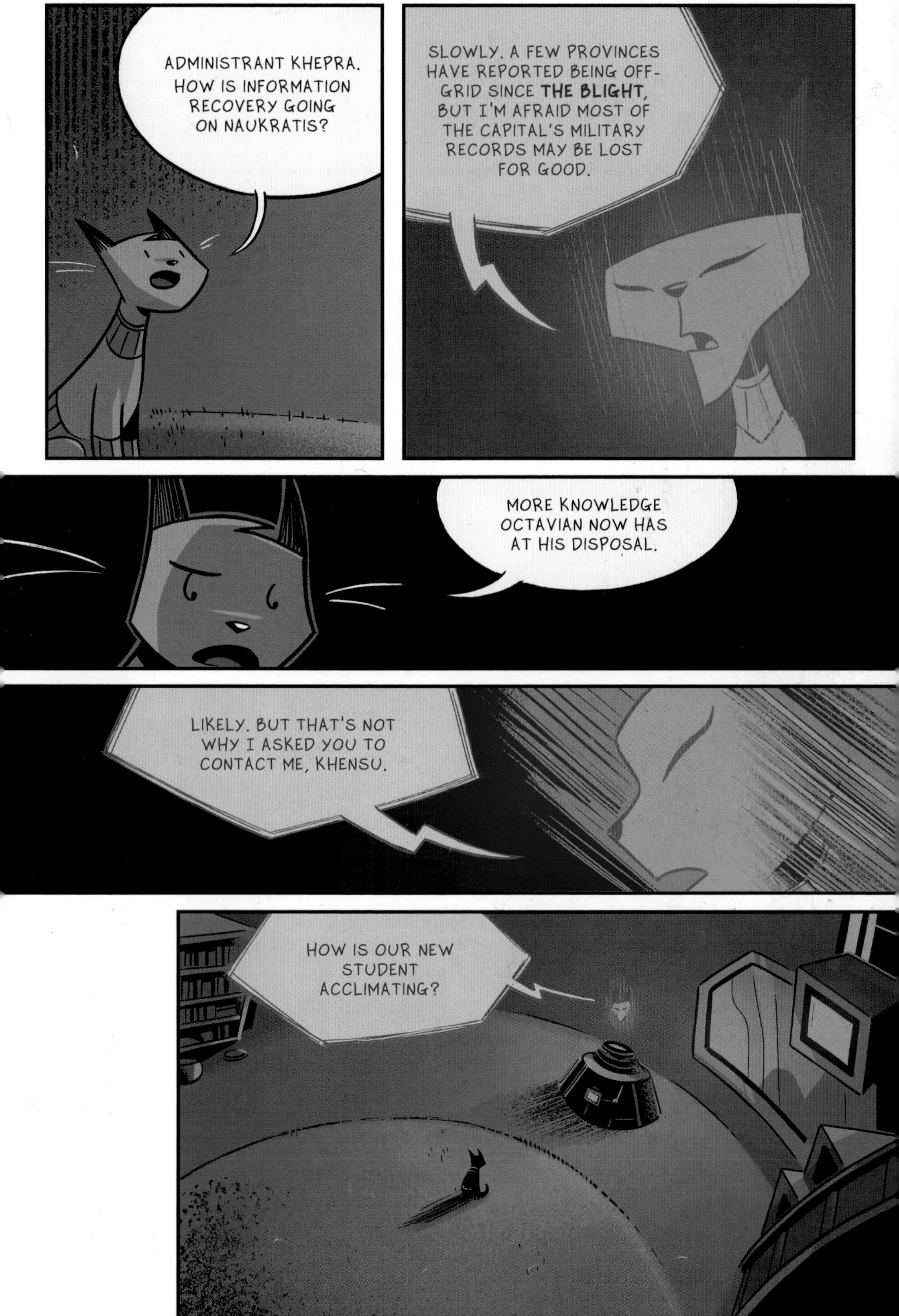
ADMINISTRANT KHEPRA. HOW IS INFORMATION RECOVERY GOING ON NAUKRATIS?
SLOWLY. A FEW PROVINCES HAVE REPORTED BEING OFF-GRID SINCE **THE BLIGHT**, BUT I'M AFRAID MOST OF THE CAPITAL'S MILITARY RECORDS MAY BE LOST FOR GOOD.
MORE KNOWLEDGE OCTAVIAN NOW HAS AT HIS DISPOSAL.
LIKELY. BUT THAT'S NOT WHY I ASKED YOU TO CONTACT ME, KHENSU.
HOW IS OUR NEW STUDENT ACCLIMATING?

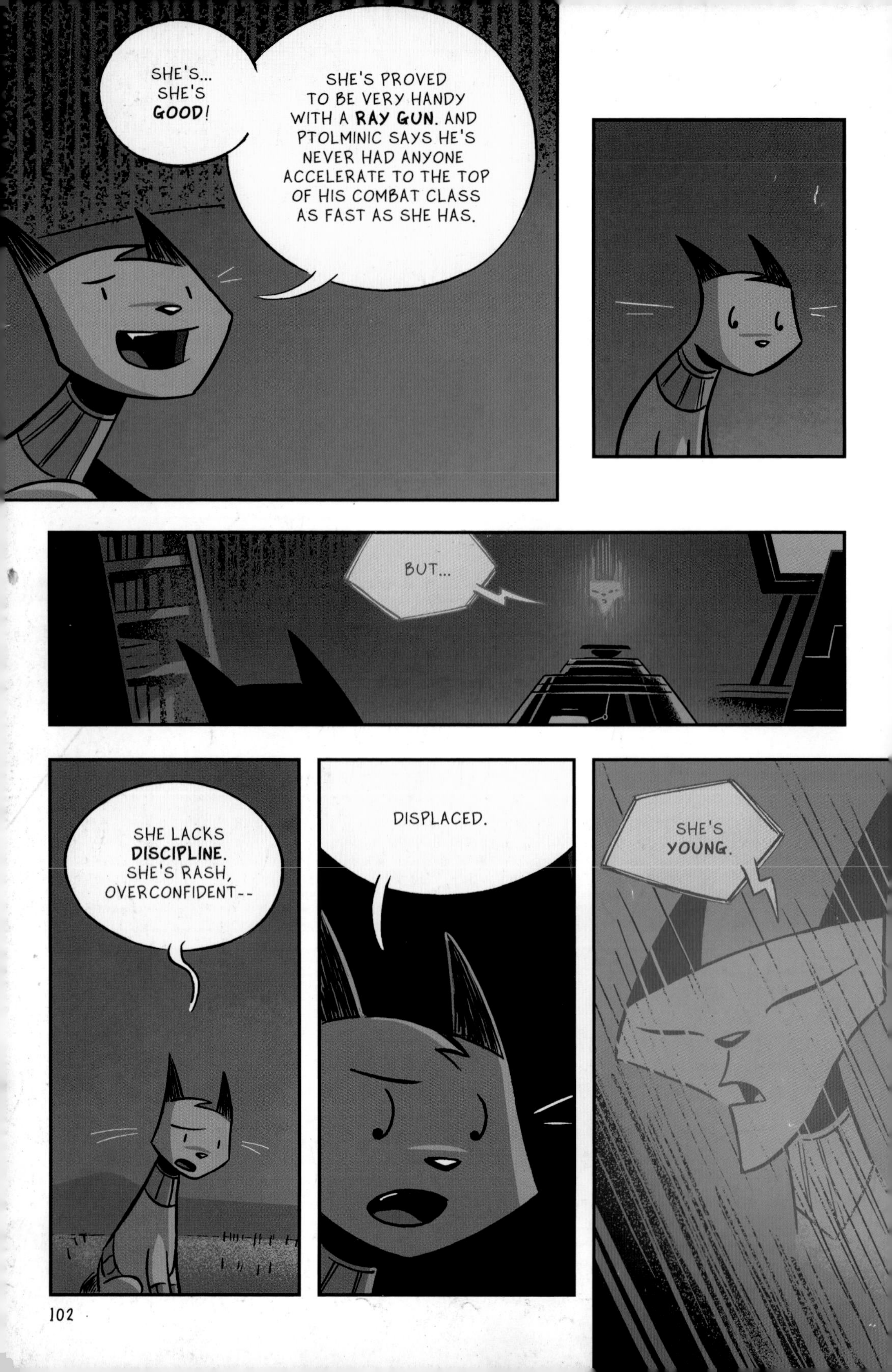
SHE'S... SHE'S GOOD!
SHE'S PROVED TO BE VERY HANDY WITH A RAY GUN. AND PTOLMINIC SAYS HE'S NEVER HAD ANYONE ACCELERATE TO THE TOP OF HIS COMBAT CLASS AS FAST AS SHE HAS.
BUT...
SHE LACKS DISCIPLINE. SHE'S RASH, OVERCONFIDENT--
DISPLACED.
SHE'S YOUNG.

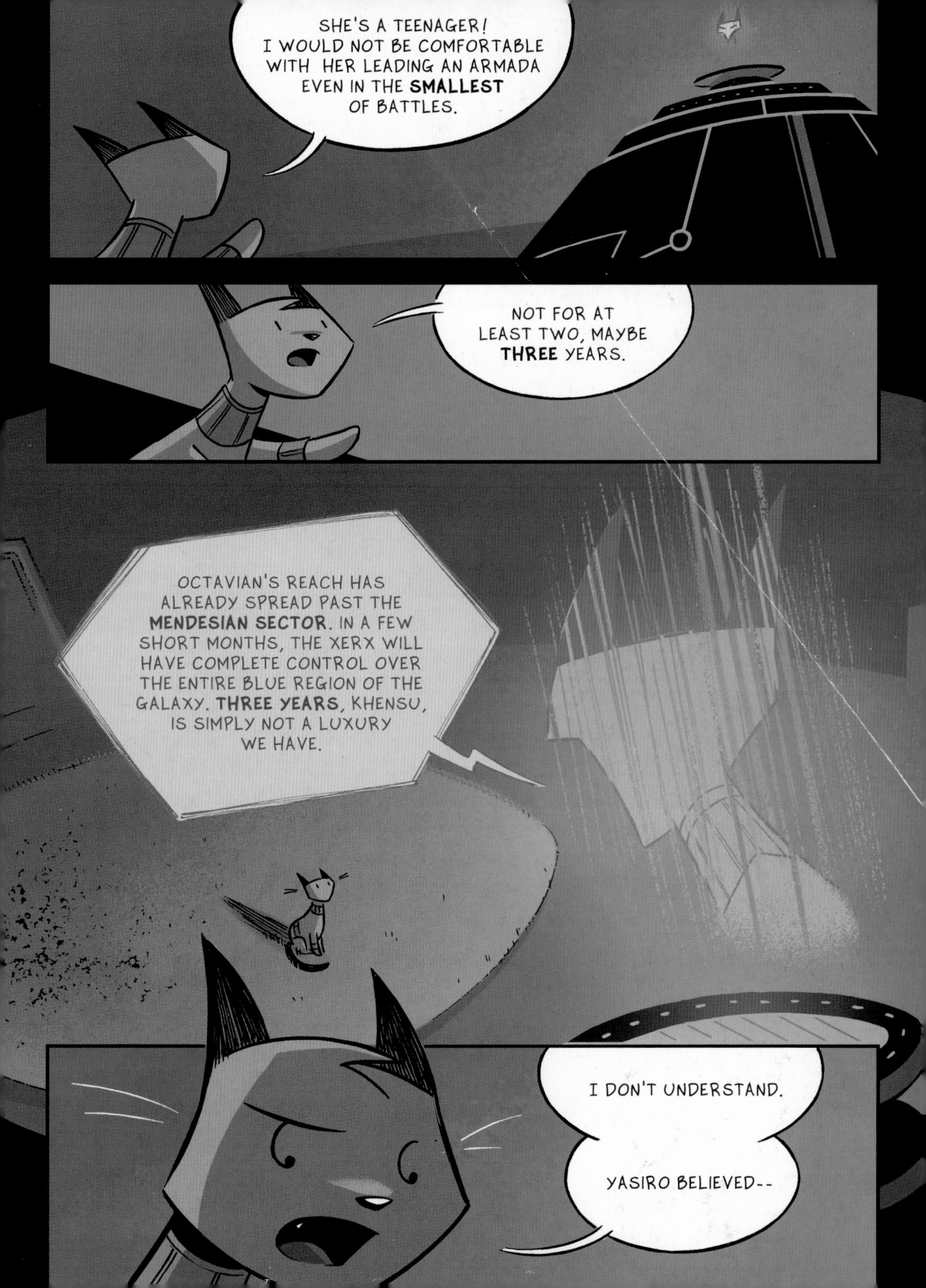
SHE'S A TEENAGER! I WOULD NOT BE COMFORTABLE WITH HER LEADING AN ARMADA EVEN IN THE SMALLEST OF BATTLES.
NOT FOR AT LEAST TWO, MAYBE THREE YEARS.
OCTAVIAN'S REACH HAS ALREADY SPREAD PAST THE MENDESIAN SECTOR. IN A FEW SHORT MONTHS, THE XERX WILL HAVE COMPLETE CONTROL OVER THE ENTIRE BLUE REGION OF THE GALAXY. THREE YEARS, KHENSU, IS SIMPLY NOT A LUXURY WE HAVE.
I DON'T UNDERSTAND.
YASIRO BELIEVED--

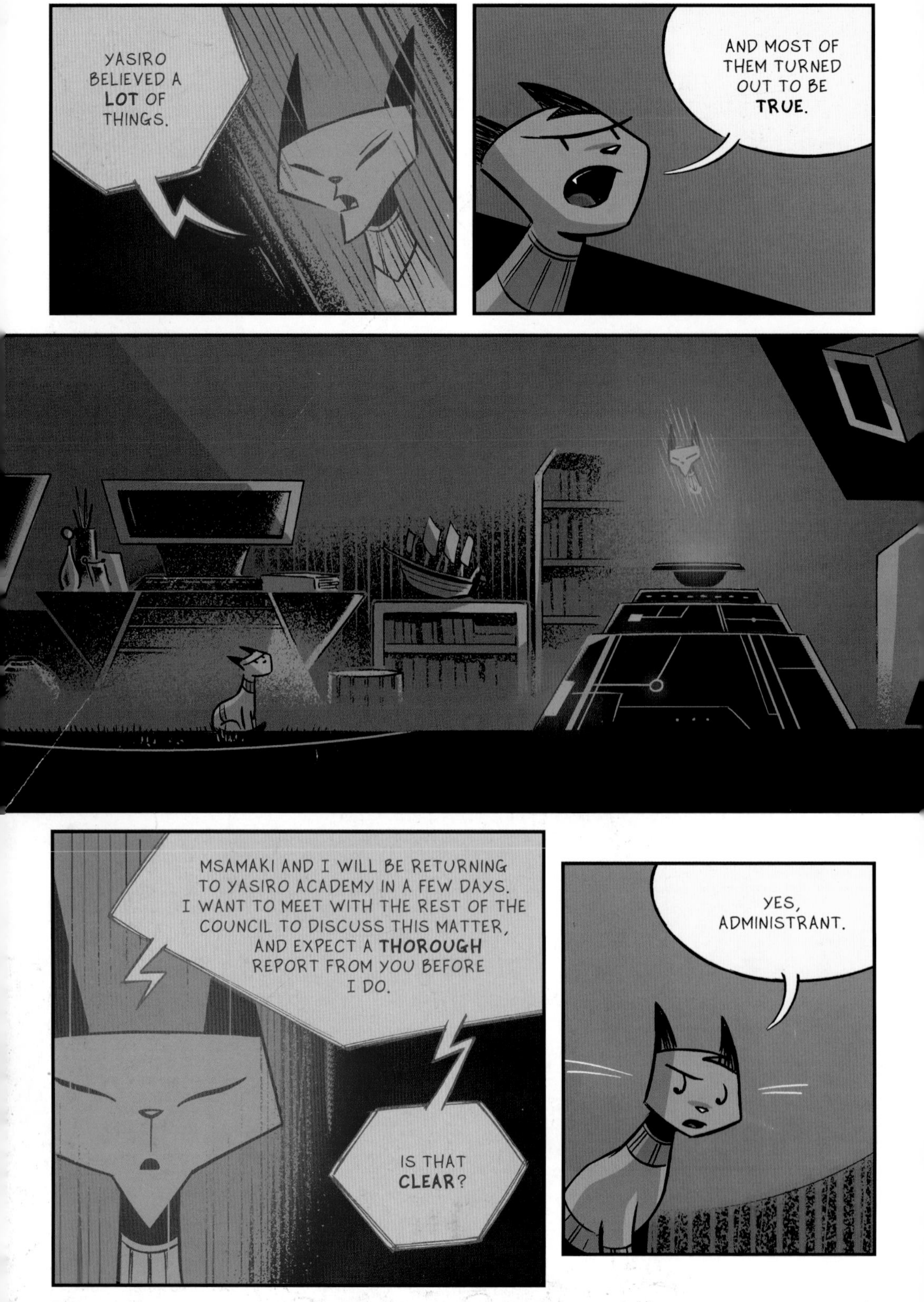
YASIRO BELIEVED A LOT OF THINGS.
AND MOST OF THEM TURNED OUT TO BE TRUE.
MSAMAKI AND I WILL BE RETURNING TO YASIRO ACADEMY IN A FEW DAYS. I WANT TO MEET WITH THE REST OF THE COUNCIL TO DISCUSS THIS MATTER, AND EXPECT A THOROUGH REPORT FROM YOU BEFORE I DO.
IS THAT CLEAR?
YES, ADMINISTRANT.

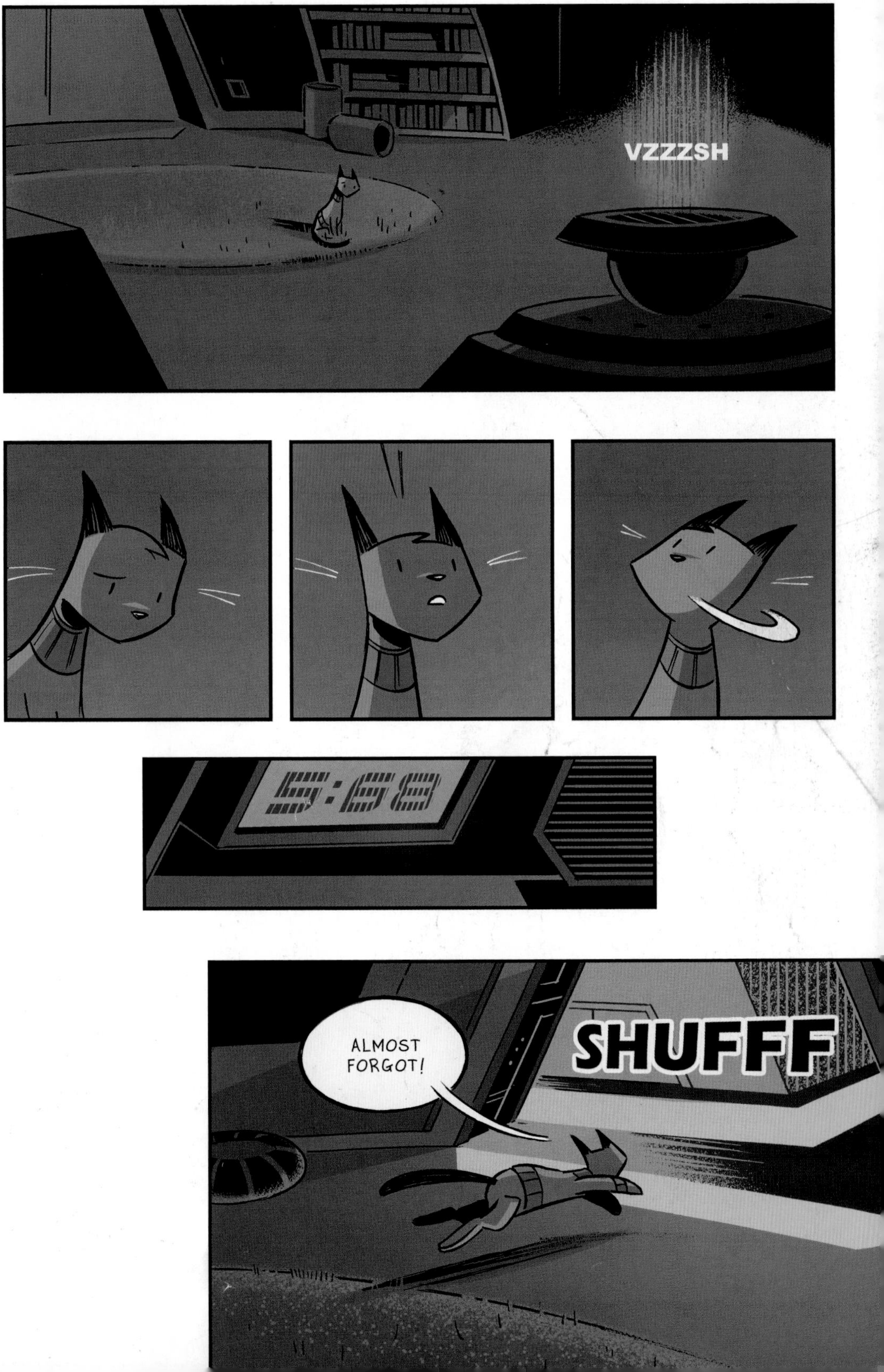
VZZZSH
5:58
ALMOST FORGOT!
SHUFFF

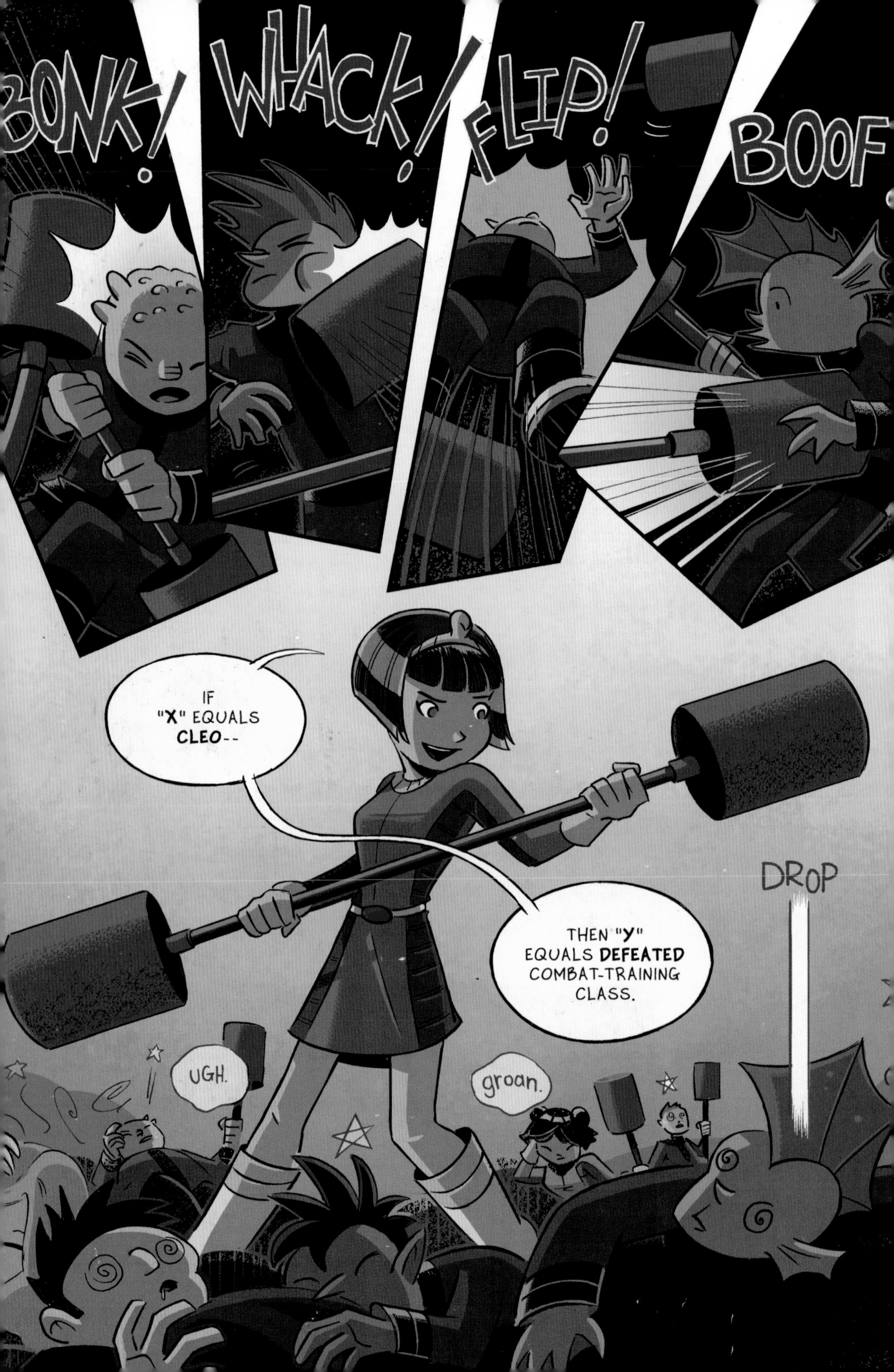
BONK!
WHACK!
FLIP!
BOOF
IF "X" EQUALS CLEO--
THEN "Y" EQUALS DEFEATED COMBAT-TRAINING CLASS.
DROP
UGH.
groan.

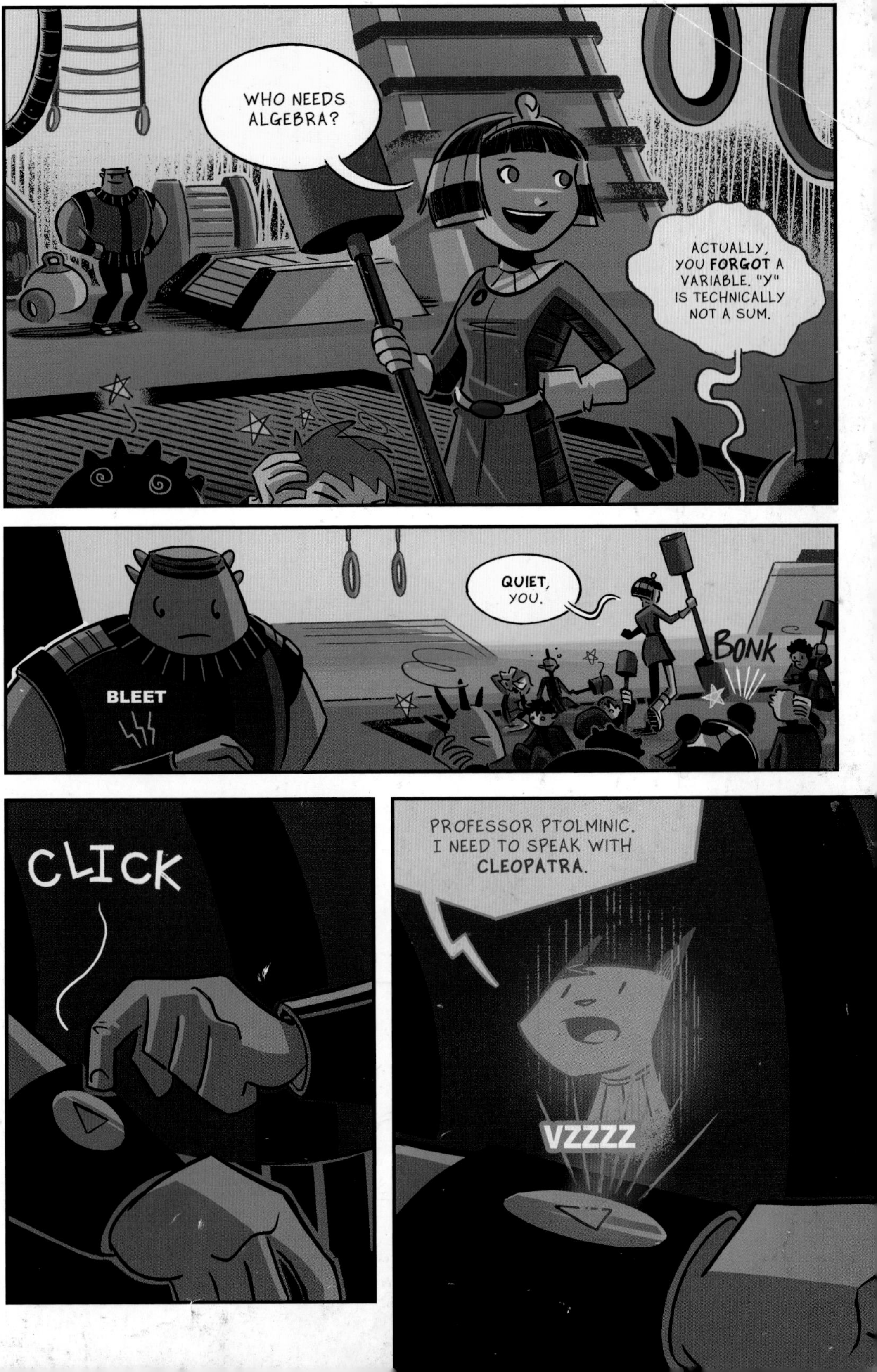
WHO NEEDS ALGEBRA?
ACTUALLY, YOU FORGOT A VARIABLE. "Y" IS TECHNICALLY NOT A SUM.
QUIET, YOU.
BONK
BLEET
CLICK
PROFESSOR PTOLMINIC. I NEED TO SPEAK WITH CLEOPATRA.
VZZZZ

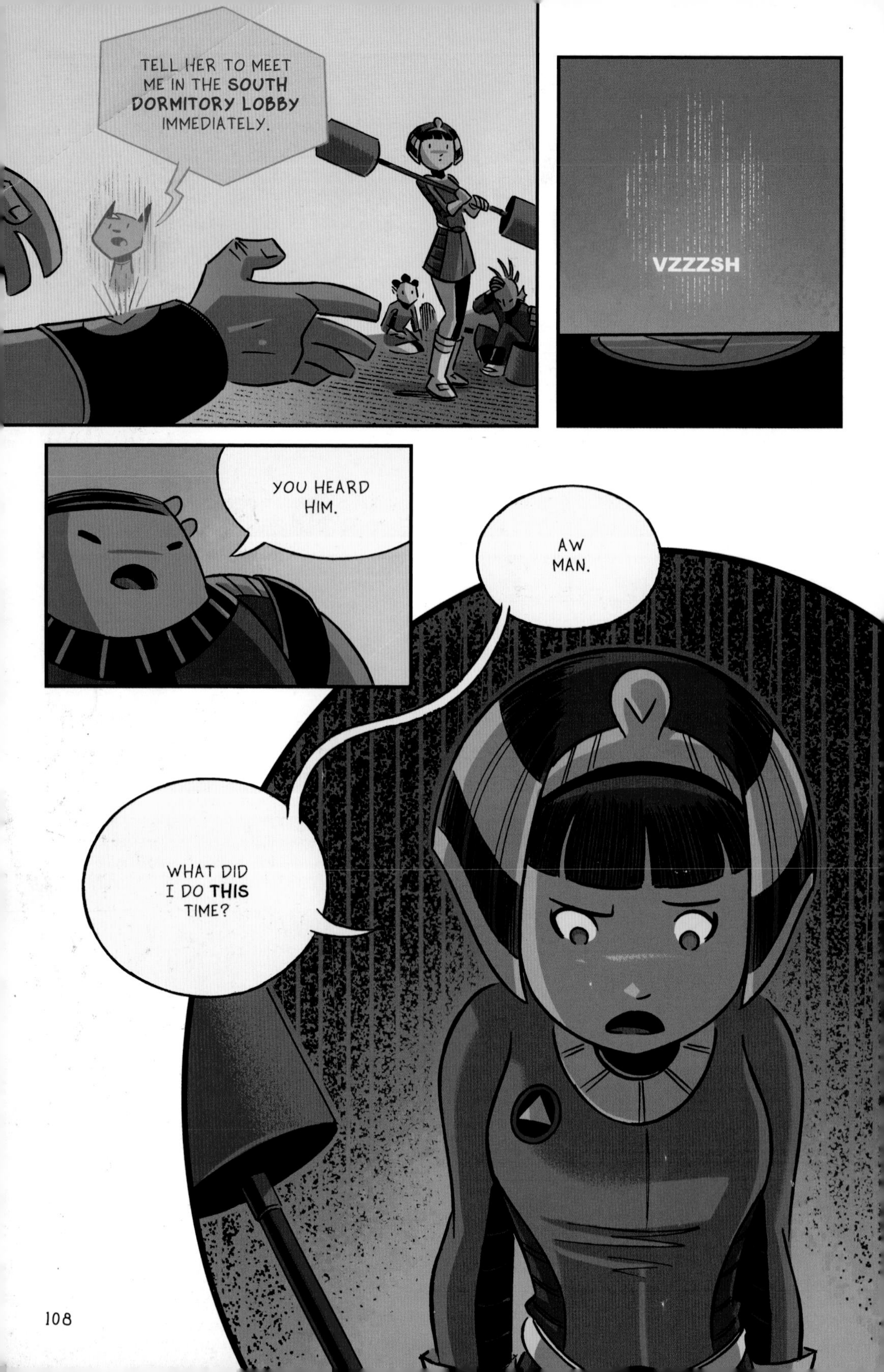
TELL HER TO MEET ME IN THE **SOUTH DORMITORY LOBBY** IMMEDIATELY.
VZZZSH
YOU HEARD HIM.
AW MAN.
WHAT DID I DO **THIS** TIME?

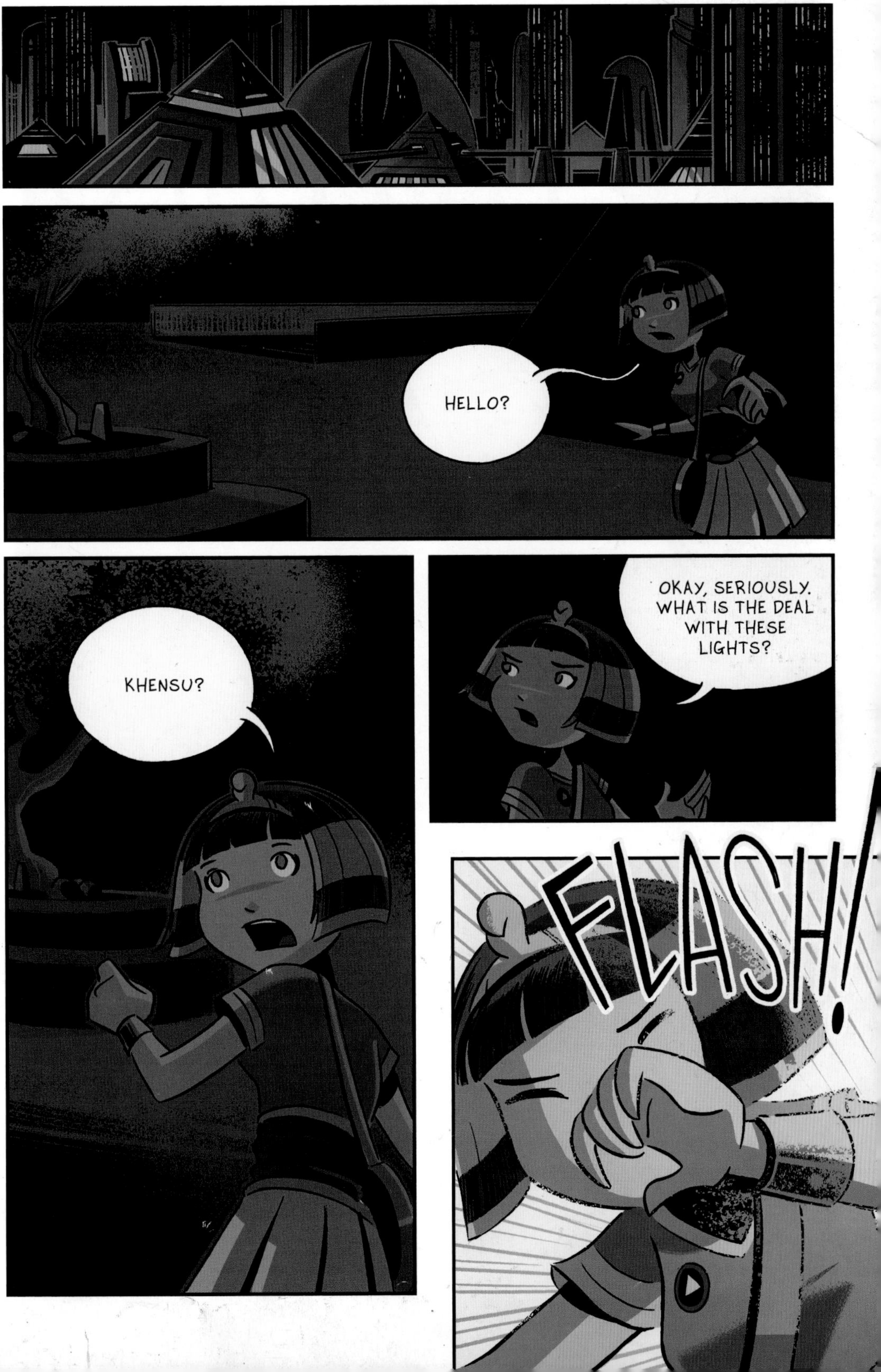
HELLO?
KHENSU?
OKAY, SERIOUSLY. WHAT IS THE DEAL WITH THESE LIGHTS?
FLASH!

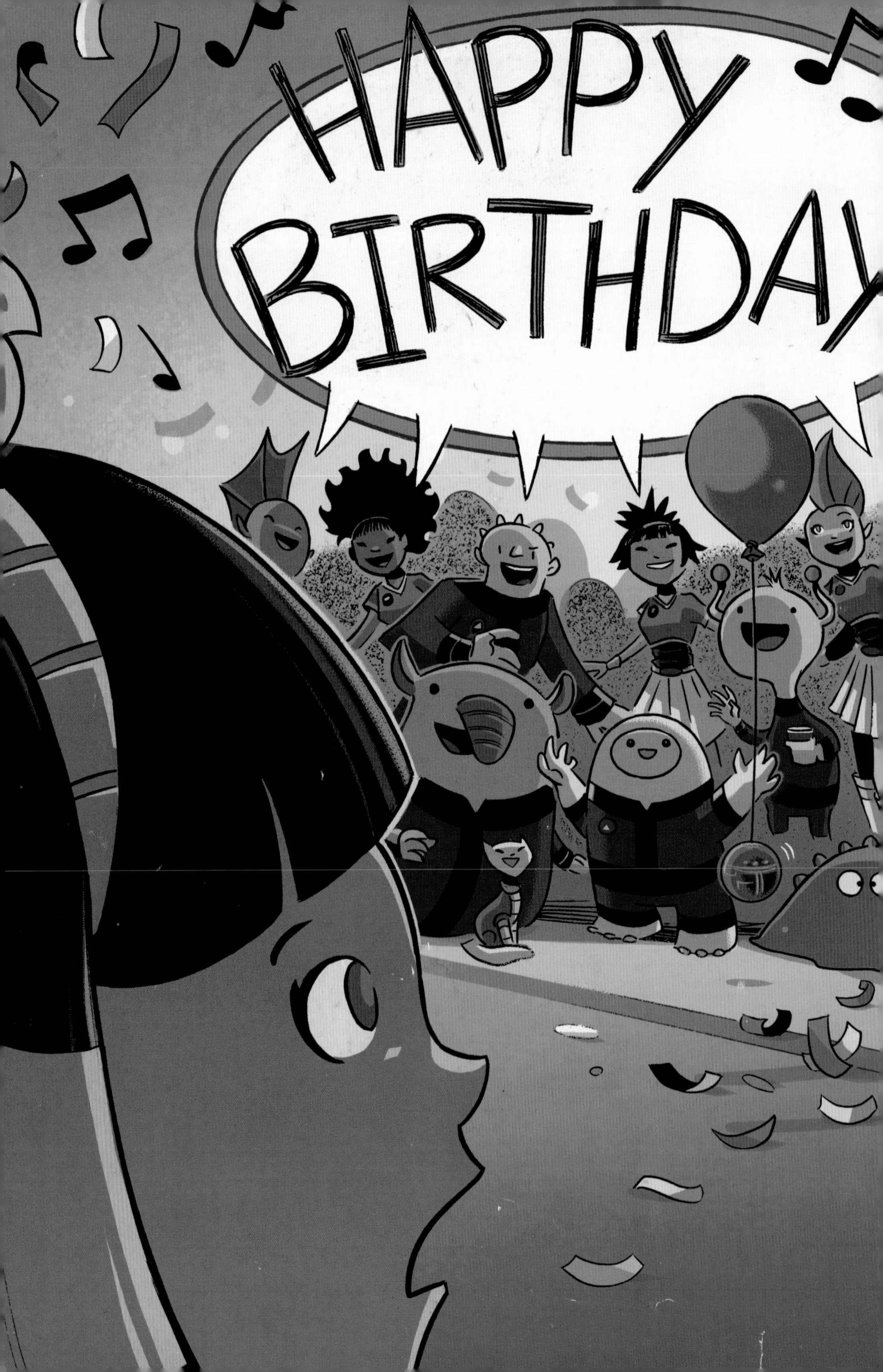
HAPPY BIRTHDAY

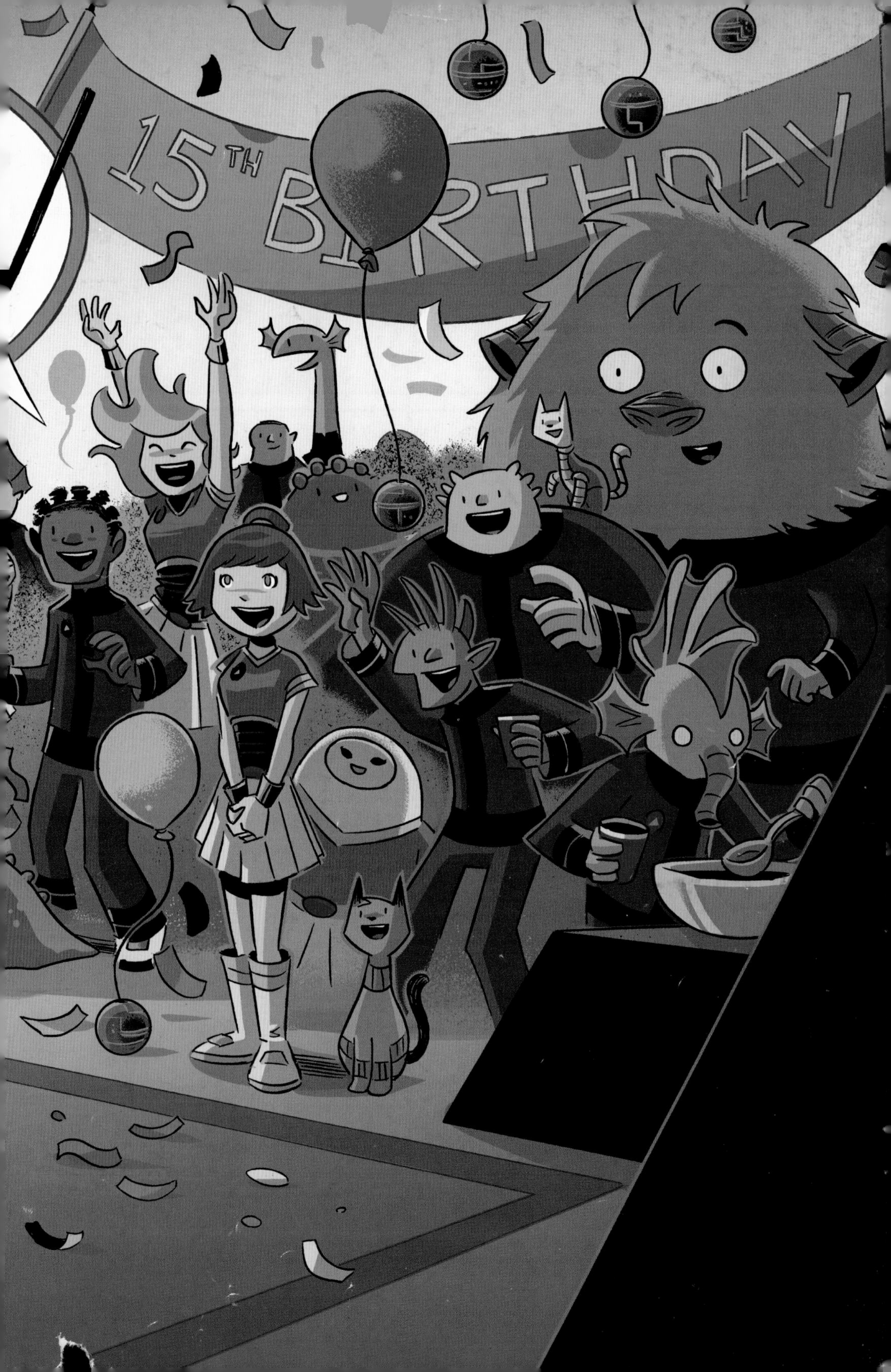
15TH BIRTHDAY

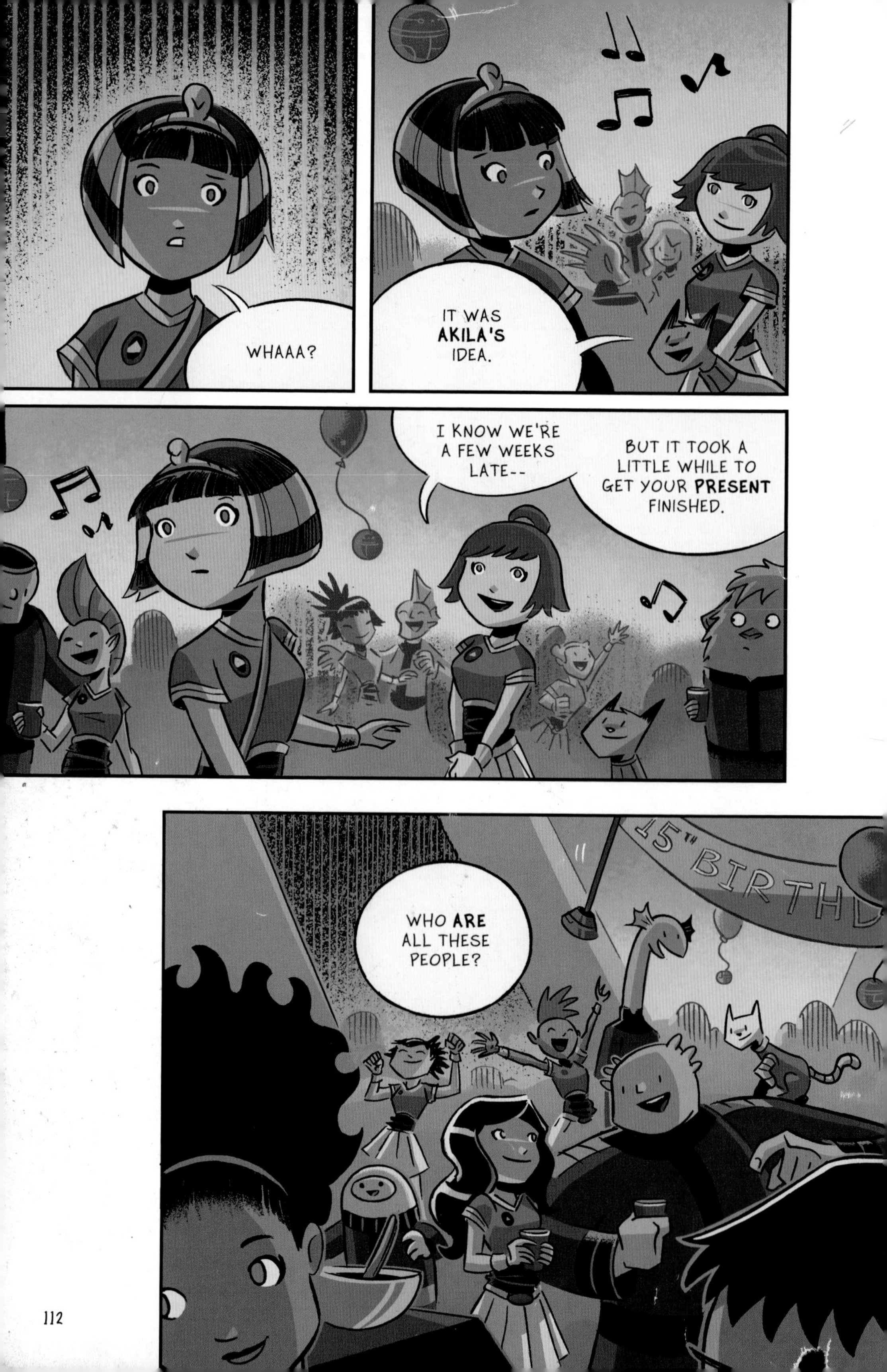
WHAAA?
IT WAS AKILA'S IDEA.
I KNOW WE'RE A FEW WEEKS LATE--
BUT IT TOOK A LITTLE WHILE TO GET YOUR PRESENT FINISHED.
WHO ARE ALL THESE PEOPLE?
15TH BIRTHD

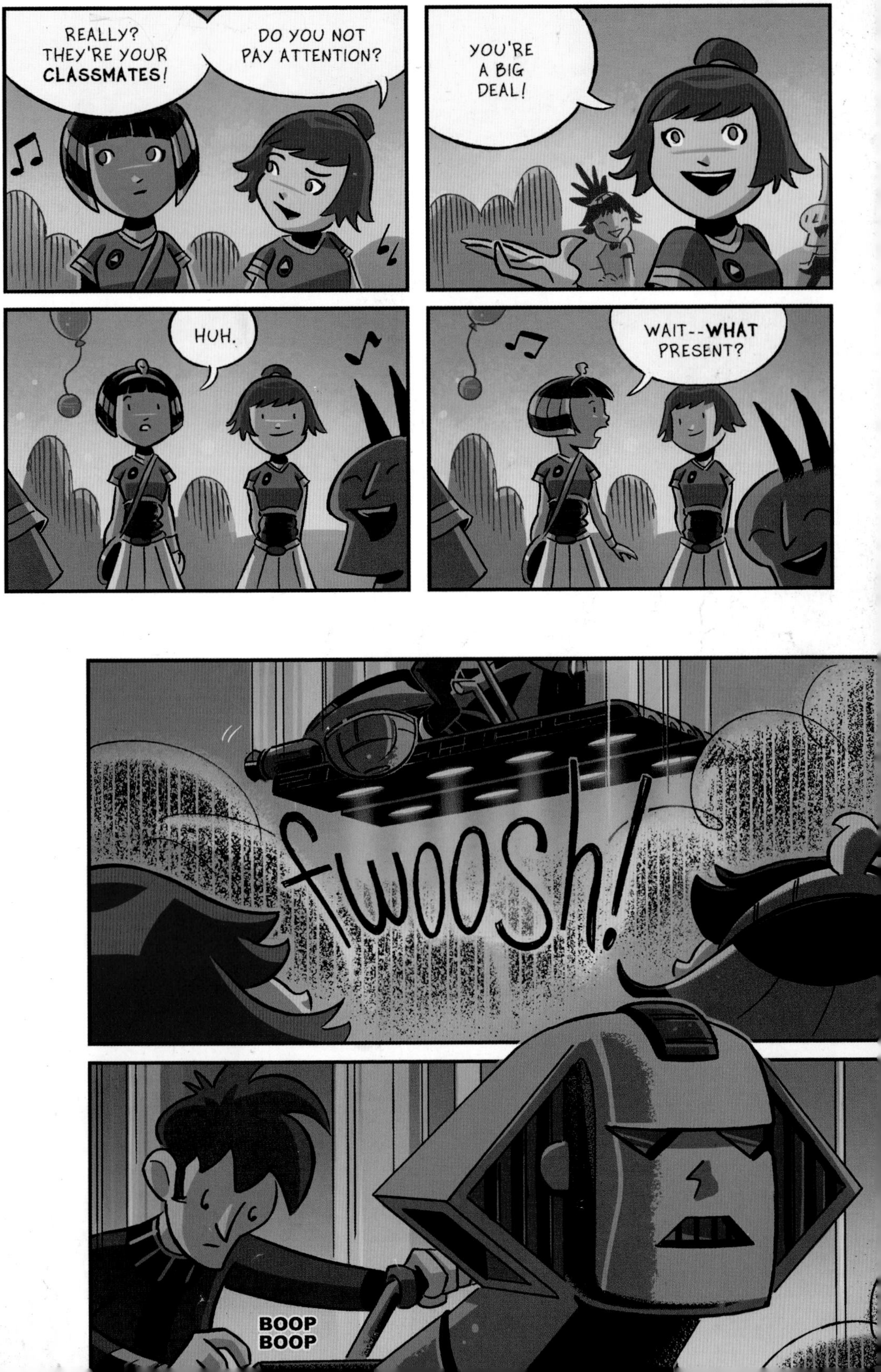
REALLY? THEY'RE YOUR **CLASSMATES**!
DO YOU NOT PAY ATTENTION?
YOU'RE A BIG DEAL!
HUH.
WAIT--**WHAT** PRESENT?
FWOOSH!
BOOP BOOP

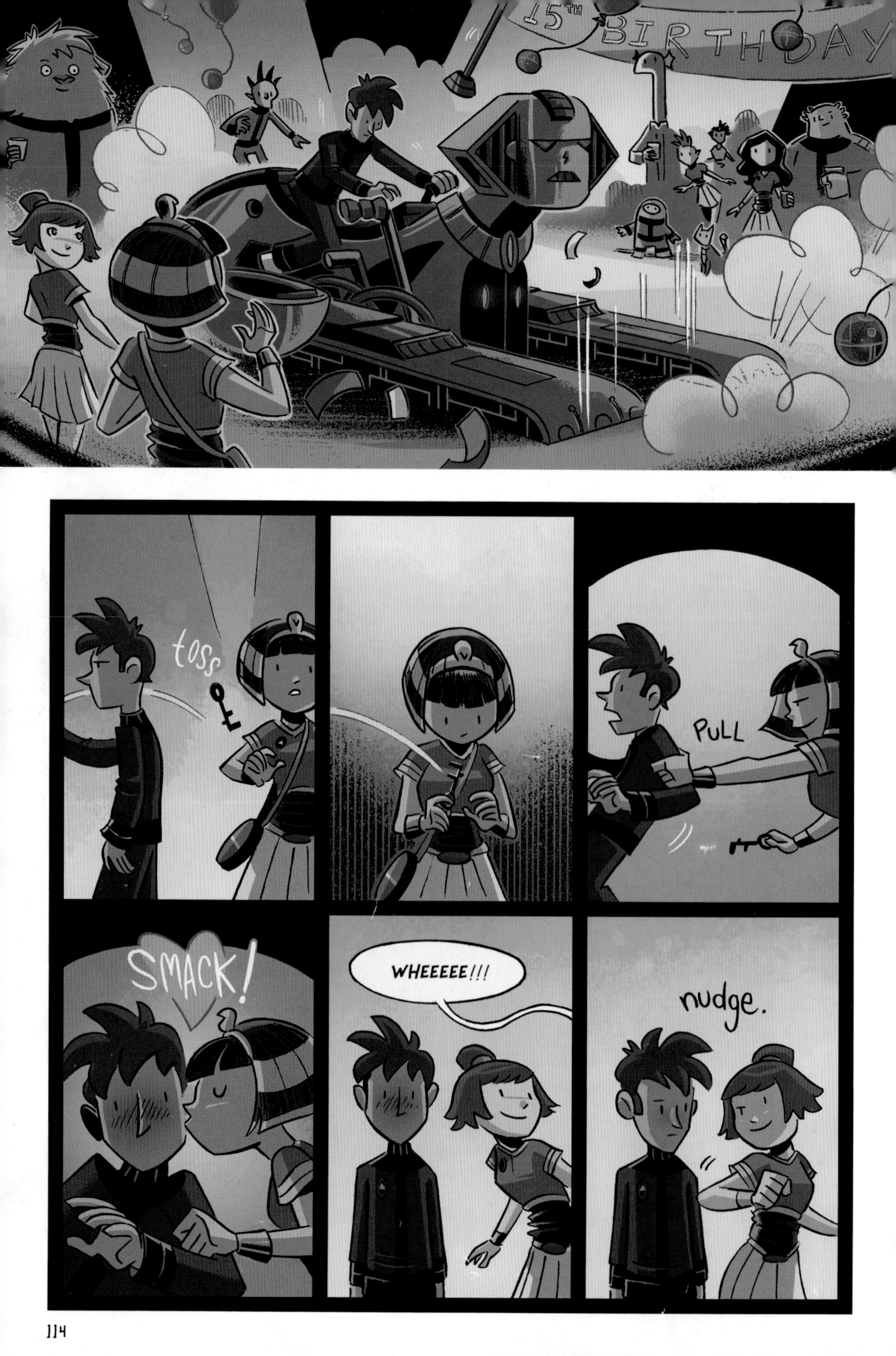
15TH BIRTHDAY
toss
PULL
SMACK!
WHEEEEE!!!
nudge.

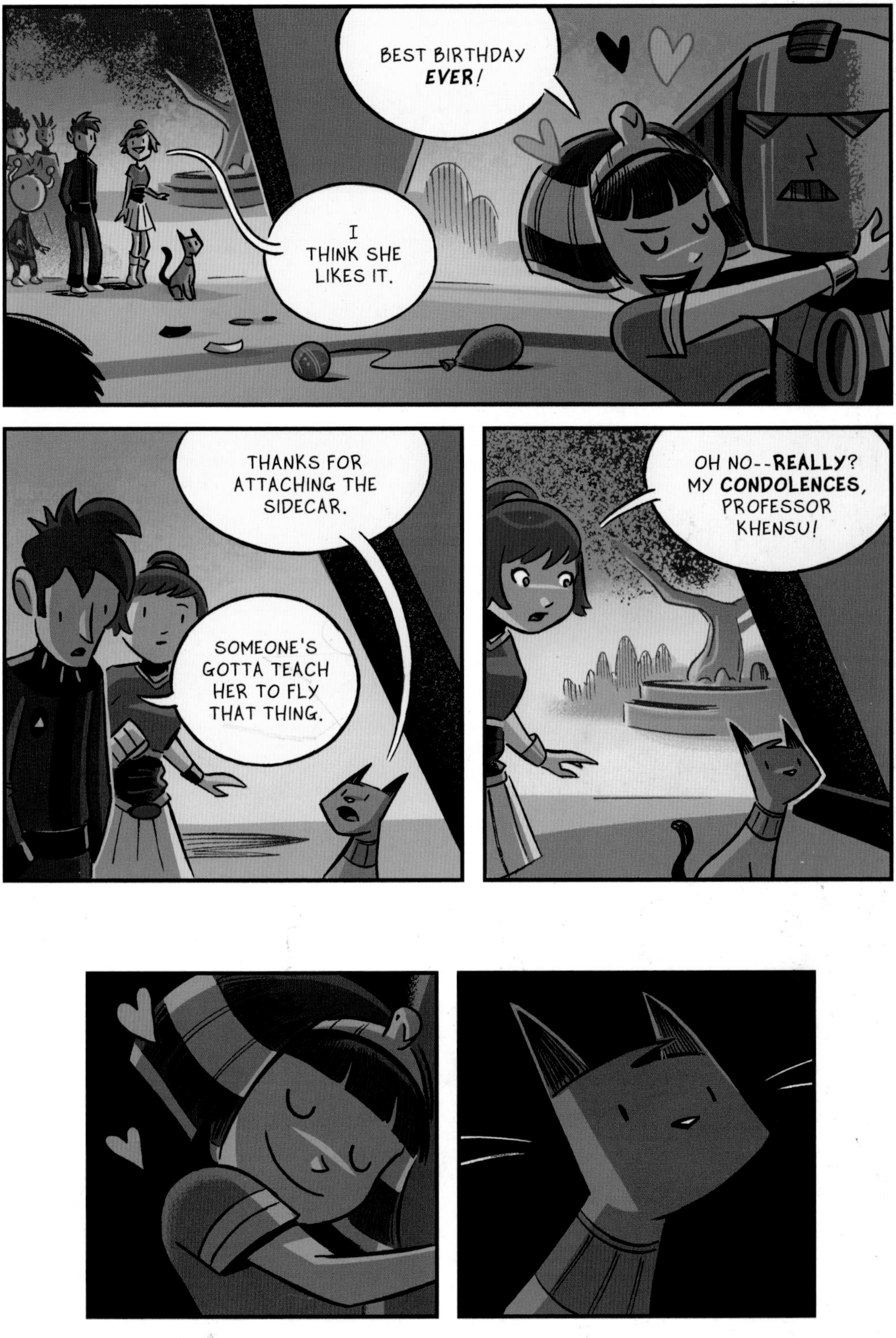
BEST BIRTHDAY **EVER**!
I THINK SHE LIKES IT.
THANKS FOR ATTACHING THE SIDECAR.
SOMEONE'S GOTTA TEACH HER TO FLY THAT THING.
OH NO--**REALLY**? MY **CONDOLENCES**, PROFESSOR KHENSU!

CHAPTER THREE

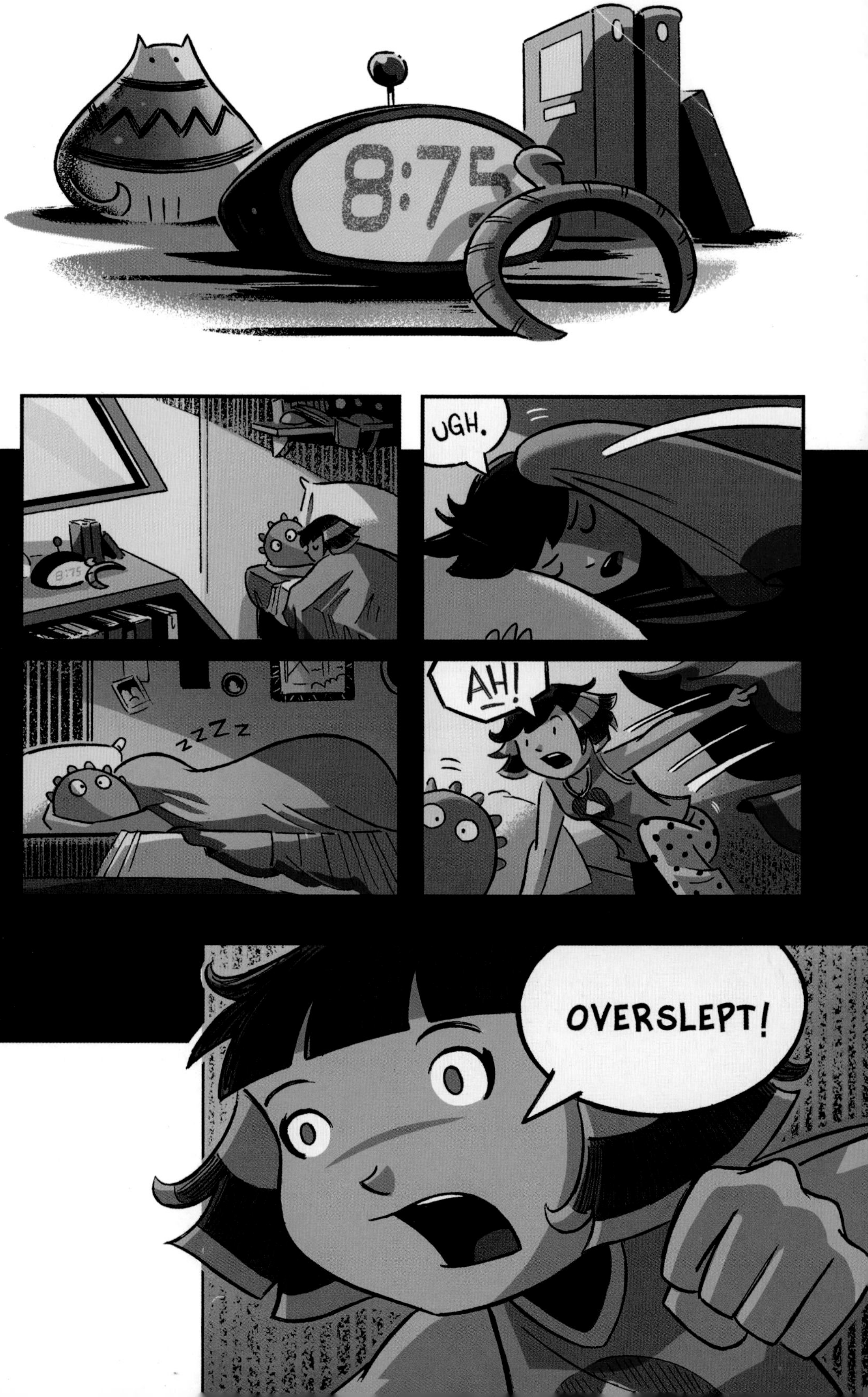
8:75
8:75
UGH.
ZZZZ
AH!
OVERSLEPT!

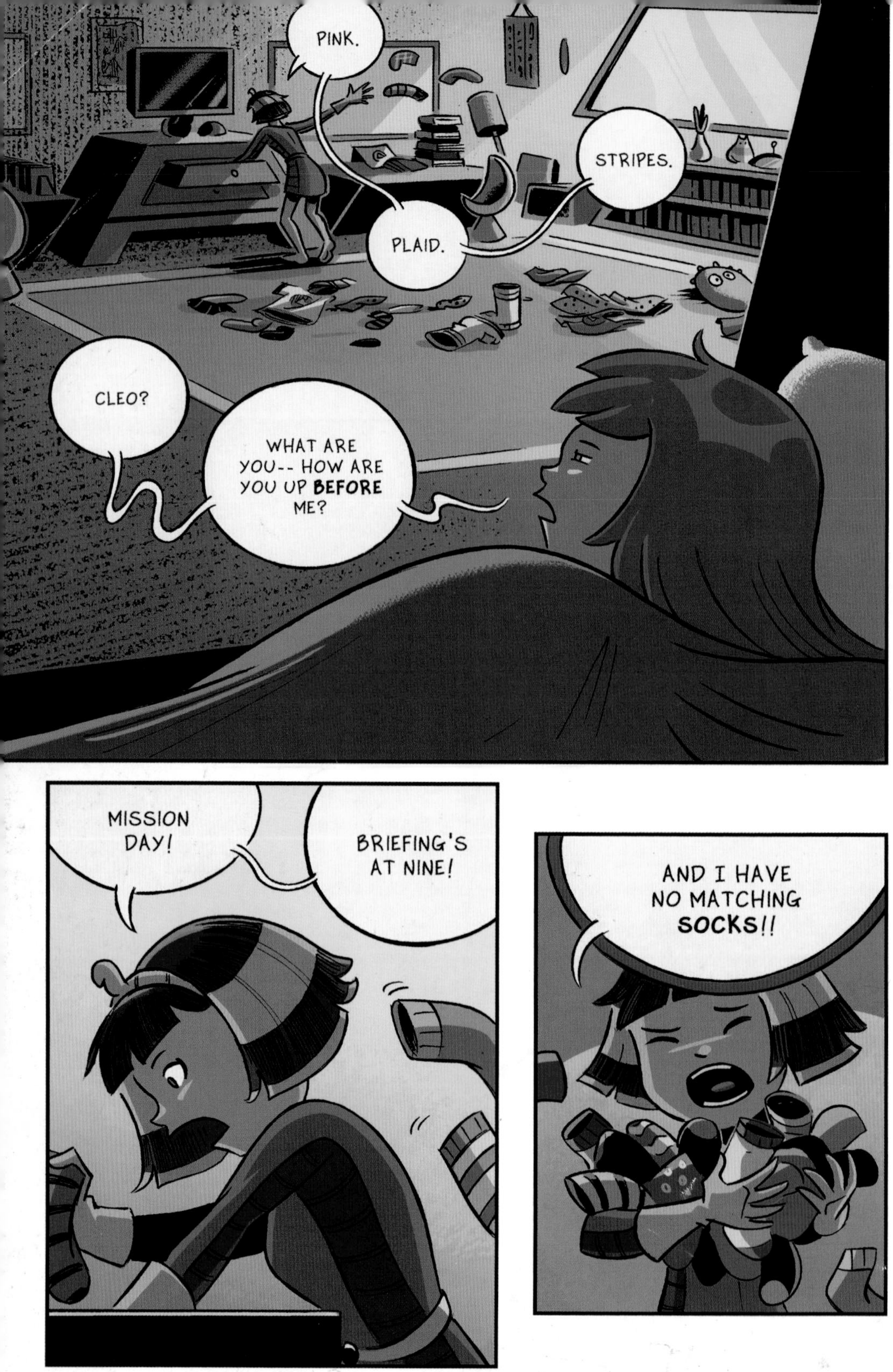
PINK.
PLAID.
STRIPES.
CLEO?
WHAT ARE YOU-- HOW ARE YOU UP **BEFORE** ME?
MISSION DAY!
BRIEFING'S AT NINE!
AND I HAVE NO MATCHING **SOCKS**!!

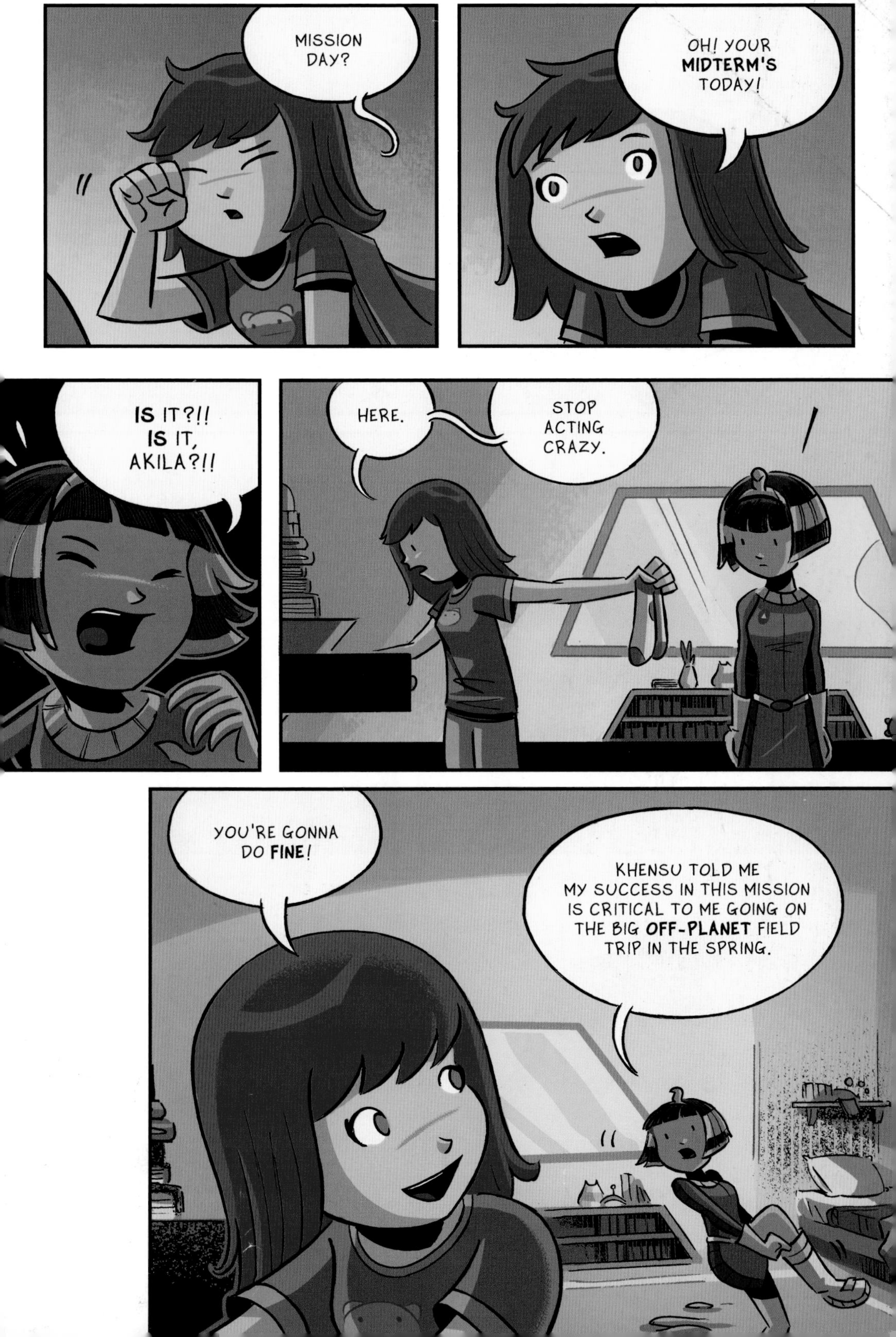
MISSION DAY?
OH! YOUR **MIDTERM'S** TODAY!
IS IT?!! **IS** IT, AKILA?!!
HERE.
STOP ACTING CRAZY.
YOU'RE GONNA DO **FINE**!
KHENSU TOLD ME MY SUCCESS IN THIS MISSION IS CRITICAL TO ME GOING ON THE BIG **OFF-PLANET** FIELD TRIP IN THE SPRING.

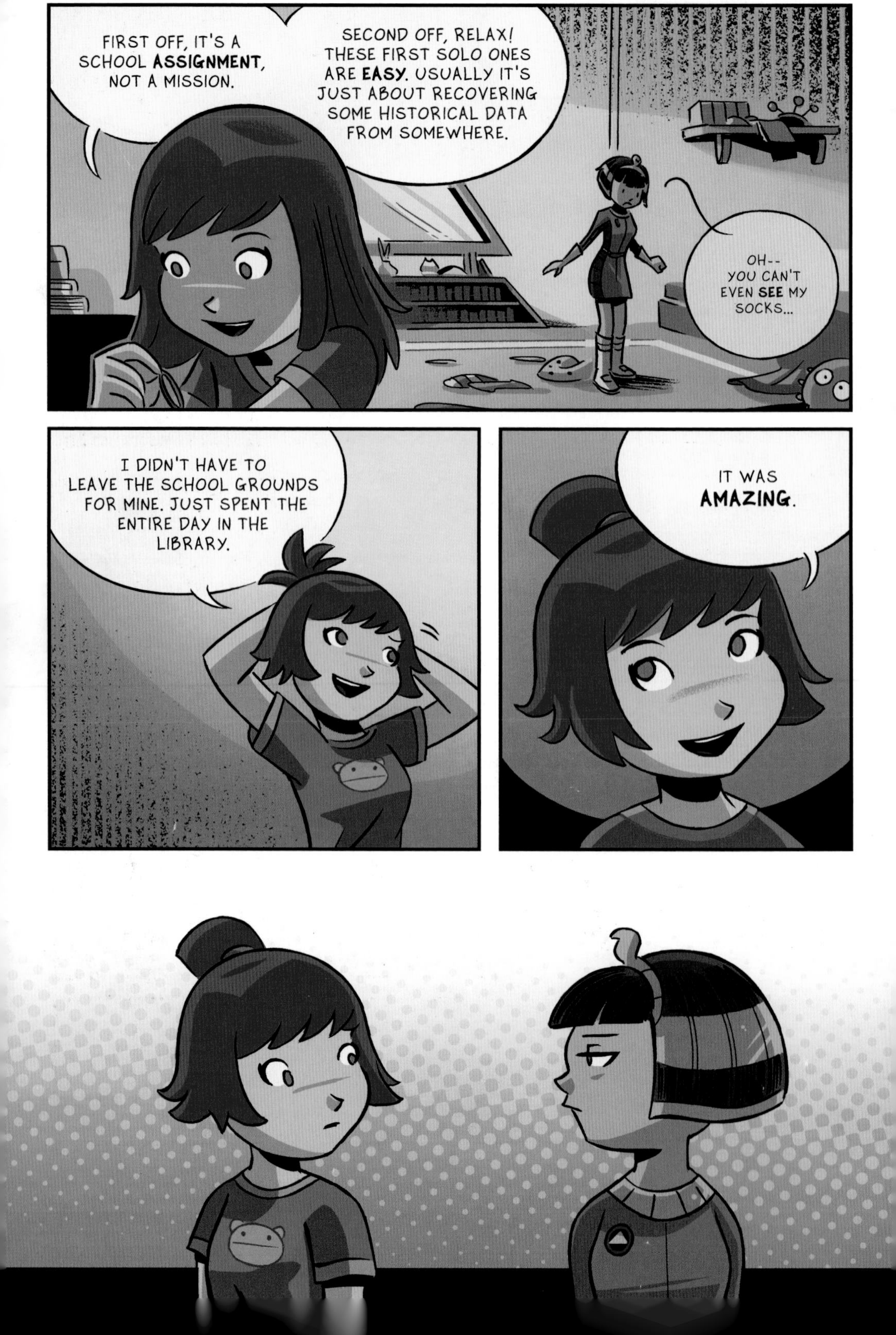
FIRST OFF, IT'S A SCHOOL **ASSIGNMENT**, NOT A MISSION.
SECOND OFF, RELAX! THESE FIRST SOLO ONES ARE **EASY**. USUALLY IT'S JUST ABOUT RECOVERING SOME HISTORICAL DATA FROM SOMEWHERE.
OH-- YOU CAN'T EVEN **SEE** MY SOCKS...
I DIDN'T HAVE TO LEAVE THE SCHOOL GROUNDS FOR MINE. JUST SPENT THE ENTIRE DAY IN THE LIBRARY.
IT WAS **AMAZING**.

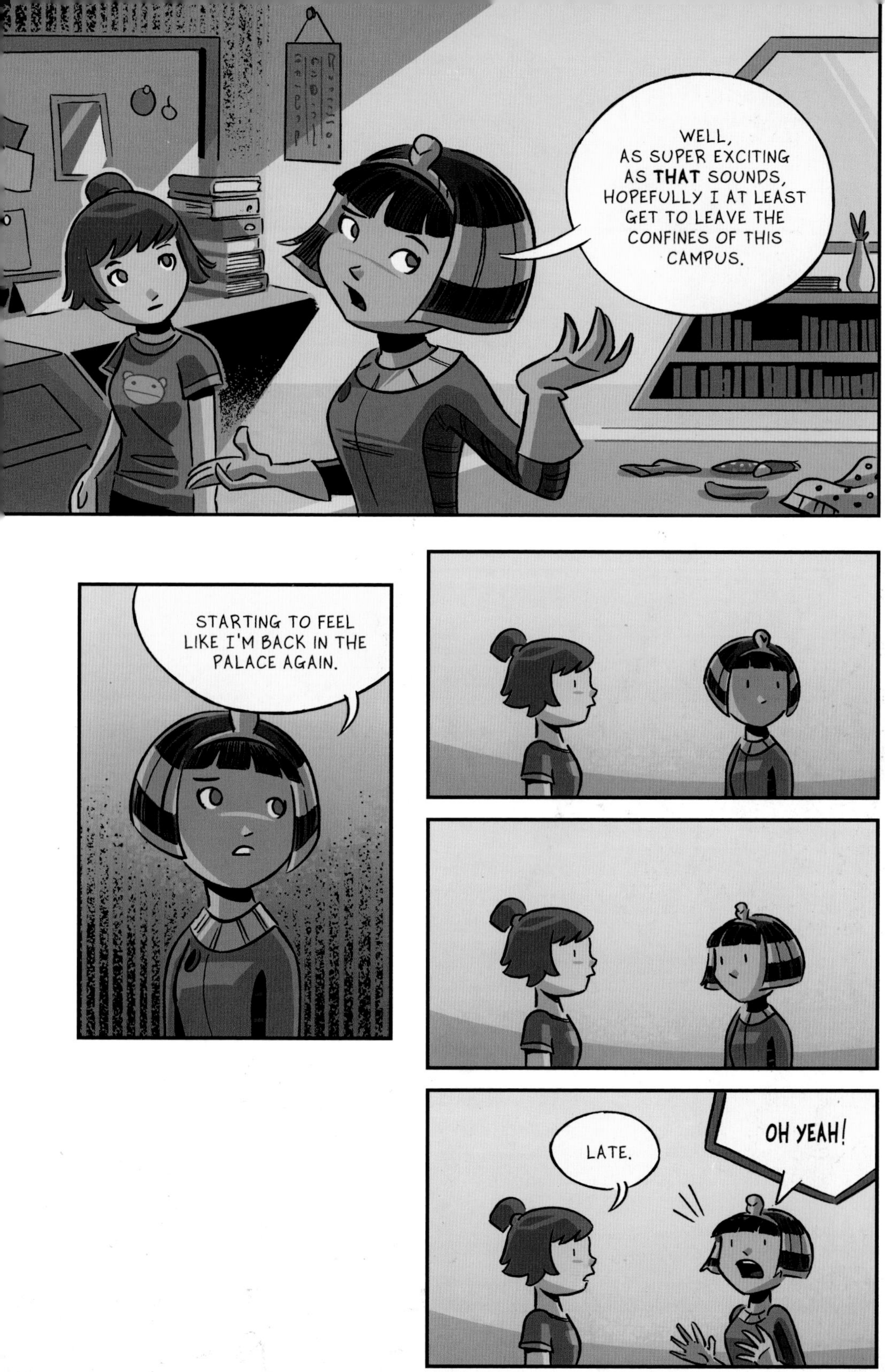
WELL, AS SUPER EXCITING AS THAT SOUNDS, HOPEFULLY I AT LEAST GET TO LEAVE THE CONFINES OF THIS CAMPUS.
STARTING TO FEEL LIKE I'M BACK IN THE PALACE AGAIN.
LATE.
OH YEAH!

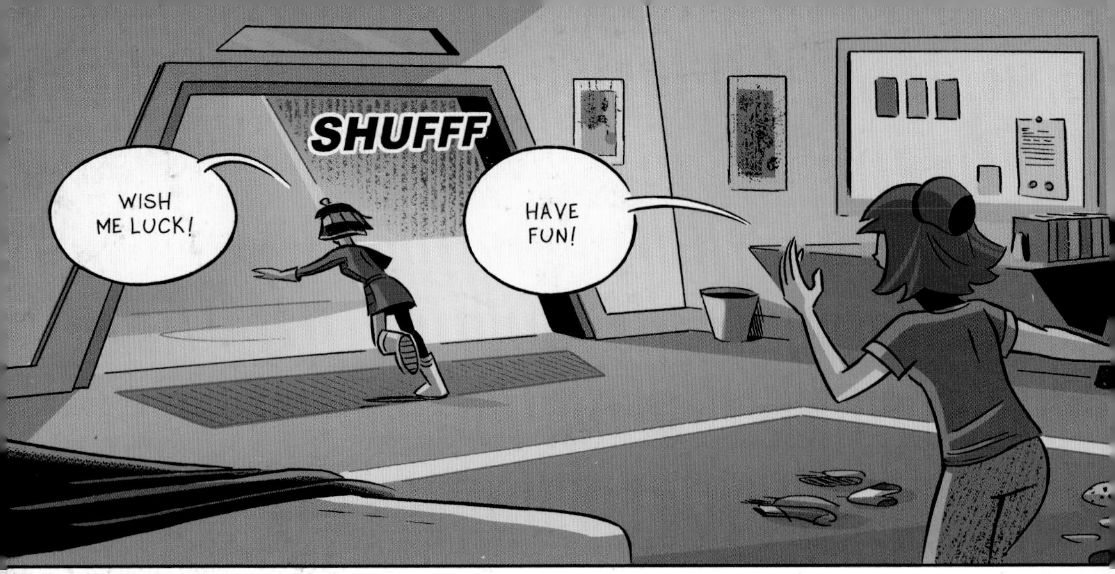
SHUFFF
WISH ME LUCK!
HAVE FUN!

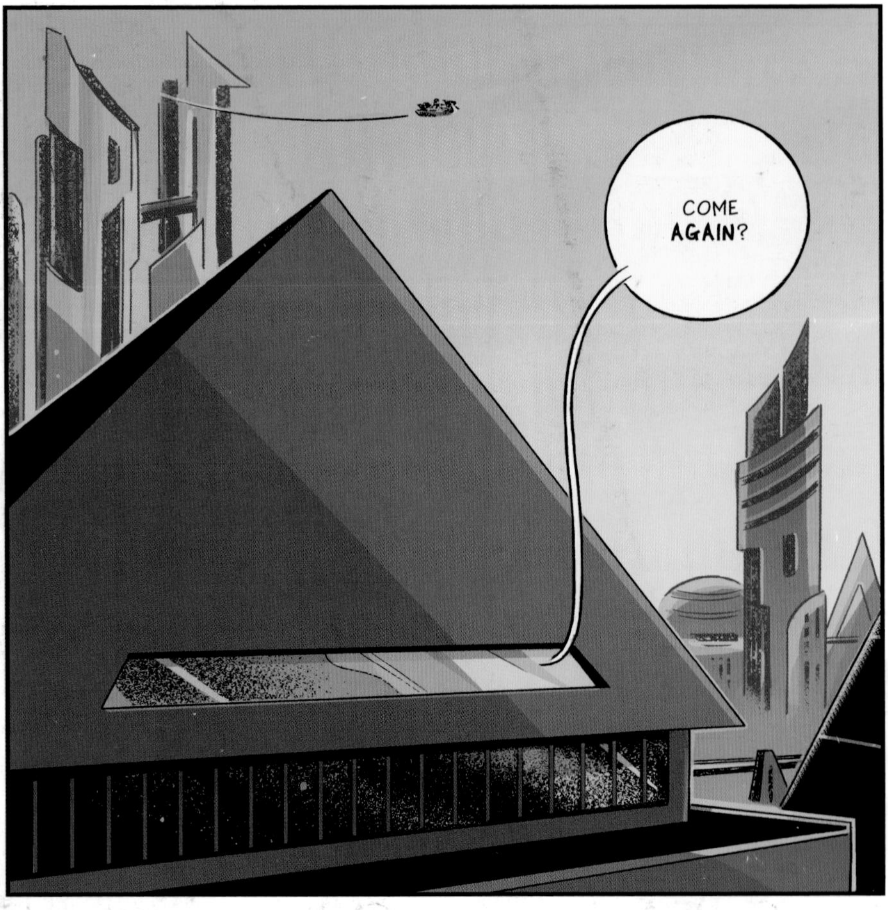
COME AGAIN?

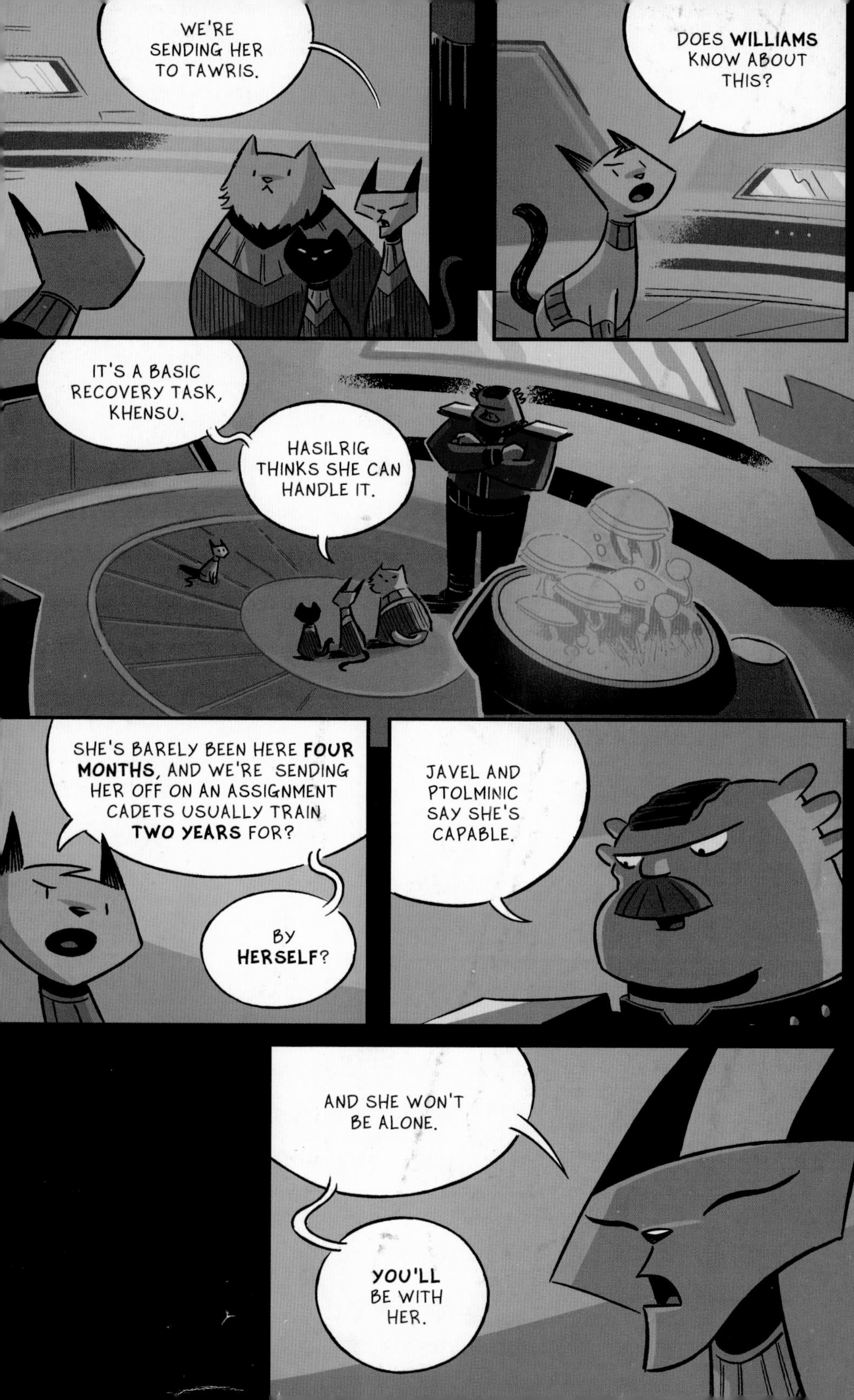
WE'RE SENDING HER TO TAWRIS.
DOES **WILLIAMS** KNOW ABOUT THIS?
IT'S A BASIC RECOVERY TASK, KHENSU.
HASILRIG THINKS SHE CAN HANDLE IT.
SHE'S BARELY BEEN HERE **FOUR MONTHS**, AND WE'RE SENDING HER OFF ON AN ASSIGNMENT CADETS USUALLY TRAIN **TWO YEARS** FOR?
BY **HERSELF**?
JAVEL AND PTOLMINIC SAY SHE'S CAPABLE.
AND SHE WON'T BE ALONE.
YOU'LL BE WITH HER.

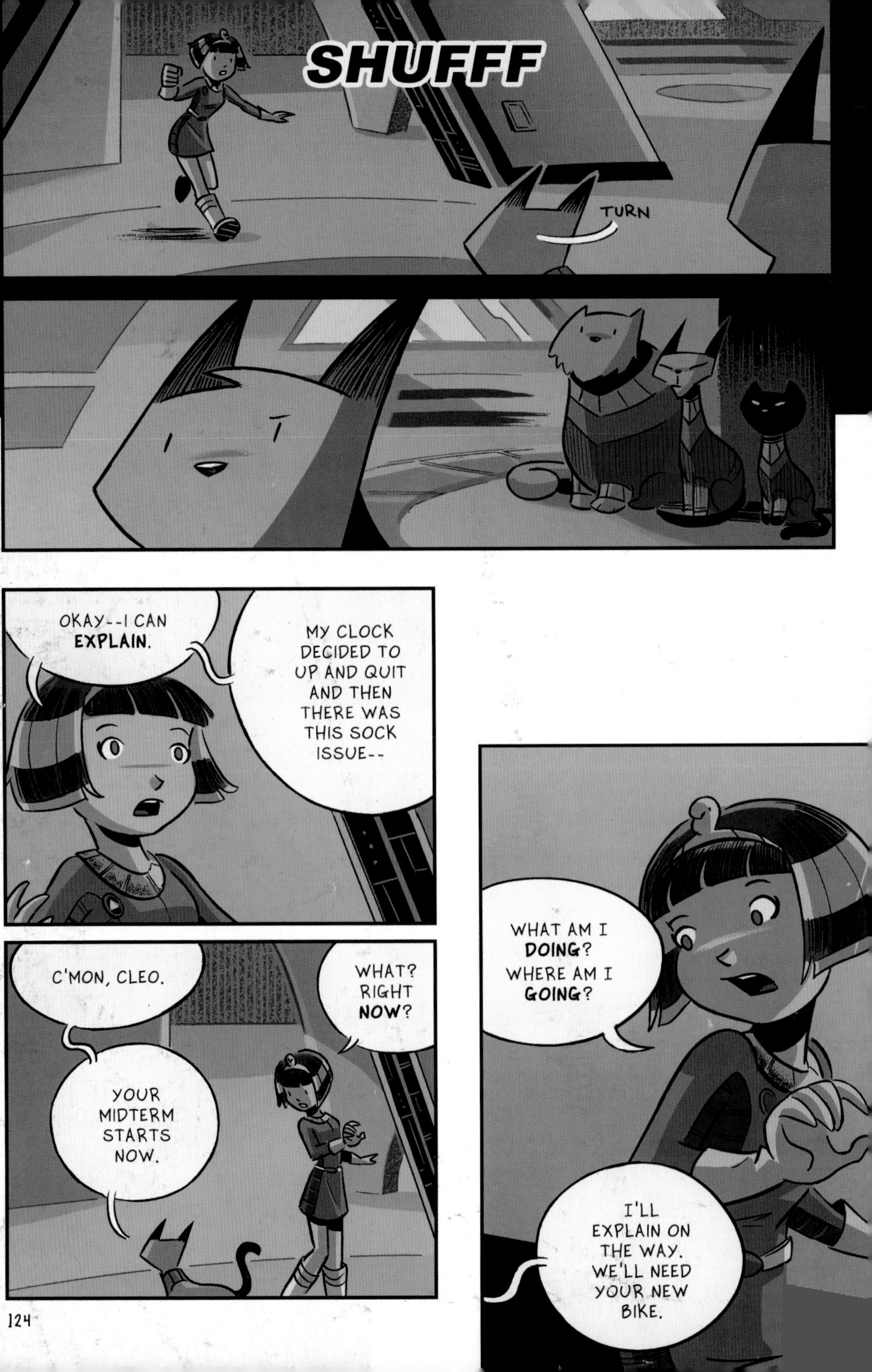
SHUFFF
TURN
OKAY--I CAN EXPLAIN.
MY CLOCK DECIDED TO UP AND QUIT AND THEN THERE WAS THIS SOCK ISSUE--
C'MON, CLEO.
WHAT? RIGHT NOW?
YOUR MIDTERM STARTS NOW.
WHAT AM I DOING? WHERE AM I GOING?
I'LL EXPLAIN ON THE WAY. WE'LL NEED YOUR NEW BIKE.

GOOD LUCK, CLEOPATRA. WE HAVE FAITH IN YOU.

UM... THANKS.

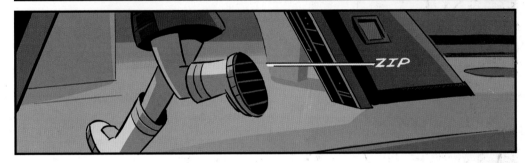

ZIP

ARE WE DOING THE RIGHT THING?

WE NEED TO BE **CERTAIN**.

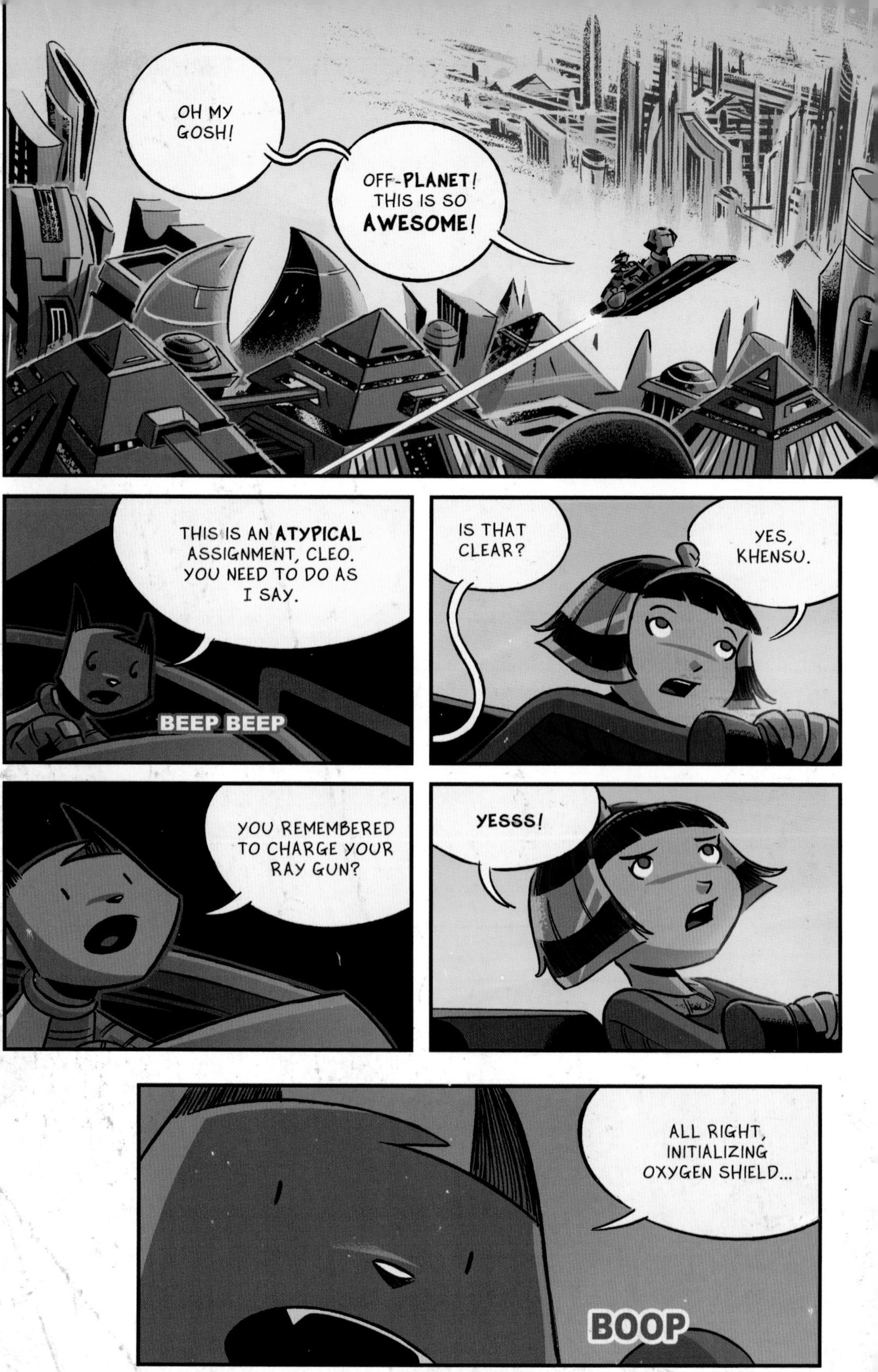
OH MY GOSH!
OFF-PLANET! THIS IS SO AWESOME!
THIS IS AN ATYPICAL ASSIGNMENT, CLEO. YOU NEED TO DO AS I SAY.
BEEP BEEP
IS THAT CLEAR?
YES, KHENSU.
YOU REMEMBERED TO CHARGE YOUR RAY GUN?
YESSS!
ALL RIGHT, INITIALIZING OXYGEN SHIELD...
BOOP

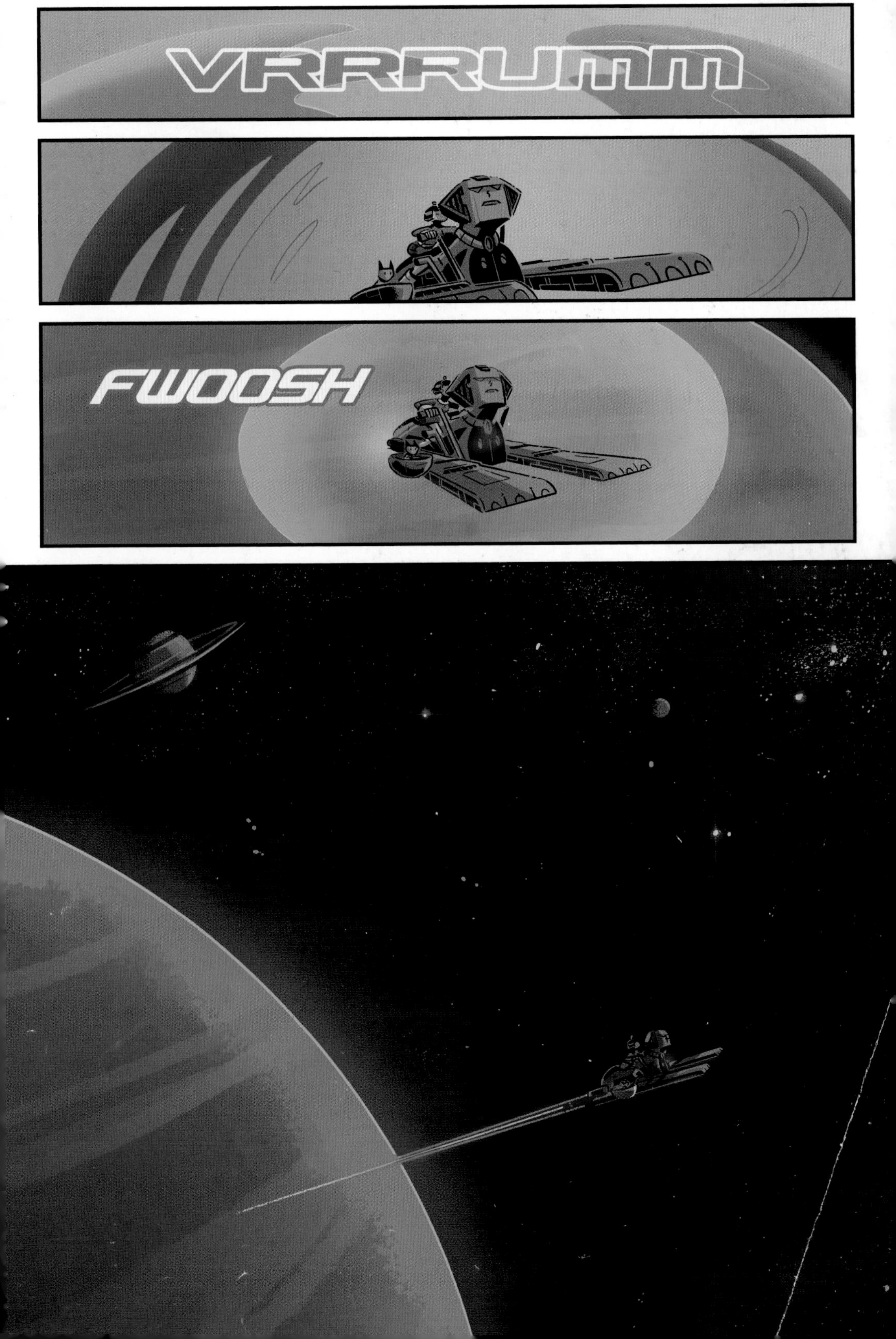
VRRRUMM
FWOOSH

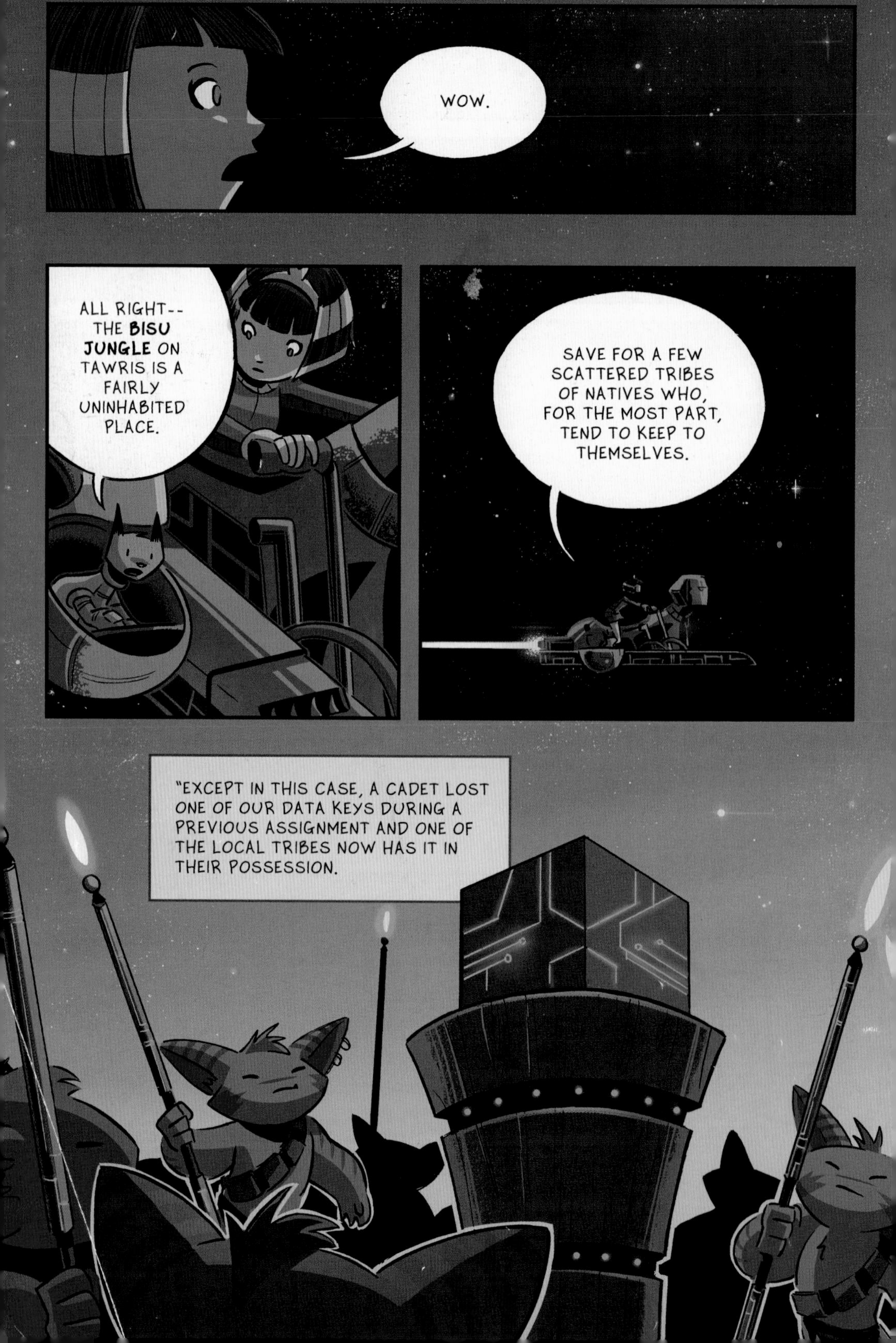
WOW.
ALL RIGHT--THE **BISU JUNGLE** ON TAWRIS IS A FAIRLY UNINHABITED PLACE.
SAVE FOR A FEW SCATTERED TRIBES OF NATIVES WHO, FOR THE MOST PART, TEND TO KEEP TO THEMSELVES.
"EXCEPT IN THIS CASE, A CADET LOST ONE OF OUR DATA KEYS DURING A PREVIOUS ASSIGNMENT AND ONE OF THE LOCAL TRIBES NOW HAS IT IN THEIR POSSESSION.

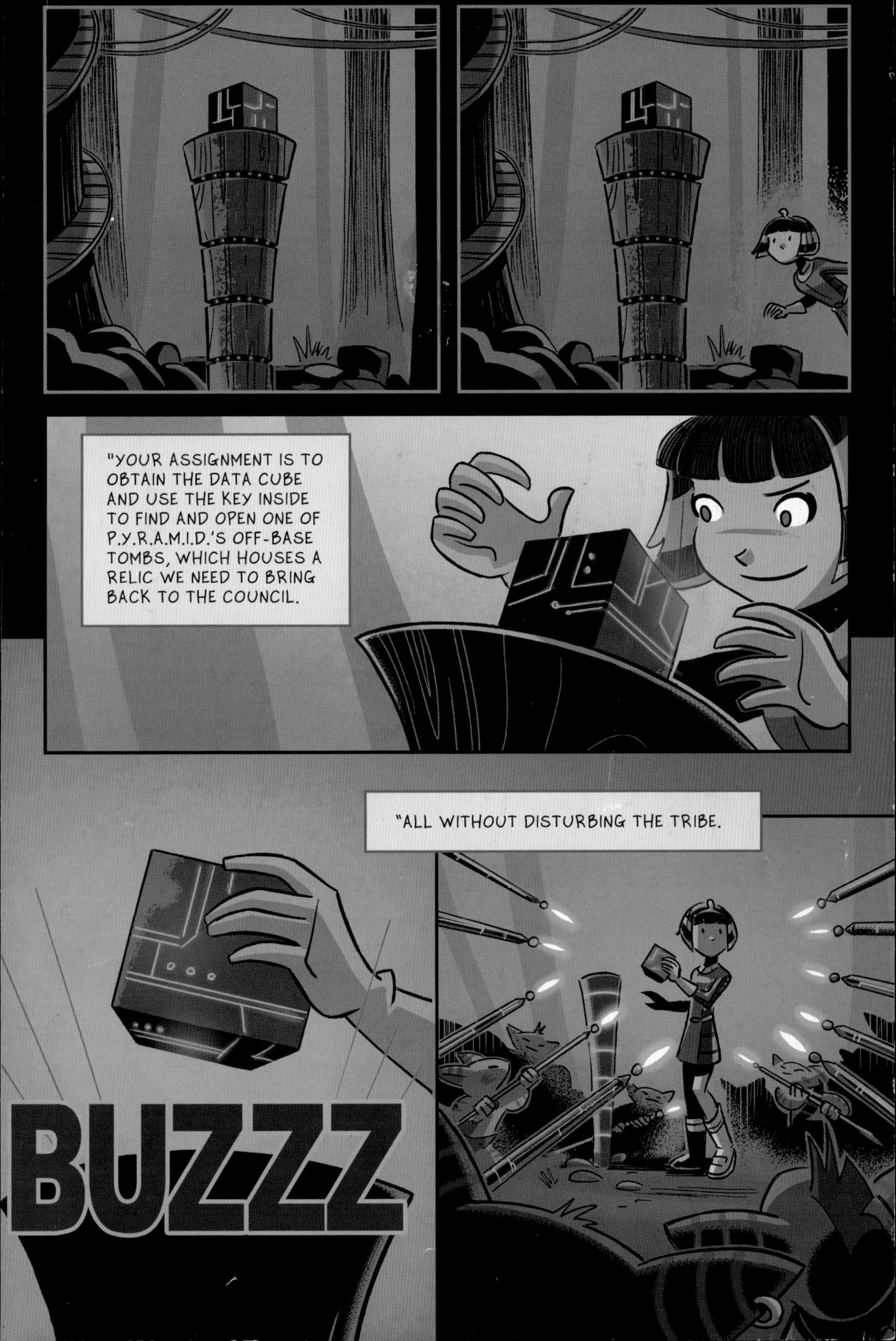
"YOUR ASSIGNMENT IS TO OBTAIN THE DATA CUBE AND USE THE KEY INSIDE TO FIND AND OPEN ONE OF P.Y.R.A.M.I.D.'S OFF-BASE TOMBS, WHICH HOUSES A RELIC WE NEED TO BRING BACK TO THE COUNCIL.
"ALL WITHOUT DISTURBING THE TRIBE.
BUZZZ

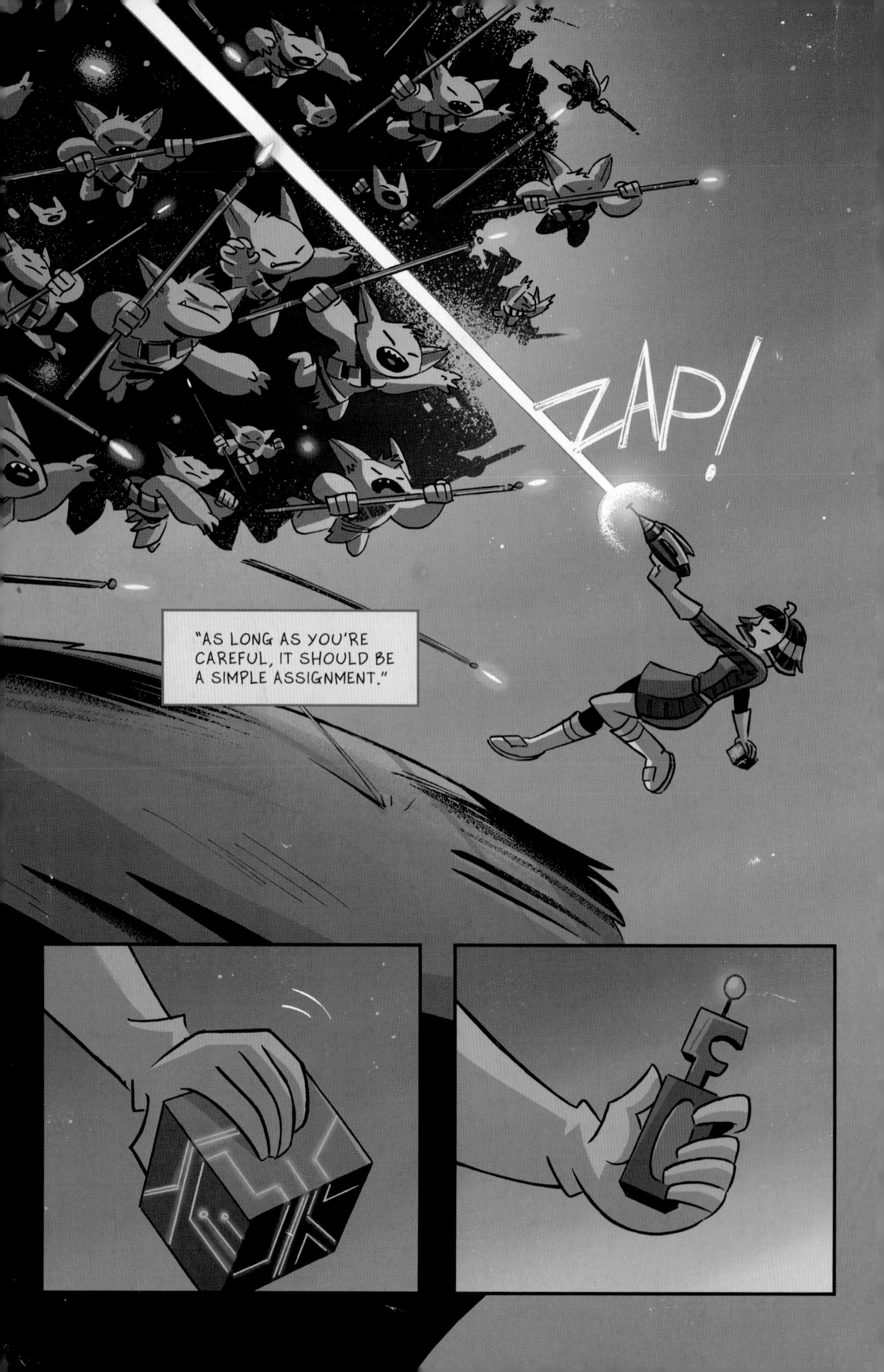
ZAP!
"AS LONG AS YOU'RE CAREFUL, IT SHOULD BE A SIMPLE ASSIGNMENT."

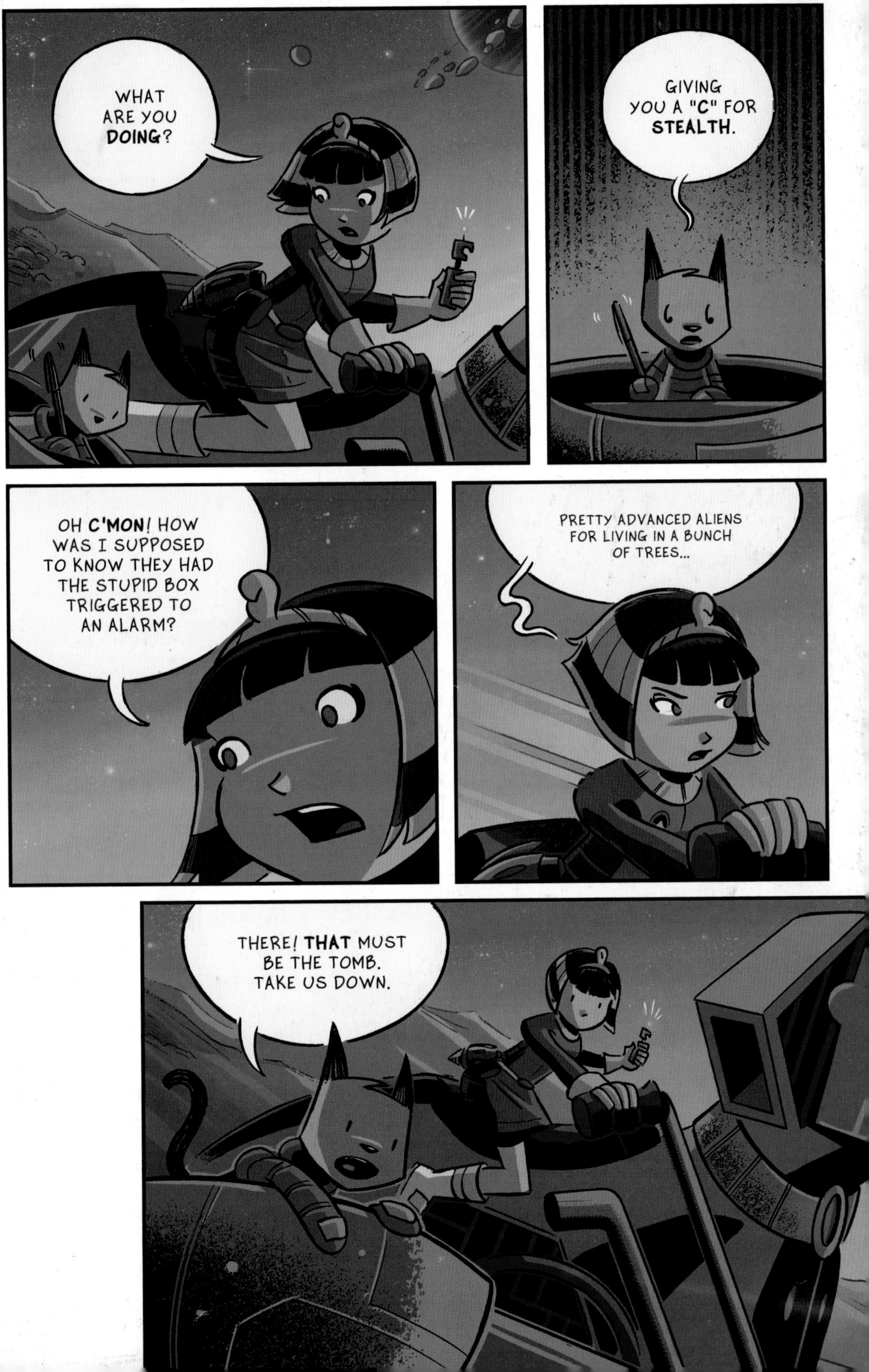
WHAT ARE YOU DOING?
GIVING YOU A "C" FOR STEALTH.
OH C'MON! HOW WAS I SUPPOSED TO KNOW THEY HAD THE STUPID BOX TRIGGERED TO AN ALARM?
PRETTY ADVANCED ALIENS FOR LIVING IN A BUNCH OF TREES...
THERE! THAT MUST BE THE TOMB. TAKE US DOWN.

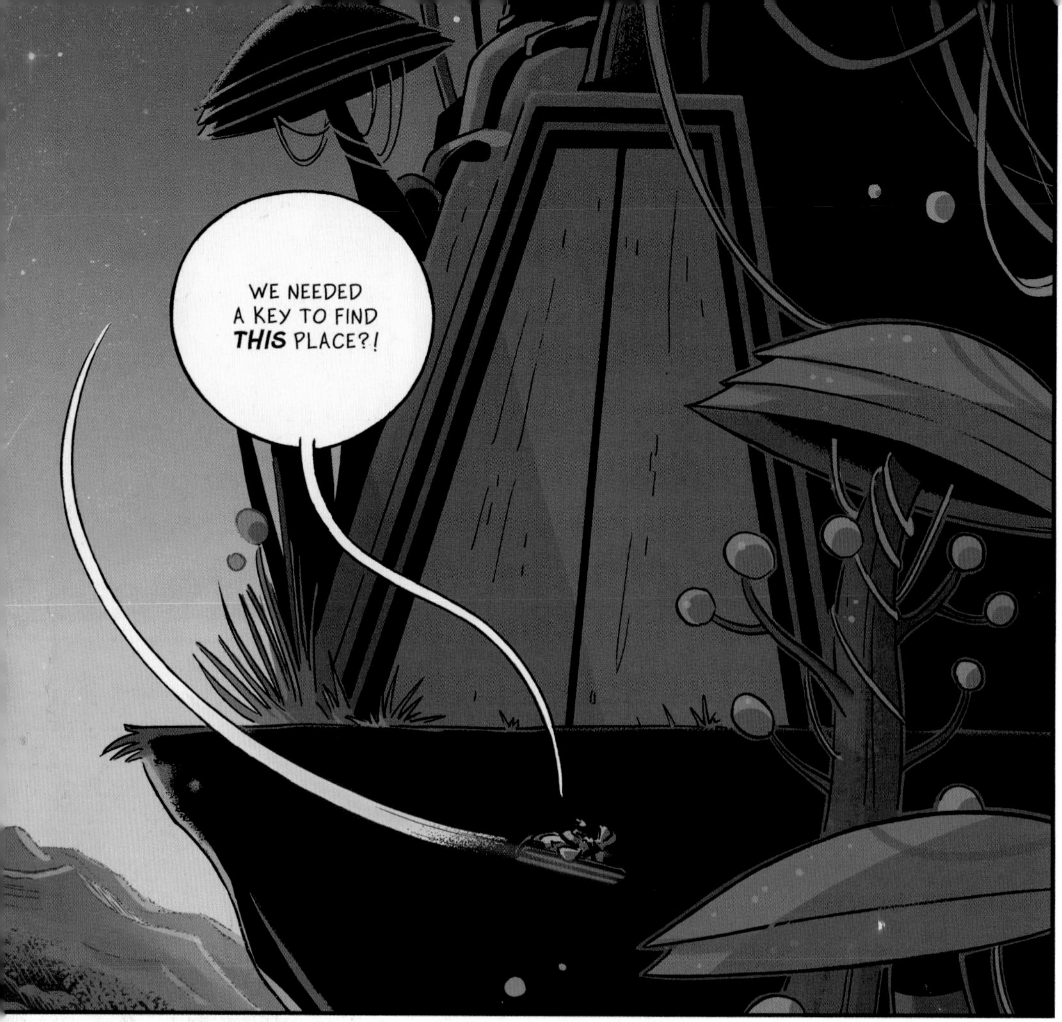
WE NEEDED A KEY TO FIND THIS PLACE?!

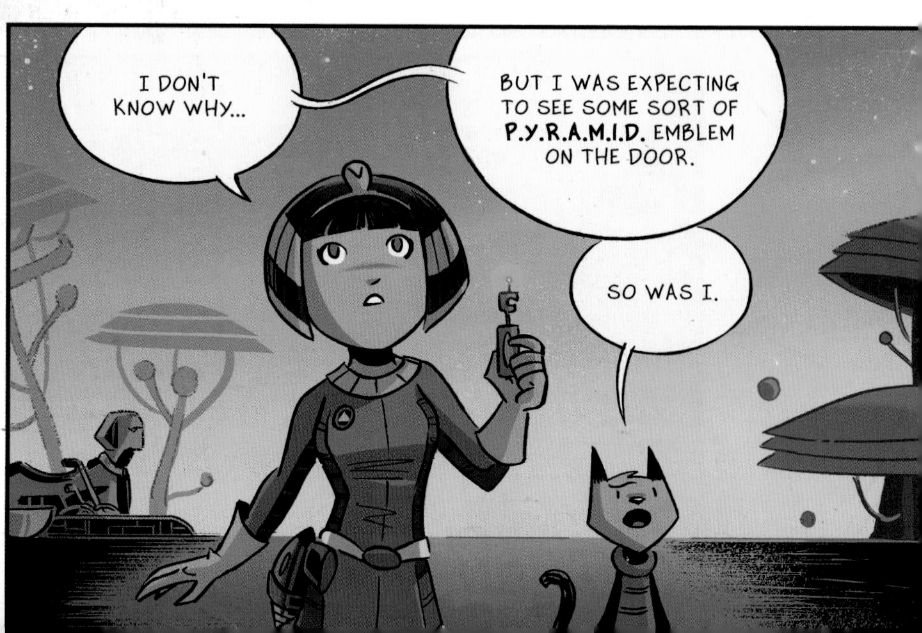
I DON'T KNOW WHY...
BUT I WAS EXPECTING TO SEE SOME SORT OF P.Y.R.A.M.I.D. EMBLEM ON THE DOOR.
SO WAS I.

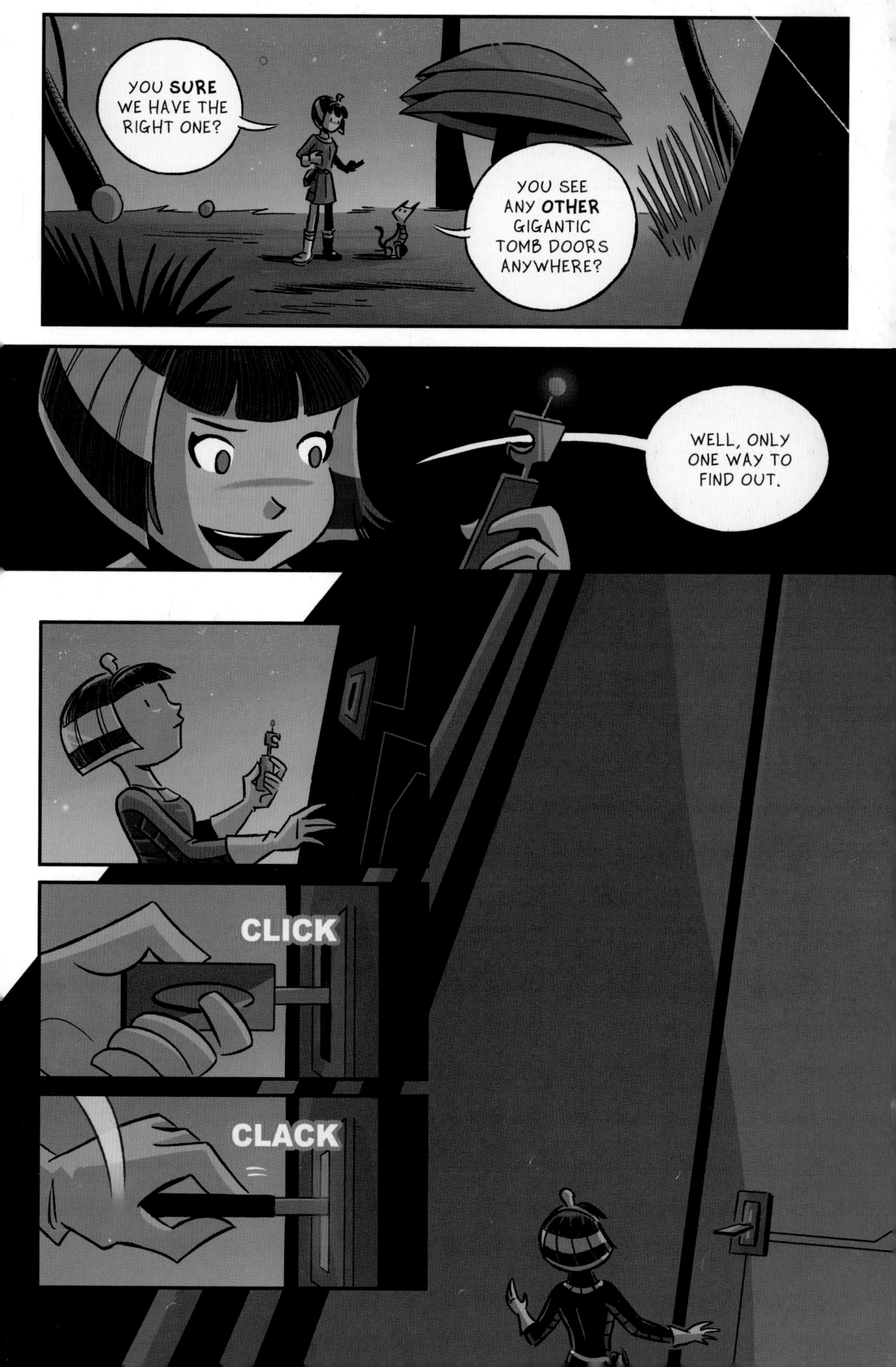
YOU **SURE** WE HAVE THE RIGHT ONE?
YOU SEE ANY **OTHER** GIGANTIC TOMB DOORS ANYWHERE?
WELL, ONLY ONE WAY TO FIND OUT.
CLICK
CLACK

I DON'T KNOW WHY I THOUGHT THAT WOULD WORK.

RUMBLE!

WHOA!

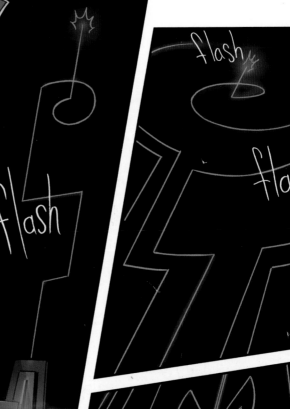

flash

flash

flash

fla

flas

flash

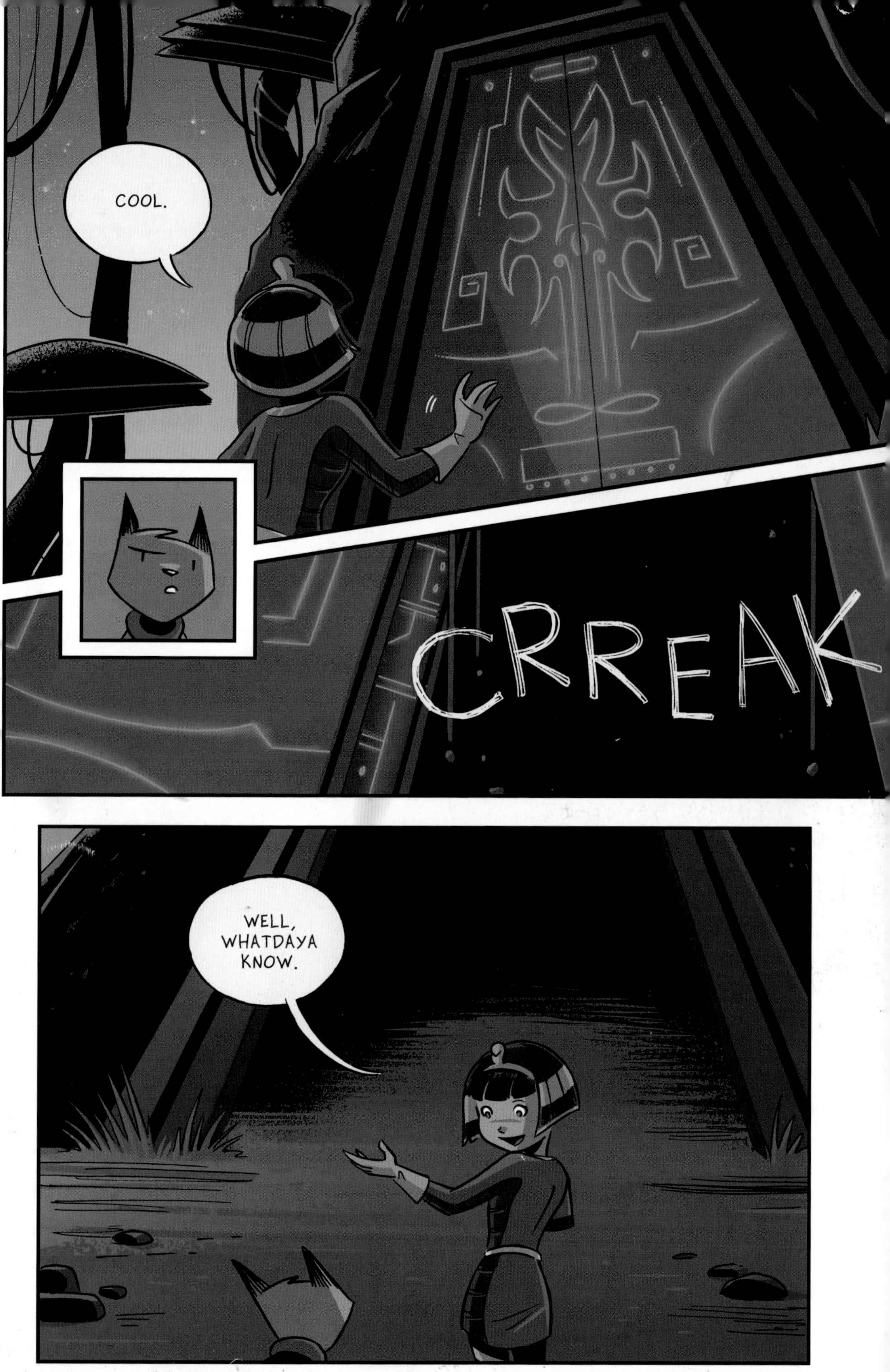
COOL.
CRREAK
WELL, WHATDAYA KNOW.

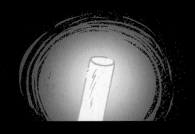

IT'S UPSETTING THAT I'M NOT EVEN **SIXTEEN** YET AND I'VE ALREADY BEEN IN MORE TOMBS THAN ANYONE SHOULD BE IN FOR **ONE** LIFETIME.

THAT'S **RIGHT.** TOMBS WERE MUCH DIFFERENT IN YOUR TIME.

WHY CALL THEM TOMBS NOW?

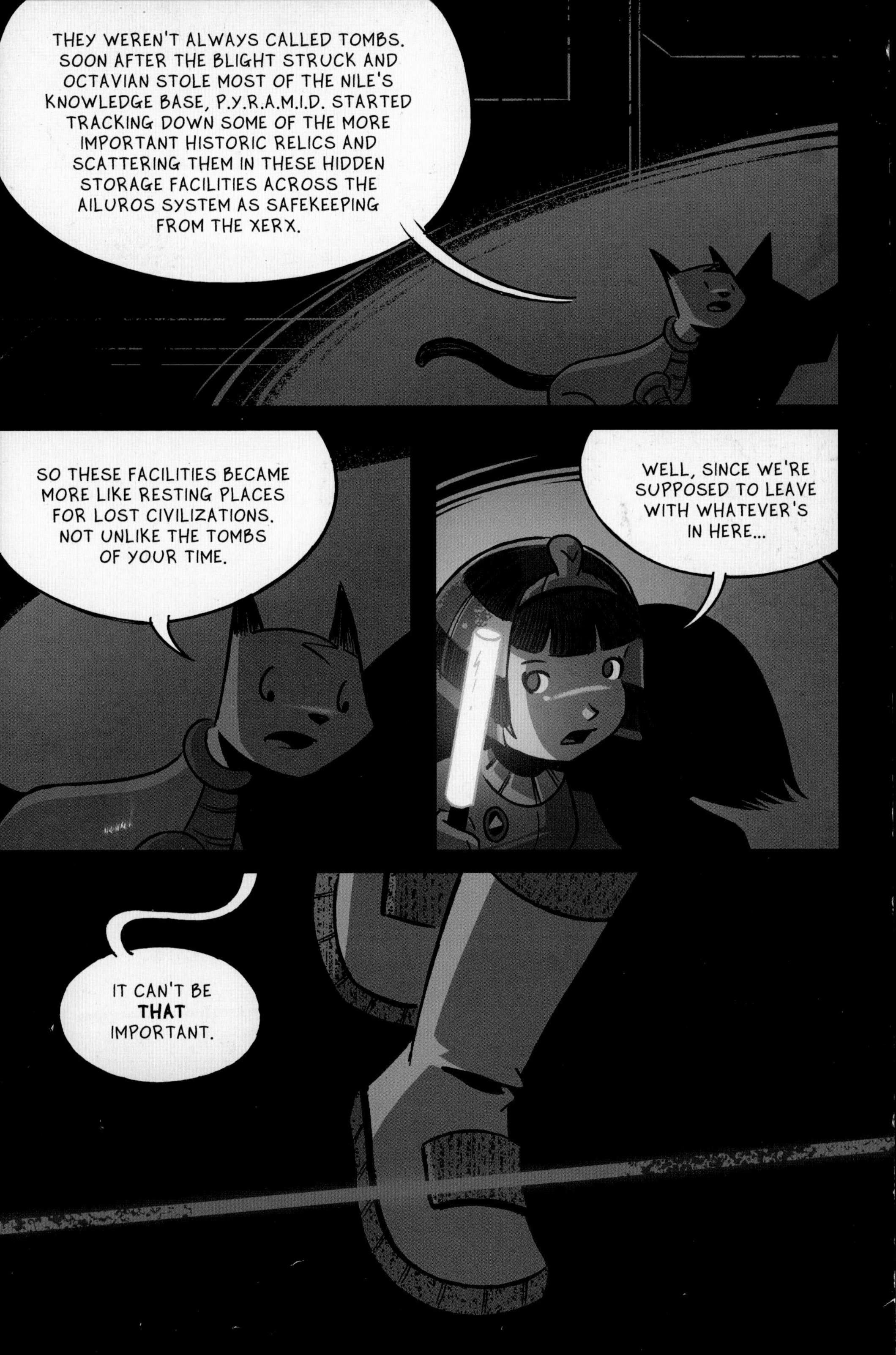
THEY WEREN'T ALWAYS CALLED TOMBS. SOON AFTER THE BLIGHT STRUCK AND OCTAVIAN STOLE MOST OF THE NILE'S KNOWLEDGE BASE, P.Y.R.A.M.I.D. STARTED TRACKING DOWN SOME OF THE MORE IMPORTANT HISTORIC RELICS AND SCATTERING THEM IN THESE HIDDEN STORAGE FACILITIES ACROSS THE AILUROS SYSTEM AS SAFEKEEPING FROM THE XERX.
SO THESE FACILITIES BECAME MORE LIKE RESTING PLACES FOR LOST CIVILIZATIONS. NOT UNLIKE THE TOMBS OF YOUR TIME.
WELL, SINCE WE'RE SUPPOSED TO LEAVE WITH WHATEVER'S IN HERE...
IT CAN'T BE **THAT** IMPORTANT.

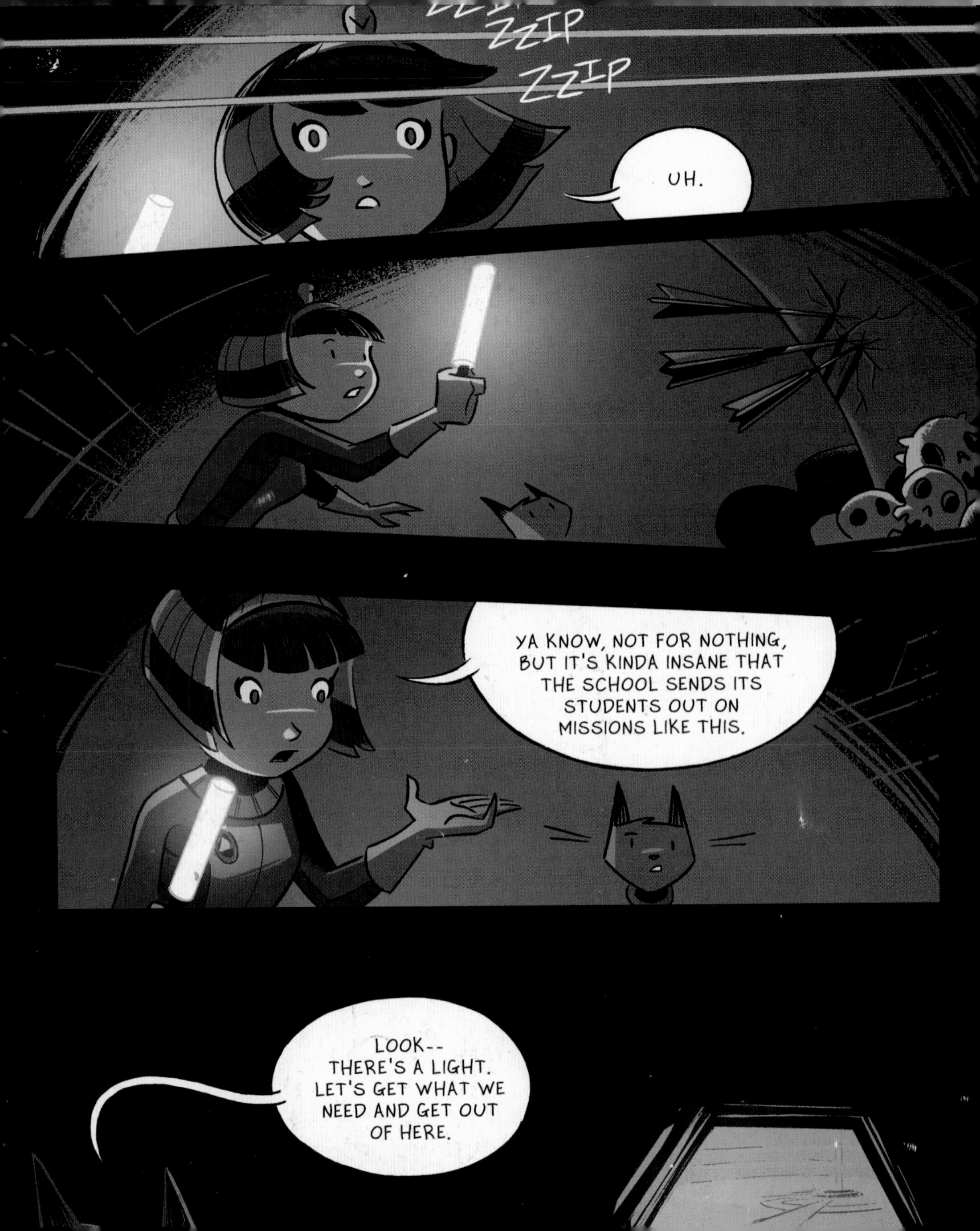
ZZIP
ZZIP
UH.
YA KNOW, NOT FOR NOTHING, BUT IT'S KINDA INSANE THAT THE SCHOOL SENDS ITS STUDENTS OUT ON MISSIONS LIKE THIS.
LOOK-- THERE'S A LIGHT. LET'S GET WHAT WE NEED AND GET OUT OF HERE.

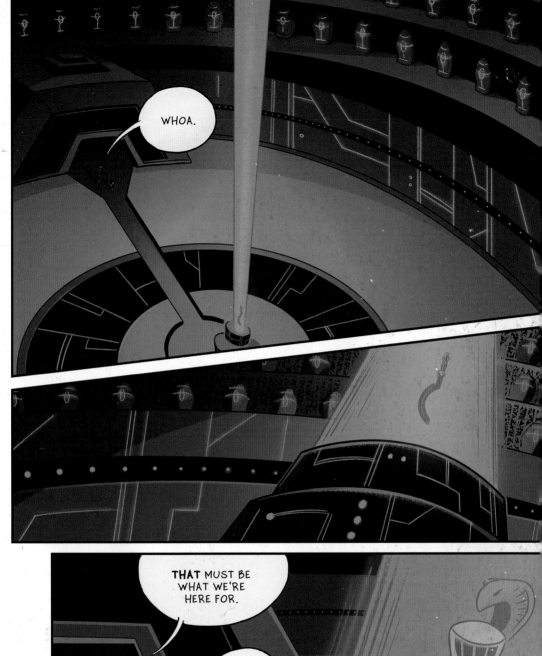

WHOA.

THAT MUST BE WHAT WE'RE HERE FOR.

CLEO, WAIT.

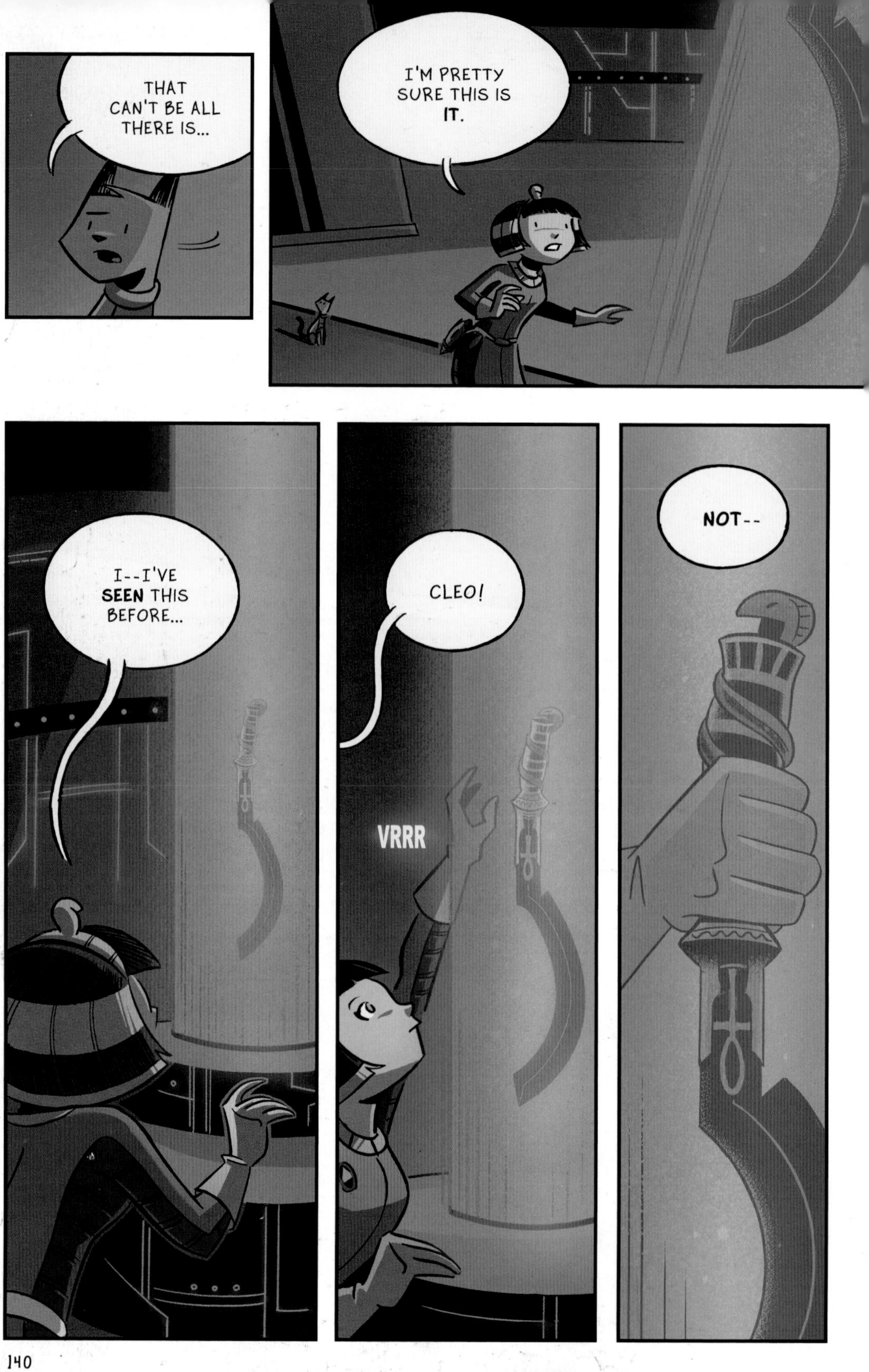
THAT CAN'T BE ALL THERE IS...
I'M PRETTY SURE THIS IS **IT**.
I--I'VE **SEEN** THIS BEFORE...
CLEO!
VRRR
NOT--

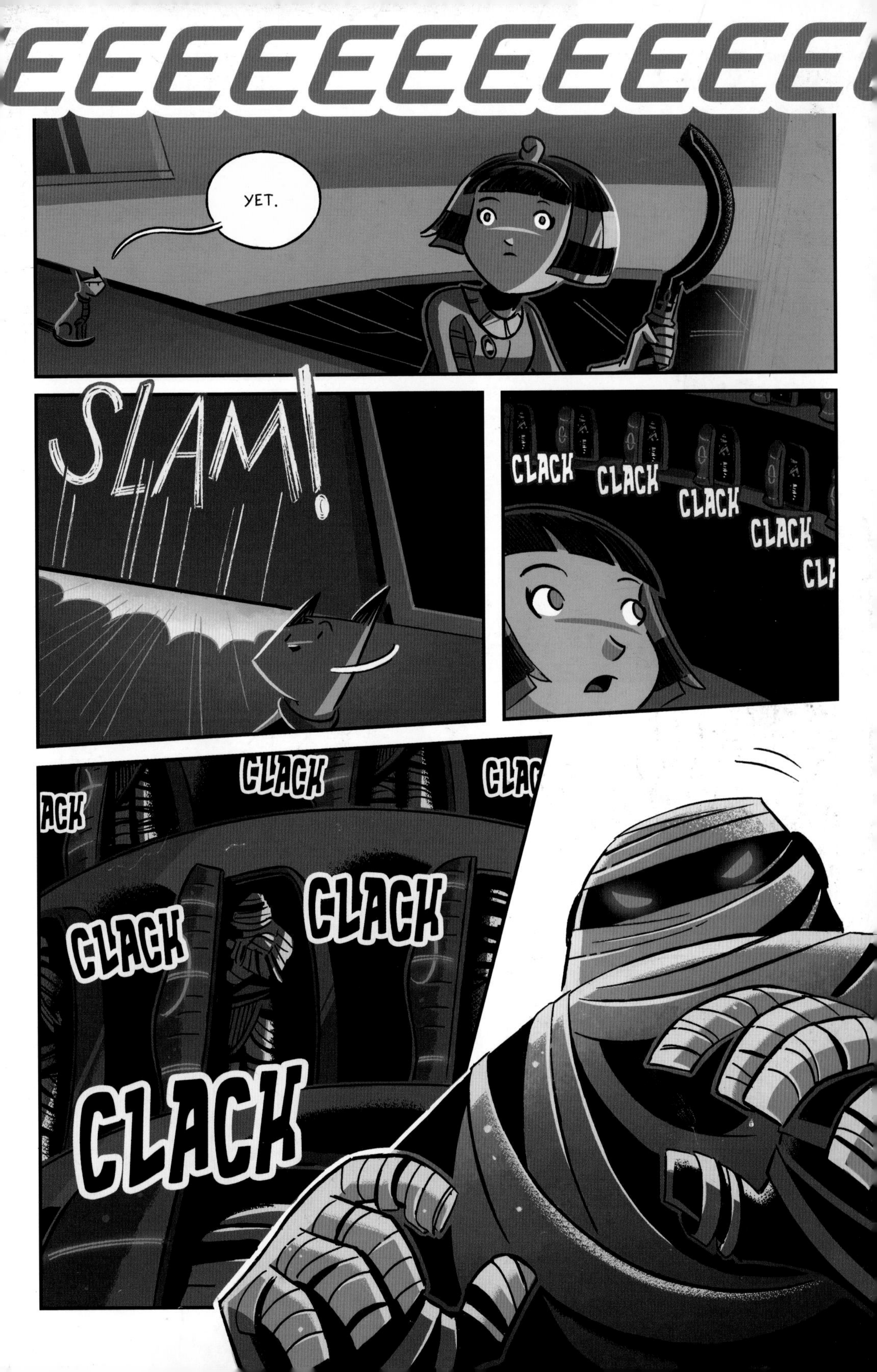
EEEEEEEEEEEE
YET.
SLAM!
CLACK
CLACK
CLACK
CLACK
CLACK
CLACK
CLACK
CLACK
CLACK
CLACK

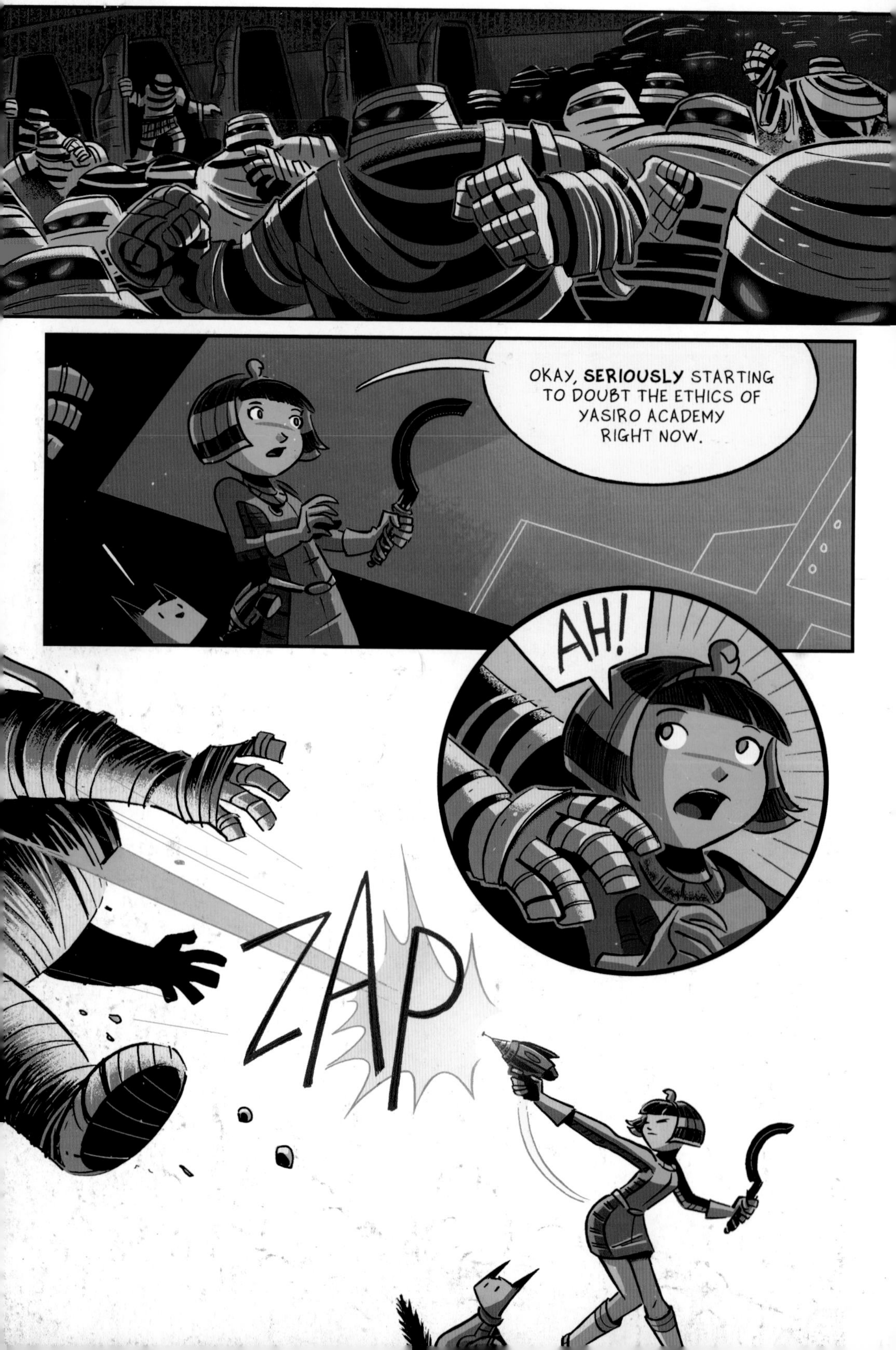
OKAY, SERIOUSLY STARTING TO DOUBT THE ETHICS OF YASIRO ACADEMY RIGHT NOW.
AH!
ZAP

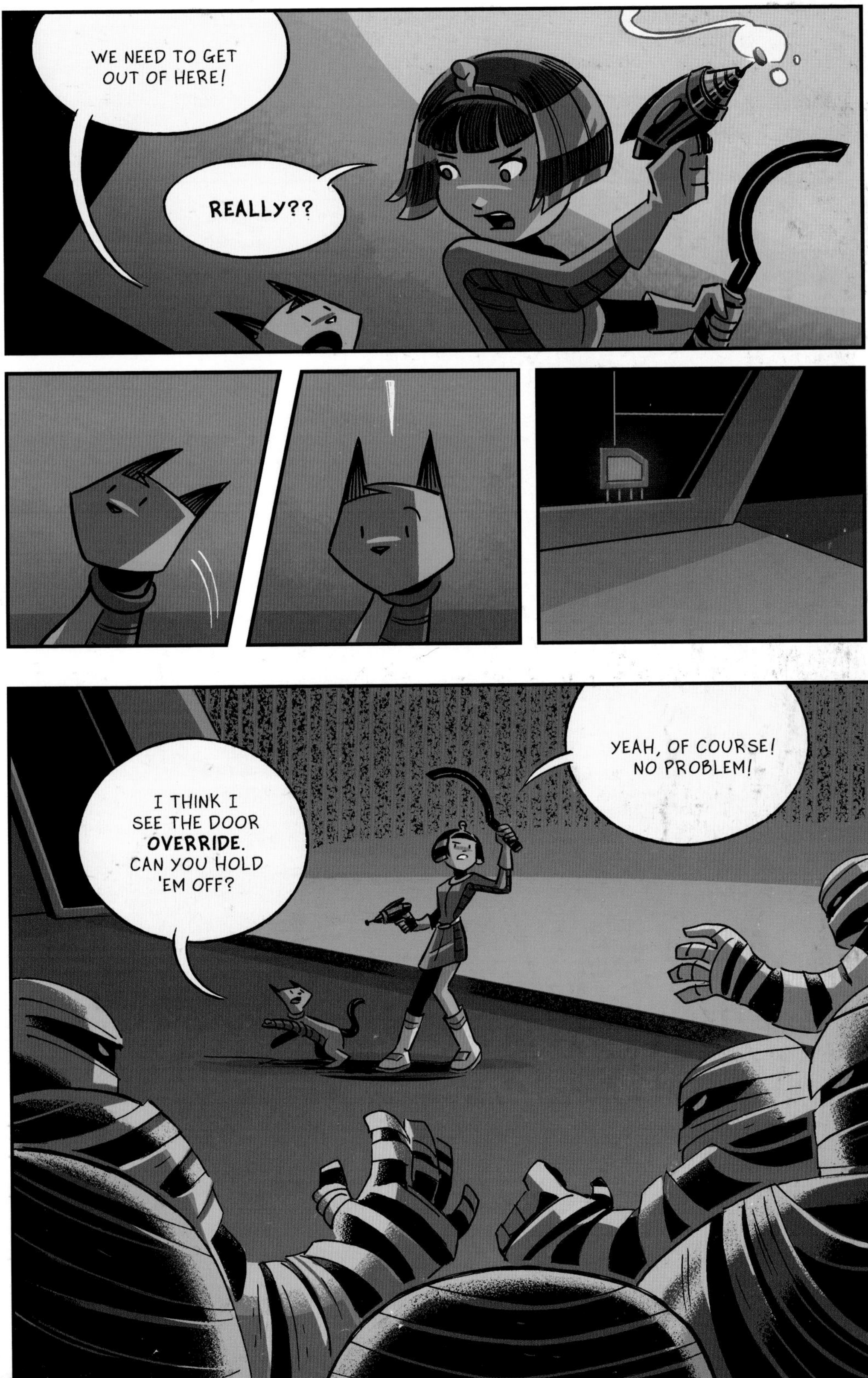

WE NEED TO GET OUT OF HERE!
REALLY??
I THINK I SEE THE DOOR **OVERRIDE.** CAN YOU HOLD 'EM OFF?
YEAH, OF COURSE! NO PROBLEM!

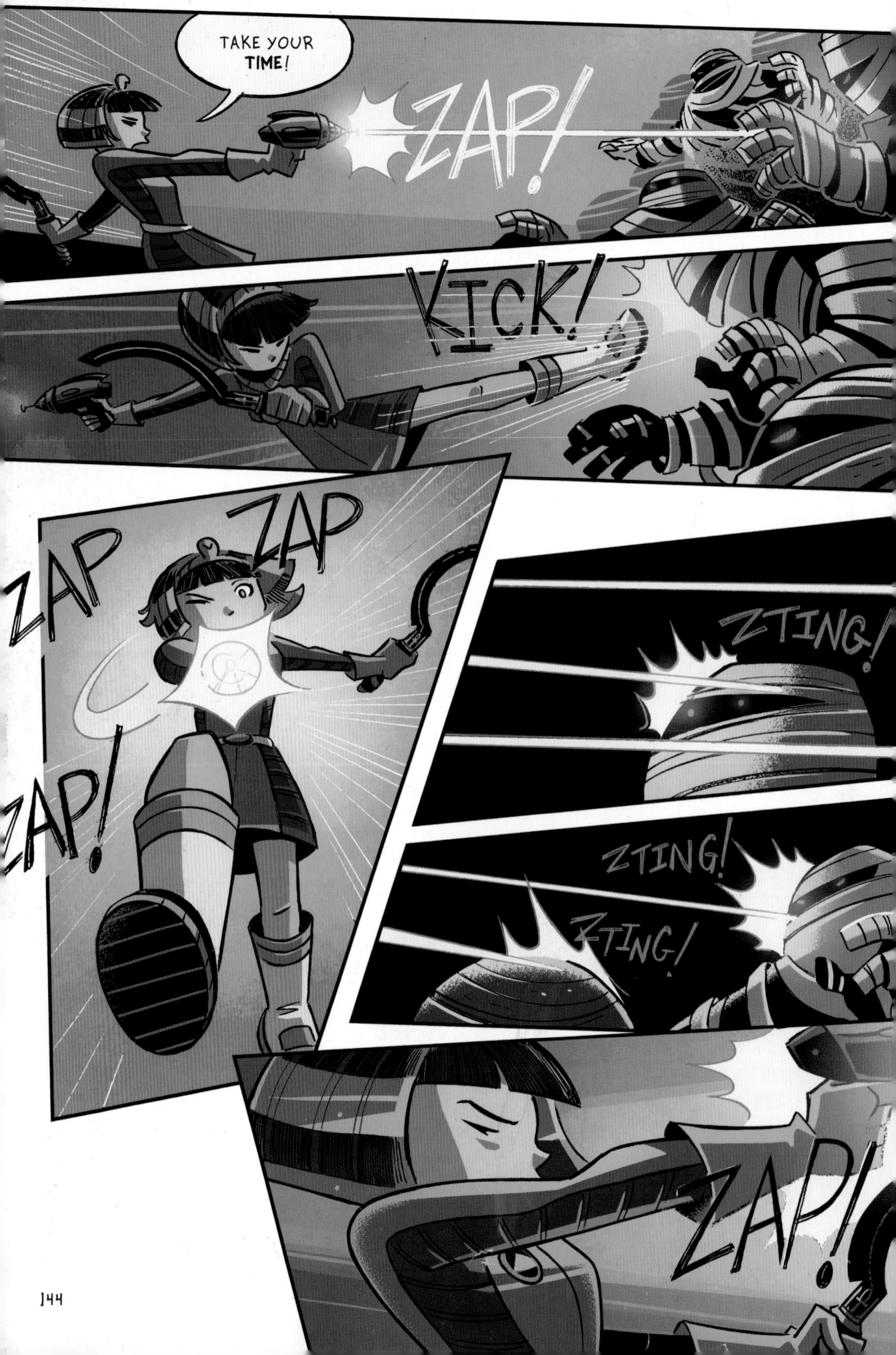
TAKE YOUR TIME!
ZAP!
KICK!
ZAP
ZAP
ZAP!
ZTING!
ZTING!
ZTING!
ZAP!

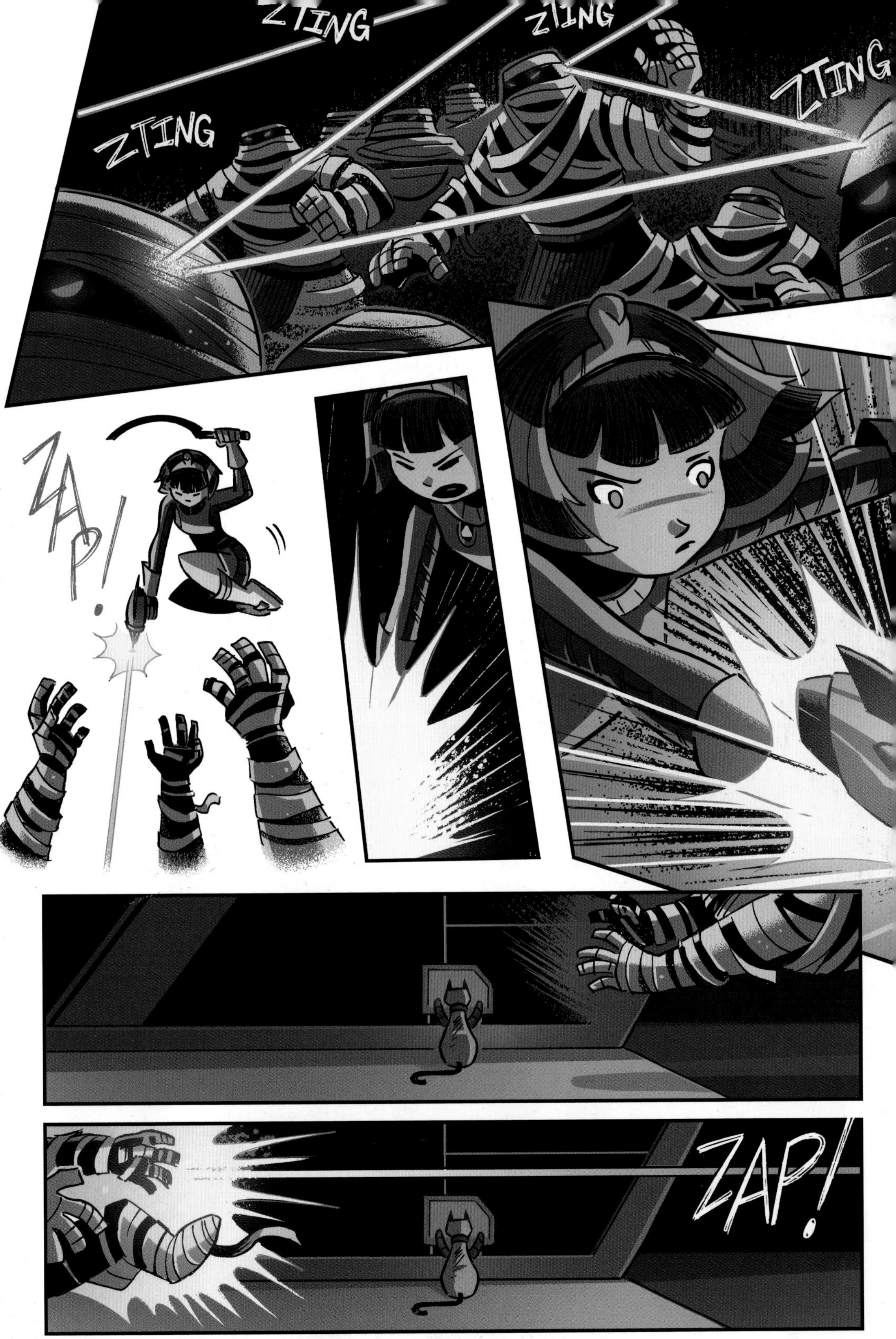
ZTING
ZTING
ZTING
ZTING
ZAP!
ZAP!

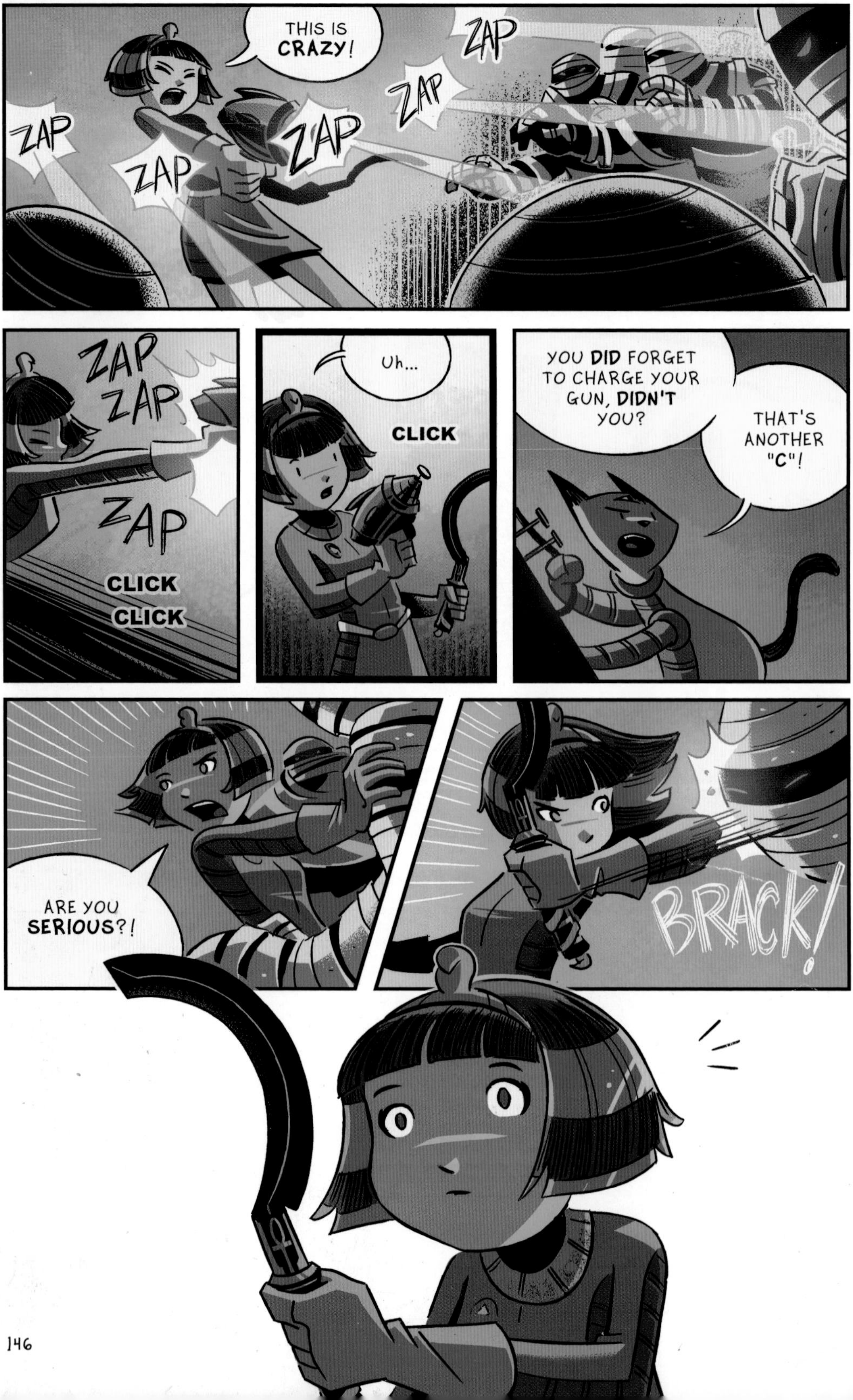

THIS IS **CRAZY**!
ZAP
ZAP
ZAP
ZAP
ZAP
ZAP
ZAP
ZAP
ZAP
CLICK
CLICK
Uh...
CLICK
YOU **DID** FORGET TO CHARGE YOUR GUN, **DIDN'T** YOU?
THAT'S ANOTHER **"C"**!
ARE YOU **SERIOUS**?!
BRACK!

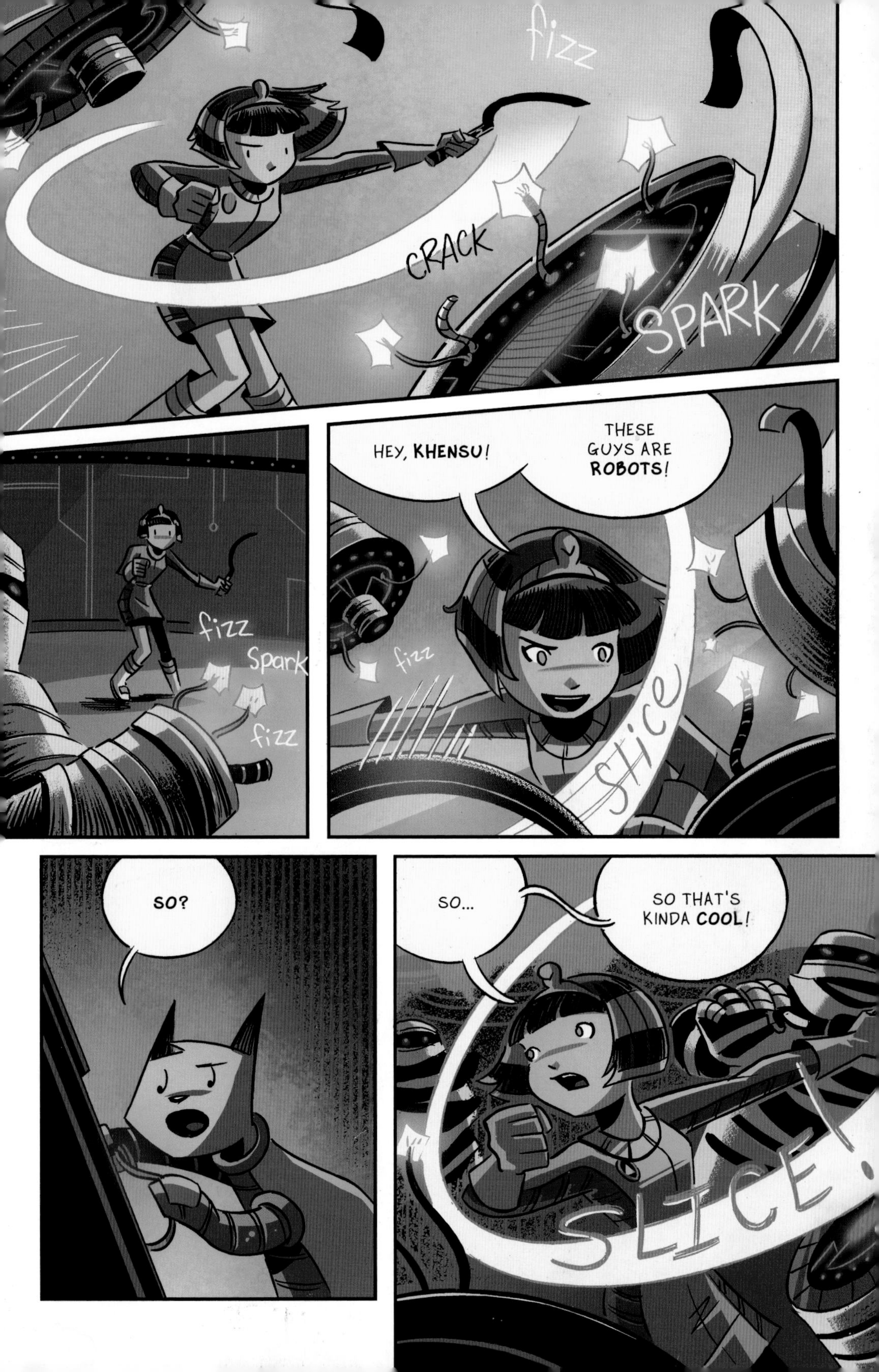
fizz
CRACK
SPARK
fizz
Spark
fizz
HEY, KHENSU!
THESE GUYS ARE ROBOTS!
fizz
Slice
SO?
SO...
SO THAT'S KINDA COOL!
SLICE!

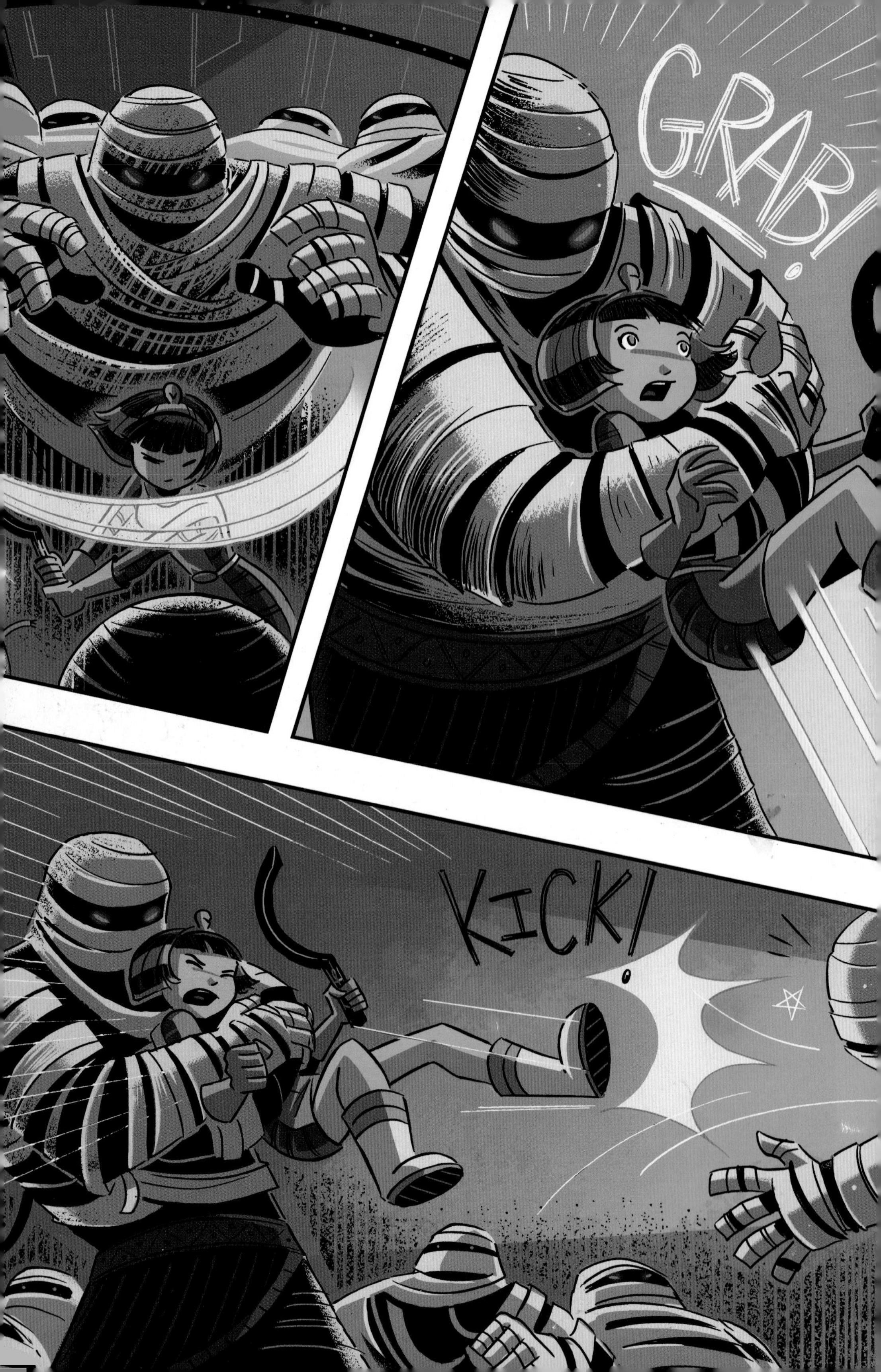
GRAB!
KICK!

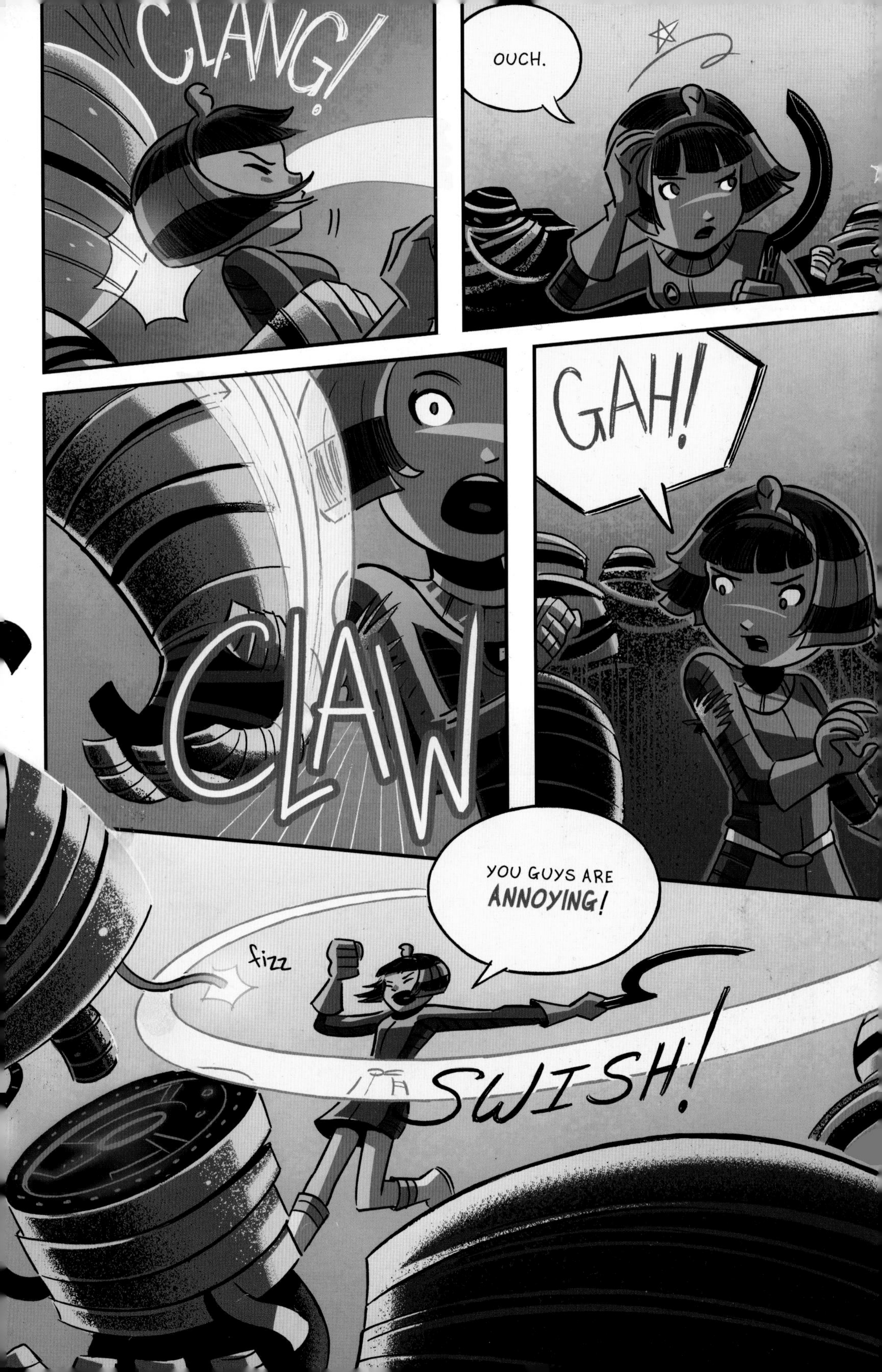
CLANG!
OUCH.
CLAW
GAH!
YOU GUYS ARE ANNOYING!
fizz
SWISH!

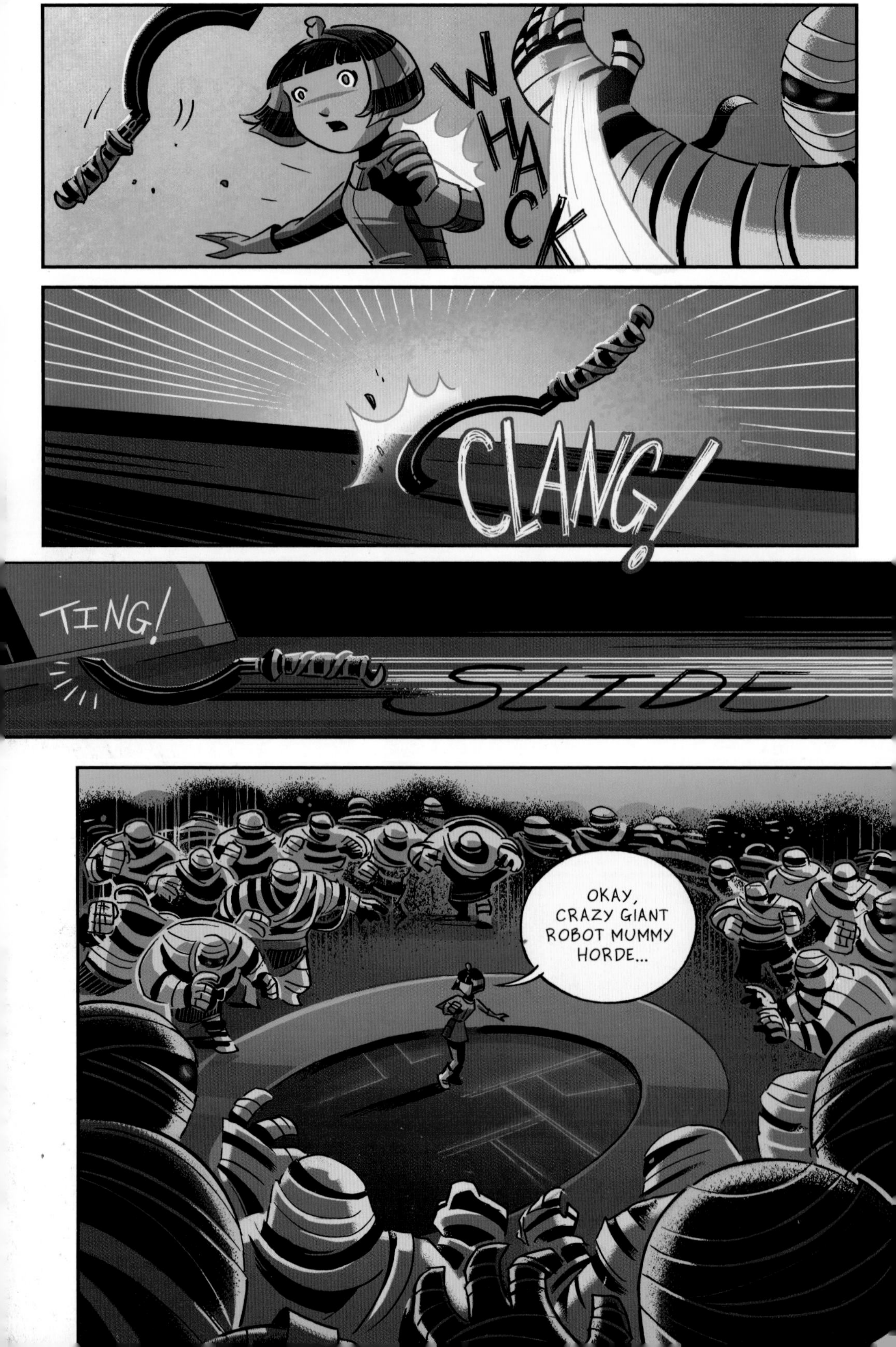
WHACK
CLANG!
TING!
SLIDE
OKAY, CRAZY GIANT ROBOT MUMMY HORDE...

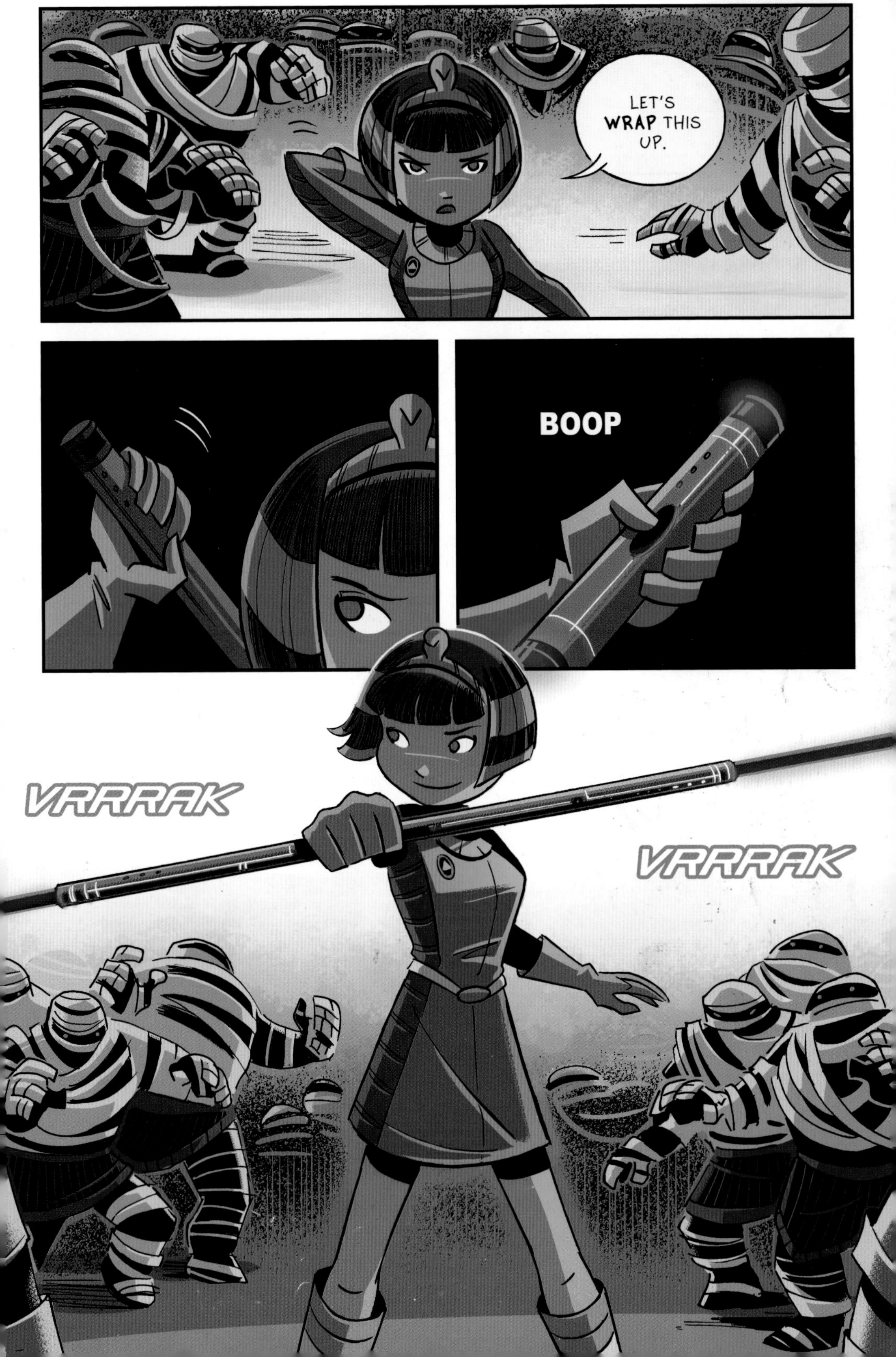
LET'S **WRAP** THIS UP.
BOOP
VRRRAK
VRRRAK

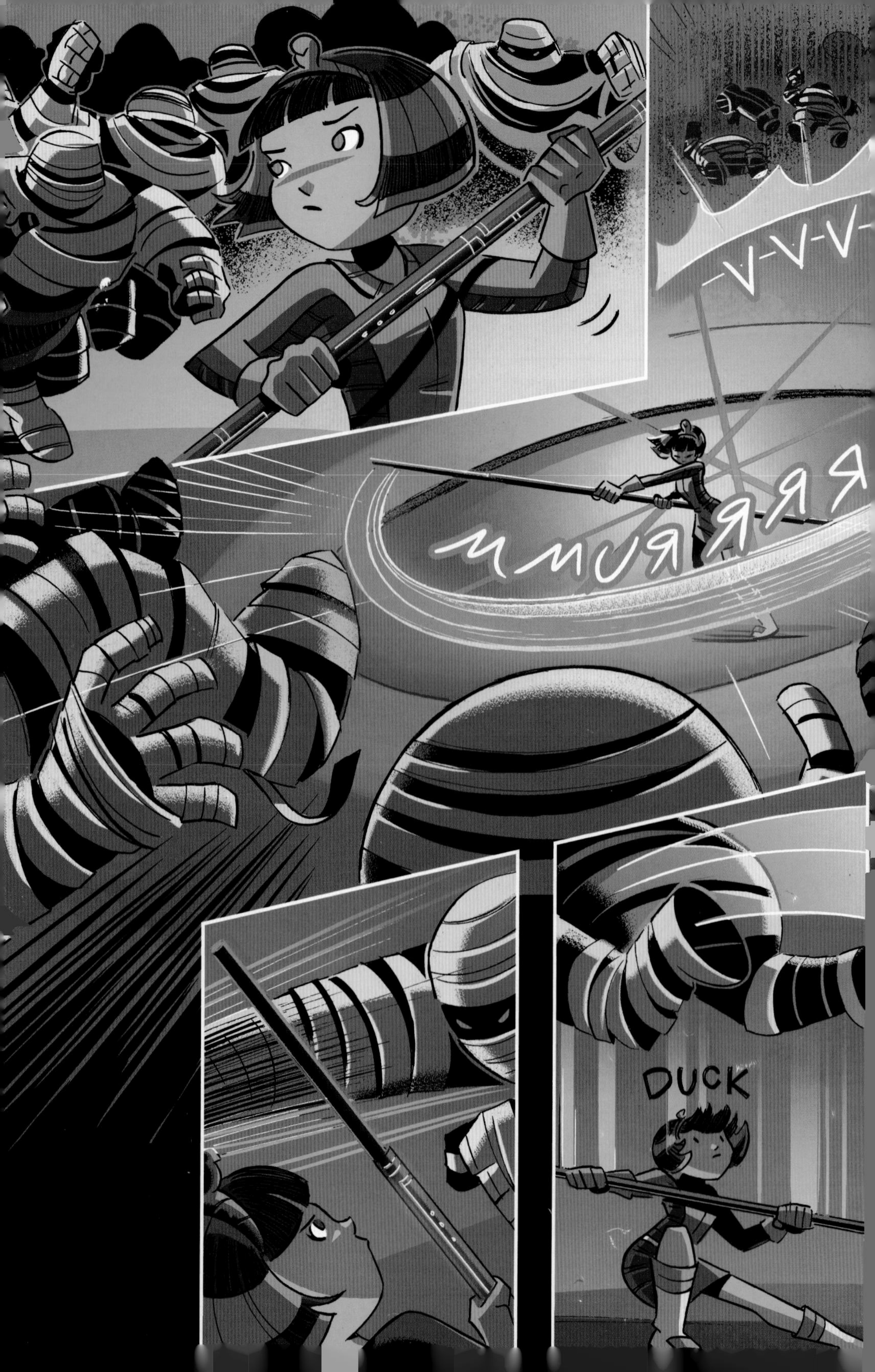
-V-V-V-V-
DUCK

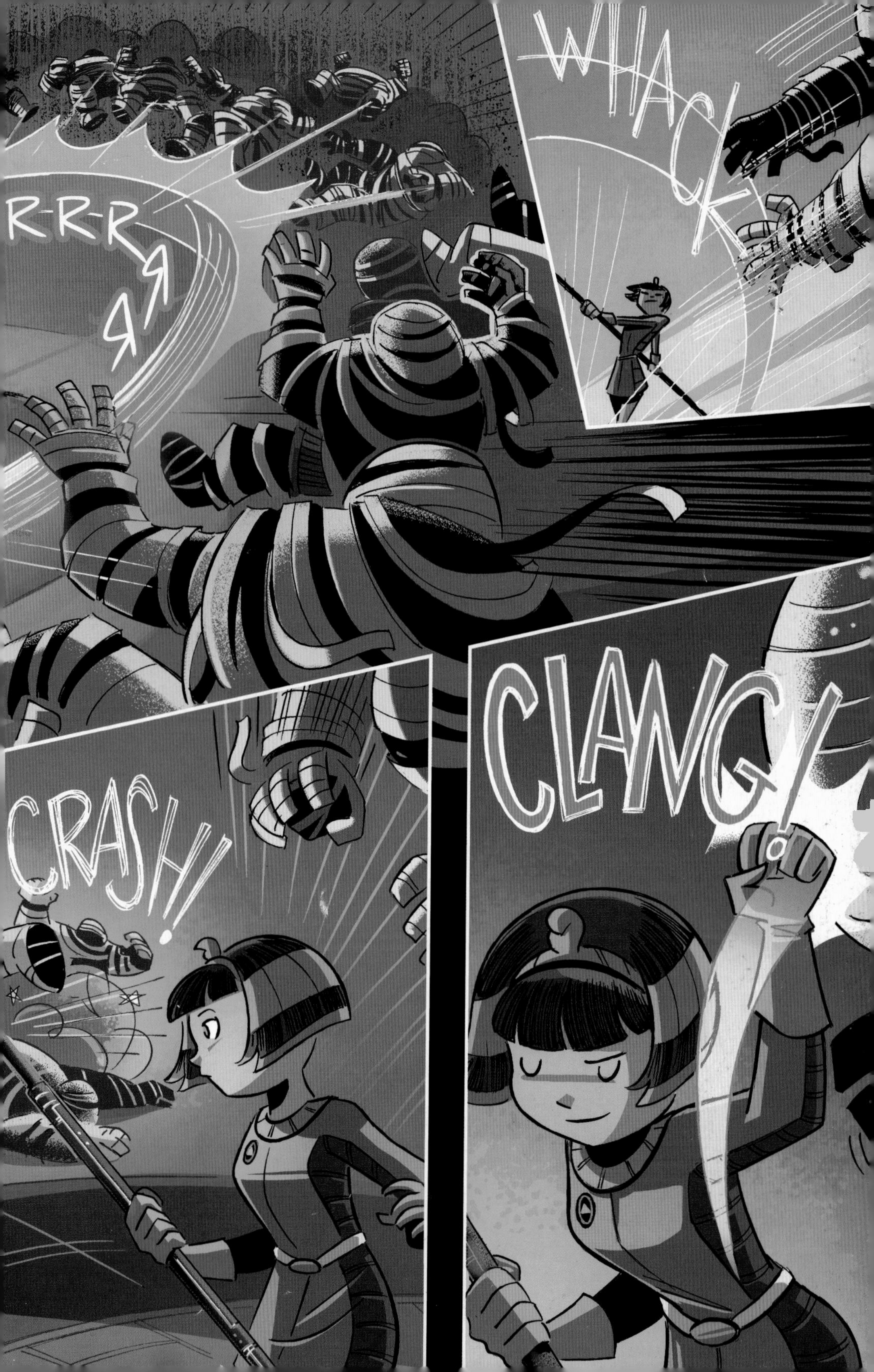
R-R-R R R R
WHACK
CRASH!
CLANG!

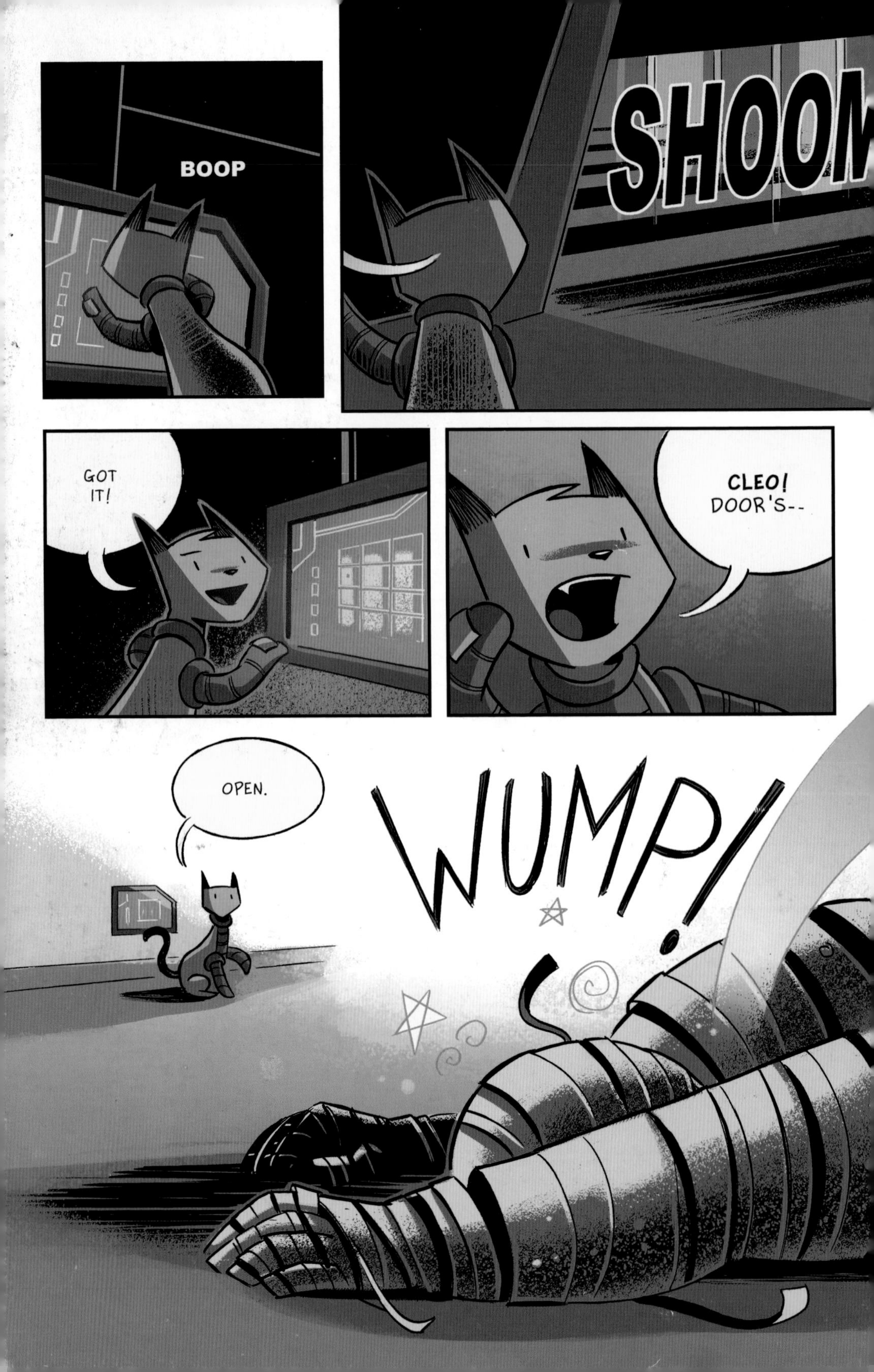
BOOP
SHOOM
GOT IT!
CLEO! DOOR'S--
OPEN.
WUMP!

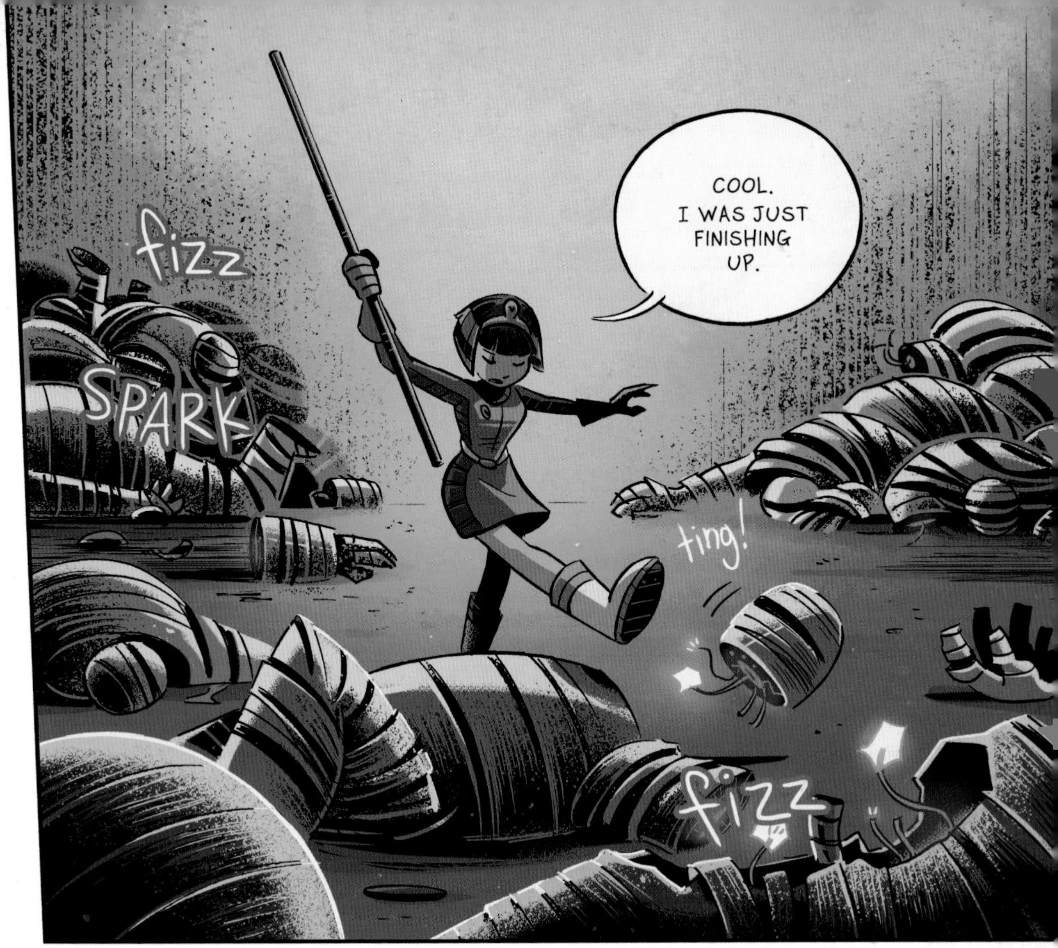
fizz
SPARK
COOL.
I WAS JUST
FINISHING
UP.
ting!
fizz

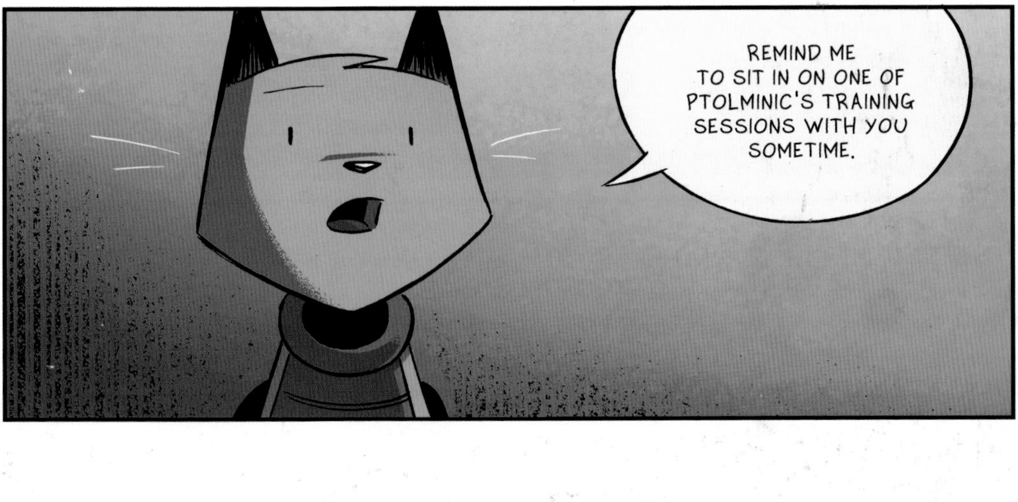
REMIND ME
TO SIT IN ON ONE OF
PTOLMINIC'S TRAINING
SESSIONS WITH YOU
SOMETIME.

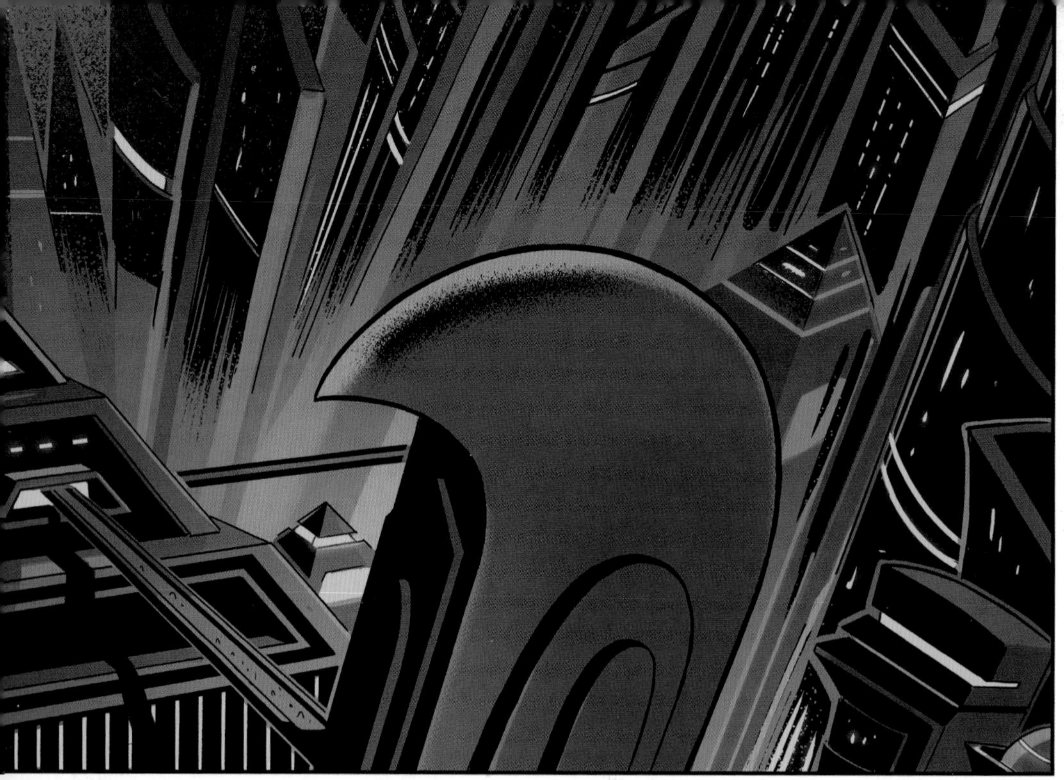

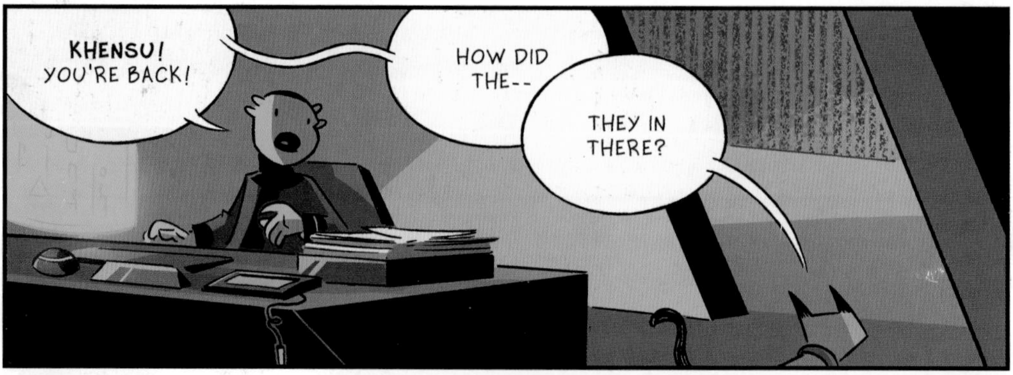
KHENSU! YOU'RE BACK!
HOW DID THE--
THEY IN THERE?

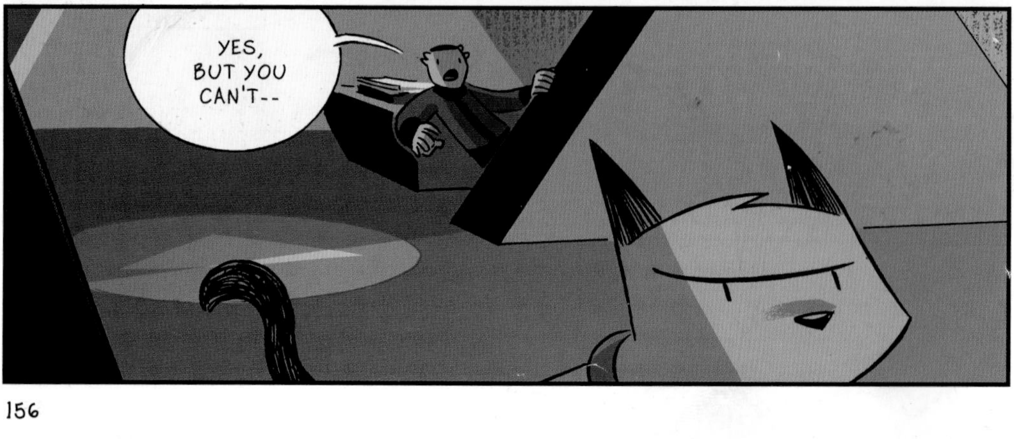
YES, BUT YOU CAN'T--

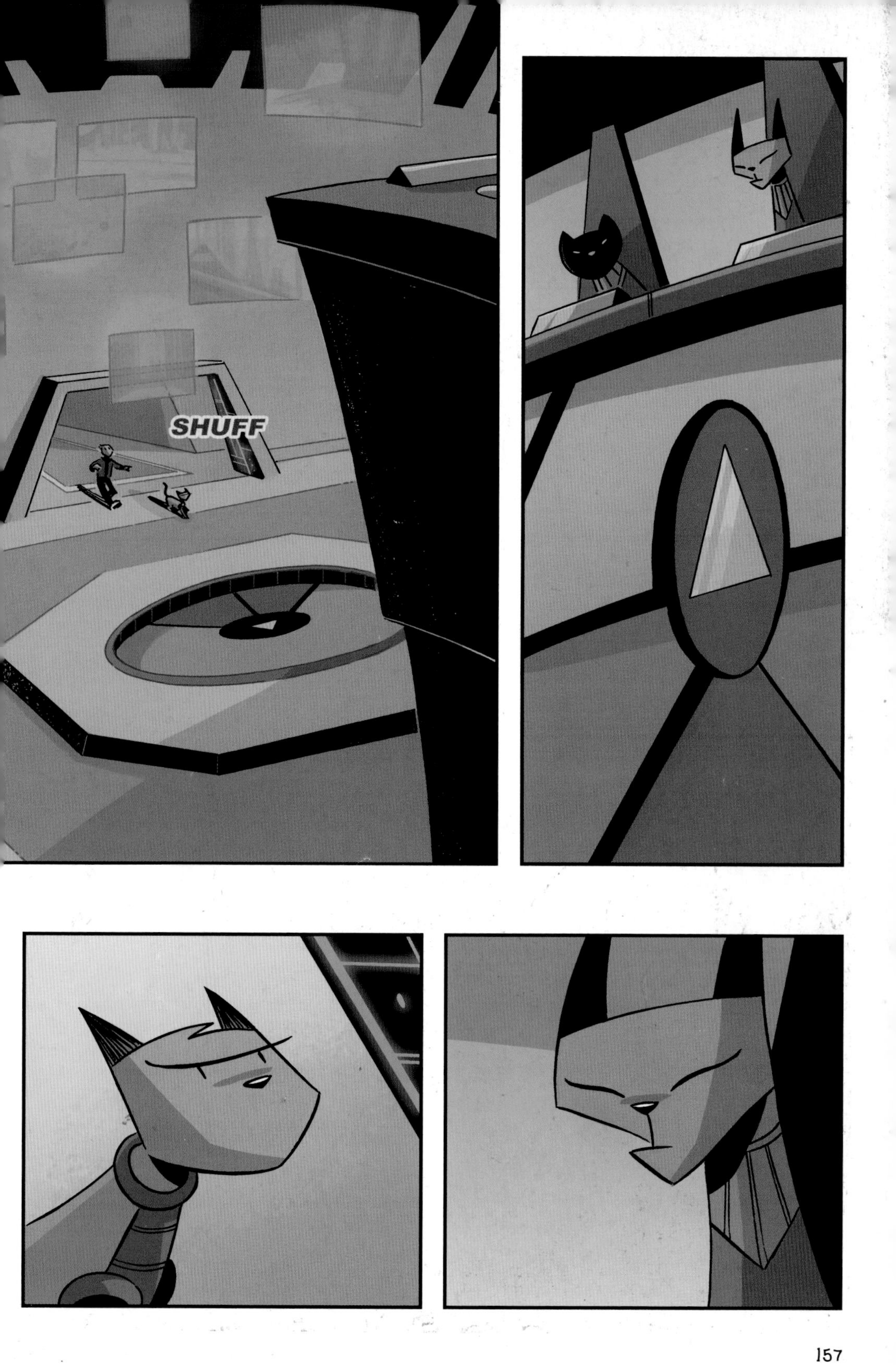
SHUFF

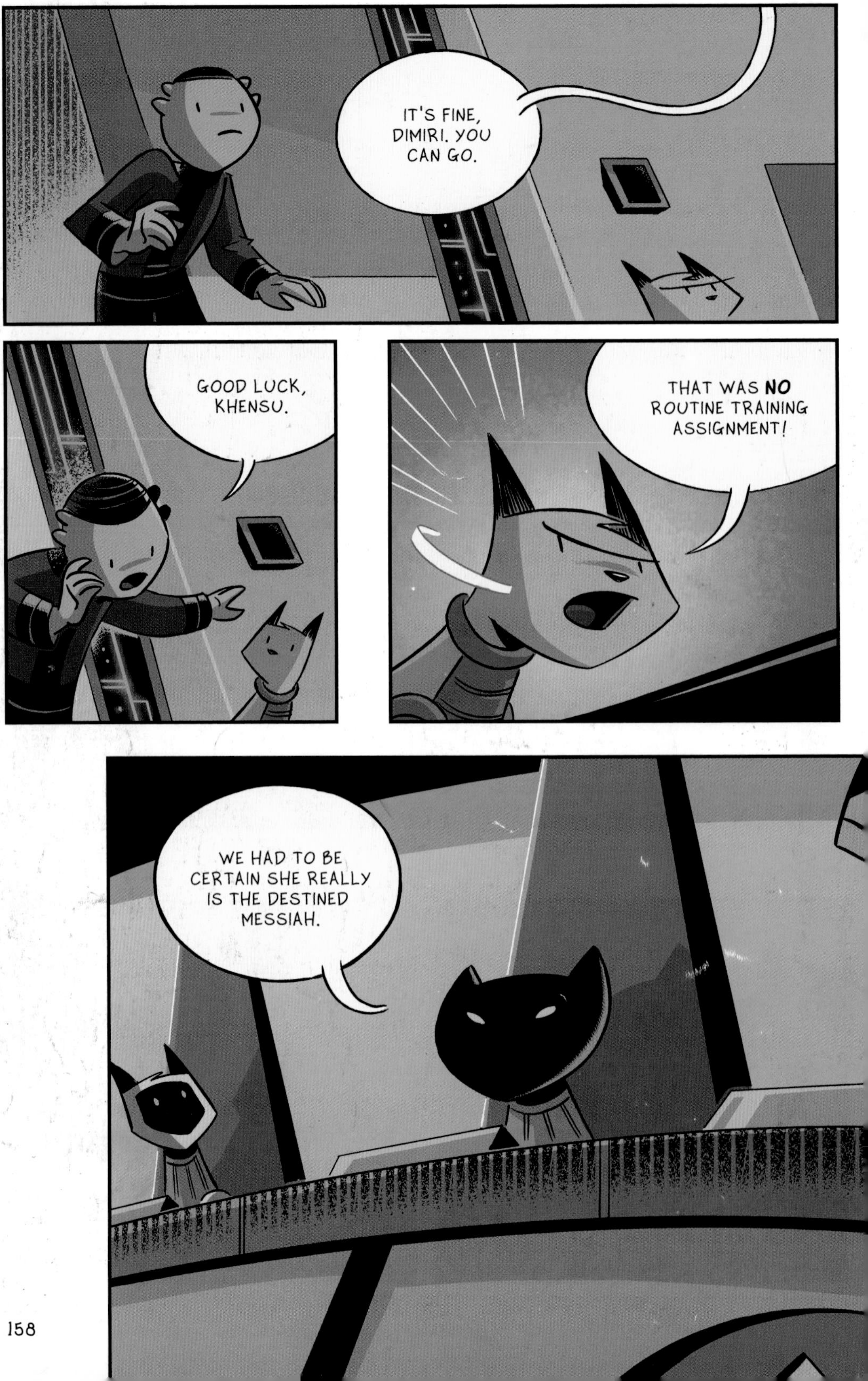
IT'S FINE, DIMIRI. YOU CAN GO.
GOOD LUCK, KHENSU.
THAT WAS **NO** ROUTINE TRAINING ASSIGNMENT!
WE HAD TO BE CERTAIN SHE REALLY IS THE DESTINED MESSIAH.

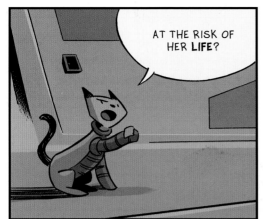

AT THE RISK OF HER **LIFE**?

AND **MINE**?

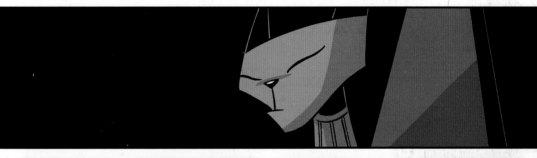

DID YOU EVEN KNOW THE SWORD WOULD **BE** THERE?

THERE WERE RUMORS.

RUMORS...

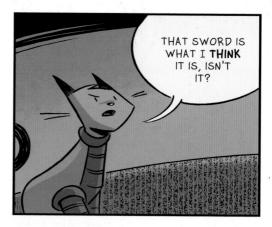

THAT SWORD IS WHAT I **THINK** IT IS, ISN'T IT?

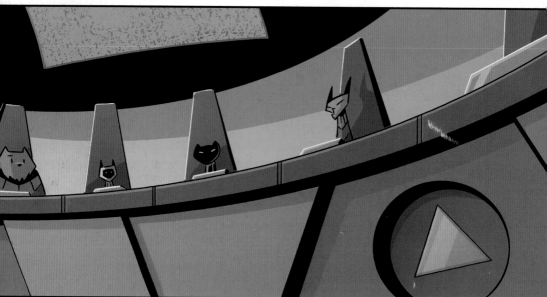

THE NEXT TIME YOU DECIDE TO SEND MY--MY **STUDENT** OFF TO SOME **DEATH TRAP** JUST TO PROVE SOMETHING WE **ALREADY**--

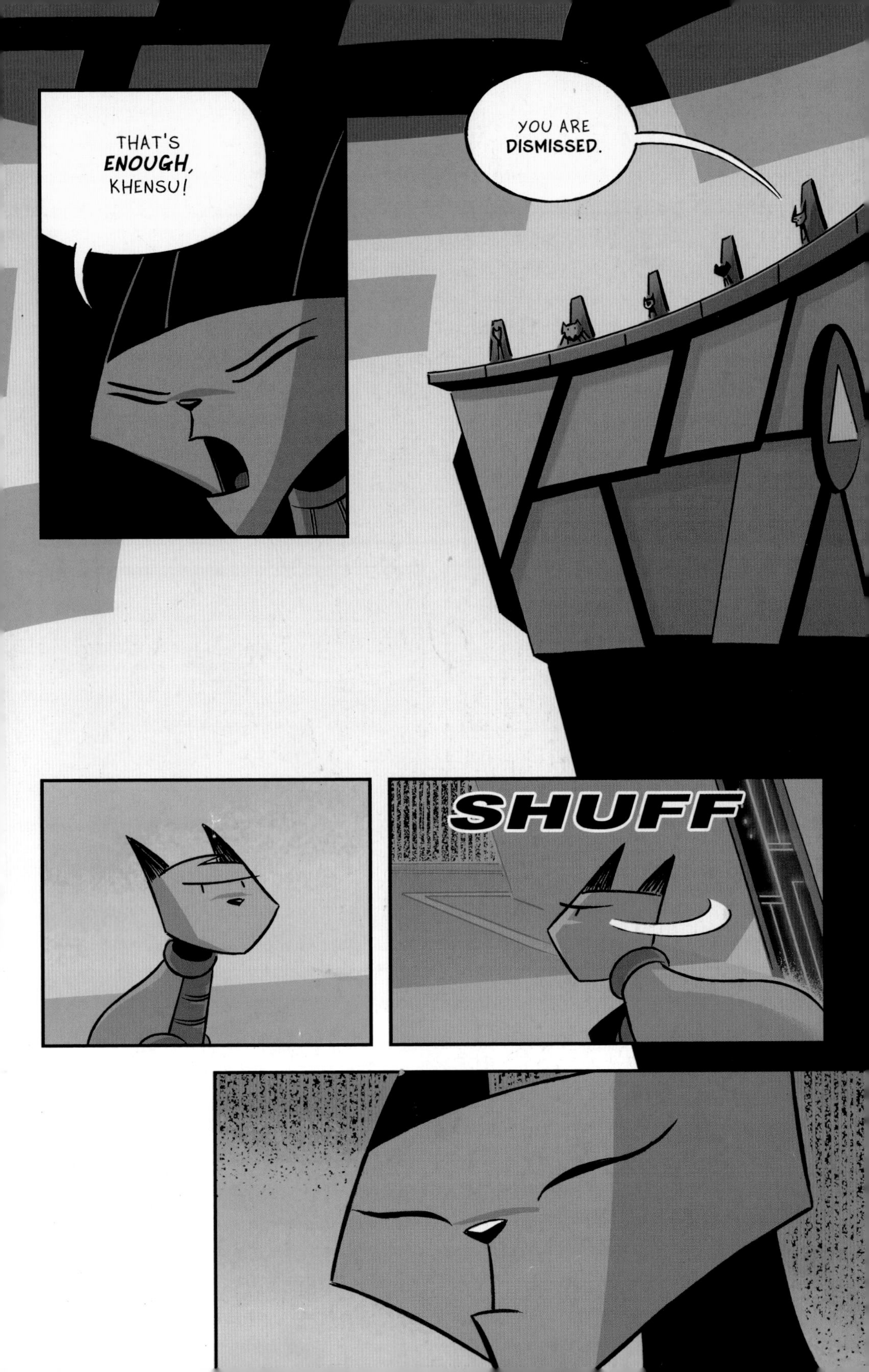
THAT'S ENOUGH, KHENSU!
YOU ARE DISMISSED.
SHUFF

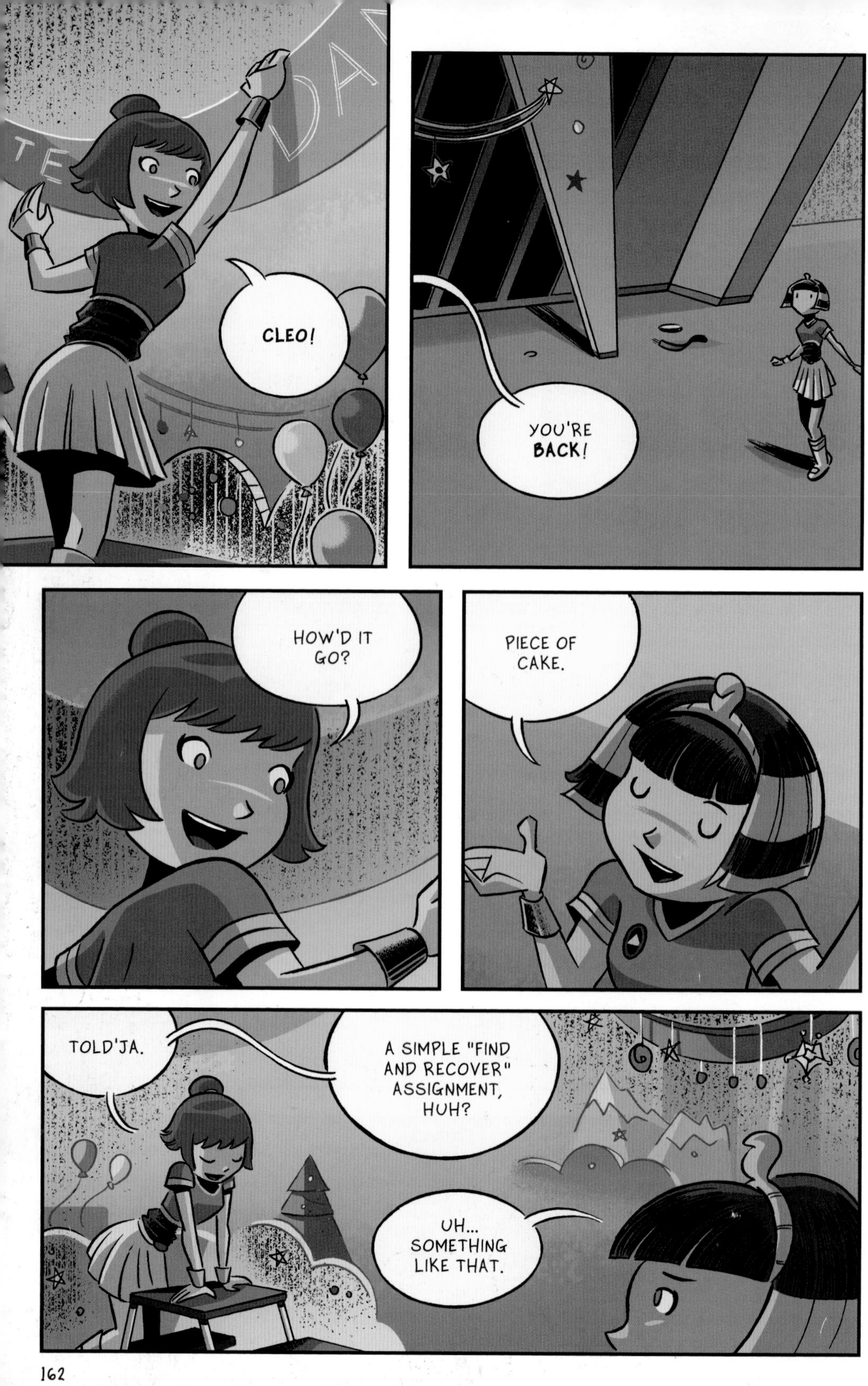
TE DA
CLEO!
YOU'RE BACK!
HOW'D IT GO?
PIECE OF CAKE.
TOLD'JA.
A SIMPLE "FIND AND RECOVER" ASSIGNMENT, HUH?
UH... SOMETHING LIKE THAT.

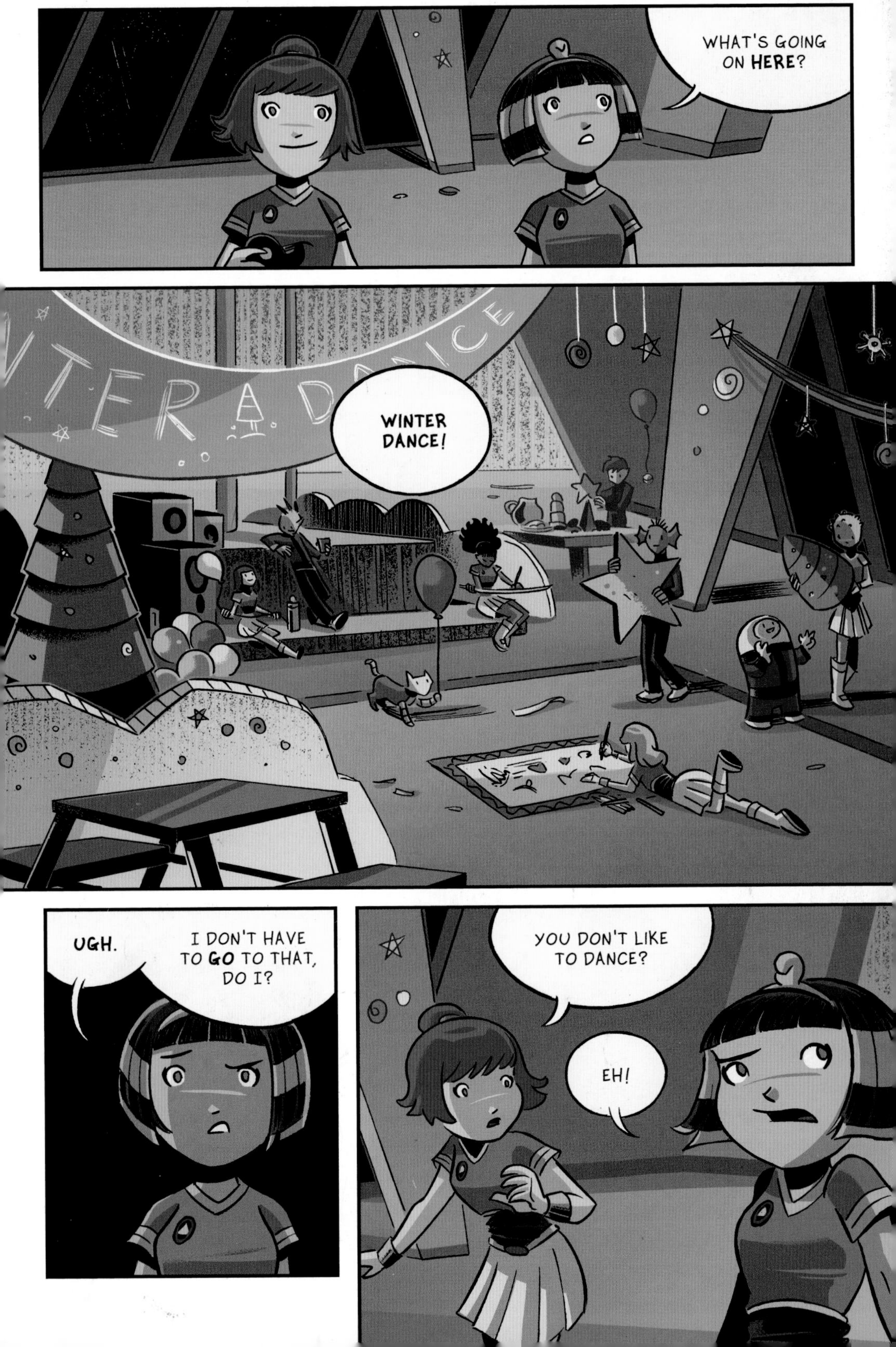
WHAT'S GOING ON **HERE**?
WINTER DANCE
WINTER DANCE!
UGH.
I DON'T HAVE TO **GO** TO THAT, DO I?
YOU DON'T LIKE TO DANCE?
EH!

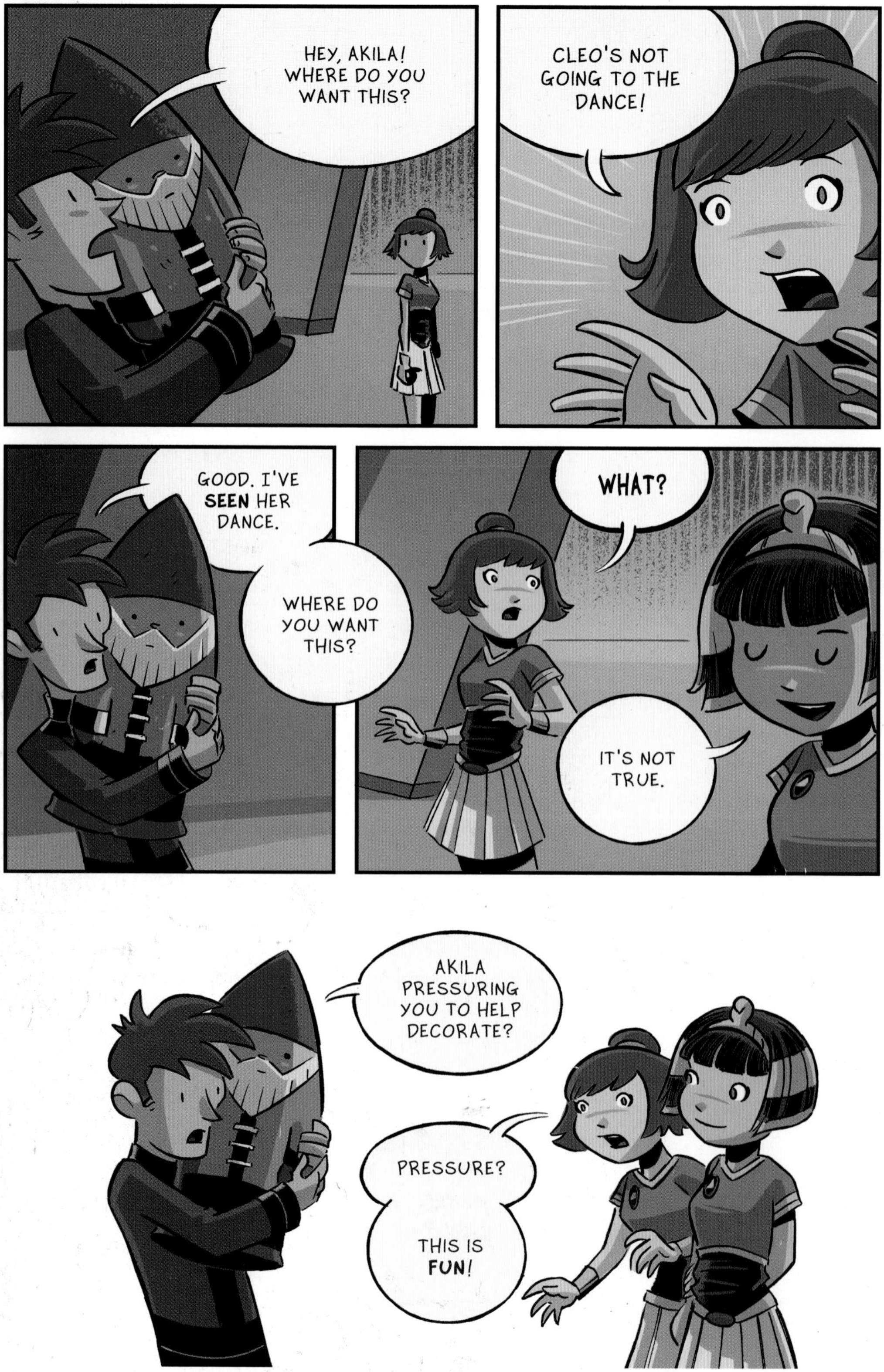
HEY, AKILA! WHERE DO YOU WANT THIS?
CLEO'S NOT GOING TO THE DANCE!
GOOD. I'VE **SEEN** HER DANCE.
WHERE DO YOU WANT THIS?
WHAT?
IT'S NOT TRUE.
AKILA PRESSURING YOU TO HELP DECORATE?
PRESSURE?
THIS IS **FUN**!

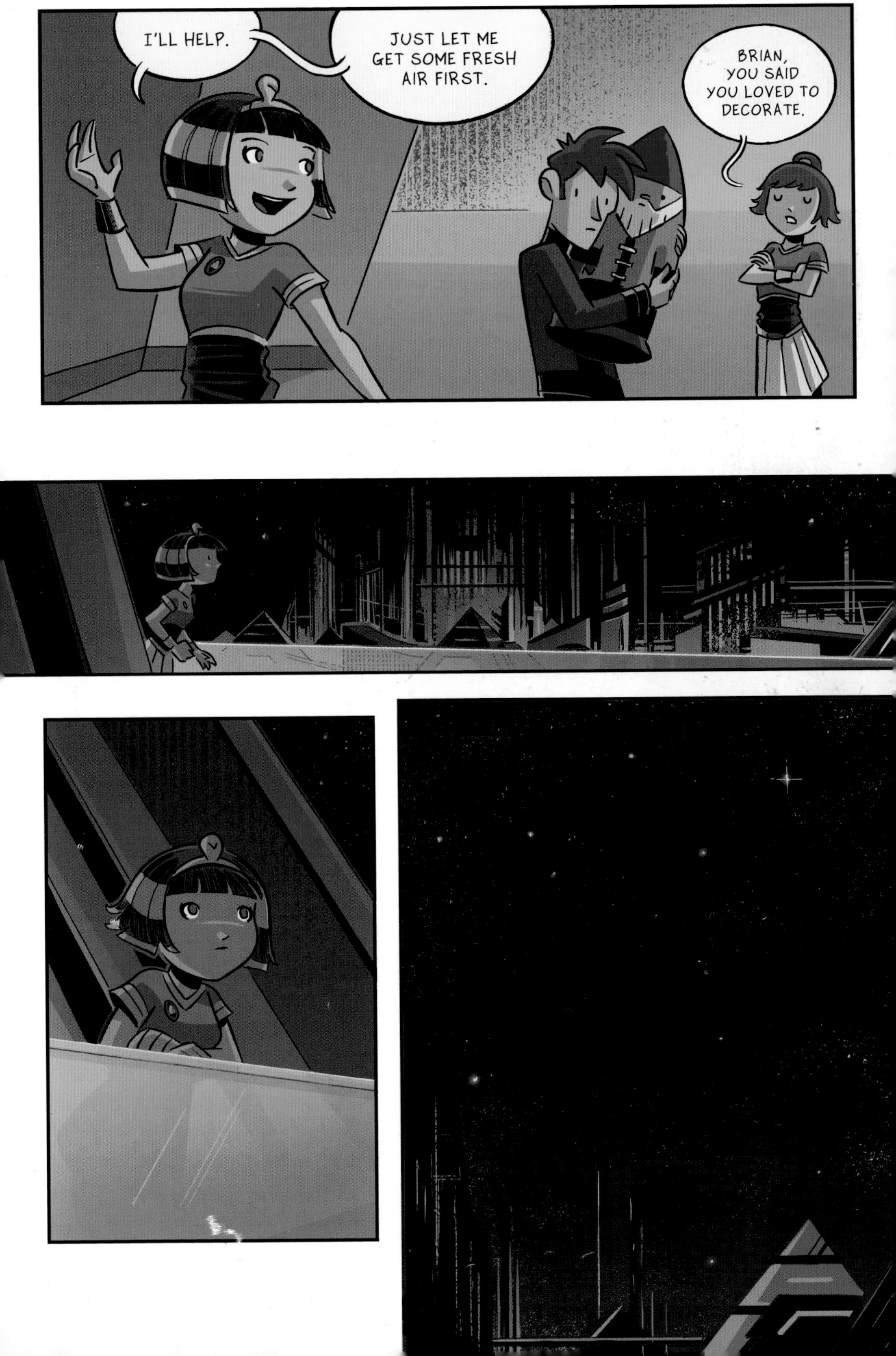
I'LL HELP.
JUST LET ME GET SOME FRESH AIR FIRST.
BRIAN, YOU SAID YOU LOVED TO DECORATE.

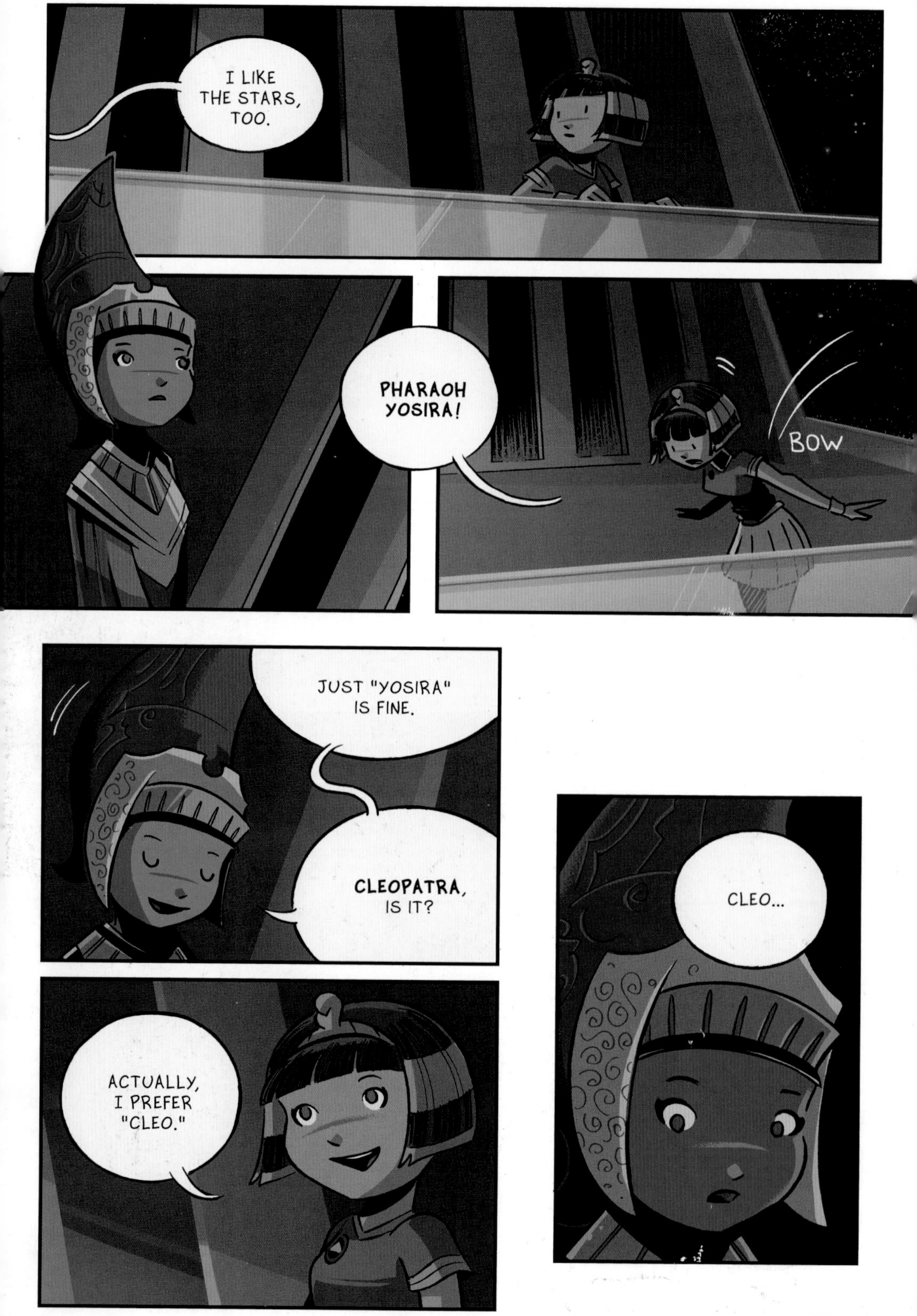
I LIKE THE STARS, TOO.
PHARAOH YOSIRA!
BOW
JUST "YOSIRA" IS FINE.
CLEOPATRA, IS IT?
ACTUALLY, I PREFER "CLEO."
CLEO...

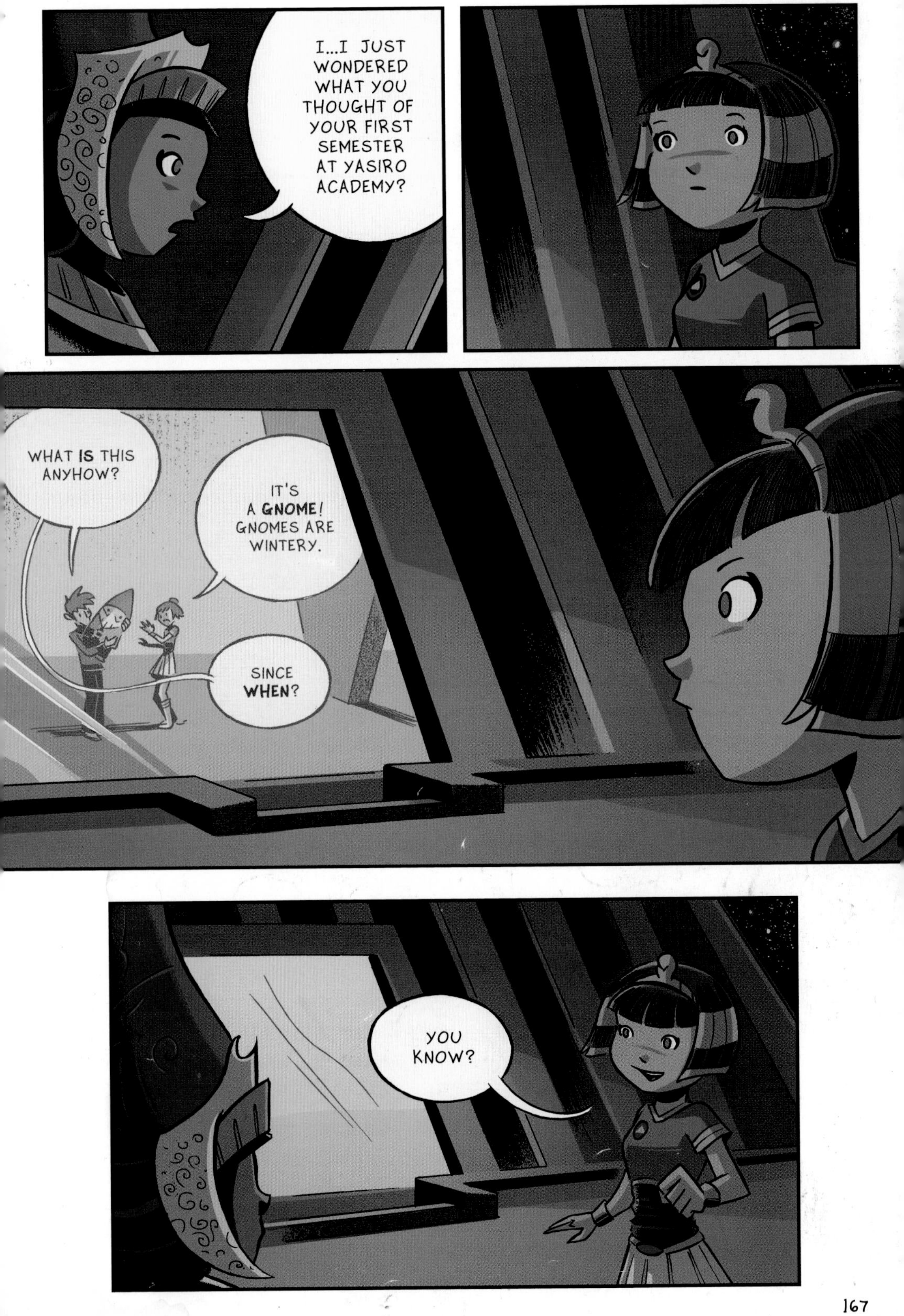
I...I JUST WONDERED WHAT YOU THOUGHT OF YOUR FIRST SEMESTER AT YASIRO ACADEMY?
WHAT **IS** THIS ANYHOW?
IT'S A **GNOME!** GNOMES ARE WINTERY.
SINCE **WHEN**?
YOU KNOW?

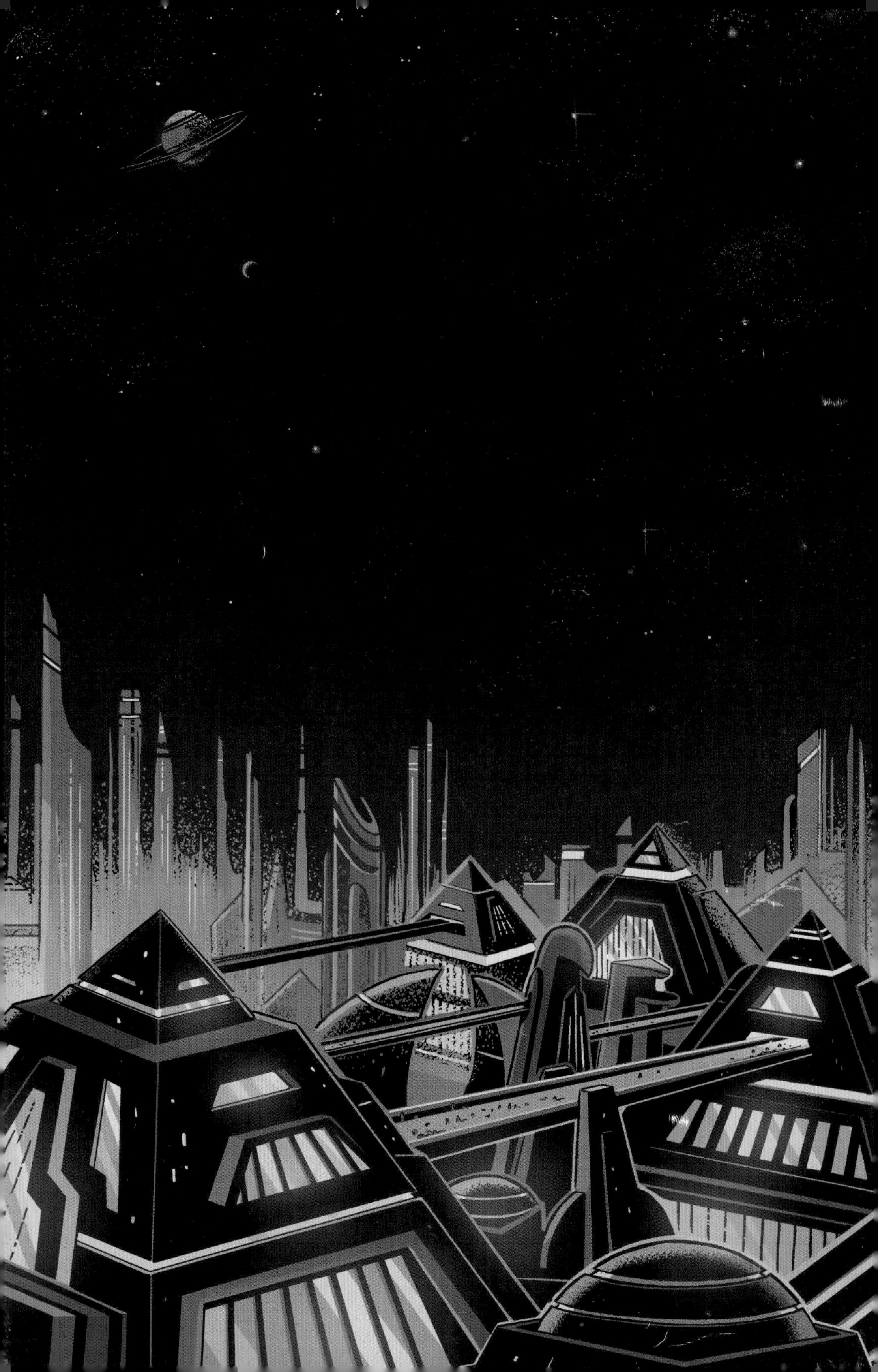

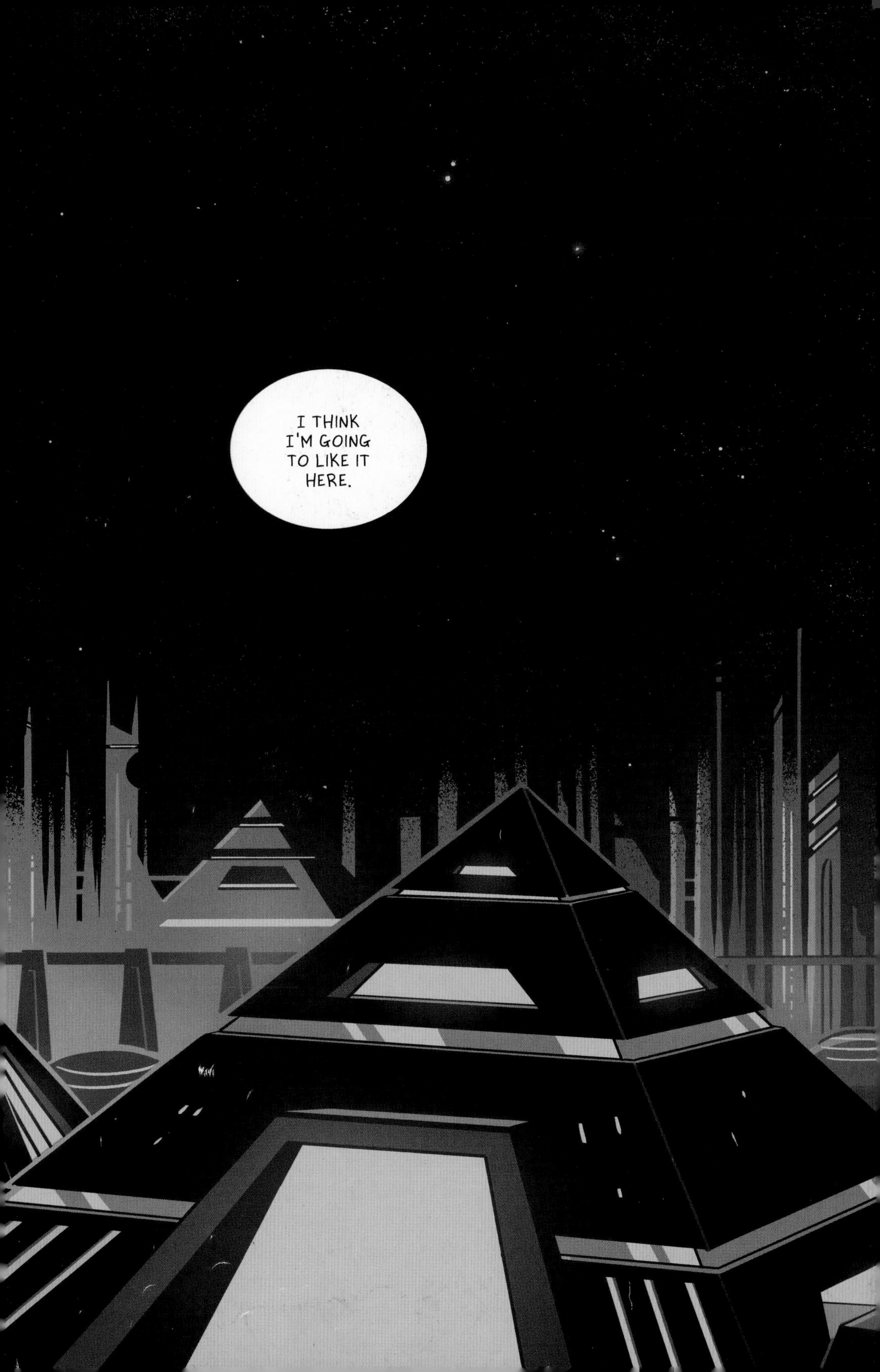
I THINK I'M GOING TO LIKE IT HERE.

ACKNOWLEDGMENTS

If not for the following individuals, this story would have been lost in space:

First and foremost, to the love of my life, Jen Maihack, whose patience and support throughout this entire creative process has been extraordinary. Also, for suggesting that Cleo's bike look like a sphinx.

To my family and friends (you know who you are!), I don't mention often enough how much your support means, but hopefully you realize it all the same.

To Cassandra Pelham, Phil Falco, and David Saylor, for not only taking a chance on me, but also pushing me past my comfort zone to create a much better graphic novel than I ever would have on my own.

To the incredible Judy Hansen, for leading me through the crazy and often scary world that is literary publishing! I continue to look forward to your guidance.

To the amazing eyes and expertise of Stephen McCranie, Sarah Mensinga, Wes Molebash, Michael Regina, and Josh Ulrich. Expect me to keep asking for your advice!

To all those who have supported *Cleopatra in Space* all these years — both on the web and off. Your importance cannot be overstated enough.

Lastly, I'd like to thank my two cats, Ash and Misty. They are pretty useless and actually were more detrimental than supportive in the creation of this book, but I felt their companionship should still be acknowledged in some way.

ABOUT THE AUTHOR

A graduate of the Columbus College of Art & Design, Mike Maihack spends his time drawing pictures of cats, superheroes, space girls, and just about anything else he can think of that might involve a ray gun or two. He is the creator of the popular webcomic *Cow & Buffalo*, illustrator of the all-ages card game Goblins Drool, Fairies Rule, and has contributed art and stories to books like *Parable*; *Jim Henson's The Storyteller*; *Cow Boy*; *Geeks, Girls, and Secret Identities*; and the Eisner and Harvey award-winning *Comic Book Tattoo*. Mike lives with his wife, two sons, and Siamese cat down in the humid depths of Lutz, Florida.

Visit Mike online at www.mikemaihack.com and follow him on Twitter at @mikemaihack.

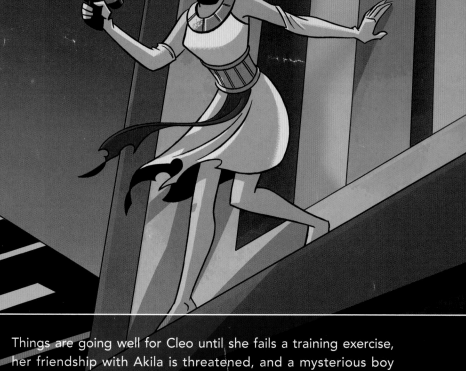

COMING SOON . . .

CLEOPATRA IN SPACE

BOOK TWO
THE THIEF AND THE SWORD

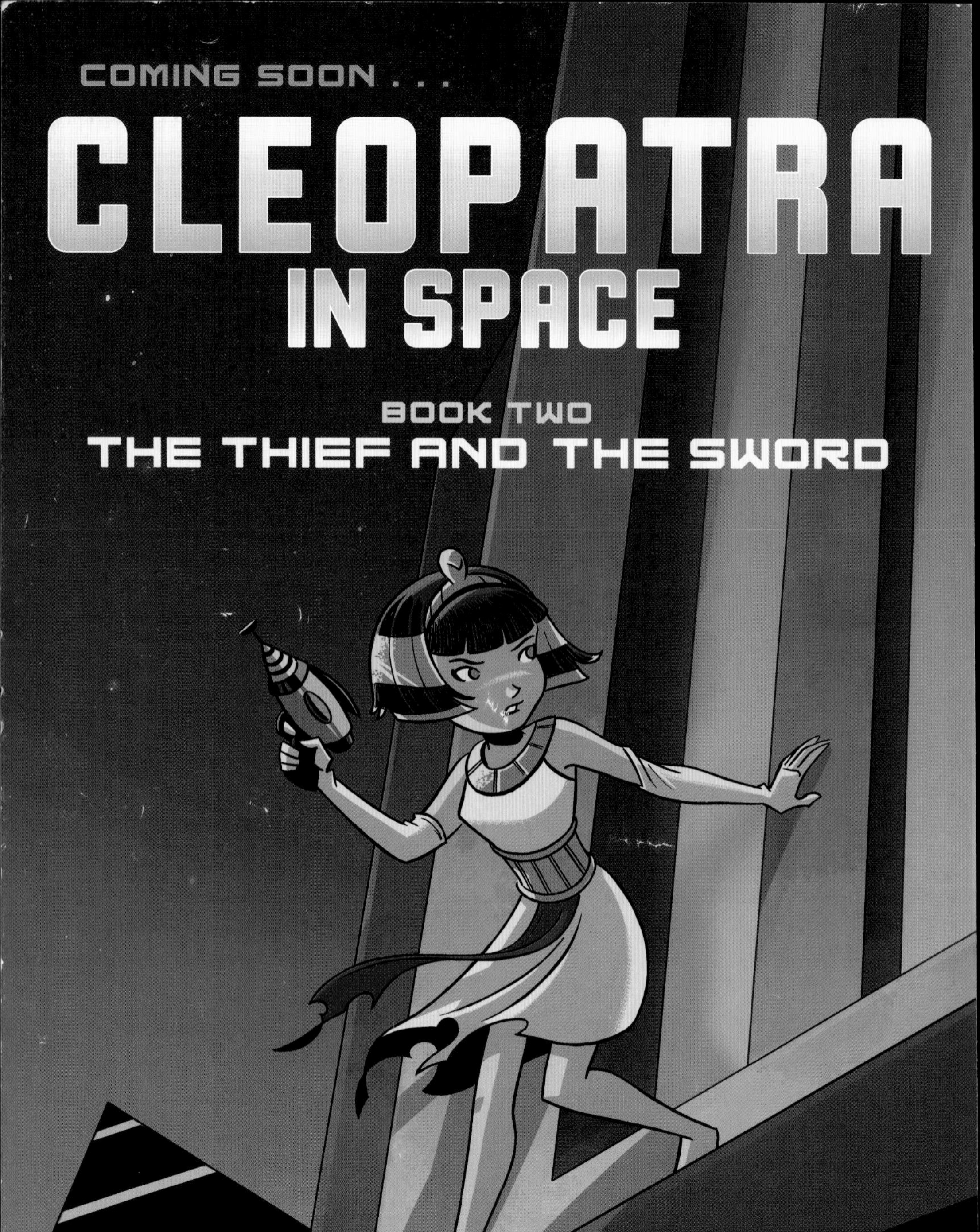

Things are going well for Cleo until she fails a training exercise, her friendship with Akila is threatened, and a mysterious boy who's working for the enemy shows up at Yasiro Academy. Find out what happens in the next book, available April 2015!